T0178726

In the Belly of the Whale

In the Belly of the

WHALE

Michael F. Flynn

CAEZIK
SF & FANTASY
ARC MANOR
ROCKVILLE, MARYLAND
✳
SHAHID MAHMUD
PUBLISHER

www.CaezikSF.com

In the Belly of the Whale copyright © 2024 by Michael Flynn. All rights reserved. This book may not be copied or reproduced, in whole or in part, by any means (electronic, mechanical, or otherwise), without written permission, except for short excerpts in a review, critical analysis, or academic work.

This is a work of fiction.

Cover art by Dany V.

ISBN: 978-1-64710-101-5

First Edition. First Printing. July, 2024
1 2 3 4 5 6 7 8 9 10

An imprint of Arc Manor LLC

www.CaezikSF.com

CONTENTS

ROSTER

Bùxiè deSōuxún, Detective Chief Inspector
Qínfèn deFēnxī, his Sergeant
Tongkawa Jones, Astrogator (jg)
Alessandro Fanghsi, "Little Face," burnsider
Winsome (Winnie) Alabaster, Eugenicist 2nd class
Dhikpāruṣya Spandhana, "Big Dhik," Enforcer of Filial Devotion
Ling-ling Barnstable, Princess of the Air
Megwan Masterson, Water Prince, Ling-ling's intended
Luis Barnstable, Commander of Air, Ling-ling's father
Sophie Masterson, Commander of Water, Megwan's mother
Ynigo "Lucky" Lutz, Staff Sergeant, first Platoon, Fleet Marines
Crowley Vermain, Ynigo's corporal, aka "Crawling Vermin"
Too Tall Goliad, Ynigo's First Sergeant
Rajalakshmi Ming-ti, tenth in-captain (blue)
Pedro san Grigor, eighth go-captain (gold)
Yves san Pedro, Pedro's protégé, Prince of *Whale* (gold)
Hamdu Organson, Lt. Commander of Liaison (blue)
Peng, Commander of Ship Security (blue)
Skybones Eframoff san Cisco, "Number One," Executive Officer (gold)
Adrienne Mei-ti, Bùxiè's Special Woman, senior quartermaster (gold)
Petronella (Peta) Patterson, a medical examiner

Dumont Ramamurthy, Vice-Commander of Eugenics Inputs (blue)
Florian Venables, tutor to Ling-ling (blue)
Reynaud Berylplume, Second Officer and Chief Astrogator (gold)
Jek Buddhathal, corporal in the Brotherhood militia
Kennett Erlanger, Commander of Maintenance (blue)
Thantos Chan, Commander of Power and Light (blue)
Gregor Vishwakarma, "Lord Argo," Commander of Food (blue)
Crewmen, officers, tutors, enforcers, mutineers, blackbirds, Marines, and Dwellers in the Outer Darkness

PROLOGUE

"Faint beneath the azure sky twilight bells do peal
Midst ruins where their echoes tone:"
We were real. We were real. We were real.
"As once they were when life enfleshed these bones,
And they fared forth to find what stars conceal."

—Méarana Harper, *Bailéad an Domhain Terra*

All this happened a great long time ago, by which we mean not merely that it was long ago but also that it was great. It was an age of drama and romance, of farce and adventure. Everything was bigger; everything was grander. Heroes were more heroic, lovers more lovely, traitors more treacherous, conflicts more conflicted. There were spaceships bigger than mountains. There were spaceships that *were* mountains.

People dared greatly, and so, failed greatly. At times, they even achieved greatly. This is the story of one of their achievements.

They flung spaceships off the Beanstalks, off of Quito and High Nairobi and Borneo and the others. The first to go was *Red Dwarf*, though Proxima was not the most promising of destinations. It was cold, and it was a flare star, but damn, it was the closest. How could they not go? Perhaps they should have awaited better technology, but it was not an age much given to waiting. As soon as they *could*, they *did*.

3

But the real prizes went to the ships they called "the Three Sisters." Hurtling southbound out of Sol, the *Whale*, the *Indiaman*, and *Big River* were aimed at the most sun-like stars in the Near Afar. This was one of those dreams that they dreamed greatly.

They called the ship "The *Whale*" both because it was large and because it was destined for Tau Ceti in the constellation of the *Whale*. She was built from a hollowed-out asteroid and outfitted with Farnsworth cages and Higgs engines. She ran a hundred Frames, fore to aft, and fifty Decks, top to orlop. Inside, her maze of longitudinal and traverse passageways was tiled with gravity plates, illuminated with power and light, refreshed with water and air, and stocked with plants and animals (both manifest and eminent). The voyagers required an entire ecosystem, for their journey would be no short jaunt. They had volunteered not only themselves but their children's children's children for, even as fast as the *Whale* would flit, twelve light years is a damned long slog.

This was in the heyday of the Audorithadesh Ympriales, and Presidente-emperor Miwell II attended the launch in his own person to bid them farewell. Orators declaimed—they were, of course, more eloquent than orators today. Women wept to hear them, and strong men sighed. Children cheered and danced in the sunlight. Fireworks soared and burst, and red-and-gold paper dragons capered through the throngs. Far above, the *Whale* decoupled from the Quito Beanstalk, and the solar powersats beamed gigawatt lasers at her combustion chambers and magnetic sails to shove her off. Then everyone went home.

In the time thereafter, bones piled upon bones beneath the grass, cities fell, and new ones rose, ashes drifted in the wind, and names that once did grip the heart in ice faded to musty memories. After a few centuries, they ceased to dream greatly, or dream at all and forgot entirely that there had ever been a *Whale*.

All the while, *Whale* hurtled on. People within her aged and died, and their children after them. Farms and industries flourished or failed. Buyers and sellers bought and sold. Swabbies washed and polished the fittings, and crew repaired the breakdowns. For a time, they wondered why they received no more messages from Earth, but eventually, they no longer cared.

The Planners had thought of everything. They had even written a constitution for the *Whale*, devised by the best social technicians Earth had to offer, laying out the duties and authorities for every rank and rating aboard. They had accounted for every contingency, for every small thing, but they had forgotten one rather large thing.

Those aboard would be human beings.

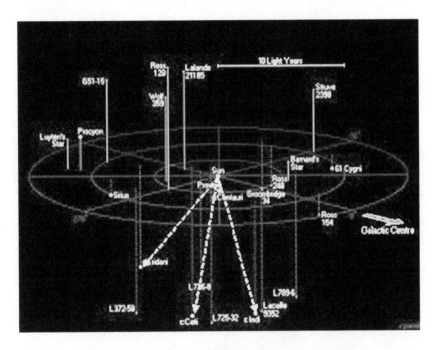

The Near Afar, based on *http://www.atlasoftheuniverse.com/12lys.html*
Tau Ceti is the midmost path, south by rimward of Sol.

1 ROLL CALL

Nobody's body—The *Whale* as she was—In the Burnout—'Excellence, we have a problem'—Damned capewalkers—Ling-ling shows her ankle—Kicking the can down the road—A pedestrian observation

Detective Chief Inspector Bùxiè deSōuxún arrived on scene in the Little Lotus neighborhood just as the sun panels were restoring daylight to the corridor. The narrow alley was already fenced off, and the physicalists were dusting for prints, testing for blood, and doing whatever else might keep them out of trouble. Bùxiè spared a glance for the darkness at the end of the block, where the lights had failed in his great grandsire's day, then ducked under the tape, where he thumbed the log kept by the scene-control constable. He came up behind his sergeant, Qínfèn deFēnxī, who was witnessing the new medical examiner's work with the body.

The corpse lay face down, head toward the blackness. It was shabbily dressed in dull brown coveralls, an old uniform issue that accorded well with the income level for this deck and frame.

"Suspicious death?" he asked Qínfèn.

"Nah," said the sergeant. "Corpse in a dim, dead-end corridor? What could possibly be suspicious about that?"

Bùxiè grunted without humor. "Fill me in."

"Deceased is male, early twenties, dead about five hours from blunt force trauma."

"To the right occipital," the medical examiner contributed without looking up.

"To the right occipital," agreed the sergeant.

"I'll know more about time-o-death," interjected the examiner, "once I get the darling fellow slabbed and jabbed. Can I roll him now?"

Bùxiè nodded, and between them, Qínfèn and the doctor flipped the body over.

The face bore a startled look. Bùxiè had noticed that before. They were always surprised when death took them. Qínfèn used his MOBI to image the face.

"I don't suppose it's a suicide."

"That would have been courteous," said the doctor, "and would it not? But no one commits suicide by bludgeoning himself in the back o' the head."

"An accident?"

"You mean, did something fall on him, or did he fall into something?" The examiner shook her head. "Then, where is the by-your-leave 'something'? He did not hide it himself, to be sure. Ah, the shape of the wound will tell us about the shape of the weapon once I mold an impression. Meanwhile, *my* impression is something tubular, like a pipe or a truncheon,"

"Patrol are searching for the weapon," said his sergeant. "But there aren't many hidey-holes along this block."

Bùxiè stared again into the darkness of the Big Burnout beyond the barricade at the end of the corridor. "Or far too many. But aren't you burying the lede here, Sergeant? What was his name?"

"MOBI doesn't know." Qínfèn waved his pocket link. "Facemaker comes back blank. It seems this body is nobody." He paused to allow the humor to sink in.

But Bùxiè was in ill humor. He had rushed to the scene without his breakfast. "Everybody must be somebody, sergeant. No damage to the face that I can see. So, why no recognition?"

His sergeant shrugged helplessly.

"DNA will give us an ID," the medical examiner prophesied. Bùxiè did not know her name, either, and tried to catch a glimpse of the doc's identity badge without being obvious.

"Have you harvested the corridor camera data, at least?" Bùxiè asked his sergeant. "If we can't learn Dead Man's identity right off, at least we can learn who parted his hair in so emphatic a fashion." But before he had reached the end of the sentence, his sergeant was shaking his head.

"*Bu hao,*" the inspector conceded. "Let me guess. The cameras are dead."

"As dead as our friend here," Sergeant Qínfèn said. "My guess: the cameras went dark eighty years ago in the Big Burnout, and Maintenance wrote them off. Why monitor a passageway that leads nowhere?"

"Or leads anywhere," Bùxiè commented.

Qínfèn brushed his hands on his smock and straightened. "No facial recognition, no surveillance footage," he said. "How do we hack this one?"

Bùxiè snapped his MOBI shut and shoved it into its scabbard. "The old-fashioned way, sergeant: detective work."

Among the images indelibly painted across the mind of Tongkawa Jones was the classic mural of *Departure Day,* interpreted in latex and acrylics by Chastity Balakrishnan. It depicted the original Command Staff in a single scene, even though they had probably not all gathered at that one time and place. Still, it had been an age that prized epic ceremonies and grand symbols, and so they might have done, and what more can one demand of legends?

Clever use of hue and shading drew the eye to the central figure of the in-captain, Joannie Chao, first of her line, who had purview over the infrastructure of the *Whale.* The artist portrayed her as regal and solidly built with a broad moon face. The in-captain's duty was to ensure that when the ship one day nests into orbit at Vishnu, Tau Ceti, there will be settlers aboard sufficient to colonize a world. What use is a successful transit if the *Whale* arrives a ship of ghosts?

Chao was painted a little right of center with mobile interface in hand and appeared to be touching off important items on the screen, as reported by her Command Staff. In fact, this was almost certainly handled autonomously by the Operating Data Base.

Surrounding her were the Department Heads: the Commanders of Water, Carniculture, Eugenics, Maintenance, Surveillance, and so on. Their poses were noble and their miens serious, as people present themselves when conscious of their place in history. They were the philosopher-kings of the *Whale*, the best aristocrats that Earth had to offer, and their bright blue uniforms were trimmed with gold.

Looking on from a mezzanine behind a single railing stood a second group in gold uniforms trimmed in blue. Dominic Dhruva was the go-captain in charge of navigation and propulsion. For what did it profit the voyagers if they thrived but never arrived? He was flanked by his Chief Astrogator, Chief Fusion Engineer, Chief Higgs Engineer, as well as by sundry other Commanders who cared for the handling of the ship. They were rendered more shadowy than the main group since, intersecting but little with the lives of the people they ferried, they were more remote and perhaps more godlike.

Each Commander bore in his hands an icon of his duty. Agriculture held a sheaf of 'ponic wheat, Astrogation, a telescope. A double helix rose from the cupped palms of Eugenics, and so on. Balakrishnan had painted them in a cyclorama around the Hexenplaza, where six passageways intersect on Twenty Deck just abaft the midline, and from a certain locus in the Plaza, viewers can experience the illusion that they themselves stood in the midst of that august gathering. Jones often delayed his arrival on the quarterdeck to contemplate these demigods. He did not regard his pause as a religious exercise nor his contemplation as an act of prayer.

But today, a gesticulating crowd had gathered before the main panel. Drawn by the hubbub, Jones ordered his cart onto the parking apron so he could suss things out before the Enforcers would arrive to disperse the crowd. Crew parted before his golden cape.

Someone had painted in bold red letters across the panel a defacing slogan: THE *WHALE* AS SHE WAS!

The sacrilege so outraged him that it was not until much later that he realized the graffito had been no more than the plain truth.

Alessandro Fanghsi owned a small face set in a large head. His eyes huddled close by his nose and mouth, surrounded by sallow, puffy expanses of cheeks, chins, and forehead, as if his ears were disinclined to hear what his eyes saw. But the wide displacement of those misfortunate auricles endowed him with a keen sense of acoustical direction, and he could hear a drink poured at two hundred meters and a passing thought at twenty.

He was a burnsider. This was not a formal rating in the crew. Officially, he was a minebot operator 2/c, but he eked out a living scouring the wreckage of the Big Burnout for relics. Sometimes, he found artifacts he could sell at a premium to a collector or a museum. Once, he had found a hand MOBI—a Mobile Operating Base Interface—that proved to be that of Rudolph Gunderson, who had been Commander of Mining during the catastrophe, and the proceeds had kept him comfortable for half a year.

Scavenging in the Burnout was not the safest vocation. The district lay largely in darkness, and lighting where it did prevail was dim and intermittent. Gravity plates had failed in many places, leaving them in zero-g—"ziggy," burnsiders called it; while in other sectors, multiple decks had collapsed and pancaked, piling up the Gs into deadly holes. Wires and cabling dangled from the overheads like pythons ready to drop and strangle the unwary. Untended hydroponic farms had overgrown their trays and now filled gangways with impenetrable thickets. Betimes, the howls of feral dogs echoed through the emptiness.

At Sixteenth Deck and Seventy-Fourth Frame, a gangway led down past a façade of balconies and overlooked a great public square. These multi-deck quarters had once been luxury accommodations for highly placed officers who had overseen operations in the aft quarters of the *Whale*. Their status had not saved them. Hundreds had died, and a tenth of the ship had been abandoned in place.

People elsewhere in the *Whale*, all forty thousand of them, now avoided the Burnout. They went around it, or under it, or over it, and thought they were safe. "Little Face" went through it and cherished no such illusion. Whatever had caused the catastrophe on these decks could happen elsewhere at any time. So why not dance *yo-yo* with death rather than wait passively? Old No-Nose would come calling sooner or later. Why duck the inevitable?

At the bottom of the stairs, he pulled out an energy bar and his canteen and sat on the bottom step to savor them. As he snacked, he listened to the rustlings of the memory metal trying vainly to reassemble itself. When bent, such materials could snap back to their original configurations, broken wires or circuits could splice, fractures could seal. But the process had to be guided, lest the broken ends connect wrongly; some deformations went far beyond the self-healing capabilities of the materials.

Material had memory, burnsiders told one another, but in the Burnout, it also had imagination.

He studied the quarters looming over him, picturing them in their glory days. Elegantly dressed Officers moving in stately measure across the Plaza amidst a throng of sturdy, dutiful crewmen. None of them with cares or worries, or indeed with any foreboding of the tragedy about to strike them. It was a time, he thought, when Officers were worth the obedience they demanded. The glories of those lost days seized him by the throat, and he wept.

Winsome Alabaster's smiles were faint, and others had to look twice to be certain they were there. Beside her, Mona Lisa flashed a manic grin. She had always been that way. Tracking her through archival images, that same wan ghost of a smile ran back to the enstrollered child. It seemed to betoken regret more than joy, as if she had found birth rather a letdown but would see the matter gamely through.

Alabaster sat within the honeycomb of carrels in the Eugenics Quarter, forward on Thirty-Second Deck and reviewed the weekly eugenics tableau with her typical fastidiousness. According to the algorithm, this case had been flagged to her attention because it wanted human judgement to resolve, though at first, nothing popped. The genome sequences lined up with a complementarity score of 95. Normally, a rubber-stamp case. Then she looked closer and saw the problem.

Ay-yi-yi, she would hate to be the *chivarist* assigned to this case! Picking up her MOBI, she contacted her supervisor. "Excellence," she said, "we have a problem," and forwarding the Commander a copy of the file, she made an appointment for the next morning's audience.

Then she disconnected her MOBI and, for a time, sat quietly at her workstation.

She smiled.

Dhikpāruṣya Spandhana—known, where it was important he be known, as "The Big Dhik"—was a massive man, as befit both his rating as Enforcer of Filial Devotion and his avocation of petty extortion. He had the visage of that very rock face where miners shaved 'stroid for the distillation furnaces: rough-hewn and thoroughly drilled and pockmarked. Few ever thought to cross him, and no one ever thought so twice. His staff of office was made of genuine Old Earth bamboo, lovingly polished and laminated in clear plastic. He handled the staff with a dexterity surprising for one so thick fingered.

The staff had also proved useful in his extracurricular activities, at least until he had been caught and sentenced to twenty strokes of chastisement himself. He had paid his debt to society but had been thinking lately of taking out another loan.

He paused his foot patrol at the Hexenplaza mural to admire the work. Not Balakrishnan's old art, which he regarded as insipid, but the unknown graffitist's newer oeuvre, which had a definite panache. The Plaza was busy at most times of the work-cycle, and the graffitist must have worked under excruciating time pressure to get in and out without being remarked. Well, the best art was always accomplished within strict limits. Dhik surveyed the cameras and noticed that they had been blinded. He wondered if anyone else had noticed that yet and decided they must have.

There would have been two of them, he noted with the professional part of his mind. The surveillance cameras had been placed to overlap their coverage. No one person could have blinded one without being spotted by the other.

He turned to go and found an Officer directly behind him.

"Step aside, Chief," the man snapped, pushing with his baton. His blazons and red cape-lining proclaimed him a lieutenant jg of facility maintenance, come no doubt to inspect the damage.

Dhik bowed and made way for the Officer, muttering, "Your pardon, Excellence," but the young lieutenant paid him no further attention. He posed before the mural, legs akimbo, hands a-hip. Then he spoke a few words to his MOBI and, without turning around, said, "Hold yourself in readiness, Enforcer. There will be chastisements soon."

Dhik harbored doubts. A vandal clever enough to evade the cameras was surely clever enough to avoid more physical forms of capture. He watched the lieutenant stride off to his scooter. The young man had not yet parsed the difference between looking important and being important.

Damned capewalkers, he thought.

Ling-ling Barnstable celebrated her twelfth birthday by playing with her friend Megwan Masterson. The play consisted of showing each other body parts that they normally concealed.

"This is my ankle," she said, pulling off her boot.

"Big deal," Megwan scoffed. "It's no different to mine." But his eyes lingered, and he declaimed:

> *"Slim, curved, and graceful*
> *Demanding no adornment,*
> *I would be your shoe."*

He made a move to touch the celebrated ankle, and the duenna, supervising the play from a stuffed chair off to the side, sat forward, warning him off.

"Thou art a bold one, Meg," Ling-ling said. She thought the poem not bad for a spontaneous composition, although he had framed it in Spanglish and used syllables rather than morae for the line counts. Her duenna sniffed disapproval, but whether for the sentiment or the syllabification, Ling-ling did not know.

They were, fittingly enough, in the Game Room of the suite known as Zephyrholm, an interconnecting set of compartments on

Three Deck, forward of Seven Frame, used by the Commander of Air. Her father was an important man, and someday the post would be hers, although she was unsure what that entailed.

"Have you gotten your draft notice yet?" Megwan asked, but with a little too much eagerness in his voice, so Ling-ling affected not to care. She extemporized a couplet:

> *"Oh, that notice best of worth*
> *Need not come on the fest of birth."*

Megwan's mother was Commander of Water, a puissant post, since next to breathing, drinking was most vital. Their parents had been conspiring all of Ling-ling's life to join her to Megwan, though she had become conscious of the deliberateness of these arrangements only in the past year. Her child by Megwan would become Joint Commander of Air *and* Water. Even the in-captain would have to pay attention to so powerful an Officer. So, she and Megwan had been tossed together like the ingredients in a salad in the hope that when their draft notices came, they would already have formed a bond.

Of course, there was the small matter of the Examinations, but she could cast a verse as readily as Megwan, and there was always *yin* privilege for moving the children of Officers up in the rankings. So long as she passed, Ling-ling did not think she need worry about demotion.

As far as that went, Megwan was not the worst choice her parents could have made for her. He was presentable and cleaned up nicely. But the Eugenics Department had the final say regarding who could copulate and with whom and when.

Her mother had instructed her in that art, too, of course, but she wasn't quite sure what that entailed, either.

Hamdu Organson, Blue Liaison to the Gold Crew, hung his cape on the hook behind his seat in the Gold Conference Room, where it dangled like an azure alien amidst the splendid golden capes of the others. The room was appointed in its eponymous color: the table draped in cloth-of-gold, the lamps and other fittings, gilded. The overall effect was one of gaudy opulence. One must look closely to notice the fraying and the tarnishing, the scratches and the burns accumulated over two centuries of use.

Eight centuries to go, he thought. There'd be naught but a few scraps of fabric by then.

Yves san Pedro, the captain's protégé and understudy, entered and stood by the empty chair at the head of the table. "The captain," he announced, "will not attend; so, if you would all take your seats …"

The Prince of *Whale* had the habit of ending his declarations with the curlicue of a question mark, which gave even his most certain announcements an unfortunate air of uncertainty. He was slight of build, too, as if to emphasize in his stature the diffidence in his speech. Consequently, the Command Staff had acquired the custom of looking to the Executive Officer for confirmation.

X/O Skybones Eframoff san Cisco was known as "Number One," a sobriquet that reflected his actual, if unofficial, eminence among the Gold Crew. The captain might command, but the X/O executed those commands.

The door warden, wearing his ceremonial leather apron, entered the Conference Room and announced, "The door is sealed." To which Signals declaimed:

> " 'The door is sealed,'
> *Says he who passed through it.*
> *Such contradiction!"*

Everyone, including Handu, rolled eyes at this jejune observation. Signals was elderly, a relic of an earlier time, but his dotage was tolerated by his younger colleagues because of his heroism during the Big Burnout. Though even heroism, Organson reflected, ought to have a use-by date,

Alone among the Senior Officers, the Gold Crew had maintained the Constitutional prohibition on marriage and property—or claimed they did. Organson did not believe their celibacy any more genuine than their poverty, but they inherited by adoption, not by blood. Hence, their "san" naming convention.

"Shall we start the agenda?" Skybones pre-empted. "Signals?"

Organson did not see the value of face meetings. Blue Crew held its monthly meetings virtually, which saved on time and distance, but in consequence sacrificed refreshments and bonhomie.

Although that might not be much of a sacrifice, given the quality of the *hors d'oeuvres* available: crackers with an indifferent paste that would not fail to appall any palate. The beverages were likewise unexceptional, being bland nectars and other soft drinks. Still, Organson filled his hand and his mouth for politeness' sake. He also kept the latter shut, again for politeness' sake.

Already, he felt trapped in the molasses of déjà vu. There was a sameness to Gold Crew briefings that was alien to the Blue. The latter were continually dealing with new things: a mural vandalized, a body dropped, as well as the normal clogs and breaks encountered in ship-running. But the last thing Gold Crew desired was the unexpected. In piloting a vessel at blinding speed, as in biting into an *hors d'oeuvre*, the last thing anyone wanted was a surprise.

An ancient sage, Machiavelli, had once said that all states were either Turkish or Frankish. The Gold Crew was Turkish. All offices were in the gift of the go-captain, or rather in that of his Executive Officer. Blue Crew was Frankish. Each Officer was a power in his own right, and alliances were constantly forming and dissolving in an incessant covert struggle to control the in-captain. Currently, Air and Water were nestled in a cozy entente, while Maintenance and Mining were allied against them. Most of the other departments maintained a wary neutrality toward both. Organson, occupying the enviably unimportant post of Liaison, had been wooed by neither side.

Mentally, he contrasted the flux of the Blue Crew against the stasis of the Gold. Li and Qi. Form and matter. Relativity or quantum mechanics. At Blue meetings, one could not step twice into the same agenda, but at Gold, he endured an endless repetition of "different day, same shit." So, Heraclitus versus Parmenides fit, too. Organson learned, as always, that no messages had been received from Earth, that the Farnsworths had been test-fired to the satisfaction of all who cared about test-firing Farnsworths, that the Higgs engines were projecting a steady field at the specified vector and intensity off the bow.

Organson nearly dislocated his jaw stifling his yawns. He presented a bored yet courteous countenance, bland and expressionless, yet with a cock to it that implied attentiveness. It was an excellent mask, and it was said that at some meetings, he would leave his countenance in attendance while he himself slipped out to take care of business.

Astrogation reported that something called BK Ceti, an F0 variable star three-hundred-and-thirty lights distant, appeared to have shifted by a nanometer on the skymap. Oh, be still, my heart! That elicited a few scowls among the Gold Crew since celestial objects were not expected to caper about, even by such trivial amounts. "The important thing," Tongkawa Deputy Jones insisted, "is that the plumb line is still fixed on the Tau."

Number One touched a finger to his earbud which meant he was receiving a pronouncement from the go-captain himself, Pedro san Grigor. The Staff formed a pool of silence into which the captain's words could be dropped like pebbles. Organson returned and sat behind his face.

"The captain," said Skybones, "has cast a poem for the occasion." And he recited:

> *"Gaze fixed on the star,*
> *He stumbles on a pebble.*
> *Feet find where eyes fail."*

Signals snorted derision. "How pedestrian."

Staff Sergeant Ynigo "Lucky" Lutz studied the shelves in the Armory with an intensity such that, could observation actually precipitate matter out of superimposed probability states, would have conjured the missing units on the instant.

It was Annual Inventory time for the Company of Fleet Marines, and verifying the physical count against the book count was a pain in the neck. Literally, in her case, since she had to crane her head back to examine the upper shelves. They should have assigned a taller Marine to the task or at least issued a foot ladder for a vertical assist.

However, the pain of taking the inventory was nothing compared to the pain of coming up short.

She imagined the multiple forms that would require thumbing, the multiple rounds of questions for which she had no ready answers, and the final *coup de gras*, the multiple dockings of her pay to cover the shortfall.

She could easily think of a *lakh* of things she would rather waste her pay on.

So, she made up the shortfall in another way.

After all, she couldn't say for sure that the teasers were *not* up there, on the upper shelves. If they had wanted her to look into those bins, they would have provided the ladder she needed. Technically, according to quantum physics, until she looked in the bins, the teasers *might* be there. As with Schrödinger's legendary cat, seeing was believing. So, on the inventory screen, where it read,

TEASER, HAND, PATEL & YOJI #6439 REVE. COUNT: 144 CASES @ 24/CASE, she thumbed, *VERIFIED.*

In an instant, the weight was lifted from her, so there must be something to this observation-existence theory after all.

Of course, she was only kicking the can down the road. Next year, there would be another annual inventory and maybe a taller supply sergeant who would discover the discrepancy. But the more she pondered it, the more she believed that last year's supply sergeant had done the same to her. Who knew how long those two cases had been missing? Perhaps they had been miscounted in the original stock-loading, and the shortage would be kicked down the road all the way to Tau Ceti.

And, true enough, except for exercises, the Marines had not needed the weapons in two hundred years.

NOBODY

The captain knows which way to go—"Near as I tell, he doesn't exist."—"Excellence, you cannot allow this."—"Dead Man get around plenty before he is dead."—There was something mighty important about that envelope.—Carpet call.

The *Whale* was much like a city: forty thousand souls jostling one another in what amounted to an enormous flying apartment block. Inevitably, they must be managed as much as a village as a crew. Tradesmen and artisans—plumbers, printers, painters, and the like—labored at mundane tasks quite detached from the celestial matters pondered by Tongkawa Jones and his colleagues on the quarterdeck or the infrastructure functions overseen by the Blue Crew.

That the go-captain's poem had possessed multiple layers of meaning went without saying. Jones took the most obvious as the caution that fixating on the Tau would lead to neglect of more immediate matters. But which matters? A second layer seemed a warning regarding the growing arrogance of Blue Crew, who dealt with those quotidian matters. Gold Crew called them "the cargo."

Focused on the stars, Gold Crew could trip on *scandala* created by Blue Crew. But again, which issue provided the stumbling block? Still, a third meaning was found in the fact that Astrogation was the eyes of the *Whale* while Engines were her feet. Had Engineering stumbled or was about to stumble? In what way?

And yet a fourth meaning might be peeled from the manner in which the poem had been delivered, interrupting Number One's management of the Face Meet. The go-captain evidently chafed at the superordination of the Executive Officer.

Under the *Whale*'s constitution, go-captains were selected either from Astrogation or from Engineering. But the first go-captain, the Excellent Dominic Dhruva, had been an astrogator and had naturally adopted as his protégé a man like himself, thus instigating the "dynasty of astrogators" that had persisted for two centuries. As Dhruva had written in one of his aphorisms, *The captain ought to know which way to go.*

He had named a Higgs engineer as his Number One, and that, too, had persisted. Just how and when the two roles had flipped, no one could rightly say. One captain had been reclusive by nature, another had disliked ordering people about, and little by little, the exec had become the captain's keeper.

That irritated Jones almost as much as did the adoption of Yves ibn Robert as "san Pedro." One advantage of the celibacy practiced by Gold Crew officers was that Tongkawa Jones was undistracted by domestic quibbles and could ponder matters more celestial. The Planners had intended that the Officer class be detached from the turbulence of domestic and commercial life to contemplate long thoughts, and so, Officers had been constitutionally barred from amassing both property and progeny. This was not easy since Wanting was the Original Void. A great deal of self-discipline was required to achieve Not-Wanting.

This had been easier in the Departure Generation, when, surrounded by like-minded companions, one could rely on the supporting examples of one's peers, but it had been a glassy discipline from the start, and cracks developed early. The bluecapes had shattered outright because they were immersed in the ordinary daily life of the *Whale*, so meditation on the Flight Plan had been smothered by quotidian distractions. Only the goldcapes had persevered. Not that none of them had tasted flesh or fortune, but their "dynasties" still ran by adoption rather than by blood.

Tongkawa's pride was that he had been chosen through merit, plucked from the mid-ship pass'ways because he had scored well on the Examination and not because his father or his mother had been an astrogator before him. His father had, in fact, been a grocer in Billy's Gate, and his mother only an able spacer with no rank or rating. Now he was living in The Cloisters and working on the Quarterdeck.

That he might have been selected not (or at least, not only) for his mathematical acuity but for his youthful comeliness did not occur to him. His mentor, Jimmy Gujarati, had never been anything but kind and attentive, but there are more ways to ensure that no progeny sprang from one's appetites than simply ignoring those appetites. They might also be redirected. Jimmy Gujarati had succumbed to a wasting disease when Tongkawa had been in his twenties, yet Tongkawa Jones seldom called himself "san Jimmy" and never really pondered why that might be so.

The problem in fixing attention on the star lay in that "the Tau" stood where it had been eleven years ago while they needed to aim for where it would be eight-hundred years from now. The *Whale* was traversing an ocean in which her ports of call did not stay fixed. The Tau was a speed demon, traversing the sky at two arc-seconds per year, more or less, which meant that when the *Whale* finally arrived, the Tau would be sixteen-hundred arc-seconds from her present position, more or less. Since it was also moving toward Sol at seventeen kilometers per second, more or less, the common joke on the quarterdeck was that the *Whale* need only hold still and Tau Ceti would come to them. More or less.

It was the *less* that kept them busy unless it was the *more*. Few measurements ran to exact intervals of the scales by which they were measured, so there was always another decimal place to add, another refinement to the ship's calculated speed and location, to Tau Ceti's calculated speed and location, and hence to their ETA. Tiny errors could accumulate over time to insuperable magnitudes so that they might do little more than wave at the Tau while they skated past.

Eyes fixed on the star—Tau Ceti, their destination—we stumble on a stone—matters beneath our feet. Ah, but which matters? The unseemly ascendancy of the Executive Officer? The bumptiousness of Blue Crew? Or something he had not yet thought of because his eye, too, was fixed on the star?

All during his watch, while he directed the quartermasters and chartsmen in their observations and calculations, Jones remained keenly aware of the irony, and from time to time, he checked for pebbles beneath his feet.

More or less.

Bùxiè deSōuxún rose to an early breakfast prepared by his Special Woman, the golden-haired Adrienne Mei-ti. This morning, she had served him a plate of baked beans, mushrooms, white sausage, and an egg enthroned on a pedestal. This he clipped on the small end with his egg clipper and placed the tip in the lap pan of Sitting Buddha. The little table statue held its hands in *vajra mudra*, the fist of wisdom, a fist every police inspector could use.

The parting kiss was more than perfunctory and floated with him as he strode off toward the precinct house. Unlike residential quarters, the nick was detached from its neighbors, with open slots on either side, and its interior ascended to the decks below and above.

Inside, the shop buzzed with constables and patrolmen coming and going, and in between whispering news to their sergeants, the net of which summed to a persistent, distracting drone.

The acid odor of coffee permeated the air. Back on Earth, in China, to bring someone in for questioning had been expressed as "invite them in for coffee." But here, that would be police brutality, for the coffee in the Little Lotus cop shop was reputedly the worst anywhere in the *Whale*. The coppers took a perverse pride in the claim.

In the carrel where they shared facing desks, Bùxiè asked Qínfèn a silent question with a cock of his head toward the hubbub.

"Oh, someone defaced the Mural up on Sixway," his sergeant explained. "And the Excellents are in a titter."

"That's outside our jurisdiction," Bùxiè said, by which he meant not only that it befell in a different precinct but that such petty nuisances did not normally rise above the Enforcers.

"You know that," Qínfèn agreed happily, "and I know that, but when the capewalkers have a knot in their short pants, everyone squirms."

"Isn't that the truth?" The term *capewalker* was modestly disrespectful, but Bùxiè did not rebuke his sergeant. His MOBI chimed, and he checked the message. "Don't get too comfortable, sergeant. The Doc wants to see us." The MOBI had also revealed the new medical examiner's name: Petronella Patterson. Bùxiè deSōuxún thought that a weird name with which to burden a child and wondered from which of the root *ethnoi* her ancestors had stemmed.

The examiner awaited them in the morgue, which lay in the lower complex on Thirteen Deck. She wore a blood-spattered yellow body suit and head cap and was pulling off a pair of blue latex gloves when the detective and his sergeant entered. She handed the inspector a large envelope.

"His effects," she said.

Bùxiè peered inside the envelope. "Seed packets?"

Patterson nodded. "Beans, maize, broccoli, carrots …. His pockets were stuffed with them."

"For what purpose?"

"You'd have to ask him. But what does one normally do with seeds?"

Bùxiè grunted and groped inside the envelope. "Where is his MOBI?"

Patterson said, "He didn't have one on him."

"So, you summoned me down here to not give me his MOBI? Any other cheery news?"

"As I suspected, the murder weapon was long and rounded, like a pipe. The attacker struck from behind, probably right-handed, almost certainly shorter than Dead Man."

"The DNA was going to tell us the victim's name," Bùxiè reminded her.

Patterson expressed irritation. "That's why I was asking you to stop by. You see, the DNA sample came back null, just like Facemaker. There's no trace of him in the Operating Base. Near as I tell, the poor fellow doesn't exist."

Bùxiè sighed and glanced at the body on the slab to assure himself of its continued existence. "What about his safety chip?"

"Which part of 'no trace' proved beyond your ken, darling?"

"He removed his chip?" That surprised the inspector. Without a locator chip, a man could be injured in some remote district, and searchers would be unable to find him. The chips had become popular after the Big Burnout when some regions had proved dangerous to rescue workers, later to curious adolescents, and over the years, they had crept slowly from popular to mandatory. Nowadays, everyone had the comfort and security of being tracked.

Patterson pointed to the corpse. "There's no scar indicating removal."

Qínfèn spoke up, "You mean a chip was never implanted?"

The medical examiner glanced at him. "I did not say so. I detected no identification signal, and there is no scar to indicate its removal. Those are the facts. That his chip was never implanted is one hypothesis that might account for those facts. But no finite set of facts permits only a single explanation."

Bùxiè understood the difference between fact and theory and the hazards of allowing the latter to scamper off too far ahead of the former, but too much rigidity on the distinction stifled the leaps of intuition necessary for good detection work.

Qínfèn said, "What about the Archival Base? Maybe you can identify an ancestor, then work your way forward to find cousins."

"Eugenics maintains the current population at, what? Forty kilo-folks? Now multiply by twelve generations since Departure. And that's assuming the Big Burnout didn't mess up the earlier files. Do you have the time for that?"

Bùxiè shrugged and pointed at the corpse. "He's in no hurry."

The office of Dumont Ramamurthy, Vice-Commander of Eugenics/Input, was decked with draperies of saffron and turquoise and with small, exquisite, faux-ivory statues set on pedestals or in niches. A morning raga, *Bhupal Todi*, played softly in the background, subtly lifting Alabaster's spirits as she sat before her boss' plasteel desk and waited politely for him to speak. A freshener suffused the air with vanilla, presumably to relieve depression, stimulate mental alertness, or enhance memory, though what the Vice-commander might have forgotten or might be depressed over, Winsome Alabaster did not guess.

Ramamurthy was as dark as his name implied and as handsome. His voice rippled like the arpeggio of a sitar. "I really don't see what the problem is, sri Alabaster." He steepled his fingers, and the light from his desk screen danced in his eyes.

He hasn't read the report closely, thought Winsome Alabaster. "Excellence," she said carefully, "you cannot allow this."

Ramamurthy smiled and bowed his head politely. "And why can I not, Lady Alabaster?" One did not tell a "capewalker" to his face what he could or could not do. Although the Vice-Commander seemed approachable, and his eyes caressed her as she spoke, there was always the social line one crossed at peril. She was crewborn; he was not.

Alabaster sucked in her breath and with it the vanilla vapor. "Please observe the difference in their ages. The putative bride is twelve, but her assigned groom is twenty-eight. That is unseemly. Sir." That was as close to impertinence as she dared come.

The Vice-Commander pursed his lips. "Unseemly? Perhaps. But surely, this fellow has been properly taught to withhold consummation until her quinceañera. It is usual in these matters for the male to run older than the female. My own Special Woman was thirteen when we were drafted. I was sixteen, and our brief time together was exquisite." He tapped the desk screen with his forefinger. "Why expect any less of this pairing?"

"Sir, have you noticed his rank?"

Ramamurthy's eyebrows rose, then lowered as he turned toward his screen. "Ah," he said with greater comprehension, "I see why your heart is troubled, my lady. It is more usual in these cases for the older male to be of *higher* rank than the younger female. I will make inquiries." He touched his screen here, there, and closed the file. "Perhaps we should discuss this matter later, in a less formal setting. Allow me to present you with a meal at the Glowering Tiger on Sixday coming."

The term "should" from an Officer often carried more weight than a "must" uttered by lesser lips. Alabaster felt a small shiver and, with some difficulty, found her voice. Since she found it somewhere below her knees, she answered in a lower tone than she normally used. "Si, Sir. I would be honored. Will your Special Woman accompany us?"

Protocol required she ask, but Ramamurthy's countenance fell. "I am grieved, sri Alabaster, to inform you that my glorious Ah Kum has passed to the realms celestial."

That explained the vanilla, then. "I am devastated to hear this," Alabaster answered.

Ramamurthy waved a hand. "It was three years ago." Then he added as if he had not already thoroughly researched the matter, "And how long has it been since your Special Man disappeared in the Burnout?"

When the Big Dhik entered Arfwendsen's Wayhouse at Sixteenth and Thirty-eighth, the other men shouldered at the bar silently made room for him. Spandhana was always pleased at this reaction because it bespoke the deference he elicited among the other regulars. "Dhik" meant "trouble" in several of the stem languages, and the regulars were never sure whether he had come to discover it or deliver it.

Fanghsi, one of those regulars, looked him over. "Off duty," he guessed.

Dhik cocked an eyebrow, which accomplished a whole skein of conversation,

Fanghsi shrugged. "You don't have your staff with you."

The Enforcer acknowledged this. "Left it home," he admitted.

"What if you run into trouble?"

"Then trouble better step away." He held his fists out and twisted them knuckles up to knuckles down. "I still got these, and these are harder to leave home."

The landlady, a hefty woman named Kunigund Arfwendsen, asked him what he was drinking.

"Make it a bottle of the Strangler." Thirty-Eighth Frame Strangler was a popular barleywine brewed on premises. Over in the corner, someone began singing a lively tune while hammering a dulcimer.

"Whether blue or golden capes we wear
Or caps or helmets crown our hair,
Whether we wear boots or shoes,
Whether we swab passageways
Or filter water all our days
It doesn't, doesn't matter what we do."

Fanghsi looked Dhik over. "Looking for a fight?" he asked.

The Enforcer turned his head to him. "Why? Do you have one handy?"

"You always look angry. No one ever sure."

"Good."

Arfwendsen struck the bar with a mug like a judge strikes the bench with a gavel.

"You here," she asked, "about that body they found over in Little Lotus?"

That surprised Dhik, who was here only for a drink. "Murder's above my pay grade," he told her. Then he thought Kunigund might have meant, "You hear?" He took a long swallow of Strangler. "Yeah," he admitted after lowering the mug. "I heard about it. Couldn't help hearing. It's all anyone is talking about when they're not talking about the Hexenplaza Mural."

Fanghsi shrugged. "I see him around."

"The mural vandal?"

"Nah. Dead man on news. Dead man get around plenty before he is dead."

"Hard to 'get around' much after," Dhik admitted. "Where you seen him?"

"Here and there."

Dhik gave him the Look. Dhik had a quiver full of looks for assorted purposes, and this one had reduced other men to quivering jelly.

But Fanghsi was not as other men, and he simply let the Look slide off his back and smash on the floor. Dhik was surprised and said, "Say, 'Little Face,' you are a staunch one. Not many men can handle that Look, let alone hand it back. What is it you know about Dead Man?"

28

Fanghsi's glance circled the wayhouse, causing men to take sudden interest in their drinks, in their mahjong tiles, or in their go boards. Gordon Wen-ti, in the far corner, drew two cards from the deck to complete his hand and studied it intently. Arfwendsen busied herself cleaning glasses at the end of the bar. Why, there were activities a-plenty in that taproom to absorb all the interest in it. When it had completed its circle, Fanghsi's glance came to rest once more on his face.

"Like I say," he admitted. "I see him here and there. Once, in Bigelow's Garden Shop over in Flowing Silk. Another time in Aishwara's Electronic Emporium in Greater Harwick. Aishwara catch him pilfering components. Chase him to drop tubes but lose him there. What value this skinny to you?"

A price for everything and everything at its price was an aphorism across the Thirty-Eighth Frame, and Dhik inquired after the street rate for information. Fanghsi quoted a discount because Dhik was not inquiring officially, and the Big Dhik paid it because the price was small and he was feeling large. As lagniappe, Fanghsi told him the times as well as the places.

Dhik bowed over his hands. "Nanri," he said, although he might not have been so thankful had he known where it would lead him.

Dhikpārusya Spandhana had only been thirsty. He had not gone to the wayhouse looking for trouble, but trouble, as always, had found him.

Ling-ling Barnstable sat on a bench with her tutor, Florian Venables, in the Greenfields, the vast park on One Deck that ran unbroken for most of the length and breadth of the *Whale*. Venables liked to hold sessions in the open air, to whatever extent "open air" had meaning in an enclosed vessel hurtling through a vacuum. But if to the stem generations who had boarded the *Whale*, the Park was a poor mockery of the True Thing, to the generations that had followed, it had truly become the Thing. If the "sky" was merely a projection onto the pressure dome, what of it? They had never known a sky that lacked a lid.

Education, it was said, consisted of a log, with an eager student at one end and Socrates at the other. The problems of education had never included a shortage of logs.

Venables was an elderly man, and white, bushy whiskers produced a reasonable simulation of Socrates, though Ling-ling, for her part, did not bother presenting one of an eager student. Eager she was, but eager to return to Zephyrholm and resume her regency over a kingdom of dolls. The thought "spoiled brat" passed through Venables' mind, but it did not pause there. He knew who paid his stipend.

"Ling-ling," said Venables near the conclusion of their session, "you have become a woman now, and it is time your lessons took a more serious bent."

The idea of "a more serious bent" stirred unease in the breast of Ling-ling Barnstable.

"At our next meeting," continued her tutor, "we will discuss the Big Burnout. It is the central event in the *Whale's* history."

Dread closed her throat. *Go to the Burnout!* and *Get Burnt!* were common maledictions among her peers, and while Ling-ling, Megwan, and the other youngsters of Third and Seventh were less than certain what such a destination entailed, they were quite certain it was unpleasant.

"What happened?" Ling-ling asked, more from the sense that she ought to ask a question than from a deep interest in ancient history.

"The gravity plates failed across several decks—and to this day, no one knows why," Venables said. "More than three hundred people are thought to have died in the disaster. Heroic efforts were made to keep it from spreading, as one sector after another failed, and people huddled in their quarters fearing they would be next." He fell silent for a moment, looking at something deep inside himself, remembering the older brother who had never come back.

But inside oneself is a place very difficult to look, and after a moment, he sighed. "Our time is up." Ling-ling jumped off the bench with unseemly alacrity; he seized her arm and spoke with quiet severity, "You will have to know these things to sit your Examinations. Be sure to read the essay by Bartholomew Chien I sent you so we can discuss it at our next session. Ask yourself why when people part, they now say *Be safe* or *Fare well* rather than *See you on Tau,* as they once did."

Ling-ling was confused. *Be Safe* was just something one said. That there might be *reasons* or that they had once said something else, confused her.

When she returned to Zephyrholm, she told her baba she wanted a new tutor.

Luis Commander Barnstable stuffed an envelope hurriedly beneath a pile, and when he turned to her, he laid his arm casually across his desk. He was an indulgent man, but in this, he would not indulge his Precious. Venables was reputedly the best tutor that money could buy—or at least rent.

Ling-ling was not the most observant of young women. If something failed to touch her directly and immediately, it did not nestle in her mind. But it seemed to her that there was something very important about that envelope.

Eventually, every can must come to rest, but Staff Sergeant Lutz would have been content had it not come to rest in her lap. Quality checkers independently audited a random sample of part numbers to determine the efficacy of the inventory. One of those random verification checks had found a discrepancy in her count of duty coveralls in the warehouse, and that had triggered a double-check of *all* her work. So, of course, they discovered that two cartons of hand teasers had walked with Jesus.

Her sobriquet was "Lucky," but not all her luck was good.

"What were you thinking?" asked Lieutenant Dingbang. The platoon called him Lieutenant Ding-ding behind his back, and not entirely because he was young. He was also called Lieutenant Dingbat by others. Lucky herself had several additional names for him.

"I thought they were there, sah." She had set her face like flint and focused her unwavering gaze on a point one thumb-length in front of her commander's nose.

"Well, they weren't." This being incontrovertible, Lucky did not launch a frontal assault by denying it but probed for a flank attack.

"I did not know, sah."

"You were taking inventory, staff sergeant. It was your job to know."

When your position is indefensible, shift your position, preferably to higher ground. "I could not check the upper bins because I was not provided with a stepladder. Sah."

"You could have gone and rousted one up, staff sergeant." Now, the Dingbat was on the defensive, but Lucky did not allow her face to relax. Speaking of faces, she wondered if the lieutenant shaved yet. He might be older than he looked.

Lucky had grown up during the devil-may-care years after the Big Burnout. She had experimented with various vapors and herbs and flirted with strange gods before settling down into a more sedate—and private—life. But that her earlier eat-drink-and-be-merry phase was a reaction to a sudden apprehension of the *Whale*'s precariousness never crossed her mind, let alone moved in and paid rent.

"Understood, sah. Where does Supplies keep the step ladders?"

"It doesn't bleeding matter, staff sergeant. You won't be assigned inventory next cycle. *And* your pay will be docked until the value of the missing teasers is repaid."

Lucky congratulated herself on achieving one objective, at least: getting out of inventory duty.

3 INQUIRIES

Shoe leather and sit-flesh—One stroke each—A bluecape in splendor—The airs of Pigwhistle—The Whale as she was—Dandi Nandi

"The basic principle of detective work," Bùxiè deSōuxún told his sergeant, "is to start with what you know more certainly and work outward into what is less certain."

Qínfèn deFēnxī pretended that he had not heard this schooling a dozen times before and said, "But, sir, in this case, we know nothing for certain, and as the sages say, 'From nothing comes nothing.'"

"Correction, sergeant: we know *next* to nothing. And what is *next* to nothing?"

Qínfèn sighed, "Something."

They sat at their facing desks in the Little Lotus cop shop, and Qínfèn reflected that they would surely not solve the case by remaining so seated. As deSōuxún often said, "It was shoe leather, not *sit-flesh*, that broke cases."

"What we know is—One: ..." Bùxiè held up a finger, "Dead Man is unknown to both Facemaker and the DNA library, which rules out the usual practice of interrogating friends and family. Two:" fingers continued to spring to attention, "he was bashed with a pipe."

"Or pipe-like object," his sergeant prompted.

"Or pipe-like object. Three: his pockets were stuffed with seed packets. Doctor Patterson-*pandit* is working on the DNA. Which lead would you pursue?"

Those were leads? Qínfèn wondered. Then he saw it. "Ah. Before entering that blind alley, Dead Man would have passed by live cameras along the main pass'way. They're mounted at each intersection and at many commercial establishments. By discovering which cameras caught him and when we can create a timeline and trace him back to his origin."

Bùxiè nodded. "That's right. But 'shoe leather, not sit-flesh breaks cases.' Assign constable Chen to track the camera data. You and I will visit all the garden shops in Little Lotus. Dead Man purchased those seeds somewhere, and once we have found that somewhere, we can use his transaction code to identify him. Ask the Operating Base to make a list of garden supply shops. *Dukāns,* they call them in this neighborhood."

But nothing was more conspicuous in Little Lotus than two plainclothes coppers roaming the gaudily decorated hallways and asking questions, nor was anything less likely to elicit prolonged conversation. The shops presented garish and welcoming facades; the shopkeepers, for the most part, did not.

Windows on the residential compartments bore soil boxes on their sills festooned with flowers—red, yellow, lavender. Hydroponic trays edged the walkways with oxygenating grasses. Bulkheads sported paisley *boteh, distlefinks,* and other colorful ornamentation. It lent the poverty-plagued neighborhood a spot of color.

"And why not?" Bùxiè asked when Qínfèn had pointed this out. "You're never too poor to tidy up."

But the Lotusens did not take pride in aiding the police.

No, sah. We are not seeing this man, no. Indeed, so certain were some that they need not even look at the image to not recognize him.

"It's not us, sergeant," Bùxiè assured him upon leaving Devandra Ovalaitis' dukān. "They eschew cooperation on first principles."

Qínfèn sighed. "How many more gardening dukāns are there, sir?"

"We must do this face-to-face, sergeant," the inspector said, answering the unasked question. "It is more difficult to cozen a man who is looking you in the eye. Dead Man hardly bought his seeds at *every* garden shop in Little Lotus. We need persist only until we find the one where he did."

At Magdalena Balasubramanian's *Eminent Flower Shoppe,* they went through the routine again, and Qínfèn wondered whether the woman would eschew the information or chew it. He amused himself by imagining Magda shoving the image into her mouth and masticating enthusiastically.

"No, I am not seeing him," the dukāndar confessed, "but I am hearing of him."

In this neighborhood, that would do for chatty, and Bùxiè leaned closer over the counter. "And what is it that you have heard?"

Now, Magdalena had the most wonderful sort of ears, for they were connected directly to her mouth. She assumed a conspiratorial posture and put her head close to theirs. "My cousin's husband's brother's niece is living in Greater Harwick and is telling me that one of your lot is asking questions there because a man of Dead Man's description robbed Aishwara's Electronic Emporium."

The two detectives raised their eyes to the overhead. Greater Harwick lay on the next Deck north. Qínfèn said, "But—"

Bùxiè cut him off before he could say, "*But Dead Man had no electronic gadgets in his pockets.*"

Outside the shoppe, the inspector explained. "It seems Dead Man was more eclectic in his purchases than we thought. Or perhaps this foray was not his first."

"If it's the same man."

"If it's the same man. Let's go interrogate this Aishwara. 'Robbed,' she said. Perhaps the seed packets were also pilfered."

"That would make tracing his transaction code problematical," Qínfèn said, not without a slice of satisfaction.

They set off together toward the manlift, where the gravity plate floated them up to the next deck. There, they stepped off into another world. The quarters were decorated in a more subdued fashion. The façades were solid, muted greens and roses in an irregular but pleasing sequence. There were no soil boxes under the windows, but the corridors were wider, and the 'ponic trays ran down their centers, dividing them "boulevard fashion." People on each side of the divider walked in the same direction: toward port on the left-hand walkway, toward starboard on the right. They did so by inclination and not by regulations. Altogether, a more orderly neighborhood than the unruly district beneath their feet, where people walked every which way. Even the smells differed. The air here boasted bread and pastry rather than cinnamon and garlic.

But Bùxiè could not help but wonder. *One of our lot?*

Dhikpārusya Spandhana entered *Baba Das Gardening Supplies* and waited patiently by the checkout. Other customers eyed him uneasily and either turned their faces away or slipped quietly from the store. No one had a clear conscience when an Enforcer appeared. They didn't know what they had done, or for whom Dhik had come, or indeed if he had come for anyone. But the best place to be when an Enforcer stepped in was stepping out. One unhappy consequence was that Dhik had a hard time striking up casual acquaintances.

But a happier consequence was that the queues on which he stood grew sensibly shorter the longer he stood on them, and soon he loomed over a clerk who, judging by the size of the shop, was likely Baba Das himself. The man was short, swarthy, fat, and sweating freely by the time Dhik came before him.

Dhik wondered briefly what the man had done or thought he had done—or thought that Dhik thought he had done—to make him shake so before an Enforcer. The First Basic Rule in enforcing filial piety was *Everyone is guilty of something.* But it was not his business, at least not today's business, and Greater Harwick was off his usual beat, anyway. He placed the thready image of the dead man on the counter. It was nice to have contacts in the morgue. Do a favor, get a favor, as they said in Little Lotus. "Y'ever seen this man?"

Das stared at the image as if he thought it would come alive and bite him on the face.

"Ought I be knowing him?" the dukāndar said, fearful of giving the wrong answer.

Dhik shrugged shoulders massive enough to trigger earthquakes, and as it was, the display rack shook a bit. "He been seen here and there," he said in a voice very much like an earthquake, "and is suspected of petty theft in stores much like this one." Dhik had been to seven dukāns in neighborhoods adjacent to Little Lotus. So far, in addition to the two shops that "Little Face" had mentioned, three more had admitted to seeing the dead man, and one, a hardware *dukān,* had admitted to being robbed. They acted as if being the victim of shoplifting was as culpable as committing it. As it might be when the annual Ship-wide Material Balance was run.

Considering this one-man crime spree, Dhik would have been obliged to deliver on Dead Man a dozen strokes with his bamboo pole. So it was his good fortune to have died beforehand.

What had begun to gnaw at Dhik was the odd nature of the thefts: seed packets, hardware fixtures, small electronic components. All things easily pilfered. But what, other than desperation or madness, would impel a man to steal broccoli?

"No, Most Excellent One. I have not seen this man, though I have experienced untoward losses in my display stock. At my wonderfully low prices, why should a man steal? Oh, my family will surely starve in consequence!"

Dhik judged the man truthful and growled, "I ain't no Excellent."

"Oh, no, sah, I see that now." The sweat was pouring off the man's face, and he mopped at it with a kerchief. Then he looked past Dhik, and his face dissolved like sugar in hot water.

Looking over his shoulder, Dhik saw two deckhands nearly as large as himself wearing the red livery of Maintenance. But they carried 'boo poles, contrary to regs.

"Okay, Lukesh," said one. "It's payment time."

No wonder Das called himself "Baba." The name "Lukesh" meant "king of the Empire," and this dukān was too paltry a domain for so grandiose a moniker. With shaking hands, the dukāndar proffered his MOBI to the intruder.

The second deckhand saw Dhik watching. "What're you looking at, crewman?"

Dhik turned full on, so they could read his chevrons. He said, "Under the Peace of the *Whale*, the right to bear 'boo poles is restricted to Enforcers."

The two men looked at each other, and the first one laughed and said, "What're you gonna do about it? Fine us?"

Unlike Das, who had been afraid for no reason, these two men were unafraid when they had every reason to be. Dhik leaned on his 'boo with both hands wrapped around it near the top, "The fine is one stroke each," he said.

"Step aside," the first deckhand said. "We're here to collect for Lord Maintenance."

"Please," said Baba Das. "I must pay them, or they will smash my poor dukān."

Dhik glanced at him, then back at the two collection men. "I'm bigger than you," he told the first man in a reasonable tone.

"Yah? But there are two of us," the second deckhand replied, just as reasonably.

Dhik's hands moved fractionally on the top of his pole, which, obeying the force multiplication of third-class levers, swung up and hard between the man's legs. He yelped and grabbed his crotch.

"One of you," Dhik corrected him.

The first deckhand had watched his partner go down. He pulled back his 'boo to guard his groin, but Dhik shifted his grip and sent the butt end of his pole into the man's solar plexus. The breath gusted out of him, and he doubled over.

A man deprived of his breath thinks of very little beyond taking another, and a man struck smartly in his 'nads thinks of very little at all. The two men lay side by side, respectively gasping and whimpering, and Dhik bent over and confiscated their 'boo poles and their MOBIs.

He scanned their names, ranks, and serial numbers. "Bearing proscribed weapons," he announced into his own link. "One stroke each applied." He entered the penalties on the deckhands' MOBIs, as well. Penalties were usually applied to the buttocks, but the Big Dhik was not about to quibble over a technicality.

"They collect from every shop on the corridor," said Baba Das. "It's a maintenance tax."

"Was it a legitimate tax, they wouldn't collect it this way. It would be a deduction on your monthly pay."

The shopkeeper shrugged. "Tell it to the capewalkers."

Dhik grunted. "Ain't that the truth." Lord Maintenance was evidently collecting a slush fund off the books. That was an issue way above Dhik's pay grade. Best not to get involved in Officer business.

Winsome Alabaster smiled when Ramamurthy came to collect her for dinner, but it was her usual sketch of a smile. It announced that she was pleased, or satisfied, or even amused. It did not pronounce her eager.

Flowing Silk neighborhood seldom saw anyone so august as a bluecape in a chauffeur-driven electric cart, bearing bodyguards on its running boards. Pedestrians paused in mid-stride, and neighbors gathered at their windows. People chattered to one another and shot unfriendly glances at the capewalker.

Alabaster was not certain what she had expected, certainly not spectacle. Why could he not have come for her in mufti! Her smile twitched slightly and became rueful embarrassment.

As a Vice-Commander, Ramamurthy was entitled by regulations to three bodyguards, and Alabaster supposed that the driver was the third. As a Eugenicist second class, Winsome Alabaster was not entitled to a howdy-do. The bodyguards wore the black of Security rather than the blue-and-pink livery of Eugenics.

Yet why would Dumont Ramamurthy feel the need to awe his own subordinate?

One possibility was that he found her attractive and wished to attract her in turn, like young men of fourteen who capered ostentatiously in the hopes of drawing a young woman's attention. But Alabaster, who did not believe she was attractive, certainly did not believe that she had suddenly become so after six years of widowhood.

Lucky Lutz decided that if she wanted to keep her nickname, she ought to give thought to creating luck rather than awaiting it.

She said as much to her corporal, Crowley Vermain. Her assistant had the most unnerving eyes, as well as a most unfortunate name.

In addition to her nickname among the other Marines of "Crawling Vermin," she had segmental heterochromia—"kaleidoscope eyes," as they were sometimes called—and if the light caught them at just the right angle, they sparkled. People who were wont to say, "Oh, she has her mother's eyes," or "her father's eyes," were nonplussed, for she had bits of both.

Lucky and Crowley were grabbing a bite at the *Pig and Whistle* after watch. They had finished their schnitzel and bok choy and were enjoying an after-dinner drink of *huangjiu* yellow wine, although the *Pig*'s version was closer to red than yellow. It pierced like an icicle in the brain.

The *Pig* occupied most of a block along the Third Longitudinal at Second and Ninety-first. Two Deck was just above the orlop, so Lesser Pigwhistle was not the best neighborhood in which to find oneself, especially after the lighting had been dimmed to evening phase. *There are forty-thousand souls in the belly of the Whale*, the proverb ran, *and not all of them can be digested.*

"Ah, the sweet bouquet of Lesser Pigwhistle," said Corporal Vermain, taking a deep breath.

Lutz decided her assistant was playing sarcastic since a deep inhalation of Pigwhistle air caught effluvia from the nearby farm vats. Seals being imperfect, the local air acquired notes of a diversity of creatures. Had it smelled solely of beef, she would have enjoyed the aroma. Even had it stank only of fish, she could have abided. But it presented an unholy amalgam of beef, fish, pork, poultry, and others, and so overwhelmed the olfactories by strength of numbers.

So, it may have been the *huangjiu*, or it may have been the company, or it may have been the airs of Pigwhistle, but Lucky Lutz had the inspiration of tracking down the two missing cases of teasers from the Armory.

"They could not all have been bent," she told Corporal Vermain. "The supply sergeants before me, I mean. When they did the annual inventory and tagged them as verified, they could not all have been fibbing."

The corporal nodded. "Honesty is not only the best policy, but the most common one, present company excluded. But so what?"

Lutz hammered back another shot of yellow wine, and it was like being whacked by an Enforcer's 'boo pole. Hey, their table was getting crowded! She could see two Vermains across from her, and she checked quickly to find how many of herself there might be. She refilled her cup from the bottle. She'd have a tomcat in the morning, for certain. "So, that means the teasers were once there."

"And now they're not. *Quelle surprise.*"

"Kell?"

"S'preez. It's an idiom my family has always used. It means …"

"Don' madder," Lutz waved her off. "If the teasers were there *then*," she held out her left hand, "but are not *now*," her right hand joined in, "then where have they gone?" Her hands came together in the space between them.

Crowley Vermain shrugged. "Why do you care, honey?" She had not downed so many shots of yellow as her boss, so while she was hammered, the nails were not driven down to the head. She reached across the table and took Lucky's two hands in hers. To still their activity.

Lutz pulled away. "Whadda I care? Whadda I care? I'm on th' hook for a couple hunnert credits. That's whadda I care! If I can fine out who tuck 'em and where they put 'em, I can slip 'em back on the shelf and not hafta pay outta pocket."

Vermain pursed her lips. "Don't you suppose Lieutenant Ding-bang is already investigating?"

"Lieutenant Ding-ding," Lutz confided in a loud whisper, "could not find his own snot on his pocket hankie. All that *chutmarani* cares about is balancing the books and throwing *kapsiao* on the Commandant."

Vermain giggled and said, "I love it when you talk dirty."

"An yer gonna help me." Lucky said this not as a request but as a statement of fact, though Vermain did not quibble. She reached out and took Lutz's hands once more.

"I'd do anything for you, Sarge."

"The cult of safety," said Florian Tutor Venables, "is a new thing aboard the *Whale*. No one whose first concern was safety would have boarded the vessel in the first place."

"True enough," said Hamdu Organson, "though one doubts they were foolhardy."

Greenfields was not only a place for instruction but a place for discussion. Its broad open areas were ill-suited for the placement of microphones. So anonymous conversations could sprout in the gaps in the coverage as well as the gaps in the foliage. Venables and Organson talked about this and that—mostly this and not much of that. Though sometimes, when they talked about this, they really meant that. You just had to know how to listen between the lines.

Surveillance Department could take six sentences spoken by the most innocent of crewmen and find something in them with which to demote him to Recycle. But first, they or their word-recognition filters would have to overhear the six sentences. So, people with something to say had learned to say something else.

"No, no, no," said Venables. "Virtue stands in the middle. That a man is not cowardly does not entail that he is foolhardy. Cowardice and recklessness are equal and opposite failures of courage."

Organson nodded. "As a man may criticize Air or Water without being a partisan of Maintenance and Mining. I understand."

"The cult of safety arose in the wake of the Big Burnout, I think. The crew had suddenly had their noses rubbed in their precariousness: a minute bubble of air, water, and power in an endless ocean of vacuum and radiation. It terrified them. Taking a chance—and remember, our entire voyage is taking a chance—began to seem insane."

Organson shrugged. "They could hardly demand the ship turn about."

Venables smiled faintly. "There were some who did. But throwing the *Whale* into reverse is not as easy as it sounds."

"You were there, were you not?"

Venables shivered. "I was a child. I knew the adults were doing mighty deeds, striving, and dying heroically, but as for the details, my parents kept me tightly swaddled."

"Would you say that was when Maintenance rose to its current eminence?"

"Certainly. Once people grasped their predicament, keeping the ship in repair became paramount in their minds, above even reaching Tau Ceti. Human beings are notoriously poor at deferred gratification."

"God save Maintenance." Organson nodded and shifted on the park bench they shared. A starling flew past them, seeking insects to harvest. "But 'hard cases make bad law.' It's ill-advised to issue new regulations in a panic."

"The desire for safety is sometimes coupled with a lack of foresight and with a reluctance even to discuss unpleasant things."

"That is not much of an explanation. And besides, those who pushed for the safety chips, for the surveillance cameras, seldom exhibited 'a reluctance to discuss unpleasant things.' Indeed, the problem was often to get them to shut up."

Venables looked left, then right. "I said 'a reluctance to *discuss*,' not 'a reluctance to posture.' Discussion implies a willingness to entertain a rebuttal, but the desire for safety and comfort included safety in their beliefs. Remember, most people feel that nothing bad should ever happen to them, and that if it ever does, someone must be at fault. Gradually, the desire for safety grew to include how your neighbor painted his quarters, or overhearing unkind words spoken by others. Have you never noticed how MOBI suppresses some stories in its newsfeed?"

"How would I," laughed Organson, "if they are suppressed?"

"When people are too comfortable with their beliefs, contrary views can feel hurtful."

"Tell me. That body I heard of …"

Venables looked around again. "In Little Lotus? It is a mystery to everyone." With just the lightest emphasis on *everyone*.

Organson dropped his voice. "Then the cache is safe?"

"They may not even know that they're missing yet." Venables stood and saluted Organson, who was, after all, an Officer. "The *Whale* as she was."

"Be safe," Organson replied.

The man who answered owned a cheerful, plump countenance surrounded by a burst of yellow hair, whiskers, and beard. A sunny countenance, indeed. He beamed as he greeted Bùxiè. "How can I be helpin' you, sah?"

DeSōuxún noticed the interrogatory. He had asked *how* he could help, not *whether* he could. Such a spirit of cooperation deserved encouragement. He displayed his warrant card. "Detective Chief Inspector deSōuxún. Are you Fireman First Class Huyo Ghontzal?"

The man's beaming visage widened. "'Deeds, I am, Chafe Inspector.'Deeds, I am. But you kin call me 'Hu.' What brings ye for'rd into Lower Black Jade from all de way aft in dat Li'l Lotus? I am not to be arrested, I hope?" His demeanor said that while he didn't expect so, he would be delighted by the novelty.

Accustomed as he was to the evasions of Little Lotus, Bùxiè was unsure what to make of him. "I came to ask you, sri Ghontzal—"

"Oh, you can call me 'Snore.' No need for all dat 'sri dis' an' 'sri dat.'"

"Snore."

"Is what we say in dese parts. Say! Kin I be offer'n ye a cuppa?"

"No, thanks. This won't take—"

"Mebbe a chug, den? I gots *Black Jade Three-two*. Dat's de brew o' d'local wayhouse here 'bouts," he added, perhaps in case Bùxiè could not add two and two.

"No, thanks. This won't take—"

"Inhalations, den?"

It became clear that the offers of hospitality would not cease until the inspector picked one. There were more ways than sullen silence to avoid answering questions. "Do you have some tea?"

Ghontzal leapt to his feet. "Immediately, I am at your service! Black tea? Orange? Green? White? I be havin' no white to hand, but the local commissary is not so far off."

"Plain black," Bùxiè said in surrender.

"I am brewing the pot forthwith! Don't go away!"

Desperately, Bùxiè shoved the image of Dead Man in his face. "Do you recognize this man?"

Snore Ghontzal paused in his mad rush, glanced at the image, then looked at it more closely. "Why, I t'ought it mebbe me, onkle Henry. But, no. Onkle never wears brown."

"It's an image of a corpse we found—"

"A corpse!" He made the sign of the wheel. "Oh, me poor onkle!" he wailed. "I am not hitherto hearin' o' dis ..."

Now it was Bùxiè's turn to interrupt. "Archival DNA tells us this man was your third cousin, not your uncle."

The caterwauling cut off in abrupt silence. Ghontzal handed the image back, "I knew it was not him."

"But you did see a family resemblance."

"What is a third cousin? Who knew dere were such t'ings?"

"It means you have the same great-great-grandparents, in this case, a great-great-grandfather."

Ghontzal's expression fell. "I don't ken who dat might be. Sorry, yer honor."

"Oh, we know who it was, given the state of the records. You had eight of them, in any case."

The man pursed his lips and whistled. "Me parents were good people, 'deeds, but to learn dat I have parents who were not only good, but great, an' not only great, but great-great, is dat not a fine t'ing, sah?"

Bùxiè despaired of explaining the point. "His name was Nandi Minkez. We were hoping you could confirm—."

"Dandi Nandi!"

"Eh? Pardon?"

"A t'ird cousin, ye say? Who knew? Me gramper tol' me of him. I always t'ought he were me gramper's gramper. He like to dress hisself up so fine. D'o I nivver laid me oculars on him, meself. A 'snazz dude' or 'bone Charlie,' dey used to say. He wore always de flower garland about de neck an' a bright, colorful bindi tween his eyes."

"Crew archives list him as 'missing' in the Big Burnout." Bùxiè managed.

Ghontzal turned thoughtful, or as close to thoughtful as he seemed capable of turning. "Dat sounds 'bout right. I remember stories gramper told us 'bout him. 'He answered da call,' he always said. But, hey, I must be making for you the tea. The brewing of him will not take long."

Bùxiè resigned himself to the ordeal.

45

4   SIGHTINGS

A walk through the wild side—Scuttlebutt in the flower market—Were they 'boo poles, or not?—Stars don't grand jete—He has the devil's eyes—This chicken was once a chicken—Crazy Eights

Alessandro Fanghsi thumbed the debit screen and left the shop with the bottle drink in his scrip. He checked his gear—specimen bag, goggles, rope, grounding staff, helmet, and lamp—and directed himself into a darkened passageway that led to an aft entry to the Burnout. Passing crewmen cast him startled looks. One, who had seen the burnsider before, grinned and made a sign for good luck.

Fanghsi turned on his headlamp and flipped down his light-gathering goggles. He had used this route many times before and could do it with his eyes closed, though that did not mean that he *would* do it with his eyes closed.

At the abandoned drop tube at the passageway's end, he detached the hazard permatape and stepped through, reattaching the tape behind him. The upward gravity plates were not working, of course, but two decks were an easy climb. He let his lamp play up

46

the rungs of the maintenance ladder and took steady unhurried steps. He tested each rung for support before he trusted his weight to it. This ladder had been sturdy when he had last taken it, but you never knew. There had been no maintenance for eighty years, and not all the bones at the bottom of the shaft were old.

At the top of his climb, Fanghsi stepped into a longitudinal gangway then turned portside into a traverse. This region of the *Whale* had been wrecked long before the fashion for decoration, and the hallways and doors were a uniform, soft beige, albeit stained now with gray-green mold. The gravity plates in this sector still functioned, as did water and sewage, but light and power were long gone. The air was as still and stifling, as in a tightly closed storage bin. No breeze or draft dispersed the warm air created by his own body heat.

He noticed some hydroponic plants creeping out of the longitudinal to port. Those had not been there the last time, and he wondered whether a tray had overflowed in an agricultural space and the plants were now advancing down the longitudinal like an invading army. The stalks were moving at a blistering pace—for plants—though he felt no need to *rankle his ankles*, as they said.

Fanghsi grunted and turned onto his well-marked route. The signs he had inscribed—chevrons scratched into the bulkhead with a ring he had made for the purpose—reminded him which directions to take at the corners. Sweat beaded his forehead in the stale, motionless air.

A heavy object clanged in the distance and he turned his head instinctively in that direction. The Burnout was still falling apart, but he was not curious enough to investigate which part had fallen.

A murmur, distant and indistinct, caught his ears and he twisted his head now in its direction. In the distance, he saw faint lights moving, and the murmurs became voices, indistinct even to his ears. They piqued his curiosity, though, in the Burnout, curiosity killed more than cats.

Perhaps the lights and voices were a maintenance crew making a long-overdue inspection tour, an eventuality not without its complications.

He opened some compartments along the way, finding a few artifacts in them. He recorded their provenance visually. Archives might be able to trace the occupancy of these quarters and thus establish who had owned the comb and brush or the desktop interface. He tagged them and placed them in his specimen bag. A skeleton rested in the third quarters he opened, and he backed out hastily, offering an apology to its spirit. He resealed the doorway so that feral dogs could not enter and scatter the bones, as they had those who had perished in open pass'ways trying to make their escape.

When he entered a longitudinal overgrown with wild hydroponics, he used the cane knife strapped to his thigh to hack through the dense thicket, knocking loose pollen that coated his uniform blouse like sifted flour and gave it an odor like stale bread. Small things scampered past his feet. Sometimes, a stalk snapped back and stung him on the face. The roots conspired to tangle and trip him. His blouse darkened with sweat.

The runaway hydroponics gradually thinned out, grew feathery, and finally failed to gather soil. Here, the gravity plates had cut out, and mice that had scampered too enthusiastically had found themselves floundering in the air, unable to gain a purchase. Unable to reach food, they had starved to death in midair, forming a noisome curtain of rotting bodies. Served them right! No one had invited their ancestors aboard back on Departure Day.

But it was not a condition he desired for himself.

While he hesitated, a mouse leapt from the tangle and, stretching its legs, deployed flaps of skin, enabling it to glide across the weightless zone. Fanghsi's eyebrows rose. He'd read that some squirrels back on Earth could pull that hack, but all the squirrels on board were eminent, that is, confined to the gene library. He wondered if this mouse was a one-of-a-kind sport or part of a breeding population. It was nice to know Darwin was no quitter.

But he didn't have wings himself, and you can't cross a chasm in two steps. He took a deep breath and leaped forward through the curtain of dead mice, knocking them aside. He flexed like a gymnast and hit the deck on the far side with both feet, stumbling only a little to regain his balance.

Hydroponics could no more grow across the gravity gap than mice could scamper, so the passageway forward was barren. He was still within the Burnout, but nearer now to its forward edge, and his progress became brisk. His markers took him around broken equipment and twisted walls, up one stairway, down another.

Until finally, turning starboard into another traverse, he found himself abruptly facing a half dozen men in tan jumpsuits wearing colored scarves. They were squatting around something on the deck. When they saw Fanghsi, they rose to their feet and spread out to block the hallway. He could see that they had been gathered around a raggedly clothed body lying on the deck.

"We have a problem," announced their leader.

Fanghsi nodded. "I can see that, but I think that fellow has a bigger one."

The leader grimaced and raised his right hand in salute. "The *Whale* as she was."

Adrienne Mei-ti presented Bùxiè deSōuxún with an exquisite flower arrangement composed of blooms of pure white and lavender accentuated with a spray of red baby's breath. Bùxiè always compared the genetically modified carnations to "blood spatter," which was a source of annoyance to his Special Woman.

"There was talk at the Flower Market," she said, inviting him to engage if he so desired.

DeSōuxún grunted as he studied the hologram on his table screen showing a mosaic of camera captures for Dead Man that Chen had stitched together. "Talk about what?" he said absently.

"The Excellent Commander Masterson plans to evict a dozen tenants abaft Third and Seventh." Adrienne spoke without raising her eyes but continued to adjust the stems in her vase.

The Operating Base had blended the camera captures by time and spatial coordinates so that it formed a three-dimensional time mosaic—except for the spots where the cameras were out. "Have the crewmen not paid their rents, then?"

Adrienne shook her head. "They paid, but Lady Water raised the rents, and they couldn't meet the new amounts."

DeSōuxún scowled and paused his hologram. He turned to face her. "That hardly seems just."

"Well, it isn't, is it? Talk is that Water wants the cubic for her son, for when he marries the Princess of the Air."

"Maybe you misheard," Bùxiè suggested, "or the gossips garbled the news."

"There was talk of going up there and protesting the evictions."

Bùxiè restarted his hologram. He could make no sense of it. The path travelled by Dead Man was impossible. Unless there were two unidentifiable men. He could not say from the camera captures. But that had ominous implications. One such crewman might slip through the cracks in the ID system, but two or more suggested more of a chasm than a crack.

Adrienne came up behind him and entwined him in her arms. "Have I your permission to go?" she asked.

Bùxiè reviewed her conversation in his head and when he had caught up, he answered, "Of course, you do. But you know you don't really need it." He turned about so he could wrap her in his arms as well. She was built like an exquisite porcelain doll. Sometimes, he thought that if he hugged her too tightly, she would fracture.

"No, I don't," she responded, "but it's nice to be asked, isn't it? You always ask my permission when you go out to the wayhouse or the dojo."

He embraced her with his lips. He could barely credit her acceptance of him. Each day still delighted him with her continued presence. It was probably time to start a child. After all, that was the reason why Eugenics had paired them in the first place, and they were licensed for one girl.

"On those evictions," he said. "If you like, I can check the Operating Base, but they probably follow the Regulations."

His Special Woman shook her head. "I'm sure they do. After all, the Excellents write the regulations."

The Big Dhik was not accustomed to intimidation, at least not from the other side of the *timidus*, but CPO Ippolito Okoye was a past master of the art. He growled and thundered like an imminent malfunction as he ripped Dhik a new one. The Dhik, for his part, endured the chewing without expression. It was the most defensive of his quiver of Looks.

Okoye's office was sparsely furnished. Dhik might have called it "Spartan," had he any notion of what Sparta was. No images adorned the walls: no Special Woman, no children, not even a cat or bird. Only official documents hung there: diplomas and certificates attesting to Okoye's sterling achievements. Dhik focused on a certificate for a training seminar in *Anger Management* and thought his boss had put it to good use. He had never seen anger more adroitly managed.

He stood to attention—his 'boo pole at parade rest, his eyes straight ahead. Because he, too, was practiced at the Art of Intimidation, he could recognize and even enjoy his CPO's expertise. Why, the man could swell up like a bullfrog, lick the varnish off his desktop, and replace it with a splat of sarcasm! Okoye's natural accent rounded his vowels so that his words came out spherical and bounced off Dhik like handballs. Some of Okoye's more blistering phrases, Dhik memorized for later use.

"Well?" his boss finished, balling his hands on his desk, "have you nothing to say for yourself?"

"Sah," Dhik answered, "would it make any difference?"

Okoye sucked in his cheeks and returned to normal size. He gestured. "Not officially, but try."

Dhik shifted imperceptibly on his feet, wishing he could sit down. But nothing was imperceptible to CPO Okoye's all-discerning eye. "Is there someplace you would rather be, Spandhana?"

"Yas, *sah*. Pretty much anywhere else but here."

The boss flashed a grin. "I like an Enforcer who can brazen it out."

"Sah, they carried 'boo poles in violation of regs."

"Did you measure them? I was told they were too short for regulation 'boo poles. They were more like erm, hiking staffs."

"Hiking? In Greater Harwick? No, sah. They were playing at being Enforcers."

"They were collecting a tax for Lord Maintenance."

"An illegal tax."

"That will be for Lady Purser to decide, not you or I. You made it look as if Enforcement were taking sides against the Alliance."

Dhik's jaw dropped. Fortunately, it did not break when it hit the floor, and when he had picked it up again, he said, "Sah! We take no side but the *Regulations*. Had the bully boys been collecting for Lady Water, I would have done the same."

Okoye sighed. "And this chastisement would have been the same. Very well, consider yourself chastised, chief. Next time, don't wander off your patch. The Harwick Enforcer was unpleased, as well."

Dhik, realizing that his censure would go no further, brought his fingertips to his temple and clicked his heels. "Sah!" Then he turned smartly about.

But when he reached the door, he had a second thought. "Sah! Their actions disrespected the Service."

CPO Okoye pursed his lips and tapped them with the fingertips of his folded hands. "So, they did, Spandhana. So, they did. I will remind Lord Maintenance of their filial duty. Dismissed." And as Dhik touched the *hoigh* plate to open the office door, Okoye added, "Oh, and Spandhana? One against two? Good work, that."

In the busy, silent bustle of the quarterdeck, Tongkawa Jones was a study in stillness. Indeed, so still was he—eyes closed, hands folded, fingers chinned—that his assistants thought he had passed on to the realm eternal. But the scowl on his face required voluntary muscles to maintain, and those, in turn, required a *voluntas*, so they did not summon Recycling to gather him up quite yet.

The forward bulkhead presented an image of the Sky Ahead, centered on the Tau; the aft bulkhead showed the Sky Behind, centered on Sol. Both images bled over onto deck, side bulkheads, and overhead. The Skyboard produced thus a reasonable facsimile of sitting in open space, save that the hatchways athwart the quarterdeck were highlighted as a safety measure.

The chartsmen, quartermasters, and assistant astrogators sat in slightly curved, concentric rows, whence they monitored their sundry consoles. The larger, centerline stations were reserved for the go-captain and the steersman, but as neither of those august personages was normally called upon, the steersman's position was occupied by the senior quartermaster, and the command chair cushioned the comfortable butt of Second Officer Reynaud Berylplume, Officer of the Watch. The two fill-ins acknowledged the importance of their roles by, respectively, playing battle chess on the console and snoring.

That placed Jones off to the port side of the deck as acting astrogator, where he faced the bale-eyed glow of BK Ceti in the Sky Ahead. Pondering that star's earlier *grand jete*, he concluded that its shift of position was either ontological or epistemological. That is, either BK Ceti really had jumped a hair or the *Whale*'s perception of it had jumped.

He asked MOBI if any other stars had shifted position, and as there were a great many of these to consider, the answer was a long time coming.

No, sah, the intelligence whispered in his ear bud, *no other stars have changed their apparent positions.*

That ruled out a sensor malfunction since that could not account for why *this* star had jumped but not *that*.

Yet, in the search for other jitterbugging stars, he became intrigued by a starless region southwest of BK Ceti.

Initially, he supposed that the stars out along that vector were simply too dim or too distant to register on the sensors, but the weird feeling crept over him that he was looking into a hole in space. The hairs on the back of his neck prickled because BK Ceti was sitting just on the edge of that hole.

An insistent beeping from the steersman's console broke into his ruminations. The quartermaster filling in there perked up and blanked her battle game, played arpeggios on her keyboard, and turned her seat to face Jones.

"Astrogation!" said Adrienne Mei-ti, "We have drifted off the plumb line! I need a steering solution."

The "plumb line" was the geodesic to Tau's anticipated future position. Though curved by the warp and woof of space-time, it was the "straight and narrow path." Jones reviewed his charts and spotted the deviation. The magnitude was miniscule, but if uncorrected, it would build up over the next eight centuries, and they would miss the Tau.

Everything that is changing ran an ancient adage, is being changed by another. Specifically, a change in motion requires an "outside force."

"Engines!" he asked.

"Astrogation, aye!"

"Have engines been redirected?" Maybe the previous watch had made a deliberate attitude change.

But the duty engineer answered in the negative. So, whatever "force" had moved the *Whale*, it was not a *part* moving the *whole*. That meant an unanticipated gravitational bending of the space-time manifold. He called up the geodesic equations on his screen.

$$\frac{d^2 x^\beta}{d\lambda^2} + \Gamma^\beta_{\mu\nu} \frac{dx^\mu}{d\lambda} \frac{dx^\nu}{d\lambda} = 0.$$

To compute the Christoffel Runes $\Gamma^\beta_{\mu\nu}$ required solving for the Metric Tensor $g_{\mu\nu}$, which in turn required solving the Ricci Tensors, $R_{\mu\nu}$. These tensors were shorthand for ten non-linear partial differential equations. Their solution was not straightforward—ironically so, considering the nature of geodesics. An exact solution being out of the question, he applied the First Rule of Astrogation: *When the going gets tough, lower your standards.*

A first approximation might be good enough for a solution. Physics often dealt with approximations: frictionless surfaces, perfectly elastic collisions, ideal gasses, and the like. Hence, the need for periodic sightings and updates.

He called up an auxiliary screen and laid out a dimensional analysis. The *Whale's* velocity was still well below relativistic levels, so he used the Newtonian approximation.

He stared, astonished at the solution presented. It did not balance to zero!

A nonvanishing sectional curvature did not *necessarily* indicate the presence of a nearby mass, but that's how the smart money bet. Something out there was pinching the fabric of space-time just a little, drawing the *Whale* off course, just a little, like a pothole in space. But there was nothing visible on the forward screen to account for the gravity.

And so, it must be the nothing that was visible: the gaping blackness southwest of BK Ceti. Exotic possibilities arrayed themselves in his mind. A rogue planet? No, a mere planet would not wrinkle space this much. A neutron star? A dark-matter star? No, they would wrinkle it more. Perhaps a super-Jovian tossed willy-nilly out of its stellar cradle in some ancient whirligig.

So, the blackness was only an occulting of the stars behind a dark body. BK Ceti had appeared to leap only because parallax from the ship's motion had brought the dark body across the star's light ray.

Gravity bends light. Not by much, because traveling at the speed of light, a photon would zip past the body before it had been deflected significantly. Hence, the image of the distant star had seemed to jump, but only a little.

I should not still see BK, he thought. *It's* behind *the dark body, but its light curves around on the geodesic.* Of course, anything massive enough to bend the light rays off a distant star would be massive enough to …

As the implications—and the go-captain's haiku—suddenly fell into place, Jones leaned forward and stared intently at the now-malign gleam of BK Ceti. The *Whale*, moving more slowly, would linger in the dark body's gravity well and be tugged farther off course. The black region now seemed a gaping maw eager to swallow him. Even if it did not pull the *Whale* to its doom, it could slingshot the ship onto an irrecoverable trajectory.

"Quartermaster!" he called.

"Astrogator, aye!" said Adrienne Mei-ti.

"A dark body off our port bow is drawing us off course. I need its mass and distance."

"Aye!" She turned. "Chartsman!"

"Quartermaster, aye!"

"Launch three swifties off the portside coil gun. These coordinates." A few touches to her screen sent the loci. "Full spectrum scans."

"Three swifties, aye!" Relays clacked in the distance as the coil gun deployed outside the asteroid's deflection shield. Jones imagined the gunners scrambling from their repose, abandoning their cards and dice to load the swifties into the armature and locking the armature into the coil.

"Where away?" asked the Officer of the Watch, who had wakened from his slumber but had not interrupted the astrogator or the quartermaster in their actions.

"Off the port bow," Jones told him.

"How soon to the bounceback?"

"That depends, sah, on how far off it is and on how large." It might be a large body somewhat distant or a smaller one close by. In space, there was no scale. Until the swifties reached it and their data streamed back, an astrogator would not know.

The Second Officer nodded as he absorbed this information. "Not an immediate hazard, then? Note it in the log, and I will inform Third Officer Tang when he comes on deck."

Jones thought Number Two was pleased any time he could defer a decision. But the body was already affecting their course, so it could not be too terribly far off.

"Meanwhile, sah, I recommend we adjust the Higgs field three points to starboard to counteract the attraction of the unknown body." Since a Higgs field gave mass to particles, the projectors created a virtual mass before the ship to attract her. The *Whale* would accelerate continually toward a pseudo-gravitational point just off her starboard bow, "sliding downhill" toward the Tau's future position. The *Whale* was, in effect, a donkey cart dangling a carrot on a pole forward of the donkey. It was an image that periodically amused Tongkawa Jones, but now it seemed they had encountered a carrot patch by the side of the road and the donkey had turned its head.

As he completed his report and saved his files, Jones was suddenly struck by the fifth meaning of the go-captain's haiku. You could also read it literally!

Ling-ling found God hiding in a digression and Satan in a passing glance.

Both befell in Greenfields while Master Venables babbled about the Burnout. Ling-ling let her tutor's voice drone through her ears. The expression "in one ear and out the other" was perfectly apt. Not that she was a stupid young woman. She had an open mind, indeed, so open that, at times, one could hear the wind whistling through it. Just now, her attention was fixed on the passing joggers on Meandering Path. She studied the ornamental shrubs and the bird that perched among them. The bird—her name was Splendida for her red, green, and yellow plumage—cocked her head and stared at Ling-ling with one eye. Ling-ling copied the gesture but elicited no response from the bird.

The gory details of the Burnout and its aftermath wriggled into her daydreams, spoiling the prettiness of the feathers. The red became blood. The green and yellow became the gaily dressed bodies that littered the Plaza before the fallen façades of the townhouses at Sixteenth and Seventy-Fourth. Finally, she snapped at her tutor, saying, "Where was God in all that?"

Venable blinked. "What?"

"Isn't God supposed to be all-good? Then how could something like the Burnout happen?"

"That would be a matter better asked of the Dalai Papa."

Ling-ling scoffed, glad to have found a topic that could put her tutor at a loss for words. "So, you don't know."

"No one knows everything, miss—not even twelve-year-old women. Don't ask me to explain the Higgs field, either."

"I don't even think there is a God!"

His response confused her. "That could be taken as two distinct sentences, young lady, both true. But as for Shangdi, *shang* means 'first or primary,' and *di* means 'God.' Shangdi is the first God, not as a god in eminence first among gods (for there can be only one) nor first in time (since he does not exist in time) but first in logical priority. He is called the 'all-*good*' because, being the source, the *shang*, of all goods, He thus contains all goods within Him, either formally or eminently, not because He is always nice. Behind everything moving stands something unmoved; behind everything caused is something uncaused; behind everything contingent lies something self-subsistent. Given that, you really can't expect Shangdi to be just like you and me."

Ling-ling, who had always imagined the Shangdi as an elderly Confucian sage with a long white beard, did not understand. "How do you know Shangdi even exists?" she blurted.

"Shangdi is Existence Itself. How can Existence not exist?"

"You have a mouthful of words for everything! But you can't *prove* it!"

Venables posted a finger. "In the ancient stem language, 'prove' meant to test, as in 'proving grounds' or the 'proof of the pudding.' So, let us test the proposition. First, everything material is a compound of Qi and Li, the active principle and the receptive principle. Westerners called these form and matter. They are grounded in the ancient principles of Yin and Yang, or as the Westerners said, Potency and Act. Qi and Li represent the unshaped versus the shaped, chaos versus order ..."

And blah-blah-blah. He went on in that vein, and Ling-ling tuned him out again. *That* would teach her to ask questions. Across the way on Meandering Path, a large hulking man had paused and stood now while other runners eddied around him like waters around a rock in an ornamental stream. He stared at her. She stared back and it was like staring into an abyss. A cold finger touched her heart. He had done nothing untoward, made no threatening move, yet suddenly, she was afraid.

"... and Celestial Li is what all men call 'Shangdi,' as Zhu Xi taught," said Venables with an air of having reached a conclusion. "Curiously, similar arguments were made by ibn Rudhd, Moses ben Maimon, and Thomas Aquinas at about the same time, and by Gaṅgeśa a little later and in a different argument, but by Aristotle earlier than all of them. Thus, we have polytheists, Muslims, Confucianists, Jews, Christians, and Hindus in very rough agreement." Then he scowled, "What is it, precious?"

She hugged his arm. "That man staring at me. He scares me. He's got the devil's eyes."

"What man?" Venables twisted, first one way, then another, but when Ling-ling looked back, the man had vanished down Meandering Path.

She might not be too sure about God, but she was now damn sure about the devil.

Afterwards, Venables mentioned the incident to Lord Air. "Do you think he was an agent of the Alliance?" he asked his client. "Might your daughter be at hazard?"

Commander Barnstable pinched up his face and averted troubled eyes. "Maybe you should hold her lessons here at Zephyrholm from now on."

Something disquieting was definitely in play, but Venables did not know whence the disquiet arose and, failing that, did not see how it might be turned to the Brotherhood's advantage.

Winsome Alabaster had not known true terror until Dumont's driver dropped them off at Twenty-Fifth and Tenth.

"This is the Palace," she said as she gazed at the brightly painted complex of compartments. She hoped she was mistaken, but who else could have quarters this magnificent but the in-captain of the *Whale?* Nearly all other compartments here had been dismantled to create an empty plaza around the Palace, filled now with planters and hydroponic trays in lush variety. Flowers red and gold and violet festooned the bushes, which were trimmed to a variety of shapes. A small crowd of swabbies in the captain's livery cleaned the deck and trimmed the hedges and polished the brightwork.

"Right in one guess," said Dumont as if it were no great thing to come here. He helped her exit the cart, for her legs had become wobbly and uncertain. Two of the bodyguards flanked them, and the driver proceeded to a cart park. Winnie watched him hum off with a rueful smile. There went her chance of a quick getaway.

"Is this why you sent me this elaborate dinner gown? I had to rewrap myself a half dozen times before it draped properly. You ought to have sent a dresser along with the dress! Why didn't you warn me?"

Dumont grinned. "I didn't want to give you a chance to beg off. Tell me true. What would you have said had I told you we were to dine at the Captain's Table?"

Winnie pressed her lips against her teeth. She couldn't say he was wrong. She knew her place in the ranks, and that was not in Palace Mainouvertes banqueting with the high and mighty. Dear Shangdi! What if she used the wrong fork?

Behind the sumptuous greenery in the Plaza stood the occasional black-clad bodyguard. The bulkheads were painted in loud, elaborate designs, so the guards stood out against it, which worked against their lurking behind bushes. But maybe that was deliberate. Maybe they were meant to be seen. After all, an unseen deterrent isn't.

Craning her neck, she saw that the overhead had been removed, so Mainouvertes Plaza was open two decks up. Above, the overhead for Twenty-Four Deck had been colored a light blue with white puffy things like cotton balls.

"Clouds," Dumont explained. "It's what the sky on Earth is supposed to have looked like."

She shivered. She had seen images, of course, but this was different—weird and alien—to see sky actually looming over her. What if the clouds fell on her? Compartments on Twenty-Four Deck were stacked upon those on Twenty-Five Deck so that they actually touched the overhead.

"Skyscrapers," Dumont told her.

The bodyguards escorted them to the reception line in the Palace foyer. Then, they departed for the servants' quarters below on Twenty-Six Deck, where the mayor of the Palace would provide a rather less sumptuous dinner. She had never learned the blackbirds' names beyond "Number One" and "Number Two," but she suddenly wished she were going off with them.

"Dumont!" she whispered as she studied the line, "Everyone here is an Officer! I'm the only ranker I can see."

"No one need know if you don't tell them. In that dress, you look as fine as the grandest lady here."

Nuts to that. Winsome Alabaster was not ashamed of who she was. She was a Geneticist second class, by damn! And if others found that a problem, it was *their* problem, not hers. She had *earned* her rating. She had not inherited the post from her father or mother as she suspected everyone here had done. So, who had warrant to feel superior to whom? Rajalakshmi Ming-ti, tenth in-captain of the Ship Imperial *Whale*, stood at the head of the reception line, wearing a red-and-gold satin *mumu*. It concealed her figure, which from what Winsome Alabaster could discern, was fortunate both for madame the captain and her guests. She was fourth of her line, her great-grandmother having seized power in a coup against the sixth in-captain after that woman's inadequate response to the Burnout.

When the Chief Steward introduced Winnie to the Captain, Alabaster found herself tongue-tied by the juxtaposition of soft, pudgy hands and hard-as-diamond eyes and managed to stammer only a clichéd "Honored to meet you, madam."

"She likes you," Dumont told her as they transitioned into the Gathering Space.

Remembering the hard eyes, she said, "Then I would hate to gain her enmity."

"Madame Raja rotates invitations to the Captain's Table among the command staff. This month was my turn. Each guest is entitled to bring a companion, and that's you. The captain owes me a favor."

The guests were enjoying a pre-prandial drink in the Gathering Space. As Officers, they were polite to her, perhaps for Dumont's sake, but they were also distant. When she tried to join a conversation, they would speak around her. The Commander of Security, the only guest to wear his uniform—a black blouse and trousers gathered at the wrists and ankles and with insignia in a lighter black—smiled and said, "So this is the geneticist's mate that Dumont has been squiring about lately." Winsome Alabaster noticed that he had spoken to her in the third person. The realization that she was now among the few who had seen his unshadowed face—a great beak of a nose between green, piercing eyes—sent a frisson of unease through her. But closer inspection revealed the nose partly prosthetic, so its true size and shape and, indeed, his eye color, even, might be wholly different.

"We've been out to dinner a few times and to the theatre."

The Commander seemed surprised that a mere ranker would speak to him, perhaps surprised that she could speak at all. Alabaster thought about barking like a dog instead but decided against it.

"Which production have you seen?" Commander Peng asked, but more it seemed because he felt the question was called for.

"*Hai Rui Dismissed from Office*," she told him. It was an ancient opera from the twentieth century, Old Calendar.

It was also a notorious one. Peng's smile turned thin. "Ah, a petty official loses his job after he criticizes his emperor. A salutary lesson for anyone to heed."

"A tragedy for the emperor," Alabaster suggested.

"What? How so?"

"An ancient Terran sage once said, '*I never learned a damned thing from a man who agreed with me.*' By dismissing Hai Rui, the emperor

61

ensured his continuing ignorance of important contrary information, and so he made poorly informed decisions."

Peng's smile broadened, this time, Winnie thought, in genuine amusement. But she was glad enough when the stewards announced the meal. There was no telling what might amuse the head of Ship Security.

Alabaster found herself seated across the wide table from Dumont. Worse, a centerpiece blocked her view of him. That was custom, he told her as they parted. One never sits beside one's own escort. Instead, Alabaster was placed between two bluecape officers whom she did not know.

The officer on her right introduced himself as Hariprasad Lord HVAC Genova. When Alabaster introduced herself and her rating, his eyes narrowed, and he pointedly turned a shoulder to her.

Winnie sighed. It would be a long dinner.

But the man on her left bestowed a friendly smile and extended a hand. "Hamdu Commander Organson," he said. "Liaison to Gold Crew." He dropped his voice. "Don't mind Hari. It's not mere 'rancor for a ranker.' Lord Air is upset over recent genetic rulings, so all his subordinates feel compelled to snub Eugenics staff."

"It's actually MOBI that selects—"

"Si, si, si." Hamdu waved a hand. "You are but a small cog in the vast machinery. I understand. Does it not grow tiresome, taking one's orders from an algorithm? Ah, the first course!"

The stewards brought out a tangy tomato and corn soup. Alabaster had been expecting something more exotic, like hoddawgs in beckoned beans or mi'loof, but the next course proved to be ordinary potato and eggplant in pickling spices. The captain seemed to prefer comfort food.

"This is really quite good," she said, more from an impulse to say something pleasant than because the food was especially toothsome. It was good but not remarkably so and, hence, deserving no remark. Organson seemed friendly and approachable, but she did not want to press her luck with an Officer by badmouthing the captain's meal.

Hamdu shrugged. "I've eaten better, but I've eaten worse—much worse if the truth be told. Dumont's Special Woman could not cook to save her life. She never knew which buttons to press." He paused.

"Despite that quibble, her death was a terrible tragedy. Has he told you how she died?"

Alabaster shook her head in silence. It was not a matter into which she had felt at liberty to probe. "I understand his loss, however," she admitted. "When my own Special Man disappeared, I had not even his body to keen over. One morning, he led his team out to conduct a repair survey in the Burnout. And that evening, he did not come back. Jaunty Alabaster was his name."

"And he worked for Maintenance? Oh, don't tell Lord Hari. Air and Water are in a great kerfuffle with Maintenance, and coupled with his recent disappointment with Eugenics, your connections may seem fraught to him."

"But I lost Jaunty six years ago!"

"Technically, my lady, *you* did not lose him."

Something in Organson's manner put her off. Perhaps it was his evident determination to find a humorous remark in every situation. Yet, she had to admit that in many ways, she had *not* lost Jaunty, only misplaced him. She kept expecting him to turn the corner and smile.

The Officer speared a forkful of spiced eggplant and spared her a look. "Tell me about him."

"I already did, sah."

"No, I mean tell me about the man, Jaunty. Tall, short? Black hair, fair? What was he like?"

Winsome Alabaster leaned away from the table so the stewards could set the chicken biryani before her. "Dark and curly," she said, using a distant and reflective voice. "He could rest his chin atop my head, and his arms were gentle iron. I could not break his embrace, nor did I ever want to. When we formally paired and chose our names, he chose the name Jaunty for himself because that was the kind of man he was. Good-humored, confident, always with style. He had a mustache you could have drawn with a pencil and straight-edge. When I learn of something new and interesting, even today, I sometimes find myself thinking, *I must share this with Jaunty*, only to be brought up sharp by an empty chair across the room. My life contains a Jaunty-shaped hole."

Hamdu nodded thoughtfully. "An impressive man to make such an indentation. Do you think Dumont is the right shape to fill that hole?"

Alabaster stiffened. "Commander Ramamurthy and I enjoy meals and merseys together, nothing more. Do you think it improper? I mean, without MOBI's authorization." But what she meant was, did he think it improper given their difference in ranks?

"Improper? Oh, no, no, no. On the scales of impropriety stand affronts far weightier than two people enjoying each other's company. Love is not the only thing in the world, though, of course, it is a very big thing. Can you cook?"

But Winnie was not certain it was love, at least not yet. She turned to her meal. "This chicken tastes funny."

Organson accepted her change of subject. "I believe because it is not from a vat."

Alabaster thought about it, then put her fork down. Her stomach turned over. "You mean this chicken …?"

"Was once a chicken, aye. Some of the stewards run a herd—herd? Is that the right word?—on Three Deck for the captain's exclusive use."

"I see. Pukka meat. Rank really does have its privileges." At least six crewmen, she thought, could be housed in the captain's foyer alone, and four swabbies would dine well just on the pickled eggplant.

Organson lowered his voice. "Not like the Departure Generation of yore."

"It does hardly seem fair, sah."

"Tell me, Winsome Alabaster, have you ever heard the expression, 'The *Whale* as she was'?"

Cards flicked across the traditional green felt cloth, five cards to each. Jen-jiao Kent, the dealer, squared the stock and placed it in the middle of the table. He turned the first card over. It was a ten of clubs. Lucky Lutz scanned her hand and pulled out a five of clubs and played it. Kanada Fishaven grunted and played an ace of clubs. Play reversed on an ace, and Lucky had neither aces nor clubs remaining in her hand. She drew from stock, returning her card count to five but was pleased to acquire an eight.

"All I'm saying," she told the other players, "is that I don't think those missing items were ever there. Why does everyone suppose that book count must be right and the supply sergeant wrong?" She threw the question out in general, but it was actually directed at Sergeant First Class Goliad, who had been supply sergeant two years ago before his promotion.

"They were there," said Too Tall Goliad. "I saw 'em myself."

"That's what *I* said," insisted Lucky.

"Yeh, but you were lying like a rug."

"And you weren't."

Goliad stiffened, and his lips compressed in anger, but Lucky said, "Relax, Too Tall. I said you *weren't* lying."

The Sergeant First Class frowned, convinced he had been called a liar but unable to find the accusation in the actual words. Lucky was convinced by his reaction, however, that he was telling the truth, and the missing teasers had *not* been missing two years ago.

"If'n yuh need extra credits to pay off the fine," said Corporal Vòng, the fourth player, "Lady Water is a-hiring extra security. Part-time work outside duty hours." As head of Weapons Squad, Vòng should have been a Gunnery Sergeant. The previous incumbent, Reginald Chang, had abruptly resigned, and Vòng was waiting for the millstones of promotion to grind out his third chevron.

Fishaven said, "Sure, a supply sergeant is just what Lady Water needs to babysit her wean."

"*Every Marine is a sharpshooter*," Lucky repeated the aphorism. "The Company's too small for spare wheels. Ain't it so, Too Tall?"

The SFC grunted and said, "Your play, Fish."

"Baby needs a new vacuum suit." Fishaven played an eight and declared the new suit to be diamonds. Vòng cursed and drew from the stock. He now had six cards in his hand, and unless his draw had been one, none of them were diamonds. Jen-jiao took the hint and played the ace of diamonds to reverse the playback onto Vòng, but the corporal surprised him by matching the ace and not the suit, bouncing the playback onto the dealer,

"Uh-oh," said Fishaven, "Here comes 'Crawling Vermin.' Too late to hide, Lucky."

Lucky's corporal had entered the wardroom and turned instinctively toward the card table. She bent and whispered in Lucky's ear. "First and Second platoons pulled two crates of teasers

65

from the armory for a live-fire exercise on the proving grounds last year. That was right around inventory time, so the two crates were tallied as 'in use' and were to be returned to the armory afterwards."

"Per book count," whispered Lucky. But finbacks to fishes, she'd bet that last year's supply sergeant hadn't bothered to open the cases to see if the teasers were within. After all, if you couldn't trust your fellow Marines, who could you trust?

5 DISCOVERIES

My sister is a freemartin—An Extravagance—A liverwurst sandwich—A meeting of the Guild—Nothing comes from nothing—A walk in the park

Although some of those in Arfwendsen's Wayhouse had claimed the game boards—a lively round of three-sided battle chess was underway—most were engaged in diminishing the supply of Strangler. The *craic* was loud and boisterous, though no fights had yet broken out.

When Fanghsi entered, still wearing his burnout leathers, a pig farmer greeted him. "Hao-hao, friend! How's the picking?"

Fanghsi squinted into the darkness. "That you, Hidaki? How's the pigging?" He was pleased with himself for punning *pigging* with *picking*.

Hidaki Thomason, redolent of the meat vats, had not yet cleaned up, nor was he likely to anytime soon. "Ah, Pig Fourteen, she ain't doing too well," he said. "What you picking up back there in the Burnout?"

Little Face shrugged. "Bagged me a tablecloth, pristine, from an officer's quarters."

"Pristine!" Hidaki whistled. "If that ain't the pig's pajamas."

"Yah. Not scorched or torn or stained. Eighty years of dust but ..."

"Now that yer a wealthy man, you can afford to buy me a drink."

"Wait up till I see a buyer, me."

Nearby, a miner spoke to an HVAC mate, the usual ilmenite. "Y'know. Titanium and oxygen."

"Could always use me more of that there oxy," someone else assured him. "I'm tired of breathing everyone else's exhalations. Some fresh molly cues would be welcome,"

"Ah, the air's scrubbed fine," said HVAC. "We pulls the CO_2 outta the air and feeds it to the 'ponics. The 'ponics suck in the CO_2 and exhale oxy. It all circulates fine. Just gotta touch it up now and then."

Hidaki raised his mug. "God save the Air."

Fanghsi let them talk around him. Nothing they said mattered much and was, anyway, ninty percent repetition of cliches and truisms. He allotted five minutes before someone would praise the district stickball team and another five after that for the first fight of the evening to boil over. He wasn't here for that. He was waiting for—

The sudden lull in the chatter that meant the Big Dhik had entered. This time, he saw, the Enforcer carried 'boo, which meant he was on duty. Even if he had come in only to wet his lips, he probably intended to whet everyone's lips. Gossip was his feedstock the way the mother-meat was Hidaki's. Sometimes he picked up info that was not strictly against regulations but was nonetheless embarrassing to its source. He had made a fair amount of cash using it in his side business before he had been caught.

Killings were above an Enforcer's rating, but Little Face did not know who else he might approach about the body he had found. The Burnout was, so far as he knew, outside anyone's jurisdiction, though by common decency, he could not just leave it there. Dhikpāruṣya Spandhana had some authority and was just shady enough to know when and how to finesse it.

Fanghsi sidled up behind him to the bar. This was easily done, as other drinkers created a Dhik-sized hole for the Enforcer to snug into. Fanghsi proffered his MOBI to Kunigund and told her the Enforcer's next drink was on him. Dhik cocked his head to look at him.

"You don't know what I'm drinking yet."

"*Strangler*, I assume."

"Never assume," Dhik told him with a lugubrious face. "God always has a banana cream pie handy." Then he ordered a tall glass of bhang lassi, Arfwendsen's most expensive concoction. They waited in silence while she made a roux of butter and ground cannabis, gently added milk and yogurt and warmed it to a simmer.

"Want it spiced, sah?" Kunigund asked.

Dhik nodded. "Nutmeg."

Fanghsi thought the nutmeg an affectation, but he wrote the expense off as an investment.

They took their drinks to a table that became available even as they approached it. "So, why moody look, Dhik? Or just keeping in practice, you?"

"Aaah, I got my draft notice." Dhik scowled into his milkshake, took a sip, and wiped the mustache off his lip with the back of his hand.

Fanghsi chuckled. "Eugenics scrubbing bottom of gene pool if they think your chromosomes worth passing on."

"Laugh all you want, Little Face. Normally, I'd welcome an invitation to the Dance, but ..." He sighed and drank his entire drink in a few hard swallows before setting the glass down hard. "It's not just that they picked a twelve-year-old woman for me—"

"Age of maturity," said Fanghsi. "For males, fourteen."

"And that's how they usually get paired," the Enforcer said. "Fourteen-year-old males with twelve-year-old females. So, why match her with someone like me? I'm twice her age. The gene combo can't be *that* good. But like I said, that ain't the worst." He raised his drink once more to his lips, realized he had already finished it, and set the glass down again. "The worst part is the woman. She's the Princess of the Air."

Fanghsi whistled. "Thought she promised to little Lord Hydro. This gonna mess up heavy plans."

"Don't I know it. That's why I'm gonna file an appeal."

"You can't fight Eugenics."

"The hell you say. I went up that way to reconnoiter a little, you know. Check her out. She saw me, and it scared her spitless. Imagine. The mere sight of me frightened the little princess."

69

"Sight of you frighten any woman. You know what you need, Dhik? You need to get horizontal."

"That's against Regulations. You can only lie with those genetically chosen."

"No, sah. There is loophole. Loophole follows: Excellents care only about unauthorized *pregnancies*. Some blah-blah about environment carrying capacity. Otherwise, take your jollies as you find them."

"Yah, but there's always the chance that the jollies will gestate. Do you know the penalty for an unauthorized pregnancy?"

"But you don't gotta take no chance." Fanghsi leaned across the table and lowered his voice. "My twin sister, she's a freemartin."

Dhik sat straighter. "The hell you say."

"Yeah, bonded and certified. She never anyone's Special Woman …"

"If she's your twin, I can see why."

"… but being naturally sterile, Regs exempt her."

Dhik nodded slowly. "So, what is it you want from me, Little Face? Don't tell me you're pimping your sister out of sheer benevolence."

Fanghsi looked left, right, behind. He leaned forward. "I have a body," he admitted.

"Not much of one," Dhik commented.

"No. *Found* body."

"Whose?"

Little Face shrugged. "Didn't ask him. He not home anymore."

Fanghsi could almost *see* the calculations running through the Enforcer's mind, and he sighed. Sis might not be down payment enough.

"So, why tell me?" Dhik asked.

"Cannot leave poor oik out there in Burnout. Recycling dead one of seven corporal mitzvahs. Might could be you help me fetch him in."

Of the three main languages spoken aboard the *Whale*—Běifāngwóng wá, Spanglish, and Taṇṭamiz, Winsome Alabaster was fluent in two and could muddle through the third. But she was uncertain what impended when she palmed the hoigh plate beside Dumont Ramamurthy's door. A kaḷiyāṭṭam meant "an extravagance," but Dumont had evidently intended a more idiomatic meaning when he had invited her to attend one.

Behind her, the autocart that had delivered her to Twenty-Third and Tenth departed for its charging station, and Winnie stood alone in the broad companionway. Unlike in her own Flowing Silk, there were no throngs of passersby, or of neighbors sitting out, or of children cavorting. The corridor was deserted. Capewalkers preferred their solitude undisturbed.

She debated pressing the hoigh plate again, but just before she did so, the door slid open, and Dumont stood there with a smile on his face. Alabaster's heart rose at the sight of him, and her smile became very nearly manifest.

The Vice-Commander was garbed in a fine pseudo-silk blouse of orange and green with the wide sleeves that had recently become fashionable and wore tight-fitting cream-colored trousers highlighted with a prominent red codpiece. From within his quarters drifted the odors of sandalwood and the sounds of *Raga Mishra Piloo*, a classic evening raga.

"Vaazhga!" he said, bowing over his steepled hands.

"Ola," she replied, extending her hand to be shaken.

It was a game they played. The scores of stem cultures that had boarded the *Whale* had been blending for centuries, and practices that had once been the provenance of a single folk were becoming the common hoard of all. Dumont offered her his arm, and she accepted. The good will of an Officer was not something to be spurned, and they had shared enough in the past few weeks to earn a few familiarities. He guided her into his quarters, where she was surprised to see a live sitar player seated on a cushion, accompanied by a tabla man tapping out the tempos. So, the music was not synthesized! An extravagance, indeed!

At least ten other people lounged about a room spacious enough to quarter three petty officers or six ordinary crewmen, not to mention a dozen swabbies. And this was only Dumont's party room.

Some guests lay on large, overstuffed cushions, others stood with drinks or inhalers at tall, skinny tables, all chatting amiably with one another. They acknowledged Alabaster's entrance with languid waves or reserved nods. All of them, she learned as Dumont introduced her around, outranked her, though none outranked Dumont. Most were lieutenants from sundry Departments, but some

71

were lieutenant commanders. There was one other vice commander: Nelson Chandrashekar, Dumont's opposite number on the Output side of Eugenics. He had purview over the chivarists, creches, and duennas. The gathering might have been intimidating had Winsome Alabaster been the sort who could be intimidated. But much as a solid punch numbs the flesh against lesser pokes, her dinner at the Captain's Table had been among far more august company, and she had survived that.

Dumont put his arm around her shoulder. "Can I get you a relaxant? Something to drink or inhale?"

" 'Ponic wine," she said.

"Flavored?"

"No, I'm a real buckaroo. I'll take it straight."

"Right. Don't go away." And he hurried off.

One of the women at the gathering drifted to her side. She had been introduced as Lt. Belika Wanderloo from Administration. She was shorter than Alabaster and had hard muscles. Winnie suspected that, like herself, she practiced gymnastics. Her fist wrapped around a decorative glass containing a ruby liquid. "Nervous?" she said. "Is this your first? Just relax and let it happen."

Ramamurthy returned with her drink before she could respond to this cryptic remark. "*Ponica* isn't really a wine, you know." He handed her the cup. "It's more like a distilled beer made from the hydroponic grain."

Alabaster knew that, of course, but she let it pass.

The sitar player was still in *vilambit*, and the slow tempo encouraged Dumont to take her in his arms and dance with her. The choreography was Western, though it complemented the music well enough. Over his shoulder, she saw that Wanderloo had hiked her skirts up and was coupling with one of the men on the cushions. Alabaster had done her duty as a chivarist, so the spectacle did not scandalize her—unless Wanderloo and the young man were not eugenically paired ....

Her glance darted about the room, where she saw other guests disrobing and caressing one another. A junior lieutenant shifted from the embraces of one female to those of another. Self-evidently, they could not *both* be his Special Woman, and that did scandalize her.

"Sah," she said. "Dumont, dear, those people over there ..." She was not so gauche as to point; a tilt of the head would do. "I don't think they have been formally paired."

The Vice-commander glanced in the direction she had indicated, and to Alabaster's shock, he shrugged. "So. If any of them give birth, you may report them in violation."

"But ..."

"There are ways to forestall conception and, failing that, prevent birth."

Alabaster stopped dancing just as the tabla man broke into *jhala*. "Sah! That may conform to the letter of the Regulations, but surely not to the spirit."

"But only the letter can be enforced." He reached for her, but she took a step away. "Winnie," he continued, "the two most basic appetites of *atman* are digestion and reproduction. That is why taking someone to dinner and taking her to bed are so intimately connected."

"Sah, those drives lie at the vegetative level. *Plants* have them. They suck nutrients and pop seeds. And you have taken me to dinner, but not ... but not ..." She pondered the matter further and said, "Eugenics must first approve our pairing."

"Oh, Winnie ... we are Eugenics. There will be no problem."

That Dumont Ramamurthy, as Vice Commander of Eugenics Intake, might put his thumb on the scale for personal advantage gave her pause.

And he is my Officer, she thought. She could not make an issue of it without hazarding her career. Besides, his attentions were neither unwelcome nor unpleasant. She was not vain. She knew she was not remarkably beautiful.

When the hoigh plate chimed again and Dumont answered the door, a dozen deckhands swinging 'boo poles burst into the room and beat the guests senseless.

Organson and Venables met regularly to "not" discuss matters. Their chosen venue, as always, was in Greenfields, where, on this occasion, they strolled along Meandering Path. They proceeded in companionable silence, the younger man holding his pace to allow the older to keep up.

"It seems to me," the bluecape said, "that we make do with less than our ancestors did back on Old Earth. I mean, technology." By this, he did not mean technology but what earlier ages would have called 'leadership' or 'the mandate of heaven.'

"Aye," said Venables, looking about. They were in an open area called The Meadow, but it was always prudent to look about. "They had *in vitro* gestation chambers, they had autonomous robots, they had the true AI." By this he reminded Organson that MOBI possessed more limited capabilities than had the fabled "Thinking Machines" of yore. But that did not mean MOBI had no capabilities at all. Facial recognition and data seining did not require intelligence, artificial or not, only relentlessness.

Organson selected a nearby bench. Venables joined him and took a sandwich from his scrip and nibbled it daintily. Organson watched him for a time before selecting a handful of vegetable sticks from his own pouch. "How's your sandwich?"

"Wurst," said Venables.

"If it's that bad, why do you eat it?"

"No, it's a liverwurst sandwich." He paused and regarded it. "Though I suppose it could be better."

Organson and Venables had worked out their object-code over a period of months, several years before, after sundry grievances had driven them to shelter beneath the overhangs of each other's confidence. Venables had just admitted that life aboard the *Whale* would have to become worse for any change to happen.

Organson shrugged. Most people put up with crap—until the crap became too deep. There was a proverb about straws and camels. "I understand liverwurst is growing more popular," he said.

Venables shot him a sharp glance. "How many carrot sticks do you have there?"

"I have four and twenty. Why, do you want some?" Each of his vegetables had a meaning, Carrots were Whalers willing to fight in the passageways. Each stick was twelve. Twenty-four dozen were not many until one recalled that a determined minority might steer a much larger whole. A deep-seated intransigence was all that was necessary.

"Well, you don't need very many to make a hand-salad," Venables admitted. "Are they washed and trimmed?" (*Are they trained?*)

"Not entirely. Some still have skin on them. But you were going to tell me why we, the *Whale*, doesn't have what our ancestors had on the Earth."

Venables smiled. "How many drinkers do you need to operate a wayhouse?"

"Eh? Why, I don't know. Is this a riddle? Like how many tutors do you need to screw in a light bulb?"

"Can't be done," Venables told him. "It's too small and cramped. I mean that a wayhouse must attract a certain number of customers to remain viable. If patronage falls too low, the landlord must close down, and the equipment and materials go back into Storage. How far would you be willing to walk to sip a cold one?"

Organson frowned. "Oh, not far, I suppose. Seven grossbeats maybe, in dodeka time." That was a little more than ten metric minutes, or a "quarter hour" in Earth time. Base twelve, base ten, and tradition each had its partisans aboard the *Whale*.

"So, draw a bubble a quarter-hour's travel in radius around your proposed wayhouse. That defines what we call a 'catchment basin.' If there are not enough thirsty crewmen within that bubble, Admin will not authorize a wayhouse there."

"Not without a hefty bribe."

"Well, the same thing is true of the *Whale* in general. She forms a catchment basin of some forty kilofolk. Old Earth had about ten *billion* people, surface, orbital, and outworlds. There are things you can do with billions in your basin that are unsupportable with mere thousands."

"Like hand salads." Organson showed he understood the code.

"Also," Venables continued, "when we reach the Tau, we don't want to be dependent on equipment and systems that can be sustained only on Earth,"

"I ... see. So, we bring plough horses, rather than auto-tractors."

"Aye, the horses are eminent, that is, contained in the DNA library, because until our descendants are actually on a planetary surface, we have no need of them. But even disassembled, auto-tractors take up room, the parts being not so compact as a specimen slide. And, too, forgoing elaborate automatons in the *Whale* gives everyone something to do for a thousand years. Idle hands are the demon's tools."

"That may be something to keep in mind."

"Depending on whose work you want done."

"Ha. So, there are lines you will not cross. I mean, the boundary lines of the catchment basin." But he did not mean the boundaries of the catchment basin, and Venables knew what he did mean: that Organson was a line-crosser.

Tongkawa Jones sat alone in a crowded room. The astrogation staff seldom gathered entirely in one and the same place. The afterbodings of the Big Burnout included an aversion to over-egging a basket. So, astrogators and quartermasters gathered virtually as holograms in one another's quarters. Jones found it challenging to arrange their images so that they did not overlap or form ribald juxtapositions. Since no one else could see from Jones' perspective, he arranged the ymagos to amuse himself.

Adrienne Mei-ti, the senior quartermaster, he positioned at his own right side, for he found her flowing yellow hair exotic and her delicate features pleasant to behold. On occasion, he even entertained carnal thoughts and, because he could not act upon them, made them as entertaining as possible.

Of course, Adrienne, being the only female in the Guild of Astrogators, would be everyone's center of attention. The Guild did not bar females, but one needed time, skill, and inclination to master the craft. Time could always be made available, and some level of skill could always be taught, but few found the beauty of tensor calculus as alluring as did Jones and his colleagues. Why coerce into the vocation one without the interest?

Yves san Pedro appeared in the queue, and Jones placed his ymago on the commode. But he expected the usual announcement that the captain had retired to meditate on the Flight Plans and was surprised when Yves said, "Be upstanding for Pedro san Grigor, eighth go-captain of the Ship Imperial, *Whale*."

Everyone's ymago rose in a posture of polite attention, and Pedro snapped into focus directly in the center of the room. Jones sucked in his breath. Everyone else was clad in their everyday duty uniforms, pale gold coveralls, but Pedro san Grigor had appeared in his full-dress whites—gold cape and gold trim, epaulettes, sword, and medals replacing ribbons. MOBI played the trumpet flourish, *Captain to the fore,* and the assembled astrogators and quartermasters put their right arms athwart their chests.

When the last notes had died away, the go-captain said, "May your geodesics lie straight before you,"

"Direct to the Tau," the others chorused.

"The Tau be with you."

"And we at the Tau."

Tongkawa Jones wondered at the ceremony. Normally, such formality in a Guild meeting was reserved for installations, retirements, awards, and the like. The other ymagos looked puzzled as well, save for Reynaud Berylplume and the abominable Prince of *Whale.*

The go-captain said:

> *"Our encounter nigh has brought to our attention*
> *A fellow now who merits our good mention."*

He means the dark star, thought Jones. *I'm to receive a commendation for detecting it.* His mind all a-roil, he tried to cast a poem of acknowledgement. A haiku, a couplet, *anything.*

The Guild Master—he was not acting as captain—continued.

> *"And what could now best crown our thanks*
> *Than to endow advance in rank."*

After that rather forced couplet, Pedro fell back on prose. "Senior quartermaster, Adrienne Mei-ti!"

"Aye, captain?" spoke her ymago. The captain's ymago reached forth, and MOBI so adjudicated the various images that he touched Adrienne on the collars and sleeve. "Now Apprentice Astrogator Adrienne Mei-ti." He looked about. "So say I."

77

The meeting chorused, "So say we all," before breaking into a hubbub of individual congratulations and well-wishes.

The ex-quartermaster flushed and smiled at the adulation, and Tongkawa was pleased for her even though the commendation ought to have been his. After all, Adrienne had merely reacted to MOBI's warning, while he had realized the problem earlier from lesser cues and had worked the tensors. He knew a flash of jealousy but suppressed it as unworthy.

He did not understand why Yves san Pedro was smirking at him.

Bùxiè deSōuxún waxed philosophical at his desk in the Little Lotus cop shop. "Life goes on," he told his sergeant. "Crime, especially in this district, will not await the resolution of one case before pressing upon us others." There had been a string of burglaries, an assault, and another murder, but with the aid of MOBI, he and his sergeant had resolved all three in quick order. The first because the burglar had not been so clever as he had thought in avoiding the cameras; the second because it had been a drunken impulse in a wayhouse and not the plan of a criminal mastermind; and the third because the killer had broken down upon confrontation and confessed in remorse.

Even so, and despite the accolades he and his team had gotten, the unresolved case of Dead Man niggled at him like a loose object in his slipper. All they knew of him was that a third cousin, the aggressively servile Huyo Ghontzal, lived in Lower Black Jade.

"Naturally," said Sergeant Qínfèn. "Solved cases don't keep us awake at night. 'Mysteries of the Explained' would lack ... well, mystery."

Bùxiè's lips quirked. His sergeant was quick, alert, and resourceful on new challenges, though he could neglect the routine. "But Dead Man, he is explained!" Bùxiè cried. The other sergeants and constables looked up at his exclamation. "Why, you yourself explained it on the very first day."

"Sah?"

"*From nothing comes nothing*, you said, but you had gotten it the wrong way round. Sri Dead Man was the *second* nothing."

Qínfèn frowned, but only for a moment, for he really was quick. He sucked in his breath as the realization hit him. "Ah! No wonder he was filching seeds and small electronics!"

"There can't be too many of them, after all, and they likely lack many capabilities."

Constable Chen approached them. "Excuse me, sahs, but there is a man to see you." He handed Bùxiè a card, which the inspector glanced at just long enough to take in the name. "Show sri Spandhana to us." Then, he turned to his sergeant. "If Dead Man is nothing, where did he come from?"

"From nothing."

"And where is nothing?"

"In the Big Burnout."

Bùxiè became aware of a massive presence by his desk. The man struck the deck with his 'boo pole and said, with some surprise, "Then, you already know about the body?"

Never let them see surprise, the adage ran. "Of course." Bùxiè invited confidence with his demeanor.

The Enforcer handed them a still image of a body. Bùxiè noted immediately that it was not Dead Man. "I hoped that you could run this through Facemaker for me."

"Because ..."

"Because he was beaten to death, and that is beyond my remit. His body was found by a burnsider during one of his forays."

Bùxiè accepted that for the time being and inserted the image card into the identifier and let MOBI seine the face-base. The console light turned amber.

Qínfèn pointed at the Enforcer. "You were the one investigating Dead Man on your own, weren't you?"

"Oh, no, sah. I was investigating petty pilfering in and around my bailiwick. It only so happened that the thief was Dead Man."

Bùxiè was not sure how much of that to believe. "Constable," he said to Chen, "a cup of tea for our guest."

"Or coffee," said Spandhana.

Chen bowed and left. Qínfèn said, "You'll be sorry." When Spandhana cocked a questioning look, he added, "You haven't tasted our coffee, have you?"

The Facemaker light turned green, which surprised Bùxiè a second time. He had expected another Nobody like Dead Man, but an identifier card slid out of the slot. He picked it up and studied it.

"Jaunty Alabaster," he read.

Megwan Masterson was not the most insightful of young men. Few men of fourteen are. But for almost his entire life, he had been groomed to be Ling-ling's Special Man, and now she seemed to have cooled to the whole idea. He didn't know why, and no one would tell him. All Ling-ling would say is that Eugenics had thrown a spanner in the works, but she did not specify the size and nature of the span, so how could he set things right? His precious Intended went about now with a haunted look.

Megwan's mother, the Lady Water, told him to pay no mind and she would take care of Eugenics. That disturbed him almost as much as Eugenics' spanner. Megwan's mother was hard as adamantine. Growing up, he had always feared her. But he had been taught that Eugenics had the final say in such matters. How else to cultivate the population? That his mother would put herself above Eugenics struck him as both frightening and believable.

His teacher, Constant Tutor Weepwillow, was no help beyond a bromide about the proper sequencing of chicken enumeration. That, and scolding Megwan for his taste in reading material.

Most of the files the young man scanned were what his tutor disparaged as "escape literature." Megwan did not see the problem. Wasn't escape the point of all literature? But Megwan's preferred genre involved tales of domestic life on Old Earth. So, its settings were colorful and diverse—the Granpublic Americano, the Paris Caliphate, the Audorithadesh Ympriales—and the daily events and personal conflicts that had engaged them.

"You ought to read realistic fiction," Tutor scolded him. "Tales of life aboard a starship, stories set in interstellar space."

But ordinary life was boring. Why should he spend his free time reading about things that he saw for himself every day? Sergeant Lutz, whom Mama had hired to beef up the security detail, seemed to agree with Megwan. "Exotic settings of oceans and forests, or tales of lions and tigers and bears, those excite the imagination. Our descendants will have to deal with them when we reach the Tau and start living again on the outside of a world," she said.

"Oceans—" Megwan had said with confidence. "They're like the Great Pond up here in Greenfields, only bigger?"

Lutz had only shrugged. "Likely so. We know that planet Vishnu is about twice the mass of Earth, so it will probably have oceans. The lions, tigers, and bears—as well as the forests—we must supply for ourselves from the DNA library. The go-aheads will have already salted the world with the basics."

Lutz had the superpower of conducting a conversation while maintaining a keen lookout, or at least while maintaining the appearance of doing so. Tutor Weepwillow believed this a front intended for self-promotion and speculated (albeit carefully) that Lady Water had other purposes beyond household security for amassing such a large platoon of "heavies."

Although Megwan could not call Lutz a "heavy." She was, in fact, quite lithe and excited him as not even Ling-ling Barnstable did.

But on the way home to Undine House, they found a small crowd of crewmen shouting and gesticulating on the Plaza. To what end was unclear to Megwan since no one appeared actually to be listening.

A tall, lanky man who seemed all gristle and bone shouted, "Justice or blood!" and shook an impotent fist at the palace façade. Someone else hollered, "Down with Princes!"

"Now, you will see," said Weepwillow, "how the lower ranks behave when not properly led. They chant three-word slogans and make little use of reason."

"Hell no, we won't go" was more than three words. So was "A man's quarters are his palace!" But Megwan did not contradict his tutor. Lutz unshipped a quarterstaff and stepped to the fore, saying, "Follow close on me. Make no eye contact. Do not engage the crowd. And hands off the pricker."

Someone cried, "Get that rotted little Princeling!" and hurled an overripe fruit for emphasis. But another protestor, a porcelain doll with flaxen hair, said, "The children are not at fault. Let him pass."

Megwan seethed. Children? Why, he was an adult. He even carried a dagger, his pricker. The mark of an adult among officers was the right to bear sidearms. But his stomach trembled, and his knees wobbled. He knew, even without Lutz's caution, that waving it around would not be the optimal tactic. He pulled the tail of his jacket down, the better to conceal it. Against such a crowd, what good would it do? He did not mind being spared their wrath, however insulting the reason. "What do they want?" he asked.

"They don't want to lose their homes," his guard said.

That did not seem at all unreasonable to Megwan, but when Lutz and Weepwillow reported on the incident to Lady Water, she fell into one of her icy rages and said through clenched teeth, "How dare they threaten my darling boy!" Weepwillow fawned and told her she was right to be concerned, but Lutz said no more than the potted plants that lined the family hall.

6   INVESTIGATIONS

That's really not his best side—A curvaceous grandfather—All gristle and bone—Fort Freedom— Let nature take its course

Detective Chief Inspector deSōuxún was not sure what to expect when he called upon Winsome Alabaster in Flowing Silk but was considerably startled to find her bruised and bandaged and sporting two black eyes.

"Some nosy parkers," she said in answer to his unasked question. "They busted up a party, and I was in the way."

DeSōuxún nodded but knew a mild curiosity since he had seen no such event on the Ship-Wide Incident Report. Flowing Silk was out of his jurisdiction, and he might have easily overlooked it, though riotous acts did generally catch his attention.

"I am DCI deSōuxún," he said, proffering his warrant card, "and this is Detective Segeant deFēnxī. May we come in?"

Alabaster stepped aside. "I've already told Ship Security what happened at the party."

"Oh, no," Bùxiè told her. "We're up from Little Lotus on another matter." But he wondered: *Ship Security?* What business had they dealing with a mere breach of peace? That was a matter for the En-forcers or, at most, the local precinct. He told himself it was none of his concern.

Alabaster led them into the sitting room and offered them tea, which she served from a samovar intricately decorated with reliefs of shipboard life. He and his sergeant lowered themselves into com-fortable, parabolic "sling" chairs.

"This is quite good," he said of the tea.

"It's a white tea. A particular friend of mine gave me a canister. Now, I cannot imagine what assistance I can render Little Lotus. I don't believe I have ever been back there .... Oh!"

"Oh?"

"Does this have to do with the Spandhana draft notice? He lives back there, I think."

Bùxiè tried not to show surprise. What had Spandhana been up to? "Nothing so fraught as eugenics," he said, "but a body has recently come to our attention, and we would like ..."

"But no one was killed!" Alabaster exclaimed.

"I'm sorry to say that not a day expires in the *Whale* without some *Whale*r expiring with it, and who often enough has been has-tened on his way by another."

"I was there," she said, pointing to her wounds. "All of us were beaten pretty badly, and Wanderloo's forearm was broken, but no one died, and the bodyguards rallied and drove the ruffians off. Ab-sorbents will resolve the bruises in a few days."

It was now clear that Alabaster was talking about something else, although that was the only thing that was clear. "I'm sorry, sri Alabaster," the inspector said, trying again. "This is only a routine notification. We have positive identification on the corpse through Facemaker, but we also like to have a personal identification. And as a matter of courtesy ..." He handed the image to the eugenist. "Well, we thought you should know."

Alabaster set her teacup aside and took the image with a frown. She glanced at the savagely beaten body, then gasped and stared. "Jaunty!"

"That was your Special Man, then?" said Sergeant Qínfèn.

"Si, though he was so much prettier. This is not his best side. Where did you get it?" She clutched the image to her with both hands.

"A burnsider came across him last week while he was prospecting. He captured an image and gave it to his friend, who then brought it to us." He did not mention that the "friend" was Spandhana, though he did wonder why the burnsider had not come to him directly. But, one complication at a time. "We're going into the Burnout to retrieve the body and conduct a postmortem."

"Then, I'm going with you," Alabaster announced. It was not framed as a request.

"It's a dangerous trek, sri Alabaster. We'll be taking medical people, some Marine guards, a guide …"

"Then, I should be perfectly safe with such men about me." She handed the image back to Bùxiè, who at first demurred. "No, take it," she insisted. "I don't want to remember him like that. Inspector, it's all wrong."

Bùxiè knew that, but he was curious what Alabaster thought was wrong. "Why is that so, madam?"

"Jaunty disappeared in the Burnout six years ago. But this image is not that of a six-year-old corpse. What was he doing out there all that time?"

Bùxiè nodded. That had been his own question.

It seemed proper to Tongkawa Jones to take the new apprentice under his wing and name her Adrienne san Tongkawa. If he could not enjoy the recognition for identifying the "pothole," then he could enjoy the mentoring of the delicious Adrienne. As a quartermaster, she had exercised certain routine duties on the quarterdeck—daily piloting, calibration of clocks and instruments, and the preparation, maintenance, and correction of the charts—but as an astrogator, she would need a deeper understanding of celestial navigation and tensor calculus.

Since part of the adoption process was to familiarize himself with her personal background, Jones invited her to dinner at *The Glowering Tiger*. He knew a little disappointment but also a little relief when she brought her Special Man to escort her. Jones had taken a vow of celibacy when he had donned the gold cape, and as he found Adrienne intensely attractive, was not ungrateful for the insulation. He got a chuckle from her Man's office-name, which meant "Relentless Search." An apposite name for a police detective to use.

The Glowering Tiger was decked to resemble a jungle back on Earth. Broad, leafy plants, both faux and real, burst from trays and pots between the tables. Fauna lurked amidst it, but all of these were faux. No actual tigers stalked the diners, only a stuffed mannequin that went by the name of Tony. After two hundred years, Tony had grown tatty from all the hands that had stroked his muzzle for luck.

(No one had ever tried to pet the python, a faux-serpent three arm-lengths long that coiled around a mock-tree branch as if ready to drop on passing diners, so its stark reptilian glare was unmarred. Tigers are far more cuddly than pythons.)

Jones lifted a flute of the *madhu* wine for which the Tiger was so justly famed. "To our newest apprentice! May all her stars align!" Bùxiè echoed him, but Adrienne, as was proper for the celebrity, did not join the celebration. To the faux animals and faux plants, this would have added a *faux pas*.

"Your Woman," Jones told the detective, "discovered our course deflection in time to correct it." He did not mention that he had detected the obstacle before its effect on their course had become noticeable. Such self-aggrandizement was unseemly.

Bùxiè nodded. "She mentioned something about it, Excellent, though I did not understand the maths."

"It was nothing," Adrienne said.

Silently, Jones agreed. Turning to Adrienne, he said, "You need have no concerns over the adoption. You have been grandfathered."

"What does that mean?" asked deSōuxún. "She has been turned into a grandfather? She is too young and curvaceous for that."

"This tiger steak is rather tough," Adrienne said, which was an answer of sorts.

"Top predator usually is," said Jones. "The vat tenders try to replicate the precise texture of the actual animal."

Her Man had been growing visibly more aware that Adrienne had not answered his question, so Jones volunteered.

"Grandfathering means she is exempted from some of the regulations governing the gold cape."

"So, my Woman will be a grandfather …. You should have seen my mother's father. He was rather less cuddly. What regulations?"

Adrienne coughed a little under her breath, but Jones did not know what she meant.

"The promotion puts her in line for a cloak, and goldcape officers cannot couple with Special Women—or Special Men, in this case. But since she was already coupled prior to her induction, she may keep you."

The inspector smiled, but it seemed to Jones a cautious smile. "How … fortunate," he murmured.

"But you cannot found a dynasty. That is strictly forbidden to the Gold. Had she already done so, she would have been rewarded in some other fashion than a cape."

"*Found a dynasty*," deSōuxún mused. "That means birthing a child, doesn't it?"

"Correct," Jones agreed. "Have you already been licensed? Eugenics will be notified so they can adjust the population balance. Perhaps the license can be transferred to some fortunate couple."

"Some fortunate couple." DeSōuxún looked across the dining room. Something there caught his eye, and Jones sent his own glance in that direction.

Tony peeked through the fronds behind a robot waiter serving a bluecape officer and woman, both looking the worse for wear.

"*The Glowering Tiger* is famed for its robot waiters," Jones contributed, assuming the object of deSōuxún's attention. "Other venues have long abandoned them. Too much effort was required to maintain them. Humans are self-replicating."

DeSōuxún cut a piece off his tiger steak. "Provided their licenses are not transferred," he said.

Lucky Lutz wore mufti. She was not sure why she had done so this morning, but she had an intuition that her uniform would lock more lips than it would loosen, and she had so advised Vermain. She and Crowley took the express trams aft to Milkhoney Hard, afore the Burnout on Twenty-Five Deck: a noisy, bustling neighborhood of warehouses and transshipment yards, busy with humming lorries coming and going, gravity carts and lifts, and thick, hard men shifting clattering goods about. It was conveniently located near the Central Tramway with shuttles to the Starboard and Port longitudinals, as well as access to the local gangways by which smaller lorries could work their way around the Burnout where the major tubes had been broken.

"Watch out, there!" someone cried, and Crowley pulled Lucky into an alcove on the aft side of the traverse corridor just as a goods lorry floated past loaded with crates of beefstuff from Pigwhistle.

"We shoulda come down on Twenty-Fourth or Twenty-Sixth Deck," Crowley complained. "People and trams shouldn't be mixing in the same passes."

"Look sharp," Lucky responded. "The surveillance cameras lost track of the crates somewheres 'round here." It had taken meticulous screening of archival video to find where the teasers had gone astray after last year's live-fire exercises. As near as Lucky and Crowley could tell, they had gotten mixed in with some empty crates, and the empty ones had been shipped off to the Armory. And that meant the teaser crates were stashed here with the other empties.

"Easy place to lose a crate," said Vermain. "We should mark ours with Marine red-and-white so they stand out."

"Why not locator beacons like people have? I'll put it in our report to Ding-ding. Keep your eye peeled, corporal. Remember what we saw on the archive video—a narrow pass'way to aft."

Crowley pulled her aside once more to escape a gravity cart moving some crates of ball bearings from break-bulk operations to an LTL lorry. If the Higgs field were to fail on that cart, it would spill an awful lot of traffic hazard across the double-wide corridor, not to mention on themselves. "You should stop calling the boss 'Ding-ding,'" she said. "One day, you'll forget and call him that to his face."

"Pay attention. That side pass' will be on this side of the traverse."

Three men in a sweaty hurry pushed past them. The *Whale* carried forty thousand souls, and it seemed as if every one of them had come to Milk-honey at the same time. A gravity crane three decks high hoisted a pallet up to Twenty-Three Deck to a waiting lorry there. Lucky reminded herself not to walk under it. She trusted her luck but did not want to taunt it.

"It's not that crowded here, boss," said Crowley. "But everyone's bustling 'round so much there seems more of them. Motion is a force multiplier."

Lucky swatted her backhanded on the arm and pointed. "This is it. This is the pass' where they shove the empties. Dark down that way, easy to forget a crate ..."

"Hey, you!" A tall teamster who seemed all gristle and bones called out to them. "That there pass' is off limits. Authorized personnel only!"

Lucky turned away, which gave Crowley a chance to capture a light-gathering image down its length. "Sorry, sir, we didn't notice the postings." Since the passage was festooned with candy-striped signs reading DANGER, KEEP OUT, and NO ADMITTANCE, that seemed disingenuous at best.

Certainly, Gristlebone did not buy it. "Look, ladies, ya want some privacy, go up to Twenty-Four Deck. Chumwater Flats—they got rooms to let. Cost you a half-credit for a metric hour, but that passage there dead-ends in the Burnout, and that would cost you a helluva lot more."

As she and Crowley left to find the manlifts to the next deck, Lucky said, "Good thing I *didn't* wear my uniform."

Crowley Vermain gave her a quizzical look. "Why?"

"That fellow back there, he didn't recognize me."

Alessandro Fanghsi entered the Burnout from Twenty-Three Deck at Sixty-Eight Frame. This was an easy entry compared to some others, and thrill seekers often used it to get a taste of life-in-their-hands danger. Some tasted it only once because it slipped through their hands. In some ways, the more fraught entries were safer. One was less likely to lower one's guard.

But Little Face was in a hurry, and this was the shortest route to the Brotherhood's redoubt. He slung his specimen bag over his shoulder, turned on his helmet lamp, flipped down his light-gathering goggles, and set forth.

However, there was no sense in making access to Fort Freedom easy, so after a few turns and ladders, the passages waxed more perilous. One lateral corridor was canted, where the bulkheads had buckled, and the deck had twisted. Cables hung like vines from the overhead, and the stale, musty odor of long-dead fires, electrical shorts, and the rotting bodies of rats, mice, and feral dogs and cats permeated all. Small wonder Maintenance had given up on repairing the region. They would have needed shipyard facilities and the resources of a planet to restore the Burnout—more resources at least than an isolated village of forty thousand could muster. One had to accept the Burnout, embrace it even. If one did that, the region ceased to terrify and became, in some small way, beautiful. The chaos of the region could be your friend—but first, you had to befriend it.

Little Face did not know too many of the Republican Brotherhood. He was a loner by nature and could not throw himself unreservedly into the Struggle. But also, you could not betray, whether by torture or accident, what you did not know. The Brotherhood was segmented into "cells" of five. Only one's cellmates did one know by name. Each cell leader knew the leaders of three to five other cells, forming a pod. Each pod leader likewise knew three to five others. And so on up the chain.

How far up this chain ran—and consequently how large the Brotherhood was—Little Face did not know. This, he suspected, was by design. The Brotherhood might not strike with confidence if its members knew how few they actually were, nor strike with intensity if they knew how numerous. "Many hands make light the work" was an adage in several of the stem cultures. People worked more lightly when they thought others would take up their slack.

At the edge of the Redoubt, a lanky man, all bone and sinew, stepped out from behind a fallen overhead panel and held a teaser to Fanghsi's temple. "The password, brother, or I'll put holes in your head."

"No thanks," said Little Face. "Already got one. Besides, you have tough time doing that with safety still on."

The sentry could not help it. He had to look, and in that instant, Fanghsi seized his wrist and twisted the weapon from his grip. "Follow protocol," he told the sentry. "First, you give me sign, *then* I give countersign. What they teach you nowadays in revolution school?"

The sentry wore an arm brassard that proclaimed him a corporal of militia. Fanghsi was unsure how he felt about self-appointed soldiers in a do-it-yourself army. Stringbean could call himself "generalissimo" for all it mattered.

"The wily fox abides her time," the man growled.

"Patience is a cunning strength," Little Face replied. "See? Not hard do it right."

Apparently, no one had thought to change passwords lately, for the corporal conducted him to Fort Freedom. Once a mess hall, it was now a mess. Camp lamps had been hung in ad hoc fixtures or mounted on the wall on sconces, so Fort Freedom was an oasis of light in the darkness of the Burnout. Fanghsi thought it just made the night outside blacker. One of the mess tables had been converted to a desk at which Group Leader Reginald Chang labored over paperwork. Other tables had been made over to beds, and on these lay various injured or sick.

"You would think the Revolution, she would do away with the paperwork." Chang spoke without looking up and waved his stylus at the material before him. "But no. There are hospital reports, after-action reports, pay records, menus .... *Menus*, for love of Shangdi."

"You could automate it all with MOBI," Little Face suggested straight-faced.

That got Chang to look up, just to see if Fanghsi had been kidding.

"Now *you* gotta come and add your mustard," Chang said. "Alright, courier, what's the *xìnxī?*"

Fanghsi wondered if he ought to salute but decided the hell with it. He saw no reason to replace kowtows to bluecapes with kowtows to coveralls.

"First things first," said Little Face. "You got collectibles for me?" He lifted his specimen bag and shook it suggestively. Chang pointed his stylus at the next table, and Little Face went over there to see what was available.

"Hey, old-style MOBI unit! Very valuable." He flipped open the cover, but of course, the unit was long dead. "You got provenance images?"

Chang did not bother answering and waited while Little Face bagged his ostensible reasons for prowling the Burnout. Collectors and museums paid well for properly attested Burnout relics. Maybe a clever hack could discover whose MOBI this had once been. That would increase its value twelve-fold.

"Come to give you heads up, Group Leader. Remember body you find? Turns out, medium important worker, him. Posse coming 'take him home.'"

Chang concealed his joy. He laid his stylus down. "Who's coming?"

"Policeman, pathologist, A couple strongbacks. Plus, Burn-out guide."

"Meaning you, I assume. You're not going to lead them *here*, are you?"

Little Face did not dignify the question. "Just say where you cache body. I take 'em there."

"2891 Conniption Pass'way."

"That on Nineteen Deck, no?"

Chang bobbed his head, and Fanghsi, having secured the information he needed and having ensured that Fort Freedom would not be startled into rash action by the incursion, turned his attention to the injured men lying on the pallets. The clandestine drill site was necessary to familiarize the volunteers with teasers and small-arms tactics. But not all the wounds looked like teaser burns, and surely not all were training exercises gone awry. "Anything Big Blue needs to know?" he asked casually. "I pass skinny up line." Big Blue was the unknown commander of the Mutiny.

Chang's demurral was too swift, and he sent an orderly to bring some tea. Over a cuppa, the Group Leader asked about the protest demonstrations in front of Undine Place. So, wounded men were apparently not a topic for learned discussion.

Little Face shrugged. Not his problem. "Growing routine," he told Chang. "Now attraction of tourists. Food vendors showing up. Someone make song."

"A song ..."

"*Lady Water's Lament, or the Bustle at Undine Palace.* Only sung *a cappella*. No bands yet."

"Bands ..." Chang covered his face. "Any sign Lady Water may cut back on the evictions?"

Little Face shrugged. "She not whisper me her plans on love pillow."

Chang's mouth settled into a grim line. "We may need to up the ante."

The session with her tutor took place in the playroom, although Ling-ling did not grasp the subliminal nature of the choice. It meant, though no one but Venables realized it, that her lessons—history, philosophy, gas chemistry, poetry, and the rest—fell into the same category as play.

"I have dispatched further reading material to your MOBI," Venables said. "I would like you to read the indicated selections before we next meet." Ling-ling fluttered her eyelashes, smiled, and bobbed her head from side to side. The gesture meant assent, just as did his own custom of nodding, but Venables could not help reacting as if she were shaking her head *No*. And a good thing, too, since the young woman had no intention of such boring labor, and so the fortuitous combination of her deception and his perception happily combined into a short lecture.

"An ancient folk saying," said Venables, whom Ling-ling regarded as himself an ancient folk, "holds that 'only the mountains last forever.' But mountains do pass out of being through erosion, and the *Whale*, being herself a sort of flying mountain, is no exception. Her appurtenances were designed to endure a thousand-year transit, but that is an average, and half the time, one is below average. With millions of components comprising the system, some were bound to fail early."

"Is this a math problem, *pandit*?" Ling-ling inquired, introducing a tremble into her voice. "I don't like math."

"No." Venables almost said *No, child*, but that would have been a grave insult now that his student had reached her majority. Yet she must get past her fear of numbers if she was to one day be Commander of Air.

"In the 120th Year of the *Whale*," he said, "something failed." This was a mistake on his part, for Ling-ling had heard him say not "the 120th Year" but "prehistoric times," and while her eyes remained politely attentive, her spirit took flight and soared into the empyrean.

But the Burnout had been a mere fourscore years past, and Venables himself had been touched by the penumbra of it. He had been a child, younger than Ling-ling was now, and the Terror had engulfed him like a fog. *Quiet, yngling,* he had been chastised. *There's a crisis going on.* And grown-ups, normally confident, wailed, "*A tenth of the ship, she is lost!*" He remembered people weeping in the gangways as they fled the wreckage, the miserable bundles on their backs the only possessions they had salvaged. He remembered his elder brother, Moe, leaving quarters garbed in thix armor and lime-yellow phosphorescent helmet, the brother who never came back.

The crisis had marked Venables, as it had marked all who had gone through it, and he had grown up afterward a subdued and contemplative boy.

"Those whose vocation is to run toward the flames," Venables said, "responded with vigor. Fires were suppressed, people rescued from the wreckage, and a new generation of heroes arose to rival the philosopher-kings of the Departure Generation." Again, the spirit of his brother flitted through his heart, and he knew with a pang that he would never be the hero Moe had been. They would raise no statues to Florian Tutor Venables.

Ling-ling was perfectly happy to allow her tutor's eyes to turn inward and his lips to fall silent. It meant a short respite from the pain of learning.

And pain it was, for learning entailed ripping out old beliefs. Since 'belief' was an old Anglic word that meant 'belove,' the extraction always hurt. When he came to himself, Ling-ling knew her tutor would redouble his instruction, as a metal worker who has paused in his work will strike harder upon his resumption. Since she found the Burnout too disturbing, she decided to divert him with an irrelevancy.

"Why can there be only one?"

"Eh? One what? One Burnout? Pray there is only one. This voyage has eight hundred years yet to go."

"No, Tutor. Only one Shangdi. We were talking of Shangdi earlier." That had been in Greenfields when she had seen the man with the scary face, but perhaps Tutor would confuse the timetable.

Venables was not confused and was quite aware of Ling-ling's ploy, but he decided to loosen her leash anyway and allow her a small triumph. Besides, logic was as important as its quantitative extension in maths.

"You recollect," he said, confident that she did not, "that Shangdi is Celestial Li or Pure Act as the Westerners said. That is, he is entirely actual, with no potential to be anything other than what he is. Like the ancient cultural hero, Popeye the Sailor, who rescues young ladies from hulking brutes, he is what he is." And *that* should provide a hook of interest, for Venables recalled the context quite well.

"Well, now," he continued, "suppose there were two distinct Shangdi. Call them A and B. If they are truly distinct, then there is some feature, attribute, or power X possessed by A but not by B. Or vice versa, of course. For example, A is *here,* and B is *there,* or A has a MUSTACHE, and B does not."

Ling-ling giggled.

"But then Shangdi B would be yin—in potency, the Westerners said—with respect to X. B would be potentially here or potentially grow a MUSTACHE, and that falsifies the supposition that B is Celestial Li as previously established. When a hypothesis entails a contradiction, it must be false. For your homework, cast the argument into proper syllogistic algebra."

At that point, the hatchway flew open, a distraction heartily welcomed by Ling-ling. The distraction came in the form of Lady Water prodding her son, Megwan, in the small of his back. Behind her stood Ling-ling's father, looking distressed.

"You, Tutor. Out!" said Sophie Water Masterson.

Venables looked to Commander Barnstable, who was, after all, his employer, and Lord Air bobbed his head silently, adding more quietly, "You, too, Tildy." The duenna closed her reading tablet and, with a worried glance at her charge, followed Venables out of the playroom.

Lady Water stepped out with the others, pulling the hatchway closed behind her, and stood athwart it. "Now, let nature take her course."

7   PREPARATIONS

"It's just that you worry me so."—Orders are orders—
The answer was 'very'—"Money and mouth should
co-locate"

Adrienne fussed at him all morning. Bùxiè had hoped to be packed and gone before reveille, but his Woman, knowing his plans, rose with him. She wanted to ensure he was prepared. "It's just that you worry me so," she said as she straightened his collar.

"I'll be fine," he answered. "We'll have an experienced guide, and I've asked the Commandant to supply some Marines who are trained in rescue and recovery work."

Perhaps it was a mistake to say so, for experienced rescuers implied the experience of rescue. "Why is it," Adrienne asked, "that those stepping into danger are less concerned than those they leave behind?"

"I worry when you go up to Undine Place." Bùxiè made what he thought was a reasonable comparison. "The demonstrations have been growing more unruly, and Lady Water has hired extra guards."

"It's hardly the same thing."

So, not reasonable, after all. Bùxiè countered her objection with a long kiss, which was harder to rebut.

"Why is it," he said when they had parted, "that those stepping into danger are less concerned than those they leave behind?"

She laughed and swatted him on the arm. "Do you have everything you need, pretty man?"

He wanted to say, *I won't know that until I need it,* but he sensed that might be an impolitic thing to say. Instead, he reviewed the checklist Dhik's friend had passed along. Hard hat, headlamps and jùggies, ration bars, climbing harness and rope, and so on. But everything that he took to keep himself safe only confirmed for Adrienne that he needed safekeeping.

"Do you remember that *mersey* we attended last month?" she asked him.

It seemed a non-sequitur, and he responded playfully, "I remember what we did last night."

"I'm serious, pretty man. The sensory immersion experience about that fellow—Jumble Jacques, he called himself—who went 'off the grid' so he could 'live free' in the Burnout. He died because the brook he was drinking from was leakage off a 'ponic farm contaminated with runoff chemicals, and he gradually poisoned himself. It was a true story."

"It was *based* on a true story." Bùxiè took his Woman by both arms. She had cried at the end, though she had known it was coming. Bùxiè had nearly cried, too—at Jumble Jacques' stupidity. "I'm not going out there to live, and we're bringing our own water. Just one day. We'll be in, out, and done."

"Take care of Peta and Qínfèn, will you?"

Adrienne often made him dizzy with the way her concerns could pivot on a pinhead. "Qínfèn isn't going. He'll be helping DI Ramjan hold down the nick while I'm gone."

"Must you go?"

Bùxiè remembered she had said the same thing on their first evening together when he had lost himself in the depthless pools of her eyes and the blinding light of her smile. He hadn't been going anywhere hazardous back then; he had only been going.

I am only half myself when you are gone, she had later confessed. Perhaps that was why she held him so close when they were together.

Youth did not know what love was. One required perspective to see it clearly, and that meant a little distance from time to time. Bùxiè, too, was not entire when they were apart.

And yet, there was his duty. He was a Detective Chief Inspector, God Save the *Whale*. He cupped her chin and tilted her head back. "You know why, dearest one. I have to examine the body *in situ* and check for forensic evidence. That's why Dr. Patterson is going too. She's bringing a strongback to operate the autogurney so we can retrieve the body."

She swept his arms aside and pulled him tight against herself. "I worry that I will never see you again. The Burnout is so treacherous."

A timeless kiss followed, during which he lost himself in the velvet of her lips. Her breath in his ear sounded like life support, and she, his ventilator. No wonder her absence left such a void!

But eternity ended, and hefting his harness, he left their quarters. "Be safe!" she called after him. His steps seemed oddly lighter. Surely, the gravity plates had not been turned down!

The pass'way was already trickling into life, and the morning watch bustled around him on their way to drop tubes and tramways. He wondered if Adrienne had caught last night. If she had, the child would disqualify her for a gold cape unless they let it for anonymous adoption. But that would seem contrary to the whole idea of conceiving a child. As the proverb ran: *Don't do the deed if you can't fill the need.*

Adrienne would be a fine mother. As he strode toward the drop tubes, he entertained the image of Adrienne nursing their baby.

"Orders are orders," First Sergeant Goliad told Lucky across his desk. "When a capewalker says 'should,' the Commandant hears 'will.'"

Lucky stood at ease but felt distinctly ill at it. "The Commandant wears a cape, too," she muttered.

"What's that, Staff Sergeant? I couldn't quite make it out. It wouldn't have been something insubordinate, would it."

Lucky admired the way the First Sergeant ended his questions with periods. "I just hate the duty, is all."

Goliad leaned back in his desk chair and tossed his stylus down. "Technically, Staff Sergeant, it's not a 'duty.' It's a bit of extra-curricular moonlighting—that you *volunteered* for, let me add, and if the work were anything else at all—shifting cargo at Milkhoney, shaving meatstuff in Pigwhistle, schenking beers in a wayhouse—your undeployment would be ever so much smoother. But no. You had to go and sign up with Lady Water, a notorious freak-of-control. If she wants Ynigo Lutz up on Undine Place, then Ynigo Lutz will duly appear on Undine Place."

"But Sarge," Lucky entreated her supervisor, "I've always wanted to see the Burnout."

Goliad sighed, picked up a booklet he kept on the desktop, and flipped through it. "Lucky, I like you. I do. But," he laid the booklet open on the desktop, "show me in the Regs here where your wants govern Fleet Marine policy."

Lucky took a deep breath. "Permission to speak freely, sir?"

Goliad appealed to the overhead. "And since when have you ever asked permission to do that?"

"Cards on the table, Sarge. I think we tracked down the missing teasers. Crowley and I reviewed security footage and followed two pallets from last year's live fire exercise to the transshipment center at Milkhoney Hard, where they seem to have been shuffled into a passageway they use for empties. Since *we* got the empties, the originals are probably still down there. Depending on where this body recovery team is going, we may have a chance to look at that pass'way from the other side and maybe recover the pallets with no one being the wiser. Or at least not too many being too much wiser."

Goliad nodded slowly, and Lucky tried to remember if nodding meant 'yes' in the culture in which Goliad had been raised. "That was good due diligence, Staff Sergeant. Does Lieutenant Ding-ding know? Well, let's not tell him until we find out one way or another. I'll command this detail DCI deSōuxún requested, and since Corporal Vermain helped with the tracking, I'll take her with me. No need to broadcast the news that two crates of teasers are loose in the *Whale*. Has Vermain had rescue and recovery training?" He made a notation on his screen. "I'll check her file."

Lucky knew when to stop struggling, or at least, she often did. But going into the Burnout? She envied "Crawling Vermin" the adventure of a life.

99

Winsome Alabaster had just finished with her packing when her *hoigh* plate sounded, and she discovered Dumont Ramamurthy at her door with two of his three escorts. The third remained at the tiller of Dumont's gaily caparisoned cart in the lateral pass'. The foot traffic, though light this early in ship morning, squeezed past the idling cart. A delivery lorry, unable to do so, waited patiently in the cart lane. No crewman was such a fool as to vent his spleen at a capewalker or his blackbird.

"Dumont!" she said. "What brings you to Flowing Silk? Quickly, I don't have much time."

The Vice-Commander looked over the accouterments she was stuffing into her rucksack and sighed. "I couldn't talk you out of this, could I?"

Not that he hadn't tried repeatedly, though he knew defeat when it stared him in the face. Pro-absorbents had reduced the swelling and bruising from the beating, so defeat found that face more pleasing to stare into. "I have to see where he died."

"You know how dangerous the Burnout is. Do you have a teaser to jangle feral dogs?" When she indicated she had not, Dumont motioned to Number One, and the blackbird handed her a weapon.

As Winnie studied it, her throat welled up. "Don't worry." She coughed so she could speak. "Don't worry. I've trained on its use." Surely, he must care for her to give such a tender-hearted gift.

"I knew you had, or I would never have given you one." He looked away. "If I could not prevent your going out, I could at least help ensure your coming back." And so saying, he gave her another gift, one that left her speechless when he departed.

How bad were the dangers of the Burnout? How badly did she need to see the place where Jaunty died? How immensely stupid and stubborn must she appear to Lord Helix? She looked again at his parting gift and decided the answer to all three questions was "Very."

The Big Dhik met Little Face in Arfwendsen's Wayhouse, where the burnsider welcomed him with a bottle of Thirty-Eighth Frame Strangler.

"How you like Sissy?" Little Face said.

Dhik was feeling large, not least because of Fanghsi's freemartin sister. "We hit it off real well. She and I are running off together to set up house down in Pigwhistle. Maybe that will make me unworthy of the Barnstable bint and get me off the hook with Eugenics."

Fanghsi took the remark no more seriously than Dhik had cracked it. Besides, he knew Ai-lin would never give up so profitable a business. "Why not like marry money, you?"

"It's more that money won't like me marrying it." He tilted back his bottle and let the barleywine slide down his throat like a stream of velvet. "For all I know, Lord Air already has his blackbirds out cruising the pass'ways, tracking me down through my locator." He patted his buttock where the chip was implanted.

"Lord Air, cream puff. Lady Water, watch your back. She do *something* to stop this pairing. My words, be marked by you."

Dhik took another pull. This time when he finished, he looked at the second burnsider who stood beside Little Face, a barrel-chested man with a red beard, denim coveralls, and a blue bandana tied around his head. Dhik's looks had reduced strong men to unset gelatin, but the stranger, like Fanghsi himself, proved immune. Dhik supposed that to a man accustomed to the perils of the Burnout, the perils of filial correction could be perceived as small beer. He decided that this was neither the time nor the place to correct the misperception.

"So, who's yer mate?" Dhik hooked a thumb at the second burnsider.

"Tan Lùzhě, him. Name means 'Finder of paths' in stem language. Worm got two ends. I take point, he take drag, guard against stragglers and mavericks."

Dhik proffered a hand, but Pathfinder only looked at it, and after a moment, Dhik dropped it. "A man of few words," he commented.

"His endearing quality. Most people got too many. Pile up in mouth and dribble out."

Dhik did not need many swallows to finish the Strangler, and his body was taking on a fine hum when Little Face complained about leading too many *niyōs*.

Since the corpse had clearly been beaten with methodical severity, the need for a police presence should have been unsurprising, though an inspector, a medical examiner, and a medtech strongback with an autogurney was perhaps more of an unsurprise than he had expected.

"Not surprise," said Little Face. "Just don't like nursemaid gaggle of *niyōpaiṭṭukaḷ*."

"I could stay behind." Dhik offered, feeling generous. "I'm a *niyō*, too. Don't know why yer draggin' me along, anyhow."

"Because this whole romp your brain-hatch. I ask you help drag body back for sake decency. Wanted to know who drag it to. Instead, you bring posse."

"I needed their help with Facemaker. How was I to know they would make such a double-yu out of it?"

"So. Money and mouth should co-locate."

8 EXPEDITIONS I

"What this shit?"—Winsome Alabaster's superpower—
Twelve are too many—"In Burnout, no easy routes"—
Walking on wall not so easy as it looks—A rest stop

They gathered in a wardroom on Twenty Deck afore the Burnout, and Dhik was chatting with Little Face.

Fanghsi scowled at the hatchway. "What this shit?"

Three Fleet Marines had entered the wardroom. What, indeed? "You guys lost?" Dhik suggested to the sergeant.

"This the body retrieval gang? I'm First Sergeant Goliad, and these are Corporal Vermain and Lance Singh. You in charge?"

"I ain't in charge of nothing," Dhik said. "DCI deSōuxún over there is in charge. Except for guiding us through the Burnout. For that, this fellow here, Alessandro Fanghsi, is the leader."

"You call me 'Little Face,'" Fanghsi said.

Goliad smiled. "I see. DeSōuxún is the in-captain, and you're the go-captain for this expedition."

"Go out, grab carcass, drag back," Fanghsi complained. "Already got autogurney and strongback. Why more niyōs?"

"This is my fault," deSōuxún said, joining them and introducing himself to the sergeant. "I asked the Commandant for an escort to protect my people. Doctor Patterson and her tech are not practiced in the burnside arts."

"And you are?" Fanghsi said. "Told you dangers to discourage *you*, not so you bring extra baggage. Soldiers no help out there. Dead bodies not fight back. Well, not often."

"Don't be too sure," said Goliad. "I mean that we'd be no help. I'm agnostic on the dead bodies. We're trained in rescue work, climbing, obstacles. Also, we know how to follow orders." He saluted deSōuxún and Fanghsi. "Sah!"

Dhik watched unease struggle across his friend's brows and cheeks, entrench in his lips and eyes. Like the sheets of a man writhing in his bunk with a nightmare, his visage grew rumpled. Dhik tried to cheer him. "Look on the bright side, Little Face. At least you don't have …"

"Not say it."

"… that widow to burden you."

Little Face sighed and turned once more to the hatchway. "You had to go and say it."

Winsome Alabaster had discovered her superpower. She could impress her own quiescence upon her environs. The chatter in the wardroom died off as the personnel in it noticed her arrival, though perhaps what snatched their attention were the two black-clad bodyguards who preceded her and sidestepped left and right of the entry. The ghost-smile on her lips turned to embarrassed. The "blackbirds" were not her idea, but Dumont had insisted on providing her with his own escorts for extra protection. They obeyed her in all things except to go away.

"They not do you no good," said their burnside guide. "Martial arts wrong skill set."

The blackbirds made no rebuttal to this evident criticism, but Number Two shifted his shoulders and snugged the coil of climbing rope that hung there. Winnie knew he was positioning himself against a possible attack by Fanghsi.

104

I never enter a room, Number Two had told her once, *without a plan to kill everyone in it.*

What if you can't find a weapon? She had asked him, but his answer had been only a bleak and empty look, and Number One had explained.

What makes a thing a weapon is the intent of the one holding it.

Chief Inspector deSōuxún took her in hand and introduced her to the rest of the party. The blackbirds followed like shadows. They came at last to Dhikpāruṣya Spandhana, whose 'boo-toting presence puzzled her. Why was deSōuxún bringing an Enforcer? To ensure filial piety on the team? Surely, breaking discipline in the Burnout carried its own consequences.

"It was Dhik who brought your Man's body to our attention," he explained. But Dhik was no burnsider, and Winnie wondered who had actually found the carcass that had so lately housed Jaunty Alabaster. Probably one of the two scouts who would shepherd them. Neither of them, she could see in their faces, welcomed her company. Then Spandhana's name clicked, and she looked him up and down. "I can see where the lady might have a problem. Your left leg alone is bigger than she is." Her remark puzzled everyone but the Dhik, who checked her chevrons and rating and darkened.

Fanghsi broke the silence. "No, officer, you. So how you fly with birdies?" Anxiety oozed from him like juice squeezed from a melon. Her explanation that the bodyguards were a gift from her particular friend did nothing to reassure him, and he muttered something about waving bright colors at bees.

"The body we're retrieving," DeSōuxún explained, "is that of her Special Man."

"Would it help," she asked the guide, "if I told you I train in acrobatics? Surely, balancing, leaping, and rope-climbing may prove useful skills in getting through the jumble."

Fanghsi tossed his head. "Still bad idea. You wait here; we bring 'im back."

"Would you wait behind while others fetched your Special's body?" What drove her to these risks, however, was less piety than a need to understand why Jaunty had only so lately matriculated as a corpse. He had been missing for six years, not six days.

Fanghsi gestured helplessly. "Admire sand, not smarts."

The bodyguards followed her across the room so closely that Winnie checked to see if they had ropes attached to her.

"We are not to allow you out of our sight, *ej'māṇi*," said Number One.

"I'm not so fragile as Dumont seems to think."

Number Two spoke up. "Begging yer pardon, *ej'māṇi*. But what matters ain't what be true, but what Lord Helix deems true."

"And you don't have to keep calling me 'mistress,' *Mistar* Iraṇtu. I'm not in charge of Dumont's household."

Two pulled back a little. "A point of etiquette, *ej'māṇi*. I am 'Two,' not 'Mister Two.' 'Tis my code on this here assignment. On duty, those of us in Ship Security don't be having names. We serve those who do."

"There are reasons for this, madam," added Number One. "It's more difficult to bribe, suborn, or threaten a man whose name you do not know and so whose quarters you cannot locate. You often take 'office names.' The Dalai Papa, he weren't *born* Benedict XXXI Gyatso. So, think of 'One' and 'Two' as our office names."

To know that these two men would take a knife in the gut for her frightened her. That sort of selfless obedience could readily be turned to ends less desirable than her safety.

Little Face gathered the niyōs in the aft of the wardroom near the hatchway. *Twelve is too many*, he thought. *Someone will be distracted, someone will not maintain discipline, someone will be swallowed by the all-enveloping night.* He wondered which of them would not be coming back.

They all supposed themselves competent. And they were in their own specialties, but nothing in their lives had prepared them for the Burnout. Not police detection, not bodyguarding, not soldiering, and certainly not calculating genetic probabilities. They didn't know the Burnout. And because they didn't know it, they didn't fear it. And because they didn't fear it, they didn't love it. And the Burnout could be terribly cruel to those who didn't love her.

So, he tackled that issue head-on. "Who fear? Show hands."

106

But instead of raising their hands, the niyōs looked at one another, and of course, no one would raise his hand if he saw that no one else had done so—although he could see that the medical examiner wanted to do.

Fanghsi quite calmly raised his own hand. "Then fools, you! Too much fear paralyze, true, but too *little* make reckless. Not act when should, or act when should not. Both kill." He gestured toward the hatchway. "This easiest route to body, but in Burnout, no easy routes."

"You scouted it already?" said one of the Marines, Corporal Vermain. She had the weirdest eyes Fanghsi had ever seen. They seemed to sparkle.

"Instruct grandmother," he suggested, "finer points egg-sucking."

"Then why dincha just bring the body back then?"

Why not, indeed? That had been his intention.

"Excuse me," interrupted DCI deSōuxún, "I can explain. The medical examiner and I need to examine the body *in situ* before it can be moved. Standard procedure." Patterson's grimace announced that she would happily examine the body in any old *situ*, but she did not demur.

Standard procedure, Little Face reflected, could get them all killed because where they were going was not standardized. It was a futile errand in any event. The Brotherhood had found the body in a gangway near Fort Freedom, and he could hardly lead the party *there*. So, it was not *in situ*, at all. Yet, how could he explain that without explaining too much?

However, once the Fates had decreed, man must submit. It was just possible that *he* might be the one not coming back. He distributed holopaper maps with their route highlighted. Although flat and foldable, the maps possessed depth since their path would take them down a deck.

Corporal Vermain, he noted, studied the map intently. "We coming anywhere near Milkhoney?" she asked.

Fanghsi stifled his reaction. What did the Marines know? He spoke with care. "Milkhoney on Twenty-Five Deck. Body on Nineteen Deck."

First Sergent Goliad asked, "Then why don't we go in on Nineteen? That way, we can avoid all the goosey-gander."

That, Little Face had to admit, was a fair question. "Can't get through on Nineteen. Overhead collapse onto deck."

The strongback, Ailmer Sanech, raised his hand. "So, ain't no direct route?"

"Direct route not easy; easy route not direct. Is what we call 'trade-off.'" In fact, there was a more direct route, but it led right past Fort Freedom. For a variety of reasons, Fanghsi was disinclined to lead them that way.

Vermain said, "I vote for the direct route anyway. It would mean less time exposed to the hazards."

Fanghsi looked at deSōuxún. "You recall extend voting franchise?"

"Shut your fly trap, corporal," explained the sergeant. "We don't hire an expert so we can second-guess him."

Little Face resumed his briefing. "So. No positioning system in Burnout," he told them, forestalling another fatuous question from Vermain about why paper maps. "MOBI no use. No map functions, no reference functions, no comm functions. No nothin'. If shit happens—and it usually does—no calling of help. Need anything, carry it here." He tapped the side of his head. "Hope you not come short supplied." It took a moment before they decided he had cracked a joke.

"No side trips, no sightseeing. You get separated, get lost, sit tight. Do not try find us. Niyōs wandering Burnout, not most sparkling idea ever. Make noise. *We* find *you*. Eventually. Give you good funeral, too."

"Good thing we're not going too deep into the Burn, then," said Vermain.

Little Face tossed his head. "'How deep' wrong worry. In Burnout, quality matter, not quantity."

Vermain rallied. "Way I hear it, most personnel that venture into the Burnout return with no harm."

Fanghsi bobbed his head. "True, that. You 'most personnel'?"

The sergeant clarified the matter. "Shut up, Vermain."

Little Face continued. "Map marked where *enziggied*. That mean 'in zero-g.' Map also marked where plates *pancaked*, and gravity 2-g or more. We not go those places. Whole route no lighting, no power, some water. Do not drink the water." He paused. "Everyone has *jùguāng hù mùjìng*, light-concentrating goggles?" He was eager for an excuse to throw someone off the party and was disappointed but not surprised when they all raised their *jùggies*. After all, blackout drill had been standard practice in schools since the Big Burnout, another of those barn-door exercises in horse salvation.

"One other matter. No pet doggies."

"Oh, but I love puppies," Vermain protested.

"They love you, too. For dinner. Dogs in Burnout feral long time. Pat head, you, they bite hand off. Also, Memory materials try always repair selves, but in Burnout, sometimes repair *wrong*. So map shows what route like when scouted. But maybe different now."

Thanks to his ears, he heard Vermain whisper to Singh. "So, if he got the map wrong, he can always blame the materials." He decided to ignore her. She loved drawing attention to herself, and Fanghsi decided he had fed her love enough.

"X on map—we climb down old drop tube. Use ladders in sidewall of shaft. Rope selves together because gravity can return without send polite invitation. Do not trust rungs until test them. Now, look left and right, you." The niyōs complied, glancing at one another.

"Those two, your *burnside buddies*. Keep always eye on *buddies*. Pathfinder, check equipment. Rope, helmets, lights, jùggies. You know drill." He waited while his rear guard turned each person's lamp on and off, tugged at belts and other straps, verified the charges on their belt generators and the function of their jùggies. Finally, inspection completed, he signaled a curt assent.

"Ready?" Fanghsi said. "Light up and follow me."

Corporal Vermain said, "If that other guy is 'Pathfinder,' shouldn't he be in front?" But this time, no one chuckled.

When the guide swung the hatch open, Bùxiè deSōuxún studied the prospect thus revealed. Light from the wardroom speared into the darkness beyond, chasing shadows before it to huddle in pockets and angles.

The overhead had collapsed down the longitudinal. Conduits and wires that had once nestled quietly in the interdeck crawl spaces now choked the passage.

"Direct route," their guide announced. "Who still want go that way?"

Fanghsi stepped through the hatchway, aimed his light across the traverse passageway that ran athwartship, then gestured to the right.

Bùxiè stepped after him. Hell of a thing, being a leader. It meant you had to go first. The others followed him one by one. Light from their headlamps swirled here, there, as they gaped about, so that the illuminated area seemed a living thing, a writhing, struggling blob of light. Their jùggies dutifully gathered it and amplified it into the seeming of a well-lit passageway, strewn here and there by jet-black obstacles where protrusions blocked their beams. Bùxiè flipped up his jùggie experimentally and saw that he stood in a small bubble of illumination bobbing within an endless night. In the distance, far to portside, he thought he saw another flicker of light, but it vanished into the inky blackness, and he was not sure he had seen it at all. He flipped his jùggie down and took comfort in the restored vision. Out of the night drifted a dog's howl.

Predators usually attack prey a tenth their size or smaller. But then he remembered that dogs hunted in packs, so that meant prey a tenth the size of the pack. Another good reason not to get separated from the rest of the team.

The traverse passageway does not look so bad, thought Bùxiè. At least compared to the longitudinal. But he remembered what the guide had told them, so he regarded it with caution: Danger could wear a friendly face. In his work, he had known affable killers.

A cable dangling from the overhead sparked, briefly illuminating the passageway. A circuit had regrown, Bùxiè supposed. But without guidance from Maintenance, had done so incorrectly. Fanghsi used his wooden grounding staff to push it out of the way.

He wondered what the Marines were up to, as they were clearly up to something. Bùxiè had asked only for some guards experienced in survival skills, but the Corporal had studied Little Face's map with such care as to arouse the Inspector's curiosity. Milkhoney Hard? What had the transshipment center to do with anything? Either she was being extra diligent, or she had another agenda.

Of course, so had Bùxiè. "Remember," he said to Patterson, who followed close behind him, "stay alert for evidence of people living out here." The supposition that Dead Man had come out of the Burnout was the primary reason he had asked for the marine guards.

But the doc remained skeptical. "If there are such people, why don't the darlings just come in? Sure, it must be more comfortable in crew quarters than out here in this muckle great jumble."

They clambered up and over a pile of bulkhead panels that had once been arranged squarely into crew quarters, offices, and workshops. Coming down off them, Bùxiè gave Patterson a hand.

"Maybe they like being outside the purview of Ship Security," he told her. "Or of Eugenics."

"This much, they like it?"

Dhik was coming down after. "Who likes what?"

Bùxiè didn't answer him. It was a wild notion, but if Dead Man had been born and raised in the Burnout, it explained why he had no locator chip and why neither his face nor genes were in the Operating Base.

And he thought their guide already knew that people were living out here. The route on the map looked like it went a long way around something. *And maybe the Marines know something, too*, he thought.

Or maybe he was theorizing too much from too little data. Given no data, any theory at all can be made to fit.

One consequence of gravity plates was that "down" could be a notional concept, so at first, Corporal Vermain failed to realize when the passageway twisted. She simply followed those ahead of her, figuring that if something did happen, it would happen to one of them first.

Initially, she thought the pass'way had warped. Then, she realized that it had corkscrewed, and the deck had become the aft bulkhead. So, she was, in effect, walking on the wall.

For a moment, her eyes and her inner ears waged a bitter war for control of her balance. She almost heaved, and she almost tripped. Walking on the wall was not so easy as it looked!

The bulkheads moaned at her in a subsonic rumble. Groaning voices from the darkness whispered her name. *Crowwwllley* ... and childhood nightmares struggled awake. *The Burnout comes alive*, her parents had warned her. *It seizes disobedient children*. And what child was ever more disobedient than Crowley Vermain? Her mouth went dry, and she nearly turned about to run.

Then, she realized that the memory material was only trying to rectify itself, and its vain efforts to straighten its kinks were causing the bulkheads to creak. It was only her imagination that had converted those sounds into voices.

Her steps grew less tentative, and she began to enjoy the strangeness. "Hey, Singh," she said to the Lance behind her, "Nihpti, hunh?"

But Singh, white-lipped, seemed struggling to retain his own breakfast, a struggle which he abruptly lost, leaving a vomitous mess for Pathfinder to step through.

At the head of the column, Little Face raised his right fist, and the party stumbled to a halt. Turning, he announced, "Passageway here twist so far, he break. Small crevasse, but do not look into abyss, or it will look back at you." Pathfinder chuckled, but the humor escaped Vermain.

"Everything on far side enziggied, so I run rope, me, when scout route. No traction in ziggy, *so keep hold of rope.* Lose grip, and residual Higgs field from deck below pulls you into fold on far side, the getting-out from which, as you people say, 'mooing difficult,' maybe—so we leave you there."

Naturally each of them, when it came his turn, looked down into the crevasse, and Vermain was no exception. The rent had torn several decks apart, and the wreckage of the upper decks was in a jagged mass below. Sharp corners and saw-toothed edges waited to impale any who fell onto them. The rubble broke the illumination from her headlamp into a kaleidoscope of light and dark.

As she scanned the wreckage, her lamp pulled from the shadows, grinning skulls with eyeless sockets. The recovery teams of eighty years ago hadn't recovered everything. There had been places they could not reach.

Vermain tore her gaze away from the bones in time to see the medical examiner lose her grip on the rope and drift away, squeaking like a mouse, with her arms and legs wagging. She kept trying to get her feet under her, but they failed to cooperate. Fanghsi and the Enforcer hurled their ropes, and Patterson caught one before she slid into the crease. They hauled her to safety.

Vermain thought the affair broad slapstick and had to stifle a laugh, but she was glad of the distraction and did not look down again when she crossed into ziggy.

It was worse than Groaning Hall. Her gorge rose, and her vision spun. She cursed Ynigo Lutz under her breath and wished the staff sergeant were here. Maybe her fabled luck would have rubbed off. Then, she decided that the sergeant's luck had held—because she *wasn't* here. She had that cushy billet patrolling Undine Place.

Lucky's whole purpose in getting Crowley attached to this task force had been to scout out the aftside of the transshipment center. But they wouldn't even come anywhere near Milkhoney Hard. There was no chance of spotting the missing pallets, let alone recovering them. Unless she struck out on her own—and nothing she had seen or heard so far promoted that as a sparkly idea.

If Lucky were here, Vermain thought, *she and I would find those pallets together.* But she had insufficient confidence in either her own skills or her own luck to try it alone. And this trepidation overwhelmed even her deeply felt desire to please Lucky.

When DCI deSōuxún stepped across the crevasse, he found himself suddenly floating in midair and flailing for purchase. His inner ears hollered for instructions. But so long as he kept a hold on his wits and on the line, he should be fine. Keeping either, however, proved a challenge. Vertigo grabbed him, and his vision rolled up and up and up. Nonetheless, he took a deep breath and pulled himself hand over hand, flying forward like the ancient demigod Superman.

Ahead, where Little Face waited, the plates were working, and Bùxiè reasoned that when he came within their Higgs field, he would accelerate toward the deck at one gee. Best not be face down when that happened.

So, with some difficulty, he jackknifed feet first and torqued onto his back, judging this posture less hazardous to his nose and teeth.

His feet came within the field and dropped to the deck while inertia urged his torso forward. Little Face extended a hand and leveraged him to a standing position. The burnsider gave him a curt nod and said, "Not entirely stupid, you." which counted for high praise.

He quickly stepped aside because the others were following close on, with greater or lesser skill. The blackbirds did best of all, and Winsome Alabaster put her acrobatic skills to great use. Bùxiè, in fact, admired her poise and self-possession. Patterson lost her grip on the line and floated free like a child's balloon, albeit one wagging frantically, but Pathfinder and Dhik managed to recover her.

Two of the group blew their breakfasts in ziggy: Sanech was one, and Lance Singh would have been the other, save that he had already left his own breakfast in Groaning Hall.

"Only two barf-bunnies," Fanghsi commented. "Better than average."

Bùxiè studied the floating globules of spew hanging in the air behind them, and he shook his head. "We'll need to go through that when we come back."

"Look side of positive, Chief Inspector," Fanghsi cheered him. "Maybe you not come back."

After they had clambered down the maintenance ladder in a derelict drop shaft to Nineteen Deck, Little Face called a rest.

Like the others, Dhik sank to his haunches, grateful for the respite. The medical examiner subsided as if all the sand had drained out of her. By chance, he had been standing beside her when Little Face had them choose their "buddies," and he had been watching her closely ever since. Fearlessness was not courage; it was stupidity. Courage was pressing on despite the fear, and courage was a quality he admired.

He placed a comforting hand on her shoulder, but she started and looked at him as if he were a cat and she, a canary. Dhik removed his hand.

"Sorry," he growled. "Should I let the air come in?"

"No, stay there. I feel safer with you nearby." After a heartbeat, she added, "I should thank you for pulling me out of ziggy, back there."

"You are my burnside buddy. It was my job to help you."

"Thank you, anyway."

Her words were not words he had often heard in the Enforcer's trade, and it struck him that on this expedition, for the first time, he was not acting as an Enforcer.

He sat in silence beside the doctor. She might not survive the Burnout. Any of them might add their bones to the ones he had glimpsed in the crevasse, but the thought that Dr. Petronilla Patterson's bones might lie there disturbed him more than even his own might.

Is this what it means to be responsible for someone? he wondered. *That her well-being matters more to you than your own?*

He thought he might speak to the widow Alabaster and learn whether she could relieve him of his assigned pairing, but she had fallen into conversation with the copper. Well, there would be other opportunities. He wondered whether she could be bribed and, if so, how much she would ask and what would that buy? She was clearly cozy with someone important. Blackbirds did not grow in 'ponic tanks.

Little Face was resting nearby. "Oi," Dhik asked his friend, "Why you so worried?"

"Not worried, but not expect major double-yu with Marines and blackbirds. Make us look like invasion force."

Dhik shrugged. "So what? Who we invading?"

Little Face did not answer.

"What can I do for you, Chief Inspector?" asked Winnie Alabaster when DCI deSōuxún lowered himself beside her and offered her a piece from his ration bar. She declined before her guardians could seize the "possible poison." Whatever else it accomplished, their vigilance would work wonders for her diet.

He put his bar back in its wrapper and said, "How is my lady holding up?"

"Very well. And I'm not 'my lady.'" She waited for him to say what he had come to say.

But the saying of it seemed to discomfit him. Perhaps the words were sharp and thus stuck in his throat.

He took a deep breath, let it out. He said, "I understand Eugenics can grant exemptions to the Regulations."

She did not let the surprise show. Did he know of Dumont's attempt to undermine the Entente's plans? Had Spandhana said something about his draft notice, or had deSōuxún, like a good detective, drawn an inference from bits and pieces? "It's possible," she admitted, "but rarely done, and then only for excellent reasons." Of course, she meant "Excellent" reasons but saw no need to elaborate.

He frowned and looked at his hands, which grappled as if mortal enemies. "I noticed you last week in the *Glowering Tiger*." When Winnie made an impatient gesture, he hastened on. "My Special Woman has been given a promotion."

"Congratulations." But she still wondered what he was getting at.

"It's a position as apprentice astrogator, and since that puts her in line for a gold cape, we've been told that we cannot 'found a dynasty.'"

"Found a dynasty?" The expression was unfamiliar to her.

"We will be forbidden to have children."

"Oh! I'm sorry to hear that."

"But Eugenics licensed us for one girl, and I've always thought Eugenics rulings took precedence."

Winnie scowled and instinctively looked about for surveillance cameras before answering. "Gold Crew has its own customs and regulations. And strictly speaking, their custom in this instance does not violate Eugenics rules."

"But you licensed us for ..."

"Si, but a 'license' is a permission, not a compulsion. We can always make up the deficit. That's easier than culling a surplus. There's never a shortage of volunteers for such a duty. Chief Inspector, the Eugenics Department has three missions. One is to avoid overtaxing our resources. Another is to avoid genetic drift from inbreeding. If a pairing fails to generate children at all, neither overpopulation nor inbreeding occurs."

She had watched his countenance fall as she spoke. "You must love her very much."

"I would do anything for her."

"Mmm. Except allow her to become celibate for a gold cape. You do know love isn't necessary for a successful pairing. Only duty."

"There you are wrong, my lady. Love *is* duty, not some gushy hormonal feeling. It's quite simply 'to desire the good for the Other.' It's an act of the will, not of the glands."

She reached out to touch his forearm. "You found my Jaunty for me, so I owe you a favor."

"Oh, no, my lady." He rubbed his arm where she had touched him.

"I told you, I am no 'my lady,' and I know what I owe and what I am owed. I can promise nothing, but I will raise your problem with Lord Dumont. After all, we don't *like* underbreeding—though it is admittedly less of a problem."

9

CONSEQUENCES

A ringularity—The bloody aftermath—The Undine Place Massacre

Second Officer Berylplume brought Tongkawa Jones and his new protégé to see Skybones Eframof in face. That face was a daunting one, all planes and angles. His nose formed a carpenter's splitting wedge, his gaze was piercing, and his tongue was sharp. When he "cut to the chase," the cuts could bleed.

When the hatch swung open, Skybones said,

> *"Slippers swipe the mat.*
> *The dust of guesting feet*
> *Gathers like gold."*

Skybones occupied a suite in the Golden Horn, the trumpet cone of senior Gold residences that partly surrounded the fore of the quarterdeck. The furnishings were spare and tasteful, the artwork, minimalist and intriguing. The décor overall favored peach and black, though the incense was an understated chocolate, which made for an interesting contrast. A saikei garden occupied a black lacquer tray in one corner of the receiving room, complete with tiny trees and a recirculating brooklet.

As they proceeded thence to a table, Jones whispered to Adrienne, "If Skybones asks you a direct question, give him a direct answer. Do not elaborate or digress. And remember, the X/O is an engineer, so keep the math light. Partial differential equations, no more."

Adrienne san Tongkawa nodded modestly but remained silent, as befit her station. Her assignment for now was to shadow Jones and observe what he said and did so that by osmosis, she could absorb the astrogator's practice.

Skybones' face was not famed for its smiles, but he attempted a welcoming one. The attempt was a failure. "So, Number Two," he said, "to what does my unworthy self owe the honor of your presence?"

Jones did not believe that Skybones thought himself unworthy, but he noted how adroitly he had put Berylplume in his place. *Second* officer. In theory, the captain commanded, and the X/O only saw that those commands were properly executed. In practice, X/Os had been issuing commands for a century while keeping the captain in pampered isolation. Everyone knew this, and everyone pretended not to know it.

Berylplume glanced at Tongkawa and Adrienne, then took a breath. "Sah, we have received the feeds from the swifties san Tongkawa launched at the anomaly."

Of course, the skinny had been circulating on the whisper circuit all day, but Skybones was an engineer and not plugged in. "Sah," said Berylplume, "We have encountered a ringularity."

Skybones assumed a posture of polite interest and said, "I'm a practical man. I have always supposed a singularity to be an artifact of the mathematical model and, like infinity and unicorns, not a creature much encountered in daily life."

"A *ringularity*, sah," said Berylplume. "The Ancients calculated that a body collapsing under its own gravitation would collapse to a single point. But such collapsing bodies tend to be stars, and stars are rotating, so the distribution of the mass is not spherical."

"Why?"

"It has an equatorial bulge from the rotation, sah." Skybones nodded his acceptance of this, if not necessarily his understanding, and Reynaud continued. "It also possesses angular momentum. But a point can support neither rotation nor angular momentum. The minimal shape that *can* do so is a ring, which has a radius but no thickness. A black hoop rather than a black hole."

Skybones grunted. "That sounds like something at the edge of the maths, not the edge of the physics."

Jones would have argued the point with the exec, but Berylplume let it slide. The model was all they had to go on, Jones reflected, so they had to act as if it were real, even if reality itself was a bit more slippery. *An entity exists*, the ancient maxim ran, *if there is a term for it in the model.* Though he recalled that the ancient prophet Hawking glossed over this by saying that this did not oblige the universe to go along with the gag. There was the thousand-year success of epicycles to contemplate.

"Sah," Berylplume explained, "the ring's rotational frame-dragging twists the space-time manifold. This unexpected curvature drew the *Whale* off course, a deviation detected by san Tongkawa and calculated by san Jimmy." He gestured to Adrienne and Jones. "I have brought them with me in case you have questions."

"You brought them with you to remind me that this invisible, immaterial entity has visible, material effects—which is how an *engineer* decides something is real." He paused, then added, "So why are we here?"

"The middle swiftie disappeared."

"Disappeared? You lost contact with it?"

"No, sah. Jones?"

Tongkawa Jones took up the briefing. "As it entered the ring, telemetry from the outriders showed the swiftie appearing to rotate and grow shorter. This is known as the Lorenz-Fitzgerald Illusion. It is an epistemic effect of the finiteness of lightspeed."

The ancients had thought objects really did foreshorten as they approached lightspeed, but it was simply that photons that reached the observer at the same time had left the fore of the object a fraction earlier than those off the aft. In other words, the observer "saw" the farther end at an earlier instant and, therefore, at a closer location than the nearer end.

Impatience flashed briefly across Skybones' visage. "So we have found a cosmological curiosity. Are there practical consequences?"

Jones ventured that according to lore, "Ringularities hold open a Krasnikov tube."

"A Krasnikov tube."

"A tunnel through space. Einstein-*pandit* had said that nothing can move faster than light. But space is no 'thing,' so *space* can move faster than light.

> *"Watching from bankside*
> *Leaves fall like snow,*
> *Current sweeps them off."*

Skybones nodded slowly. "Ah. I see what you mean. Though you could have added a few syllables without spoiling the morae count. A ship might be carried along *within the tube* by the speed of space, without exceeding *c*, as a leaf is carried by a swift-flowing river." His eyes, which had hitherto been clouded, brightened as if those clouds had been parted.

Skybones' smile grew positively frightening.

Megwan Masterson stroked Ling-ling's back gently while she cried.

"I didn't know it would hurt," he said again. "No one told me it would hurt you."

Ling-ling swallowed another sob but said nothing. The sheets were stained with blood, and her most precious bedgown was absolutely ruined! She hated Megwan's mother. The woman had spoiled everything. Ling-ling wondered how she could make Lady Water hurt.

Did Megwan really think apologizing repeatedly would lessen the hurt? It wasn't even the physical pain; it was the betrayal. That her relations with her Man's mother would be fraught was proverbial. She was stepping into the woman's sandals, after all, but that her own father had assisted gave her stomach cramps.

There ought to have been a chivarist present to coach them through the procedure. But Eugenics Input had paired her with a mere chief from the aft frames, and Output would not likely cooperate in circumventing Input's ruling.

An ancient saying proclaimed, "The act makes the marriage." Everything else was mere ceremony and registration. So, she and Megwan were now well and truly married and a fig to Eugenics!

And Megwan, she knew, could not be *too* sorry, as he had quite evidently experienced a pleasure-burst. A part of him was inside her now. She struggled to understand how she felt about that.

He put his arm around her shoulders, but she threw it off, and he did not try again. She thought she might go to her own mother for comfort, yet she did not think she would find it even there.

Lucky Lutz stood with a motely of Marines, Enforcers, and miscellaneous bully-boy riff-raff moonlighting as special security for Lady Water. They formed a double line on the broad Plaza between Undine Palace and a crowd of noisy protestors, their mission being to prevent the latter from entering the former. A third line, consisting of blackbirds assigned to House Masterson, backed them up, and one of them—Blackbird Five Masterson— was in nominal command this watch.

Protestors had been congregating on Undine Place ever since Lady Water had announced her plan to raise rents on her tenants. Her action, it was said, had been less a means to increase revenues than to vacate the premises for her son. Many tenants had abandoned their dwellings already rather than pay the higher rents—*voluntary self-evictions*, the wits on MOBI had called them—while others still squatted stubbornly in their homes. Lucky had promised herself not to sign on for the involuntary evictions that would logically follow, no matter how much she needed the extra money.

She hoped "Crawling Vermin" could locate the misplaced teasers during the body recovery excursion. Lucky had always wanted to see the Burnout herself and envied her corporal the lark.

Meanwhile, the torrent of invective from the crowd gave her the jeebs. Although as abuse, it fell short of what Lucky had endured every day from the lips of First Sergeant Goliad and did not touch him for inventiveness, the jeering rubbed on her cookies, and there was always the undercurrent of implied violence.

She could live with the implication, but she wasn't sure what she could do if they actually did rush the palace gates, armed as she was with only a quarterstaff and a riot shield. She had no doubt that her conditioning would kick in but did not know what condition it would kick into. She almost wished the protestors would try something just to find out how she would respond. Almost, not quite.

"A man's quarters are his stronghold!" cried a yellow-haired woman, and Lucky wondered if she thought the security guards had not heard that sentiment a thousand times already.

"Damned swabbies," whispered the bully boy standing to Lucky's right. "Who they think they are, telling an Orficer what she can do?"

More to the point, what did the protestors think the *security guards* could do? No one else was about on the Plaza except the food vendors, and they were not interested in hearing anything but "two footlongs, with hot mustard." A fruit-and-vegetable cart was doing a brisk business.

"Quarters don't belong to the tenants, anyway," the man continued. "An' Lady Water thinks she kin get better use o' the volume by repurposing them, she's within her rights."

At least, so the Judge Advocate had ruled. Water's actions might be callous and indifferent; they might even be ill-advised, but they were not against Regulations. Lucky was glad it was not her place to choose between justice and the law. She was in the conforming/non-conforming business, not the right/wrong business.

"They're not swabbies," she ventured, *sotto voce.*

"Eh? What's that y'say?"

"I said the protestors, they aren't swabbies, not most of them anyway. They look to me like regular rankers, maybe even some chiefs."

The man turned his head and glared at her. "Whose side you on?"

"I'll check the chop on my pay stub and get back to you."

"Hunh?"

"When I take a man's money," she said, "I do the job she's paying me for."

"Quiet in the ranks!" said Blackbird Five Masterson. "Lid closed; monkey dead."

Then the protestors began that godawful song.

> *"Whether we preside, command*
> *Or shuffle papers all day and*
> *Fix whatever's broken, too.*
> *Whether we patch pipes or people*
> *Live in Cloisters or Highsteeple,*
> *It doesn't, doesn't matter what we do."*

Lucky sighed and maintained her stoicism. The duty was not very onerous, and Undine House paid well, but it was boring to an excruciating degree. She had to stand on the Plaza all day, face the noisy crowd, listen to their awful poetry and singing, endure their tedious posturing, and wait for something not to happen.

Boredom was the enemy because a bored man was liable to indulge in whimsy just to break the monotony. Half the security detail was composed of amateur tough guys: strongbacks, bully boys, gangway toughs. They expected action. They *wanted* action. It would take little to nudge them into it.

> *"Whether we proudly ride in carts*
> *Or we go on foot just as we are*
> *And toward our goals heave to.*
> *Whether crosses hang upon our shirt*
> *Or drag behind us in the dirt,*
> *It doesn't, doesn't matter what we do."*

"Of course, it matters," said the bully boy on her right. "What some of us do matters a lot more than what others do. That's just the sort of eagle-tarian self-'grandizing you'd expect from the lower ranks."

Lucky thought it odd that a hired muscle took the side of the Officers. She did not check the man's chevrons, but she did not think that what he did mattered much more than what any of the demonstrators did. "I think they mean that we are 'all in the same boat,' and freshening the air is just as important as repairing equipment or preparing meals or, hell, even swabbing the passageways. They're all necessary if we're to keep the *Whale* shipshape."

A lanky, rough-hewn man threw a rotten tomato at them, easily deflected by a shield. "Dinner's served!" the man cackled.

"Well, that wasn't called for," the bully boy commented.

The off-duty Enforcer to Lucky's left growled. "Improperly disposing of a recyclable," he said, and his fingers twitched on his 'boo pole. Lucky wondered how many strokes the penalty was.

"Stand easy," she said. "We don't want a riot on our hands." Strictly speaking, Five was in charge, but a firm word spoken in the right tone at the right moment could accomplish much. What she meant, of course, was that *she* did not want a riot on her hands. She was less certain of others on the line.

The fair-haired demonstrator admonished the tomato-hurler. "Keep it civil, Jek," she said. Lucky preferred her own pet name for the fellow: Gristlebone. She thought the protesters were as tormented by tedium as the security guards. How long could you chant and sing with no sign that anyone has so much as listened?

"Poodles!" Jek threw another fruit, which a strongback down the ranks caught on his shield. *Poodle,* Lucky had learned, was a pejorative for the hired security staff. They were lapdogs for the Mastersons. She amused herself, trying to make it a positive acronym. **P**rotect **O**n-board **O**rder, **D**iscipline, **L**ives, and **E**nterprise. Although that wouldn't work in Taṇṭamiz, which used a syllabary, or Běifāngwóng wá, which used ideograms.

"I don't like bein' called them names," the bully boy said.

"Sticks and stones may break your bones," Lucky whispered, "but words can never hurt you."

Perhaps she whispered too loudly, or perhaps great minds simply thought alike. Sticks and stones not being readily available in the pass'ways of the *Whale*, cans and bottles, obtainable in any canteen or commissary, provided a workable alternative.

A full glassite bottle packs a decent mass, and velocity is a force multiplier. One of the bully boys was slow in getting his shield up, and the bottle struck him square in the face. Lucky's neighbor cried out, "Oi! That's me, mate, there, innit?" And he charged the demonstrators, swinging his half-staff like a club.

The flaxen woman cried at her companions, "What are you doing?" just as more bottles let fly. All of them, Lucky noted, from the protesters' rear ranks.

Dropping a single seed crystal into a supersaturated solution is enough to precipitate the entire beaker. Or, in simpler terms, one thing leads to another. Blackbird Five called, "Don't charge!" But a man hears what he wants to hear, and half the line heard only "Charge!" They surged forward, waling and clubbing.

"Marines," Lutz shouted to the other moonlighters, "Hold fast!" And because she was the senior sergeant present, the five Marines in the detail obeyed. So did most of the Enforcers. The blackbirds, too, she noted, had heard Five's command clearly. Indeed, they were backing toward the palace gates.

"Form a cordon," Lucky told the others, "so the idiots who broke ranks have an escape route." She had studied the great battles in Military Science, and this reminded her of Hastings, when the Saxon shield-wall had broken into an ill-considered charge, and the Norman horse exploited the resulting gap. Even unarmed, the demonstrators could overwhelm the guards by sheer body mass. Lucky clenched her teeth. You could train all you wanted, but the moment of truth still wrang your guts.

But a mob differs from an army. It has no discipline, and the idea of organizing a counterattack and taking casualties for the sake of reaching an objective never entered their pretty little heads. They hadn't come to win any medals. Instead, they "rankled their ankles" and scattered while the bully boys waled on whomever their staves could reach.

Blackbird Five Masterson blew a code on his bosun's whistle, and the blackbirds split into two groups and hustled to either end of the Plaza, where it narrowed to an ordinary gangway. They did not block these exits but rather discouraged the crowd from congregating and chivvied them through. One of the Enforcers stepped toward the bully boys, hollering, "Enough!" Other Enforcers joined him with their 'boo poles at order arms.

"They're gettin' away!" cried one of the toughs, perhaps mistaking his own anger for the Orders of the Day. Following Culloden back on Old Earth, the victorious English had scoured the Highlands, never bothering to ask if their victims had fought in the Jacobite army or not. Lucky felt sorry for the fellow whose face had been smashed, but she could easily imagine the bully boys running wild through the corridors, wreaking vengeance on anyone they caught.

For a fraught moment, the angry guards faced off with the Enforcers, then, perhaps with a glance at the silently watching Marines, decided that driving the protestors off had been enough to satisfy their pride.

As the Plaza cleared, Lucky saw that four protestors remained, recumbent and unmoving, including a redhead whom she could not remember having seen before. Then she realized the woman's yellow hair only appeared scarlet because it was drenched in blood.

10 EXPEDITIONS II

Dead body stink after four days—The tracks of her tears—"She was *our* irritating little skite."—Are there bags enough?

The body lay in the front room of a three-room suite that must have once quartered a petty officer. It stood in a row of similar quarters along Conniption Pass'way. If crew in this neighborhood had ever thought of painting their façades or planting window boxes, there was no trace left on the moss-and-lichen-stained bulkheads.

Little Face, holding a kerchief to his nose and mouth, commented, "Dead Body, he stink after four days."

"That how long it's been since you found it?" Bùxiè asked. The burnsider bobbed his head, then froze, and Bùxiè hid a smile. So, this was Dhik's informant. But why hadn't he brought the image to the nick himself? There was something hidden yet in the affair.

The hatchway was flanked by two once-clear ceramic windows. Both were now caked with grime to the point of near opacity. Bùxiè, Patterson, and Sanech had donned their breathing filters before cracking the hatch, but the others remained in the pass' and backed away from the foul odor that wafted through the open door. Vermain and Singh tried to squeak the windows clear with cleaning rags so they could watch without gagging.

Fanghsi and Tan stood facing port and starboard. When Number Two noticed Bùxiè's quizzical expression, he explained. "If'n everyone be a-looking one direction, someone ought be a-looking in another."

The forensics team entered the suite, and Bùxiè thought the cadaverine and putrescine thick enough to swim through. Even through his filters, he could catch a whiff. Or was that his imagination? Patterson crouched over the body, inserting her omnicorder in various locations, and Bùxiè knelt beside her. He had seen immediately that the entire venture had been futile.

"Rigor has passed," Patterson announced into her recorder while Sanech captured visual images, "but there is evidence of cadaveric spasm: the head is arched back, ye see. Snap that, Sanech, darling. That is consistent with the signs of a brutal beating." She looked up, caught Bùxiè's gaze. "He didn't die in here."

Bùxiè looked away. He had not expected Patterson to miss that point. Jaunty had been bludgeoned repeatedly, and the swinging bludgeon would have spattered blood across the bulkheads and overhead like red baby's breath. That there was no spatter meant that this was not the murder room, and that meant that little of forensic value would be learned here. He had dragged the medical examiner and her assistant into the perils of the Burnout for no good purpose. "How long dead?" he asked as he rose from his knee.

"Between four and ten days but not too much longer, or the bloating would be more advanced." She pointed to the left leg. "He's been hamstrung."

Which meant there *were* people in the Burnout, for he did not expect that Jaunty had hobbled himself. The obvious inference was that he had been held captive for six years and hamstrung to prevent his escape. But "obvious" did not mean "correct," and Bùxiè kept his counsel.

He wondered where Jaunty had been killed if not here and why his body had been moved. And who had moved him? Good questions, all three, but with no good answers. He glanced at Little Face and wondered whether the scout knew them.

Winsome Alabaster, kerchief pressed firmly to her nose, finally stepped into the room, and her bodyguards immediately investigated the other two rooms. She stared at her Man's body, tugging at her lower lip. "O Jaunty," she whispered. "O Jaunty." The policeman cast her a sympathetic look.

Faint down the corridors of night drifted the mournful howl of a dog.

"Not like sound of that," said Little Face. Alabaster wondered if a feral pack, attracted by the carrion odor, was coming this way.

The medical examiner said. "At least the darling fellow was spared that indignity." She began repacking her instruments while the strongback wrestled the carcass into an odor-proof bag. "Imagine if feral dogs or cats had gotten to the body." Winnie shivered at the image. Jaunty torn apart, his beautiful body rendered into shreds.

"Maybe that's why he was placed in here," said deSōuxún.

"How ... thoughtful of ... whomever."

"No," Little Face insisted. "Not like *sound* of it. Not sound like real doggies." He and Pathfinder chivvied Dhik and the Marines into the room. All of them gagged at the odor.

"Everyone to be taking cover," said Pathfinder, and since up until then the man had not rubbed more than two words together, his pronouncement carried weight.

Singh shut the hatch and spun the locking wheel. He, Vermain, and Goliad pulled teasers from their holsters and only then looked to Pathfinder for clarification. "What's the situation?" asked Goliad.

"*Wàibù hēi'àn jūmín,*" Pathfinder said.

"That clears that up," said Dhik.

"Dwellers in outer darkness," Bùxiè translated. "Unless I miss my guess: descendants of crew that survived the Burnout." Pathfinder bobbed his head in confirmation.

Little Face tossed his head. "Hear odd sounds, lights, voices, but never see these wàihēi'jū, me."

"They not many," Pathfinder said, "and good at hide. Burnout big place."

"Dwellers in outer darkness." Vermain chuckled. "Do they weep and gnash their teeth?"

Tan Lùzhĕ squinted at her. "No. But sometimes they hock their captives." He gestured at the hamstrung body. "*You* not worry, though."

"Oh, good. Why not?"

"Females, they kill."

Winnie exchanged glances with Patterson and Vermain.

"But not males," said Bùxiè. "Why?"

Pathfinder gestured at the corpse. " 'Diversity,' they say. If captive unwilling to diversify, strap 'im to frame so clanswomen can mount him."

Vermain laughed. "A fate worse than death."

Winnie suddenly understood. She could see it all laid out before her by the cold equations. Dead females, captive males. And there would be unremitting violence, too. The Dwellers could not have been too numerous when the Burnout marooned them here, so recalling the hazards of inbreeding, they would outbreed at every opportunity. *Ay-yi, Jaunty!* In a flash of intuition, she knew what had happened to him. A captive milked for his genetic diversity, he had tried to escape back to her. They had hamstrung him, and still, he had tried to escape—a more difficult endeavor without the use of his left leg—and they had tracked him down and slaughtered him as finally more trouble than he was worth. She knew this as if she had seen it herself.

She had never cried for Jaunty, at first, because she expected him to show up any day, later, because the hurt had become too old and scabbed over. But the tears came now in quiet, controlled sobs and plowed furrows through the dust that caked her face. One and Two looked on with concern, others with puzzled or quizzical looks, but Bùxiè with something approaching understanding. She punched buttons on her MOBI, suddenly anxious to regard his beauty once more until she remembered that out here, she had no access to the operating base that otherwise permeated the *Whale*, and she threw the device from her. She hunched into herself.

A moment later, she felt the touch of a hand on her shoulder and, looking up, saw Bùxiè deSōuxún holding her MOBI with his other hand. She took it from him and replaced it in her bandolier. She could not say *Thank you*—she did not trust her voice, so she nodded mutely and hoped the inspector understood.

Goliad questioned Tan Lùzhě.

"I know four clans," Pathfinder said. "Good friends with Desolate clan, me. They help with artifacts; I help with diversity. This Pass'way, Desolate 'corner.'"

The barks and howls from outside rose and fell in a wild kind of antiphon and response. "Is how they signal one another," the burnsider said. "We call 'em 'dog whistles,' but whoever hear dog make whistles?"

"Are those your friends making the racket out there?"

Tan tossed his head. "No. Sound like Triple-X. They from deeper in Burnout but shouldering forward lately."

Goliad listened to a long howl, and as it died away, cocked his head. "Friends with them, also?"

Pathfinder made a slashing gesture with his left hand. "Triple-X not friend no one."

"Why do they kill women?" Goliad asked.

"I can answer that," said Alabaster, surprising everyone. "Too many births would overtax their resources, and birth is a function of the number of fertile females. Men are mathematically irrelevant. Twinning and such aside, a clan with fifty women can have at most fifty babies in a year regardless of whether there are fifty men or only one."

"One very exhausted but happy man," suggested Vermain.

"Resources out here must be terrible slim," Goliad suggested. "How do they get by?"

"Supplies abandoned in evacuation," said Pathfinder. " 'Ponic farms grown wild. Dogs and cats."

"Scavenging is not a prosperous life choice," Bùxiè told them. "They're beginning to raid the frontier for supplies."

"Limiting population means limiting the number of females. What do they do if too many girls are born?"

"Throw 'em down drop shafts," Pathfinder said.

Patterson gasped. "That's horrible!"

But Alabaster shook her head. "Is it more horrible than the entire clan starving because there are too many mouths to feed?"

"If they killed boys, too …"

"Can't." Pathfinder tossed his head. "Need 'em fight other clans. Chief Venslaw of Desola say, 'It matters that your warriors are brave and strong, but it matters more that there are lots of them.'"

Goliad scoffed. "It matters less *how many* show up for a fight than *who* shows up." Vermain and Singh balled their fists and said, "Woof, woof." Goliad smiled briefly, then addressed Pathfinder. "You seem to know a lot about these Dwellers."

"They know I no snitch, so they not hock me." He nodded at the body bag. "He probably tried escape."

Alabaster spoke up. "He had somewhere he needed to be." She listened to the barks from Conniption Pass'. "They must fight, *a lot*. Themselves and other clans."

"Why do you say that, my lady?" asked Goliad.

"If they cull females, they wind up with excess males. The excess males don't get domesticated by pair-bonding and congregate into what we call 'the primate bachelor herd'—gangs of young men who vent their frustrations in violence. Then, for protection against the bachelor herd, a mother needs a strong son. But if half the men die young in fights, she needs to birth *two* boys, and that means she needs to bear four children on the average. And *that* blows all their population controls out into space."

"There must be another way," Dhik insisted.

Alabaster shook her head. "War is the price they pay because they cannot afford daughters. Even in the belly of the *Whale*, haven't you noticed a penchant for rowdy and violent behavior? That's why we license freemartins and other non-procreative outlets for sexual tensions."

Goliad interrupted. "Lid closed, monkey dead. None of that helps us here and now. Pathfinder, you know these people. What's our best course?"

Little Face interrupted, "Calls grow fainter. Sound like moving away."

"When it comes to sounds," Dhik said, "we defer to your ears."

"What do you think?" Goliad pressed Tan.

"Could be going somewhere else," Pathfinder admitted, "or could be ruse."

"Oh, for Shiva's sake," said Vermain. She wheeled open the door and stepped out, teaser raised. She looked first to starboard, then to port, and slowly the tension eased out of her. "I don't see them."

A crossbow bolt pierced her neck. She looked startled, then annoyed, then the light went out behind her kaleidoscope eyes, and she collapsed in a heap. Goliad and Singh, crouching low, dragged her back into the room, fortuitously avoiding a second bolt that glanced off the doorframe at chest height. Singh closed the airtight door and spun the locking wheel. Vermain's legs kicked as her blood pressure crashed. Blood welled from her mouth, and her throat made a sound like a leaking water hose.

Pathfinder grunted. "Never do see 'em."

Goliad turned on him. " 'Crawling Vermin' may have been an irritating little skite," he growled, "but she was *our* irritating little skite. She knew that if any Dwellers were out there, she would draw their fire by exposing herself, but we had to *know*. We couldn't just cower in here not even sure if they were out there."

Sanech said, "Instead, we can cower in here *knowing* they are out there."

"Cower all you like," said Goliad. "But stay out of our way." After a contemptuous glance at the strongback, Goliad turned to Pathfinder. "What are their capabilities? Weapons, tactics, what can we expect?"

Patterson, who had sprung immediately to Vermain's side, looked up. "She's dead."

Pathfinder bobbed his head. "*That* what you can expect." Then, he stopped and added, "Crossbows, you know. Also have throwing axes, knives, stabbing spears."

"No teasers? Air rifles? Blowguns?"

"No."

"Can they mount a siege?"

"Siege?"

"Are they capable of waiting us out, physically or psychologically?"

"They need prove selves big men. No chance for deeds; get bored. Maybe Desolate catch 'em on their pass'. But—your party, many males. Much diversity. Maybe so, too big prize for pass up." He shrugged. "Maybe they 'siege' us, maybe not."

A sudden chorus of barks echoed down the passageway from portside. Then, a pause. Then, a rhythmic banging followed by more barks.

"It is a great and terrible thing to kill a human being," said Alabaster. "They have to work themselves into a frenzy first."

Goliad looked at Vermain's body. "It's not that great."

More barks, more banging, each round getting louder. Then a great howl burst forth, and they heard the sound of feet pounding up the pass'. A crush of men collided on the door. They banged on the windows with hatchets, and something struck the door with a thud.

"If they break a window," said Sanech, "we could retreat to a back room."

"Retreat, hell," Goliad muttered. "We just got here. Is there a rear door? Fire codes require two outside exits for each quarters."

"The alley out back is blocked with wreckage," said One. Naturally, the blackbirds had checked that immediately after entering.

"What about the interdeck crawl spaces?"

One shrugged. "Some might scrooch out that way, but not all."

Goliad did not ask him who he thought might scrooch and who might not. He growled, "We don't leave anyone behind."

Lights pierced the windows as the dwellers pressed against them with leering faces. Headlamps and jùggies gave them the seeming of huge insects. Their hatchets struck and struck again. Their chattering voices were a patois of antique Běifāngwóng wá, Spanglish, and Tantamiz. Goliad could make out only one word in ten, but he didn't like the ones he could. *Kill the breeders; grab the seeders.*

"Glassite ain't infinite strong," said Dhik. "Just sayin'."

"Singh," said Goliad, "They think they're safe from our crossbows, knives, and hatchets."

"Hunh? But Sarge, we don't have any cross …. Oh!"

Goliad pressed the discharge end of his teaser against the window panel, right in the face of one of the Dwellers. The Dweller did not react. "He don't recognize it as a weapon," Goliad judged. "No one touch the bulkheads!" The others stepped quickly away from the walls.

135

The weapon snapped, and sparks flew off the pane and the metal frames. The Dweller shrieked at a higher pitch and fell with a tight, black burn on his forehead.

Teasers fired nanosecond long, high voltage pulses that punched holes in cell membranes, disabling human muscles—including the heart muscle and other vital organs if the voltage was high enough. He thought the Dwellers might be confused at death without blood.

Goliad stepped away from the window, and his weapon hummed as it recharged. "Oi, Pathfinder, they have three red Xs painted across their foreheads like caste marks." He looked around the room, and his eyes came to rest on the two blackbirds. "One of you want to take Corporal Vermain's weapon?"

In answer, they snapped open pouches on their bandoliers and produced their own teasers—a different model than the Marines used but of similar voltage.

Goliad nodded, "Who else is trained on teasers?"

Alabaster raised her hand. "I know how to fire one."

"But can you fry another human being?"

"If those people out there did not beat my Jaunty to death," she said, her voice hard and pitiless, "they'll do until the killers come along."

She produced a teaser, and Goliad looked it over. "That's a 'dog-kicker,'" he said. "Useful for jangling feral dogs, not much else. Got anything with higher voltage? No?" He unclipped the lanyard from Vermain's belt and handed Alabaster the dead corporal's weapon. "The pane material will disperse the ray a little and refract it, but glassite is permeable to the beam."

Bùxiè took the smaller teaser from her. "I know which end means business."

Singh beamed a shot from the right-hand window. The blackbirds stepped up and took their shots. Then Bùxiè and Alabaster replaced them.

The Dwellers had backed away from the windows. Bùxiè aimed at a scrawny guy who was shouting and spraying spittle off his mouth. None of them seemed well-fed. He hesitated. As a policeman, he had never wittingly harmed another human being, though he knew that some men he had arrested had been demoted to Recycling. Alabaster, he noticed, did not hesitate to press the button.

136

Bùxiè fired, and his man collapsed, holding his leg. If his dog-kicker couldn't kill them, it could at least lame them. That might be better. A dead man required no assistance, but a wounded man pulled a hale man out of the fight to aid him. By then, Goliad was recharged, and he and Singh returned to the firing line.

"What's happening?" said Sanech. "Tell us what's happening!"

They fought like that for what seemed forever: rotating two at the windows, two recharging, and two ready to step up. The battering ram on the hatchway continued, and every bang pulled a cry from Peta. Dhik did not have his 'boo pole but stood nevertheless between Peta and the windows and door. But from the windows, they had no angle on the Dwellers swinging the ram.

A hatchet strike on the right-hand window started a crack before Singh could burn the hatchet man. Peta gasped, and Sanech said, "Jeez and the Bood!"

"The avatars won't save you," growled Goliad, "not even if you add Krishna and the Jade Emperor unless they appear packing high-V teasers. There's a fellow out there with a five-kilo sledge. Don't let him strike the cracked glassite."

But the Dwellers were not stupid and soon realized that the killing magic came from the besieged room. They ran to portside, out of range. No one suggested going outside to get a better shot.

And no bodies remained on the deck.

"Jeez!" said Goliad. "I could have sworn we dropped four, at least."

"They leave no man behind, either, Sergeant," Pathfinder told him.

"How many did we get?"

"Enough to make them angry; not enough to drive them off. Males disposable; easy replace."

Patterson said in a small voice, "You mean they weren't angry before?"

Dhik, standing beside her, put his arm around her shoulders. "I'm sorry I dragged you all into this, but Jaunty's body had to go to Recycling. It reads so in the Regs."

Little Face grunted. "Is that all? Filial piety? We have duty to dispose of dead written on heart." He thumped his chest.

Patterson chastised Bùxiè. "Ye dinna even have jurisdiction out here! Why should we care how or why that man died? Och! I wish I was back in the morgue."

"You may get your wish, doctor." Winsome Alabaster's voice snapped like a teaser, and her ghost smile appeared suddenly threatening. "For my part, I could not *not* come for Jaunty to pay my last reverence to his body."

"Fash it! It's not *him!*" the medical examiner told her. "It's a carcass!"

"Si, *snora*, but it is *his* carcass."

Bùxiè wondered if Adrienne would venture into the Burnout to retrieve his body for Recycling. He wondered if anyone would even learn what had become of them or where in the Burnout they had gone.

Goliad, standing sentry by the left-hand window, turned and said, "Complaints are premature. They can't break in here as long as we can burn them down through the glassite."

"And how long is that, first sergeant?" Dhik asked. "All those bastards need do is wait out of sight until we starve or die of thirst. Or our weapons no longer recharge."

Alabaster turned to Pathfinder. "Would they do that if their goal was diversity? They can't harvest semen from corpses."

"*Shi de*," Bùxiè felt compelled to add to her argument. "And you said that if they cannot perform feats, they'll get bored and go away."

"But how will we know?" Sanech asked. "If'n we don't see 'em, how do we know they're not there?"

Goliad's lips curled. "You could find out the way Corporal Vermain did."

"Dwellers also need food and water if sit-wait." Pathfinder sounded wistful as if he was trying to convince himself along with the others.

"Back in olden times," Goliad said, "when the Granpublic was expanding across the Northern Mark, or later, when the Paris Caliphate was falling apart, armies discovered—or rediscovered—that besieging forces could suffer hardships greater than the besieged."

The thought brought no comfort, and the team sat about in various attitudes, exchanging few words. Sanech pulled another bag from the storage compartment in the autogurney, and he and Dhik wrestled Vermain's corpse into it.

"Hey, you, Sanech," said Pathfinder. "You bring enough bags for everyone?"

Sanech did not respond. He and Dhik strapped both bodies to the gurney, one atop the other.

"I don't think Jaunty would like to be so intimate with a strange woman," Winsome Alabaster commented.

"And they didn't come much stranger than Crawling Vermin," said Singh. Alabaster's smile flickered briefly.

Little Face set up a camp lantern in the center of the room so they could remove their jùggies. Dhik mopped the sweat from his face. "Glad to get that thing off my face for a while," he said. "I'm starting to get a headache."

"Me, too," said Singh.

Patterson scowled and looked at Bùxiè. "How about you?"

Bùxiè rubbed the bridge of his nose. "*Shi de.* The stress must be getting to me."

"What are they waiting for?" asked Sanech. "The Xers, I mean."

"Everyone in Burnout," said Little Face, "know danger, shut up in seal rooms."

Pathfinder echoed him. "They wait us suffocate."

But Patterson corrected him. "We won't suffocate. The HVAC fans aren't working here in the Burnout, so CO_2 is building up. We'll get dizzy and disoriented; we won't be able to think clearly. We'll hyperventilate …"

Goliad cut her short. "That's enough!"

"… and we'll grow irritable and short-tempered. Eventually, we'll pass out." She paused and grew introspective. "But we won't suffocate."

11 EXPECTATIONS

Chen brings a message—An empty seat—A cat among the pigeons—A meeting of the powers—Lingling eavesdrops

DS Qínfèn deFēnxī sat at his desk in the nick and wondered when DCI Bùxiè would return from the Burnout. Not that DI Ramjan was a bungler, but he just didn't have the panache that his usual governor did. DeSōuxún could be almost comic with his schoolings, but Ramjan was serious to the point of dour. He had to admit the man's efficiency, however, and they had already made three arrests for aggravated assault.

He opened another brief on his desk interface and was highlighting key data with his stylus when he became aware of Constable Chen standing by his desk.

"Yes, Constable, what is it?"

Trembling, Chen handed him a note. Qínfèn saw that it was handwritten in Spanglish, in a firm, masculine hand on standard bond notepaper. The writer had been emotionally wrought. He had pressed the stylus so firmly against the paper that Qínfèn thought he could read the note from the backside with his fingertips.

It was from DCI Henrik Abasinian at the Cloisters nick. *Dear Bùxiè*, it read. *I thought you ought to hear this from me …*

As he read the note, Qínfèn felt the blood drain from his face. He looked to Chen, whose eyes were welling up.

"It's been on MOBI," his constable explained. "But the news vendor named no names."

Tongkawa Jones sat at the astrogator's screen while he discussed with Second Officer Berylplume the X/O's plan to enter the ringularity. Now and then he glanced at the empty seat for the astrogator's mate and wondered. It wasn't like Adrienne to be late for the watch.

"It's sheer madness," Jones suggested. "What about the spaghetti problem?"

"Skybones is an engineer," Berylplume answered. He had perched himself on Jones' console table. "He'd regard that as another example of how models go bad without necessarily dragging the universe along. Not that he doesn't have a point—the map is not the territory, and all that—but the model is all we have to go by, engineer's hunches notwithstanding."

"What does Tang say?"

"More to the point, what does the captain say? He has the final say on the ship's course."

"In theory," Jones replied, "but we all know the X/O calls the shots. I wonder what has him so spooked."

Berylplume shrugged. "A radio message, he said, but Earth has not contacted us in a hundred years. And what could they have to say, in any case?" He rose but paused and said, "Maybe the X/O should not rule the captain. He's clearly gone mad. Maybe the captain should resume his constitutional powers."

"Pedro?" Jones was not sure if the Second Officer was suggesting what Jones suspected he was suggesting.

"If not Pedro, then Yves."

It was bad enough that the wretched Yves san Pedro was the designated successor to Pedro san Grigor. To suggest he be King Stork rather than King Log was unendurable.

"Yes, Yves," said Berylplume. "What is it?"

Jones turned and saw that the Prince of *Whale* had entered the quarterdeck. His usual mocha coloring had paled, and he passed a slip of paper to Berylplume. The Second Officer read it, turned grim, and handed the note to Jones.

Jones frowned and read the slip. Then he read it a second time, hoping that he had misread it the first time. "Is this confirmed?" he asked Yves. He and the Prince detested each other, but Jones saw tears in the man's eyes. Yves struggled to speak and settled for nodding dumbly. He leaned over Jones and embraced him awkwardly. Then, Berylplume placed his broad hand on Jones' shoulder and murmured, "I'm sorry, Tongkawa. We all liked her. She was our guild-brother." Yves nodded his agreement.

Tongkawa Jones swallowed a sob as he looked at the empty seat beside him. Who had been responsible, he wondered. He would find out and ensure their punishment.

Images of the Massacre at Undine House hit MOBI within the hour, and shortly thereafter In-Captain Rajalakshmi Ming-ti hit the ceiling. She summoned Masterson, Peng, and other Commanders whose departments had been involved with the Palace Mainouvertes and there reamed them royally. Other Commanders attended as well, either for gloating, entertainment, or the fear of being out of the loop.

There ought to be a name for that fear, Organson thought, amused that he was one of them. Something-*phobia. Ektóvróchou-phobia?* He struggled to recall his schooling.

They had gathered in the Salon Rouge with its plush red draperies and mobile chandelier. Odors of chamomile and cinnamon suffused the air, but there was no music, which was ominous. Ming-ti occupied the captain's chair, formally attired in solid navy-blue trousers and a bemedaled cornflower jacket with a broad scarlet sash. That portended serious *fen-fen* waiting to glop down on someone.

Everyone save the captain was standing, for in a contest between the standing and the sitting, advantage is generally to the latter.

"Would anyone care to tell me what the hell happened at Undine Place?" Captain Ming-ti asked the question in general, but she gave Lady Masterson , Commander of Water, the squint-eye when she asked it.

"Excellent Captain," Masterson said. "The images logged onto MOBI have been edited to show my security detail in a bad light. They don't show the harassment and assaults that triggered the dispersal."

"Oh, hear the offended liverwurst," the captain responded. "But that was not my question." Hamdu thought he detected a note of satisfaction in the captain's voice. She had been playing the Entente and the Alliance against each other for years.

Lord Peng, Commander of Ship Security, spoke up. "The provocation was clearly intentional." This elicited a murmur of agreement. Peng waited a beat, then held his hand up to still the murmurs. "Some of you may be aware of a movement among the crew that calls itself 'the Brotherhood of the *Whale*.' Our reports are not clear on its extent or its goals, but they have a motto: 'the *Whale* as she was,' by which they seem to mean a return to the original order of Whalish society."

"So, are they revolutionaries or reactionaries?" asked Lady Masterson.

"Are this 'brotherhood' the ones who defaced the Hexenplaza Mural?"

Peng ignored the extraneous chatter. "Excellent Captain, public outrage against Lady Water in the comment files has begun to spill over against all Officers. We must take common action if we wish to avoid a mutiny."

Mutiny. The M-word.

"Such as what?" asked Lord Kennett, Maintenance Erlanger, Commander of Maintenance. He did not look happy at the thought of closing ranks with Water. Organson maintained a politic silence. The trick in a Captain's Council was to pass unnoticed.

"Power," said the captain.

"Captain, aye!" Thantos Chan, Commander of Power and Light, was an older man whose short, iron-gray hair crowned a granite block of a head.

"Assemble a Task Force to hammer out an action plan for how we are to turn this omelet over."

"It shall be done, captain." Such was his mien that half the assembled commanders considered the task as already accomplished.

"We can start," Water said, "by logging the security images so the crew can see how the sentries were provoked."

"They'll see," Maintenance predicted, "that my Lady Water hired untrained bully boys to face a mob. She cannot now complain that they displayed that lack of training."

"There was no time to train …"

"In other words," said Commander Kennett, "You did no contingency planning, laid out no PERT, or …"

"Enough!" said Captain Ming-ti. "That's for the after-action report. Peng, that will be your task. For now, we must focus on the forward plan. The matter is urgent, Lord Power." The granite head looked askance, and lightning flashed in his eyes. His voice was a distant rumble.

"I recognize that, Excellent Lady."

The captain had insulted Lord Power, and Hamdu noted that she did not realize it. As yet, no one had mentioned the major sticking point about the Massacre.

"They're calling it a 'security riot,'" said Lady Comm. "I mean, the info vendors are."

"Which ones?" Peng demanded. "Yank their licenses for spreading disinformation. None of *my* people broke ranks."

"Two Enforcers did," Lady Medico pointed out.

Lord Air said, "My Lady Water was forced into precipitant measures by the protestors …"

"By the *mob*," insisted Water.

"They behaved well enough until yesterday," the Purser commented.

"Who, the mob or the sentries?"

"I was well within my rights—"

"So you were," the captain interjected. "But it doesn't matter what your rights were if everything gets cocked up, now does it." Captain Ming-ti continued to hold Water's eye until Lady Masterson looked away.

No one was going to bring it up, it seemed, so Organson reluctantly spoke. "I beg your indulgences, Excellents, but there is a complication. As Liaison to Gold Crew, I recognized one of those killed as an apprentice astrogator."

There went the cat among the pigeons!

"Gold!"

"What is their involvement?"

"It's none of their damned business how I dispose my property!"

"Did he wear his cape?"

"How dare your ruffians strike a cape!"

Outrage ran in several directions as the commanders spoke over and under each other.

It would not take Peng long to learn who was who. Adrienne Mei-ti had only recently been raised and had not yet qualified for a cape. In fact, Organson wondered how much Peng already knew, not only about quartermaster Mei-ti, but about the Brotherhood and the bungled choreography on the Plaza before the Water Palace.

The committee met at Power House, just afore the residence district known as The Cloisters. While the four had never called themselves "The Elementals," it occurred to Organson that they might have done so had they been better educated in the classics. Luis Barnstable managed air regeneration and circulation. Sophie Masterson purified and delivered water. Gregor Vishwakarma, a soft, round man with a voice like syrup, had oversight of the 'ponic tanks, the carniculture vats, and related sections. And Thantos Chan, in whose palace they met, provided lighting and power.

They were Air, Water, Earth, and Fire.

Organson thought the gathering lacked only Æther to be complete, but logically, that would be the Dalai Papa, who was nominally Gold Crew. As it was, Organson himself occupied the fifth position.

For which Lady Water gave him a squint eye. "What is *he* doing here?"

Lord Power arched his back and stretched his arms over his head. He believed that this invigorated the flow of his blood and, therefore, quickened his thoughts. "Make five," Power said. By this, he meant he had broken the unluck of *four* without (Organson being inconsequential) upsetting the balance of power around the table.

I am become a mascot, Organson thought. *Or mayhap, court jester.* But it was his good fortune since he would now become privy to information he would otherwise have to learn through less reliable channels. He glanced at the swabbie servants who stood behind them waiting to be beckoned forward and wondered if Thantos would dismiss them before he began discussions.

Thantos noticed Organson's glance and said, "No worries, Liaison. They are all deaf and mute." Hamdu wondered how Thantos summoned his servants when he needed them or gave them instructions. Sign language?

However, the swabbie standing behind Thantos himself seemed far too attentive for one so deprived, and he carried the slightest smile on his lips.

"If you needed a fifth member, why not Maintenance?" asked Air. "Or Eugenics or the Purser or …"

"… Or any of dozens of commands? Pfaugh! Dozens cannot decide when to eat lunch, let alone deal with crisis that comes soon upon us."

Earth did not waken the dread that the Light Lord did, but what was worse, he lulled. He said, "We are the Four Essentials—Your pardon, Lord Thantos, but we *are* four. Lord Liaison hardly counts. *Whalers* cannot survive without breathing, drinking, eating, and power. They could survive very well without Eugenics telling them who they can couple with or without Security tracking their every move. Other commands may be useful, even vital—Maintenance foremost among them—but they are not *essential* in the way that we are."

Organson hummed to himself. *It doesn't, doesn't matter what we do.* He wondered if Lord Agro was sympathetic to the Cause or whether he only found the fat old man likeable. Any one of the four could wreak havoc in the *Whale.*

Which was why an entente between two of them had unnerved so many, up to the in-captain herself. And why, Organson suspected, Power had called this meeting. Not as a subcommittee to deal with unrest among the crew, or at least not only to do so but as an overlooked power bloc dealing with another that had gotten out of hand. Organson had heard that Eugenics had acted unilaterally, and one of its commanders had been savagely beaten in consequence by Lady Sophie's thugs.

146

She might find that more difficult going forward if Power and Agro were now aligned against her. Why, the Excellents might not need a revolution. They might overthrow themselves!

But if Thantos and Vishwakarma only intended to rein in Masterson's excesses and smooth things over—say, by buying out rather than evicting her tenants—that would be less convenient to the Brotherhood. Organson took a handful of salted nuts from the dish on the table and popped them into his mouth, one by one. This might be an interesting facemeet, after all.

Ling-ling Barnstable—she refused to call herself Masterson—knew the reasons why she was expected to move into her Man's apartments. Motherhood was always self-evident, but fatherhood, though now more easily established by DNA, was empirically less certain, and Eugenics was now unlikely to cooperate in the testing. Moving into Megwan's quarters in Undine House meant that she would live in the same residence as the egregious Sophie Water Masterson, but it was an outward sign of her promise that any child that popped out from her loins would be fathered by Megwan.

She had grown up with that future ever in view, but it had been an abstraction full of ancient ceremonies, lovely gowns, and splendid music. Faced now with the fleshy procedures involved, she thrilled less at the prospect.

She spied Baba down the long central hallway, crossing into the Small Conference Room. What was he doing here? Was Mama with him? She knew such questions were unworthy now that she was a married woman. Why, she even shawled her hair! But she knew her parents sometimes visited g-ma and g-ba, so it might not be unseemly for her to proceed down the hallway and engage with her baba.

"Baba" was for babies. She must learn to call him *"Tantai."*

She had taken a few steps in that direction, rehearsing a dignified conversation as befit a grown woman, but stopped short when Lady Water crossed the hall and entered the same conference room as Baba had done.

When she reached the door, she stopped, but her hand hovered, uncertain, and did not touch the hoigh plate. The Small Conference

Room was not exactly a closet, but it was too small to hold her and the Egregious Sophie at the same time.

Besides, the muffled voices she could hear bespoke anger. Lady Water always sounded angry, even when she was trying to sound pleasant. Her natural voice was a harpy's screech, and she spoke in curt, clipped sentences that always sounded like scolds, even when they were not.

But Baba was angry, too. It seldom showed in his voice or manner, but Ling-ling could hear it, nonetheless. Were they mad at each other? Too late, if they were, for she was married now into House Masterson.

No, they were both angry at Thantos Chan, the Light Lord.

"Who does he think he is?" Sophie's voice, even muffled by the door, was piercing enough to be heard. "Apologize to *crew*? They attacked my sentries. *They* owe *me* the apology."

Baba said something she could not make out, but the Harpy answered. "What do you mean, 'It's not enough to be right'?"

This time, she could hear Baba's reply, "Sophie, you have to be *seen* to care." She had never heard her father raise his voice. "Even if you don't care, you have to act as if you do. Lord Agro is an oily son of a bitch, but he puts on a good front, and the crew love him."

"Who cares if the crew love us?" That shrill voice was a needle through Ling-ling's brain. "All we require from the crew is their obedience to orders." More muffled voices; then: "Honey? Vinegar? What do I care about catching flies? Sometimes, Luis, I think you're a melon."

"Sophie." And this was loud and stern, as Ling-ling had sometimes heard when she had done something very wrong. "Our grandchild is to be Joint Commander of Air and Water, but we cannot go up against not only Maintenance and Mining, but Eugenics, Power, Agriculture, and the in-captain herself. Or hadn't you noticed how few friends we had in the Salon Rouge?"

Ling-ling stepped away from the door. She didn't want to hear any more. That sort of talk upset her. She turned her steps back toward her own quarters, where she found Megwan. Her Man was looking none too happy himself, and so she sat with him on a settee, and they wrapped their arms around each other, not speaking, for the first time since they had Done It, he did not try to Do It again.

12 TRIALS

A death sentence concentrates the mind wonderfully—
Professional pride—A stoatin idea

Ohik had no desire to smother, even though Peta had said that it was not technically smothering. That was the sort of distinction that passed right through him. You were dead either way, so what difference did it make? He was not widely known as a deep thinker, but a death sentence, he found, concentrates the mind remarkably well.

He had been born in Billy's Gate deep in the belly of the *Whale* and aft of the Burnout. He barely remembered his parents, who had died of the Red Rot when he was five. He had been raised thereafter by a negligent uncle and the wide-open passageways. Mocked by the other pass'waifs for his size and his slow demeanor, he had schooled them in the applications of large size to small persons. A few such lessons had sufficed to win a greater respect in the corridors and even renown in the pass'gang.

Though too large for pickpocketing or snatch-and-run, he had shown skill in harvesting from passers-by donations to the gang's

Benevolent Fund. Even then, his voice had the timbre of the rock pulverizers in Mine Town, though less melodic. It helped that he also had the build and demeanor of a rock pulverizer.

Even so, he would oft seclude himself at night so that when he cried over half-remembered parents, the others would not hear him.

He might have lived his life in the pass'ways of Billy's Gate and perhaps ended it there, as well. For what else could a pass'waif expect besides a short life of meaningless struggle? But then Jonesy, the grocer's son from just down the pass, scored well on the Examinations and had been summoned Forward, and Dhik glimpsed a glimmer of daylight.

Not that he would ever qualify for a brain post like Jonesy had done, but there were other possibilities. So, one day, he turned confident strides into the local Enforcer's station and asked to be enrolled. Old Emicho Drinkwater had taken one look at the young mountain of a boy, seen something in him, and sent him on to the School of Enforcement. There, he had learned to modulate his strength with dexterity, and he also learned that he was not as irredeemably stupid as he (and his uncle) had always believed.

He learned also that some Regulations were to be enforced to the letter—sorting recyclables, saluting officers—while others fell within the Enforcer's discretion. Who, after all, suffered from a dice game or a wager on the neighborhood stickball team, provided the element of chance was not discounted too blatantly? However, collecting a fee for closing his eyes had proven an error, and he had been more judicious since then.

"Hey?" he addressed Blackbird One. "What's it like out the back door?"

The man looked at Dhik curiously. "A compact mass of wreckage. Can't wriggle out through that."

"I ain't built for wriggling, Friend. But then the Xers can't wriggle in that way neither?" He directed this question to Pathfinder, who tossed his head without speaking.

"Then why did we leave the back hatch closed? Those are airtight doors. The HVAC fans aren't working in the Burnout, but cracking the door ought to get a little air circulation going and maybe help disperse the CO_2 'cumulating in here."

The others gave him startled looks, and Peta struck herself on the thigh. "I should have thought of that." Grabbing Dhik's hand, she squeezed it and whispered, "That's the second time you've saved my life."

"It ain't saved yet," he whispered back. "You told us the CO_2 buildup would impair our thinking. Just be happy I didn't have enough thinking to impair."

"You do yourself a disservice."

One had gone to the back hatch already. Goliad suggested, "If I crack the main hatch, too, it might get a cross draft going." It was not quite a question.

"Xers *can* wriggle in that way," Pathfinder reminded him, proving that he had been listening, too.

"I said 'crack it,' not throw it wide open. If they're out of our sight, we're out of theirs. Turn off the camp light, put our jùggie lamps on low, and they might not notice when the hatch opens."

When no one objected, Goliad spun the locking wheel and eased the hatchway open about a finger's width. Little Face went to the door and listened. A minute passed. "No reaction."

"I can feel a draft," Winnie said.

DeSōuxún clapped Dhik's shoulder. "That was good thinking."

No one had accused him of that before. Dhik passed it off. "Someone else woulda thought of it, sooner or later."

"Maybe so, Chief, but you did."

Dhik's spirit swelled, and he felt improbably lighter as if the swelling had filled him with helium and he had become a balloon. It was a very different feeling, he decided, when they weren't afraid of you.

Little Face squatted by the hatchway, cloaked in shame. He remembered all the times he had noticed distant voices, fleeting lights, remnants of camps. But he had thought each an indication of other burnsiders or even of adventurous niyōs. He was no better than a niyō himself to have missed the signs and may as well have been back in the pocks, shaving 'stroid like his old man.

But he could not have gone back. Mining the asteroid had been mind-numbing work. A man could immerse himself into the vibrations and rhythms of the drillbot until they took on the aspect of voices, and his thoughts took wing. Until one day, those thoughts had alighted in the drill pocks themselves, and a conviction had swollen in him that he would drill too deeply, pierce the *Whale*'s asteroid shell, and open a hole into the void of space itself. The vacuum would suck him out through the hole into the sleeting radiation and the endless cold that enveloped the ship, where he would gasp for just an instant before his head exploded.

Never mind that the shell was not so thin as that; he had been spooked below the level of rational thought, and you couldn't really argue with the irrational. You also could not work in Mine Town if you were afraid to drill.

So, he had sought refuge from his fears in the Burnout, amidst the detritus of other people's lives—only to get sucked into another sort of vacuum: the Brotherhood's revolutionary folderol. Not that he had any great love for capewalkers, but he did not see that the likes of Group Leader Chang or Jek Buddhathal marked any significant improvement on them. It seemed to him the chief purpose of any revolution was to erect a better regime than the one being replaced, not merely to install a different gaggle of mendacious fools.

Now these Dwellers swarmed around him. The Burnout was growing right crowded, though all he had ever asked of it was solitude. He remembered the injured men he had seen that day in Fort Freedom and decided that the Brotherhood militia had stumbled upon the Dwellers and found themselves in a fight in which they had come off second-best. Group Leader Chang should have reported the encounter up the chain, but like so many subordinates, had been reluctant to mention problems to his superiors.

When he saw that deSōuxún was speaking with the Big Dhik and out of earshot, he leaned toward Pathfinder. "Tan Lùzhě," he said, speaking in Běifāngwóng wá, a tongue in which he suspected only the inspector fluent. "*You knew.*"

His colleague grimaced. "I tell Desola we be coming with opportunity for much diversity. Not expect you bring blackbirds and Marines with teasers."

Little Face had not expected to bring them, either, but was happy now to have had them. "You plan sell me as sex slave, too, or just the policeman?"

"Cannot not go back, you, if lose your whole party."

"So, doing for me favor, you?"

Pathfinder shrugged. "Expected Desolate, not Xers."

Little Face held up a hand, palm out. "Hush. Doggies bark." He leaned into the crack of the hatchway. The sounds were distant, not approaching. A howl lifted over the chorus.

"What is it?" Goliad had joined them by the doorway, his hand on the butt of his teaser. "Are they coming?"

"No. Fracas down pass'. Big fight." Little Face could move his ears the way others could move their eyes. "Different calls," he decided.

"Maybe so," Pathfinder suggested, "Desola find Xers in their pass.'"

Fanghsi had not decided whether he would leave Tan's carcass to feed the feral dogs of the Big Burnout or simply beat the man senseless for his treachery. If what he heard was a dogfight between the Desolate and the Triple-X, it made no never mind who won. Both proposed to kill the women on the team and enslave the men. He could not allow either because the niyōs were under his protection. He had led them into the Burnout, and by damn, he would lead them out. It was a matter of professional pride.

"We will settle what lies between us," he told Pathfinder, still in the birdsong twitter of Běifāngwóng wá, "at a time more convenient for us both."

Goliad crouched beside them. "After which," he added in the same tongue, "you will settle with me."

And Winsome Alabaster added over his shoulder, "Ránhòu Peta hé wǒ huì bǎ nǐ biàn chéng nǚrén."

Fanghsi raised his eyebrows and said to Pathfinder, "And how will your friends in Desola treat you if your diversity sliced off?"

Goliad did not so much assume command as accept a command that came bounding to him like a bouncing baby. He did not remind anyone that the Fleet Marines had seen little action aside from riot control since Departure Day, and the riots had been in the aftermath of the Burnout, well before his time. What often matters is not what is true but what people believe is true. If he had no more practical experience in combat than anyone else, he had far more theoretical knowledge of it. He was First Sergeant of First Platoon of the goddam Imperial Fleet Marines, and never mind that the Imperium was two light-years behind them and two centuries in the past, Here and now, he was all his compadres had.

So, when he ordered everyone to gather by the main hatchway, no one questioned his authority. "This distraction," he told them, "is an opportunity, but we must move fast. We're going back up the pass.' We'll do it single file and in the dark so we don't attract attention from the Dwellers. Juggies on dim. Rope yourselves fore and aft and 'rankle your ankles.' Little Face takes point because he knows the route. But Singh and I will take the rear guard in case the Dwellers notice and come chasing. We can provide teaser cover. Pathfinder will go in the middle."

"Gag him so he not call friends?" asked Little Face.

"Xers not my friends," Tan Lùzhě insisted. "They catch me, they hock me, same as you."

"What if Desolate win dogfight?"

The burnsider took on a grim look. "Not holding breath."

Winnie said, "Number One, Number Two, remain with the rear guard since you also have teasers."

"We are supposed to guard *you*, ej'māni?" said Number One.

"Which you can best do by safeguarding our rear."

"You be having a teaser, too, ej'māni," Number Two pointed out, "but we don't cotton to you exposing yourself in the rear guard."

"I will post myself near Pathfinder, and if he takes a deep breath to holler, I'll kill him."

Goliad would rather have the Dwellers mad at him than Winsome Alabaster. But Pathfinder's plan would have condemned her to death, and that might irritate anyone.

Bùxiè raised the 'dog-kicker' he had taken. "I'll stay in the rear, too."

"No," Goliad told him. "You stay in front in case we run into anything in that direction. No guarantees that all the Dwellers ran portside."

Once they were roped together, Goliad said, "Maintain a steady beat so we don't get tanglefooted."

Sanech activated the autogurney, which rose on its repellors. He quickly extinguished its running lights. When he saw the others staring at him, he said, "It's why we come here, aina?"

They went dark and filed out the hatchway, lining up in the pass'. Everyone could hear the sounds of the fight now. Overlaying the howls, yips, and the, frankly, human screams were high-pitched snaps and whines, and in the portside blackness, fireflies winked like jewels on velvet.

"Those are teaser discharges," Singh exclaimed. "The Marines are here. It's a rescue!"

"Quiet, You." Little Face swiftly stifled Singh's exultation with an arm around his shoulder and a hand across his mouth. "Think. *Is wrong direction.* If rescue party enter Burnout, it come from starboard past our little fort."

Goliad decided Fanghsi was right. How would such a party know where they were, let alone that they needed rescue? Those must be the Little Lost Teasers that Lucky and Crowley had been tracking. One of the burnside clans had found them. Probably Desola. Had the Xers had them, they would have used them through the windows earlier, and the team would have been goldfish in a bowl.

"Briskly, now." Goliad whispered a cadence, "Left, left, left. Keep in step. Whoever wins that fight back there will win the teasers, and we'll be jangled but good."

"Nah, boss," said Singh. "They'd prob'ly 'lectrocute themselves. You need training to handle teasers safe."

The Lance was correct, but then Goliad wondered, *who had trained the Desolate?*

Or was someone else wielding those teasers down at the end of Conniption Pass'?

As DCI Bùxiè deSōuxún hustled through the twilight, mice and rats spooked through the 'ponic weeds that had sprouted in corners and angles. An occasional bird took wing. With everyone's lamps on dim, his goggles had little light to gather, and the hatchways and longitudinal intersections they passed were barely discernable in the false-color gloaming. Once, Bùxiè saw the bright, reflective eyes of a feral cat watching them from a broken bulkhead. Now and then, a dangling cable sparked where the memory material was trying vainly to reconnect, and it seemed as if a great flash bulb had gone off, leaving a sharp electric odor.

The first time that happened, Bùxiè spun about, convinced they had been spotlighted and the fighting clans had seen them escaping. He imagined them loping through the night behind them, axes and crossbows at the ready.

Little Face, clipped to his front, grunted at the unexpected tug. "Eyes front," growled the scout. Then, "Relax, Chief Inspector. Marines warn if anyone come after us."

They soon turned off from Conniption Pass', and the sounds of battle faded with both the distance and the corners. When they reached the drop shaft to climb to Twenty Deck, they turned their lamps back up. That's when they noticed that Pathfinder was gone, and the clips that had fastened him to the autogurney in front and Alabaster behind were now clipped to each other.

"How did he do that?" Alabaster asked. "I was keeping an eye on him."

"Should have kept both eyes," said Fanghsi. "Pathfinder moves in blinks between our attentions."

"I had plans for him."

"Probably why he gone."

"He might have gone to tell Desola where we are," said Bùxiè.

But Little Face tossed his head. "No. Pathfinder promise them easy pickings. Desola maybe think he trick them. Maybe he burrow deep in Burnout, hide there."

Sanech had been eyeing the shaft. "It will be *apuro* to lift the autogurney up that. Bottom's too far down for the repellors. You sure there's no stairwell we can take?"

Bùxiè saw the difficulty. They'd be lifting two bodies without the assistance of antigravity. Folded and compactified, Sanech could carry the gurney on his back, but he could hardly climb the ladder with two bodies strapped to it.

"Sanech," said Dhik, "you carry the gurney up the ladder. It's only one deck. I'll go with you, and we'll lower ropes. They can buckle the ropes to the handles on the body bags, and the two of us can haul 'em up, one at a time."

"That's a stoatin idea, Dhik," Patterson said. "I'll climb up wit' ye."

"You go first, Little Face," Bùxiè added. "Make sure there are no unpleasant surprises up on Twenty."

The burnsider cast him a hurt look. "Not Pathfinder, me," he said.

Bùxiè was not listening. He took Dhik aside and whispered to him and to the medical examiner, "Keep an eye on him so he doesn't cut out like his friend." He turned to the Marines. "Goliad, take Singh and go stand watch over the traverse pass'way. It's still possible that the winners of the fight in Conniption Pass' might come after us."

"One, Two, go with them," added Alabaster.

"Ej'māni ..."

"You can guard me better by keeping the Dwellers away from me. The inspector and I can fasten the bags to the ropes." She turned to look at Bùxiè and said, "Let's make this happen, Chief Inspector."

When Dhik and Sanech lowered the ropes, she swung gracefully out to the ladder, and Bùxiè recalled that they were twenty decks above the orlop. But her motions were fluid, and she swung back with the rope as if dismounting from a balance beam. They snapped the end to Crowley Vermain's bag and signaled to Dhik and Sanech to hoist away.

After a time, the rope snaked down once more, and again Winnie fetched it. She evinced no problem snapping the line to her Man's remains, but wrestling the bag out into the shaft proved difficult, and she swallowed a sob while assisting him. "Farewell, Jaunty," he heard her whisper. She made the Sign of the Cross and Wheel and bowed her head in prayer.

The feral dogs of the Burnout were a wily lot, and successive bitches had taught their pups to watch for inattention. So, once Winnie had closed her eyes, a large, gray dog sprang for her out of the shadows. Where in the darkness it had been lurking, Bùxiè could not say, but he yanked the "dog-kicker" from his pouch and fired.

The dog yelped and dropped into a curl. The blackbirds came running back from their watch.

"Did a Dweller get past us?" One asked.

"No. This was an actual dog," Winnie said. "DCI deSōuxún took care of it." Her smile broke through.

Bùxiè thought he understood, at least a little, why Alabaster's *particular friend* would do much to see that melancholy smile of hers blossom.

13   TRIBULATIONS

Don't go home—Broken carrot sticks—They were only on loan—The long farewell—"Perhaps he intended to brace her."—"We'll just have to go and fetch them."

When the body recovery team reached the wardroom on Twenty Deck, it was raining on the traverse pass' outside. A squad of swabbies, mops in hand, were huddled inside the wardroom hatchway, waiting out the downpour—all but one, who stood out in the pass'way itself, arms spread wide and moon face upturned to the sprinklers in the overhead, laughing as the water cascaded off him and soaked his hair and coveralls.

Their bo'sun turned with a look of astonishment when the team entered from the Burnout.

The team's MOBIs had come out as soon as they stepped within the wireless zone, and who they tried to contact sketched the boundaries of their lives. Patterson contacted the morgue, Sanech, his parents. Winnie called the parents of Jaunty Alabaster; the blackbirds contacted Dumont Ramamurthy.

159

Goliad called Lt. Dingbang and reported the death of Corporal Vermain and the circumstances surrounding it.

"So, you think these jumble outlaws have found the teasers? That makes it stolen property, and that's a hefty fine."

That would do for a first approximation, but Goliad was uncertain whether the Dwellers would pay the fine—or who would collect it and how.

Bùxiè got no response from Adrienne, which likely meant that she was standing watch on the quarterdeck. He left her a message and told the Operating Base to contact Qínfèn.

"Guv'nor," his sergeant said when he answered. "You're back!"

"Don't sound so surprised, sergeant. And get your feet off my desk."

The pause that followed brought a smile to Bùxiè's lips. But then Qínfèn said, "Guv'nor ... don't go home, yet. We'll be right down to fetch you."

DeSōuxún put his MOBI away and immediately tried to parse his sergeant's voice. Had a major case broken during his brief absence? He noticed Dr. Patterson staring at him as she holstered her own MOBI. Her face had gone slack, and her skin seemed drained of blood.

Definitely a major case. He sighed. No rest for the weary,

The rain outside shut off abruptly, and the sun panels lit up. The swabbies went to work, whistling while they mopped the puddles into the scuppers and swabbed the deck clean. Swabbies were generally recruited from the mentally challenged. They were limited in their skills and thinking. Consequently, their decision-making was owned by others. The bo'sun directed them with select profanity, and the swabbies bobbed their heads, smiled, and ignored him. The pass'way had the fresh smell it always possessed after a rain.

The Little Lotus nick was not far, and Bùxiè wondered how long it would take Qínfèn to arrive, but he noticed that Goliad, too, was staring at him. Bùxiè's body vibrated like a plucked *koto* string, as it always did at the beginning of a new case. He couldn't wait to learn the particulars.

Organson met Venables this time in Fu-lin's Wayhouse in High-steeple, known as "Pursuit of Hoppiness," where the talk was high and the patrons as well. Highsteeple, on Ten Deck abaft Thirty-Two

Frame, formerly a prestigious address, had become tatty in the present generation. Lord Kennett, Commander of Maintenance, had lived there, and it was said, though not very loudly, that Lady Water had cut back on the rainfall cleanse, and the drinking water had acquired an unpleasant tang. The problem with infighting among the Excellents was that ordinary crewmen could be discomfited as well.

Venables looked around the tap room, which buzzed with animated conversation. "Is it safe to talk here?" In case anyone was listening, he contrived to make the question sound like a clearing of his throat. Peng had ears everywhere.

He and Organson occupied a table for two by the starboard bulkhead. Although not an aficionado of such places, Venables judged Fu-lin's an upscale instance of its kind. Organson signaled to the nǚfú, who seemed to float to the table as if she rode a gravity board. He checked her feet and saw that they did move and wondered how she achieved the effect.

"*Shi de*, honorable sirs. What will it be my privilege to bring you?"

Organson held up two fingers horizontally. "The Black," he said.

This sign evidently meant two long glasses of porter, for that was what shortly appeared, brought by the same waitress. Venables thought a well-fed mouse could scamper across the foam head without sinking, although, once having thought that, he searched in the murky depths for an indication of whether the experiment had been attempted.

"What do you think went wrong?" Organson asked him.

For a moment, Venables thought he meant the experiment with the mouse; then, he realized Lord Hamdu was asking about the massacre at Undine Place, and he coughed his first cautious sip of porter. "Hush," he said between hacks.

"Florian," Organson gently chided him. "All that anyone is talking about today is the Massacre. Peng's keyword algorithms will be overwhelmed with tags. Remember, MOBI flags only syntactical constructions; a human must still screen the flags for actual semantic content. Peng would be hard-pressed to listen to twenty thousand recordings."

But Venables found the habits of years difficult to slough off and took refuge in evasive phrasing. "I wonder if it was deliberate."

"Some jek-ass probably exceeded his instructions." By mispronouncing 'jackass,' Organson had told him who was responsible.

Venables thought Corporal Jek could be a problem when the time finally came for the Mutiny. His zeal was too emotionally loaded. Twelve years earlier, Jek's mother had been molested by a capewalker, though what Jek found more unforgivable was the way Officers had closed ranks and dropped a veil of silence over the incident. That had shifted his hatred from the perpetrator in particular to Officers in general.

Venables had known the mother, and she had not been above spinning a tale or two to cover for her alcohol usage. She had been vague regarding time, place, and identity and might as easily have accused anyone of the groping. He wondered at the reliability of a Brother whose impulse was more personal than political.

"So, now that Lady Water has relented on the evictions—"

"Probably because other Officers leaned on her." Organson's tone indicated that he knew this for a fact.

"—the protests are over." Venables found it a most unsatisfactory victory. He had expected more of the affair. Chao or Barnstable or the others would hardly provide a *casus belli* as clearly as had the volatile Commander Masterson. He felt that with this step forward, they had somehow taken two steps back.

"Oh, it's not over yet, my friend. The captain has asked me to sit as prosecuting magistrate on the trial of the sentries."

"You!"

"Because one of the victims was Gold Crew. The captain feels that because I am Liaison, I can help sort any ill feelings on Gold's part. I am at liberty to choose who I want for the defending magistrate."

"That will hardly be a popular assignment."

"That is why I want you."

"Me? No! Away with you!"

"Hear me out, Venables. You're a well-known scholar. 'The best tutor money can buy.'"

"You know what that means? The better ones can't be bought."

Organson waved off the objection. "… with a reputation for fairness, objectivity, and good judgement. If it gets played right …"

"Most of the accused are actually innocent."

162

"Then you will get them acquitted. But the acquittal might leave a bad taste in people's mouths. They'll feel that—somehow—Lady Water has 'got away with' something but won't be able to put their fingers on quite what it was." Organson turned and gave the waitress a different hand signal.

Meanwhile, a lean woman with dark hair took a seat on a small stage in the corner of the tap room, where she uncased a lap harp. The regulars in the room hooted, clapped, and called out requests. "Drunken Nights," "Star of Lower Black Jade," "Highsteeple Races," and other popular titles. The harpist patted down their applause, saying, "Patience, friends. Chandra plays all in good time. But first, here's a tune that's grown popular of late here in the belly of the *Whale*." And so saying, she plucked the harp and sang "It Doesn't Matter." When she came to the fourth verse, however, she altered the refrain.

> *"But whether we build something novel*
> *Or only change how much we grovel.*
> *Drinking in the same old stew,*
> *Whether we renew the Whale*
> *Or chug another pint of ale,*
> *It really, really matters what we do."*

Venables muttered, "Clever."

"We thought so. It contrasts what we do in the sense of our ratings with what we do to change things."

"Tell me—" Venables broke off as the waitress brought a nosh plate of raw vegetables, but when he reached to take one, Organson slapped his hand lightly and gathered a handful of carrot sticks for himself. Venables nodded thoughtfully, then asked, "This Brotherhood the news vendors has mentioned as possibly behind the protests—do you think they'll try something else now that Lady Water has backed down?"

"Possibly."

"You know, most revolutions eat their young. Those who erect the guillotines wind up on them. Beria was shot."

"Who?"

"Never mind."

"You rely on history. But how reliable are records from back in the Dark Ages?"

Venables wondered if his friend was serious. "We call them 'dark' because we cannot read many of their records, not because the people suddenly became stupid and ignorant. They were written with operating systems that soon became obsolete."

"Really? I had always thought it was because they fought a great war. Two of them."

But Venables tossed his head. "Many scholars believe there was only one 'Great War,' not two. To fight a second one so shortly after the first really would have been 'stupid and ignorant.' They think the tale—what has survived of it—was reduplicated. Probably different authors told it. They call them the J-version, for Jurman, and the E-version, for English."

"Those were the Doish and the Anglics in Yurp?" Organson folded his hands on the table and presented Venables with an attentive look.

"The two versions are much the same, as you would expect if they were drawing on a common source. A small country in the middle of Yurp fights the rest of the continent—and holds them off for four or five years."

"That hardly seems likely," Organson said.

"Well, it isn't. In both versions, one of the Opposition collapses. Roosiya in the J-version, Fransáy in the E. But E seems more mythic since it is populated with clearly symbolic characters. Noble Wolf—the Doish name was 'Athalwolf' or 'Adolf'—descends on the hapless sheep of Yurp until only one remains standing, like 'a church on a hill.' The Church-Hill people hold out valiantly alone—that's why we call it the E-version. It valorizes the Anglics. They receive assistance from the wealthy 'field of roses' until Noble Wolf turns on his former ally and smashes himself on Steel. The others rally and attack, led by a figure called 'Iron-Hewer,' clearly connected with northern legends of the thunder god. The Fransáy come back, led by an exiled prince whose name is simply an older name for Fransáy. The trope of the exiled prince who returns as savior is familiar in folklore, as is the Stalwart Holdout, the

Wealthy Benefactor, the impregnable Steel Wall ... and the Big Bad Wolf. The whole narrative is obviously allegorical."

Organson smiled. "And that should take care of anyone listening to a recording of this conversation. They will never listen all the way through."

Venables humphed and fell silent. He wished Organson would show more respect for scholarship.

Organson broke several carrot sticks in half, and Venables understood. *Casualties.* But how?

"Sometimes, you're minding your own business," Organson said, "and you stumble into someone else's quarrel."

"Whose?"

"No one seems to know. It's a game of *tiaoqi.*"

"*Tiaoqi?*"

"You may know it as 'jump-chess' or 'Chinese checkers.' What I mean is that there are multiple players." Organson placed two broken carrot sticks on his left and two on his right; then, he pushed both pairs into the center. (*Someone may put two and two together.*) Then he looked at his watch and said, "We better wrap up here." (*We had better act soon.*) "So, I'll tell the captain you've agreed."

Venables knew how to play jump-chess and knew when he had been jumped. But he really, really wished there had been a question mark at the end of Organson's sentence.

Winsome Alabaster browsed the aisles of the Flowing Silk Commissary, noticing as she did so the tendency of her neighbors to fall silent at her approach and break into whispers in her wake. No one addressed her save to say Ola or Nǐ hǎo or some other greeting or to flash a brief and superficial smile. Usually, her neighborhood crackled with chatter and cheer. Only Old Lady Vishwakarma spoke to her, and then it was merely to scold.

"Gettin' airs above yer station," said she.

"I'm not sure what you mean, Vish."

"Ah, don't come the raw prawn wi' me, deary. I saw them birdies wi' ye. Since when do the likes of you merit a pair of Peng's Poodles?"

Winnie shifted her shopping basket to her left hand. "I was going into the Burnout to recover my Man's body, and my supervisor loaned me two of his bodyguards for safety's sake. Afterwards, they escorted me back to my quarters."

Vishwakarma wagged her hand horizontally. "Listen to madam 'look-at-my-boyfriend,' so important, she is. Your Man disappeared years ago."

"But they only found his body recently." She reached past her neighbor to snag a box of milled 'ponic. She didn't really need the flour, but it enabled her to interrupt the conversation.

"Just be careful who ye 'sociate wi,' dearie. An' ye lie down wi' dogs, ye get up wi' fleas. Remember, ye don't wear no blue cape yerself."

Later, at Dumont's palace, she told him that being seen with his blackbirds had not flown well with her neighbors. Dumont frowned and said, "Had you been harmed out there, I would have felt devastated."

At that point, Two entered the room and stood to the right of the hatchway with his hands clasped before him. Alabaster waved to him, but he made no response. His gaze danced across her and focused instead on the distance between her and Lord Helix. Alabaster remembered something he had once said. "*I never enter a room without a plan to kill everyone in it*," and she shivered. She was no longer Two's assignment. He had only been on loan.

She tried to see the room as Two saw it: an informal armory. She considered each object in it as a potential weapon. The chairs were obvious, and her head could be bashed against the desk. Pillows could be used for smothering as easily as for sitting, and the curtain cords would make excellent garottes. She had to think a moment regarding the stylus with which Dumont had been writing until she remembered it had a sharp tip and could serve as a poignard if thrust into a soft area like the base of her throat. The only safe object she saw was the sheet of paper on the desk, but then she wondered if that was because it actually was harmless or because she lacked sufficient imagination.

Bùxiè deSōuxún sat in his quarters and tried not to think. He had turned the lights to low, and in the dim shadows, he could convince himself that his Adrienne sat in her accustomed chair just across from him. Qínfèn was mistaken. That was the only sensible explanation. Qínfèn and Henrik and all the others who had been pestering him with "condolences." They would feel foolish when Adrienne came off watch and normal life resumed.

He checked the time, and it was only five minutes since he had last checked it. He realized he was missing the memorial service for Jaunty Alabaster, and he had promised Winnie that he would attend. But that had been before he had gotten the confusing news regarding Adrienne. Winnie would understand.

That night, he heard Adrienne's soft breaths in the bed beside him. As he was drifting off, he heard her voice crystalline and clear: *pretty man*. Her favorite name for him, and he smiled a little as he fell asleep. She was home at last.

Two days later, reality had intruded and asserted her dominance. He no longer believed it was all an awful case of mistaken identity, though it did remain awful. The memorial service was held in the Cathedral of St. Brendon the Navigator, which confused Bùxiè, as he could not remember having made the arrangements. "St. B's" was a splendid space, draped in white and saffron banners bearing the Cross and Wheel and other imagery.

Columns soared three decks high to be lost in clouds of incense. The upper decks were painted with devas and cherubs that floated amidst them. Murals evoked the realms to which souls could transmigrate: Heaven, Purgatory, Limbo, or Hell. In the Heavenly realm, the soul would be reincarnated in a new, glorified body, and Bùxiè chose to focus on this.

The Three Persons were portrayed on the transept walls: on the left as Brahma, Vishnu, and Shiva; on the right as Father, Word, and Spirit. The avatars of the second persons—guru Krishna and guru Iesu—looked on with kindly benevolence.

He wondered if Qínfèn had made the arrangements. He thought Adrienne would have preferred a humbler ceremony at St. Guanyin's chapel in Little Lotus.

An acolyte swung the wooden mallet on its chains, and the Calling Bell tolled—two, then five, then three. A funeral. Bùxiè turned in his seat and was astonished to see a large crowd of mourners had gathered behind him.

Jackson Mei-ti and his clan, of course. He recognized women from the flower mart and other places Adrienne had frequented, as well as his own colleagues from the nick and friends from the dojo. But there were also strangers garbed in bright golden capes. He turned to Qínfèn, "Who are all these people?"

His sergeant placed a hand on his arm. "They came to pay respects to Adrienne."

Looking closer, he recognized Tongkawa Jones and supposed the other goldcapes with him were also Adrienne's colleagues off the quarterdeck. Jones was visibly sobbing.

He saw Winsome Alabaster, escorted by a bluecape—her *particular friend*, he supposed. One and Two were with them. He felt a pang of guilt for having missed Jaunty's memorial. That so many had come to show respect for Adrienne brought Bùxiè near to tears.

When the celebrant proved to be the Dalai Papa himself, he could not contain a sob. The altar bore a picture of Adrienne shopped into the company of the Buddha and the Christ, who embraced her on either side. Papa Benedict sprinkled the reliquary with holy water and intoned the introit gatha:

> "*Out of the depths I cry to you, O Lord.*
> *If you, O Lord, should mark our guilt,*
> *Lord, who would stand?*"

And concluded with:

> "*Eternal rest grant unto her, O Lord.*
> *Let perpetual light shine upon our beloved sister, Shi Paṇi*
> *Malaisu Jackson san Tongkawa, as she is reborn into the*
> *country of assurance and joy.*"

Bùxiè was impressed with the dharma name the Papa had chosen to bestow. A long dharma name bespoke a meritorious life, and 'Snowy Mountain' was peaceful and serene.

Snatches of the readings—sutras and gospels—nestled in his attention as Papa Benedict called upon one or another of the mourners to read a passage.

"The souls of the just are in the hand of God," read Tongkawa Jones, though his throat caught a bit when he did, "and no torment shall touch them. They seemed, in the view of the foolish, to be dead, and their passing away was thought an affliction, and their going forth from us, utter destruction. But they are in peace."

May she escape the Wheel, Bùxiè prayed, though he knew she had not escaped the *Whale*. From whole organs to residual water, the undertakers in the Recycling Department were thorough, and nothing vital went to waste.

During the eulogies, Bùxiè trembled that they might call upon him to laud his Woman. He was not sure he could do that without breaking. He could contemplate her passing. He thought he could even write about it. But to speak of her aloud was beyond his abilities.

Jackson Mei-ti described his daughter's childhood. A woman named Hydrania Axelrod spoke of her skill at *ikebana*, or flower arrangement. Tongkawa Jones spoke of her performance as chartsman and quartermaster and how she had detected a ringularity in time for the *Whale* to avoid it. Bùxiè thought he heard an ironic note in Jones' eulogy, but it was gone before he was certain. A bluecape officer named Organson addressed the fellow feeling that had led Adrienne to protest at Undine Place.

Finally, a man whom Bùxiè did not know arose and said, "Be upstanding for Pedro san Grigor, eighth go-captain of the Ship Imperial, *Whale*." And an elderly man in splendid golden robes trimmed in red strode up the aisle to the altar. Bùxiè could not believe it. The go-captain himself! At the altar, the captain made an ablution to Shi Pani Malaisu and informed the congregation, "On the recommendation of my protégé, Yves san Pedro, I raised quartermaster Mei-ti to apprentice in the Guild of Astrogators. She had barely begun her new duties when she was brutally struck down while performing a *mitzvah* for strangers. Nonetheless, it is the custom of our Guild that a member is raised one grade upon his passing, and so, I pronounce her now Astrogator Junior Grade Pani Malaisu. So, say I."

The goldcapes responded in chorus. "So, say we all!"

At that, Bùxiè sobbed without restraint. She had gotten her gold cape at last and would never found a dynasty.

After the ceremonies, he stood before the altar with Adrienne's family to receive condolences. "She was a gentle and caring Woman," he told Jackson, who replied that she had been their particular treasure. The words seemed banal and spitless, but they were words that wanted saying. He and Jackson embraced, then both faced forward to endure the condolences of others.

That included the high and mighty: the Dalai Papa himself and the go-captain, as well as Hamdu Organson, who, Bùxiè now noted, wore blue-and-gold pinstripes marking him as Blue/Gold Liaison. Most of the mourners had barely known Adrienne, and some not at all. They had come to her funeral out of form or because, like Big Dhik or Too Tall Goliad, they knew Bùxiè.

Bùxiè was laminated in glassite; nothing in the world could touch him, nor could he touch the world. People appeared before him, and then they were gone. He longed for the ordeal to be over.

And then suddenly, Winsome Alabaster stood there. He had not seen her approach; she had simply appeared, *ex nihilo*. She took his hand in both of hers, and for once, her sad semi-smile did not seem misplaced. "I never met her," he heard her say, "but you spoke of her so lovingly."

Bùxiè searched for words, found them. "I'm sorry I missed Jaunty's memorial."

"You had other things on your mind. I remember what that was like."

Over her shoulders, he saw One and Two and supposed they had come out of solidarity from their time together in the Burnout. "It was good of you to come," he told them.

"Our master came," One said. Two looked as if he wanted to say more but held his peace. The dark and handsome bluecape with them engulfed Bùxiè's hand in his own and squeezed.

"You saved Winnie's life," he said. "That earned my everlasting gratitude. I was devastated to learn that you returned to such awful news as this."

"Thank you, Excellent, sah." Ramamurthy had spoken the right words, but there was something off about them, though Bùxiè could not say what.

"Lady Water must be made to pay," Lord Dumont said. Then he, Winnie, One, and Two took their leave.

Next in line was a young couple. The man wore the uniform of a lieutenant (jg) in hydraulics; his Woman was badged for air. Bùxiè added two and two.

"You have nerve coming here."

"Sah?"

"You're Lord Hydro, aren't you? I thought so. And this must be the Princess of the Air. My Woman was killed protesting the evictions that were to provide you with a palace."

"Please, sah," said the earnest young man. "That was neither our intention nor our plan. We would happily live wherever my income can afford. My mother …"

"The bitch," added his Woman.

"… she's a hard woman to like."

The Princess snorted derision.

"But she never intended this tragedy. She wanted to offer her condolences personally, but our lawman said that it might be too inflammatory."

"So, she sent you?"

"No. She doesn't know we came. But I thought someone from the House should show how sorry we are."

"You've done so. Thank you. But you understand how painful it is for me to be reminded of the events. So. Goodbye."

The youngsters showed the hurt in their faces, but Bùxiè was past caring. Afterward, he found Henrik Abasinian in a conversational knot with Organson and others and drew him aside.

"Henrik," he said. "Do me a favor. Send me a complete set of surveillance footage from Undine Place for the afternoon of the riot. Unedited. Raw images."

His former mentor squinched his face. "You know I can't do that, Bùxiè. It's against protocols. You're too involved with the crime."

"Involved? Why, yes, I suppose you could say I am *involved*."

"Please, Bùxiè. This affects Excellent people. We could both get into serious kimchee if we don't follow the protocols to the letter. Don't worry, I'll handle things."

Bùxiè turned away. A hand closed on his shoulder, and he spun back. It was Tongkawa Jones.

"What!"

"Gold Crew wants this investigated, too," the astrogator said. "We'll get a copy of the surveillance for you. Our Signals Department can access the Operating Base."

Startled by this unlooked for help, Bùxiè stammered thanks, and they exchanged MOBI links.

Afterward, Qínfèn found him and told him the nick was holding a funeral buffet to celebrate Snowy Mountain's life.

"It's fine, sergeant. You can still call her 'Adrienne.' If her ghost hears the old name and comes back from the dead, I wouldn't mind that at all. But there is one favor you can do me. Run a background check on an Excellent Dumont Ramamurthy of Eugenics. Deep dive, but keep it 'on the orlop.'"

Qínfèn did his best to look unsurprised. "May I ask why?"

Bùxiè tossed his head. "I don't know yet."

The footage showed the sentry struck squarely in the face with the glassite bottle. Tongkawa Jones winced. "That had to hurt," he told his guest.

The police inspector agreed. But it wasn't the man with the busted nose who broke ranks and charged the protesters. He was too busy howling and holding his face. It was the man standing beside him who shouted and ran forward, swinging his staff.

"I've seen hits like that playing full-contact handball at the dojo," Bùxiè said. "That's why we wear cage masks over our faces and thix armor on our groins."

Jones winced again. "Does it help? The thix armor, I mean."

"A little. The impact is dulled, but you still feel it."

They sat together in Tongkawa's spare but comfortable quarters in the Cloisters. Chetwin's *Air in G-minor, The Void* played in the background. Tongkawa always derived a chuckle from calling music about the interstellar emptiness an "air." But then, he had been bread-and-buttered in a neighborhood where such music was seldom heard. He favored it now because he found it mathematically intriguing.

"Would you like another cuppa?" Bùxiè asked him.

Meaning the inspector wanted another. Jones made to rise and fetch it. But deSōuxún said, "I saw where the samovar stands. I'll pour it."

"Guest is god," Jones told him and bid the inspector remain seated. He carried the empty mugs to the samovar himself and returned, handing one to the inspector. Jones noticed how the cup wobbled and splashed a little. The inspector was "holding it together," but barely.

"'Guest is god.'" Bùxiè repeated the aphorism thoughtfully. "I've never been treated as a god before. I suppose I should enjoy it, but it actually makes me uncomfortable. I'm accustomed to treating guests like family, meaning that they're expected to pitch in and help."

"Is that why you brought the cookies? You weren't obligated, you know." He picked up one of the cookies and bit into it.

"Well, I'm not used to the manners up here."

Jones smiled. "It took me a long time to fit in. 'Gold is the mold.' We don't inherit our posts. We win them through the Examinations."

"So do we. At least the chiefs, mates, and such. Officers run about fifty percent exam versus birth. So, you came up from somewhere else, then. I was wondering about the accent."

"I thought I lost that accent long gone."

The inspector sipped his tea. "Mostly, you have, Excellent. But I heard hints of it."

"Can you guess from where?"

"Mmm. No."

"Billy's Gate."

"Really? That *is* a long stride to the Cloisters."

"Ain't it just," Jones said in his childhood accent. "What about you? Did you always live in Little Lotus?"

"I've been posted in several cop shops over the years, but I was born and raised in Highsteeple, back when it was a tonier district. My father was a chief warrant officer," he explained. "In Electronics."

"You never had a yen for that, yourself?"

173

"No. How about you? Did you always want to be an astrogator?"

"Never gave it much thought. When I sat the Exams, I took the Aptitude Tests, and those said I had a bump for math. Then Jimmy Gujarati reached into the pool and pulled me up onto the quarterdeck." Jones paused and said, "We're putting it off, aren't we? Are you sure you want to see the rest?"

Bùxiè swallowed and bobbled his head, so Jones switched to the next camera angle, from a post across from the palace.

They saw the bottle thrown again, this time from behind the bottle-thrower. "No facial ID," Bùxiè commented.

"Not for the back of his head, no." All Jones could see was that the man—he assumed it was a man—was tall and skinny.

And there was Snowy Mountain, turning sharply about and shouting something at the bottle-thrower even as others let fly. Shouting what? Encouragement? Her face was creased with anger and, in Jones' opinion, had never looked more lovely.

He froze the image and noticed that Skinny had grabbed her by the wrists. Perhaps he had intended to stiffen her courage, but the practical effect was to hold her immobile with her back to the charging sentry, one Khemla Shezmat, according to the face data.

Jones had asked the inspector if he was prepared to watch his Woman's death but suddenly discovered that he himself was not, and when Bùxiè reached across to toggle RESUME PLAY, Jones snatched his wrist and held it fast.

DeSōuxún pulled loose from his grasp. "We have to watch," he said, "regardless how it hurts." Jones heard the pain in the man's voice as he reached for the toggle.

In the replay, Skinny held Snowy Mountain for only a moment or two but it was long enough that Shezmat's quarterstaff struck fairly on the back of his protégé's skull. Sorrow welled up once more in his throat.

Jones said, "If Skinny hadn't tried to brace Snowy Mountain, she could have run off in time."

But Bùxiè tossed his head. "Adrienne was never much for running. Maybe it's the copper in me talking, but to me, that looked like Skinny held her as a human shield. Shezmat was coming for the bottle-thrower, and he held my Woman in the way."

Jones ran the sequence through again, this time with the inspector's comments in mind. And yes, he could certainly see how someone could read the actions in deSōuxún's way. "We need to find a camera that catches Skinny's face so we'll know who to interrogate."

"DCI Abasinian has the case," the inspector allowed. "We should pass this on to him."

Jones pulled his lip. He hadn't seen where Skinny had actually broken any regulations. Yet, surely, he had been as morally culpable as Shezmat for Snowy Mountain's death, and some penalty should be extracted from his hide. "Should we?" he mused. "Should we really?"

When Lucky Lutz entered the Barracks, Fishaven, Vòng, and the others pounded her on the back, shook her hands, or otherwise indicated their approval.

"We knew you'd get off the hook!"

"It was a bogus prosecution."

"Welcome back, Lucky!"

The tumult attracted the attention of First Sergeant Goliad, who came from his office expecting a melee. When he saw it was Lucky, he grunted, "Bout time you got back. You can't expect us to cover your duties forever."

"Hey, Sarge. Glad t'see you, too. I coulda been sentenced to Recycling, y'know."

But Too Tall shook his head. "Naw. The fix was in. I watched the trial myself, and it seemed to me that the prosecuting magistrate was lobbing softballs to the defense counsel."

Lucky shrugged. Her luck had held. Enough surveillance had been found to exonerate her, not only of participation in what they were calling a "security riot," but that she had actively refrained and kept others from breaking ranks. The only uncertainty had lain in what she had said to the bully boy beside her just before he attacked the demonstrators. Although the bully boy had claimed she said, "Go get 'em," defending magistrate Venables had found a lip-reader at the school for the deaf who was able to interpret the surveillance images. She had said, "Hold fast!"

175

"Do you have a minute?" Goliad asked.

"For you, first sergeant, I have fifteen minutes. Hey, I see Vòng finally got his stripe. Congratulations, *Gunny!*" As Lucky followed Too Tall into his office, she racked her memory for some recent infraction that would explain the invitation.

"Close the hatch," Goliad said, "and have a seat." He perched himself on a corner of his desk. So it was not to be a reprimand. Too Tall seemed to search for words for a moment, then took a deep breath. "You must have been told about Crowley."

The words were a punch in the face. She had been trying not to think about her corporal ever since she had been briefed about events in the Burnout. "Yes, first sergeant. I heard."

Goliad nodded. "You've had your own worries in the meantime, but I know the two of you were close."

Not as close as Crowley would have liked. But her corporal had been an eager and loyal henchman. Lucky had cried when she had heard the news and wondered if the plan to hunt out the backside of Milkhoney Hard had in any way contributed to her death. That would make it partly her fault, and Lucky regarded responsibility as one would an importunate brother-in-law.

"I've put her up for the Wounded Lion," Goliad added. "Stepping out into the pass' to discover if the Dwellers were nearby—that was the bravest act I've ever seen."

Or, Lucky thought, *the most clueless.* She could easily imagine the corporal exposing herself for no better reason than exasperation, but of this, she said nothing to the First Sergeant. *About the dead, say nothing ill.* They were liable to take offense and come back to haunt you, and of all the Hungry Ghosts Lucky could happily contemplate being haunted by, "Crawling Vermin's" was not to be numbered.

And yet, she felt a deep regret. She would miss the little sycophant. She brushed her eye quickly where some dust had gotten in it. "So, what can I do for you, First?"

"I saw it happen," Goliad mused. "I'll never forget it." He shook himself. "So. Well, someone in the Burnout has the missing teasers, someone who knows how to use them. The lieutenant wants to take the platoon out to fetch them back. Stolen property, after all. I want you to lay out the logistics. What supplies the platoon will need. I want to go in heavy. Thix armor. Bolt cannons. Dispersal mail. The works."

"Dispersal mail."

"They've got teasers."

"I guess you don't think they'll just hand them over."

"It doesn't seem the maximum likelihood."

Lucky bobbed her head. "*And* thix armor on top of it? That'll be hot and uncomfortable."

"They have crossbows and flying hatchets."

That made sense. Thixotropic padding hardened on impact. Hard enough to blunt a crossbow quarrel? She would run some experiments on the firing range to find out the pad density required.

"And you'll need to draft an engineering squad and their equipment," the first continued. "We have to build a redoubt so we can patrol in different directions. The lieutenant wants light, power, comm."

"Not exactly a sneak attack then."

Goliad shot her a sour look. "I don't think we could slip in unnoticed regardless how little foo-foo we make. Pull the draft from Lord Thantos' crew. Oh, and grab an HVAC technician while you're at it and a squad of Maintenance with their gear."

"Why don't we just move the whole crew into the Burnout?"

"I was there, Lucky; you weren't. It's dark and comm silent and twisted into a jumble. Just entering the region was rough going. Lieutenant wants to clear a road in, raise a redoubt, then find the teasers."

"Was the lieutenant in there, too?"

"You know he wasn't."

"Yeah. I was just wondering if *he* knows it."

"Won't matter to you, Staff. You aren't going."

Normally, being struck from a dangerous detail filled Lucky with joy supreme, but not this time. "I wouldn't mind," she said, "counting coup on Crowley's killers." *Oh, Lucky, what are you talking yourself into?*

"Sorry, Lutz, but if you read the reports, you know what Dwellers do with female captives."

Lucky smiled. "I should be okay, then." Goliad raised an eyebrow in inquiry, and Lutz told him, "Because first they'd have to capture me."

14 SETBACKS

Back in the nick—Through the Bubble—Inter legere—
Ling-ling sits her Exams—Mulligatawny

"**Welcome** back, guv'nor," said Sergeant deFēnxī.

Bùxiè settled into his accustomed seat at the nick. He shifted some items on his desk—a stylus, a paperweight, a stack of notices—mostly for the satisfaction of moving things around. He thumbed through the notices, most of which he filed directly in the shredder.

"Why do they send out hard copy notices when there are electronic copies?"

"Are you feeling alright, sir? Maybe you should take more time off. You are entitled to more grieving time, you know."

"The allotted time is too long and too short."

"That makes no sense, sir."

"Oh, bless your pure and simple heart, sergeant. You still expect life to make sense. I will be grieving my beloved for far longer than the allotted furlough time. But if I had spent one more day in those empty quarters staring at the places she would occupy no longer, I would have gone barking mad." He gazed around the nick and saw how the other coppers were carefully not looking at him. Did they think him so brittle that normal human interactions would shatter him? Quite the opposite, he thought. To be closed into the closet of his own memories would render him far more breakable.

He had dreamed last night that he and Adrienne were in a long line of people shuffling toward some unspecified destination, and Adrienne had run off ahead. He could see people farther up the line jostle as she passed through the press. In vain, he had tried to catch up with her.

One needn't be a Detective Chief Inspector to understand the meaning of that dream. He thought he should speak with the Alabaster woman and learn how she had coped with this.

"So, Qínfèn," he said. "How have matters proceeded while I was on leave?"

Qínfèn studied him briefly, then picked up his notes. "We've had five assaults, four of them fights at wayhouses. Three burglaries of quarters. One armed robbery of a commissary. You'll like that last one."

Bùxiè cocked his head. "I will."

"It seems to have been another raid by a—what did you call them?—a Dweller?"

Constable Chen stopped at the desk and gave Bùxiè a mug of coffee. "It's nice to see you back, boss." Bùxiè grunted thanks and sipped from his mug.

"I see the coffee has gotten no better in my absence. Have a seat, constable. The sergeant was bringing me up-to-date on recent irregularities in our bailiwick."

"And sixty-three disorderly conducts," Qínfèn finished. "All of them stemming from, erm, protest demonstrations."

"What were they protesting?"

Qínfèn and Chen exchanged glances. "The, erm, acquittals, sir."

"What acquittals? Go ahead, Qínfèn. You can say it. It won't send me under the black dog. The acquittals of the sentries at Undine Place, right?"

His sergeant hunched his shoulders. "We can see the justice of it in some cases. The Marines and blackbirds did not participate in the riot. Neither did most of the Enforcers. But it wasn't right to release the others as well."

Bùxiè smiled but without humor. "I followed the trial. I had a keen personal interest in it, as you know, and I can see why the magistrates ruled as they did. The sentries were badly provoked."

"That's no excuse, sir. *Constant under pressure.* Isn't that the motto?"

"For the blackbirds. Not for pass'way toughs. They don't have mottos. No, a negligence fine on Lady Water for posting amateurs with no screening or training, and a goodly assortment of blows with the 'boo on the bully boys for reckless endangerment and 'conduct unbecoming.' Otherwise, the ancient adage comes to mind. *Don't throw shit at an armed man.*"

The constable spoke up. "The crew doesn't like it."

"Neither do I, Chen. Neither do I."

"Oh, one last thing, guv'nor," said Qínfèn. "That matter you asked me to look into … the report's on your desk."

The crowd was singing as they jostled out the wayhouse door. Diners at the *Pig and Whistle* looked up from their meals and frowned at the boisterous throng across the pass'way. It was too early in the day for singing. Then they caught the tune, and one by one, the diners joined in, which increased the volume—if not the harmony.

> *"Whether in our skulls are brains*
> *Or in our hearts the fire remains*
> *To set the blaze a-brew.*
> *Or whether we 'hind bulkheads cower*
> *Or stand up tall with all our power*
> *It really, really matters what we do."*

Jek Buddhathal snickered as he slipped past the singers and found the entry to the Burnout on the orlop deck. Did they think singing was going to change anything? Though he had to admit that whoever had planted that song had known what he was doing, If the complement of *active* was *passive*, the complement of *action* was *passion*, and passion was the readiness to receive the act. So, the silly song was surely preparing people's minds for the Direct Action Faction.

He passed by the huge stowage spaces where miles of superconducting cables laid coiled like enormous serpents against the day when they would be called upon to break the *Whale* against Tau Ceti's magnetic field. The cabling had not been used since Departure when they had aided the *Whale*'s acceleration. No one anymore knew the art of their use, and Jek did not believe the archives could teach anyone the practice. Arrival was likely to be a fiasco.

Not that he cared, personally. That was more than seven hundred years down the road. The crewmen had not been born who would be grandparents to those who would have it to do. Tearing down the degenerate capewalkers *now* was all that mattered. The *Whale* would not cross the Tau's heliopause for many more generations. If the dead were left to bury the dead, the unborn could be left to midwife their future.

Jek rode a manlift from stowage to Thirty-Eight Deck, where a seldom-used pass'way presented itself. He checked the dust, saw no footprints save his own, and grunted in satisfaction. The frame ahead was blocked with the rubble of a cave-in—or appeared to be—the reason why this pass was so untrod. He did not think anyone knew of this route: not the Brotherhood, not the pesky burnsiders, not even the wildmen who had so lately thrown a spanner into the works. The Burnout was a wide and wild ruin, and no one knew it all.

He pulled open a bulkhead panel, behind which a winding crack led through the rubble. Closing it behind him, he squeezed between the wreckage. A rumble marked the passing of a tram through the adjacent tramway. Jek froze a moment, then hurriedly scrooched the last few arm's lengths onto an open pass'way, where he let out the breath he had sucked in. Vibrations from the tram might have caused the wreckage to shift, crushing him and leaving countless capewalkers unslain by his righteous arm.

He was in a sector of the Burnout he called the Bubble, where random chance had left the region untouched. The corridors were clear, lights and gravity functioned, and he could kick dust all the way forward to Seventy Frame.

He passed workshops and crew quarters and the skeletons of those who had been trapped in the Bubble until their food had run out. Jek suspected that the food had lasted as long as the people, for many of the skeletons showed signs of having been butchered. Another crime to lay against the abominable capewalkers. They should have rescued these people.

Finally, he reached a zone where the lights had failed, and, as he did so, he pulled a dog-kicker from his pouch and flipped his jùggie in place. Up ahead, the overhead had collapsed, and rubble really did block the pass'way. He clambered up the pile until he could reach his favored drop tube and then climbed the maintenance ladder to Twenty Deck. After that, it was a clear walk to Fort Freedom, where he reported for duty.

Group Leader Chang was less than pleased to see him. "Sit down, corporal," he said.

Headquarters was quiet. Only a handful of freedom fighters were present, cadre awaiting the next group for basic training. Like Jek, they spent most of their time here at the Fort, where their locator chips could not be tracked. Some, again like Jek, had had their chips replaced with dummies so that when they went out on missions into crew quarters or officer country, "Peng's Poodles" could not identify them.

"It was a big bust," Jek told him. When Chang said nothing, Jek added a reluctant "sah."

"We heard about the acquittals. You made the provocations too blatant. Even most crew sympathized with the sentries that were struck. They still didn't like the evictions, mind you, but thanks to you, they didn't blame the violence on Lady Water. Had you stuck to taunting, sooner or later, one of the poodles would have broken."

"Later rather than sooner, I think. Sah."

"Did I hear the word 'think' cross your lips, corporal? Big Blue is not happy."

"Big Blue can blow—"

"—his own horn. That's what you were about to say, wasn't it? You managed to get a Gold Crew member killed."

"I didn't know that then. Goldcapes are just as bad as bluecapes, swanning about with their superior airs. Sah."

"They don't 'swan about.' Mostly they keep to themselves and don't bother anyone. And she was ordinary crew, like you and me. If we want to restore the Constitution, we must all work together; and that means we must all work from the same script."

"I heard you had a run-in with those wildmen."

Chang nodded. "The courier conducted a larger force than he had promised. Not just a copper but an Enforcer, two blackbirds, and three Marines. So Wennel Ku took the squad down there to keep an eye on them and ran smack into a turf fight between two of the wildmen gangs. Gently Amberson took a crossbow bolt in the gut, but we routed them with teasers. Since they know the Burnout better than we do, we have to keep keen watch for them. They could pop out of any hatchway or corridor. You're posted to sentry duty at the corner of Twetny-First and Watchitough Pass'. Report there at four bells and relieve Lance Shwarmawallah. Usual password."

"I pulled sentry duty on my last rotation."

"Then you should be getting good at it."

"Is this assignment a punishment?"

"Only if you let yourself be surprised by the wildmen. We're on watch-and-watch until the next band of Volunteers shows up for basic."

"I protest."

Chang touched his screen. "Protest noted."

Jek shut up and added Chang's name to the list of those who would one day suffer for the injustices done him. Right after the courier who had tried to humiliate him over the password.

DCI Bùxiè deSōuxún knew how to read between the lines. *Inter legere,* the ancient Roman term, had become *intelligence* in Spanglish. It was the faculty of putting two and two together, even when "four" was not explicitly stated.

But because his own quarters had grown oppressive, the emptiness haunting, he took Qínfèn's dossier to *Jambles,* his local way-house, and settled into a booth in the back corner to study it, well away from the chatter and the game boards. Jambly, the landlady, knew him and had set his preferred potion, a brandy, on the table almost before he had taken his seat.

Qínfèn had assembled a quite comprehensive dossier on Dumont Ramamurthy, though because there was no official case, he had pulled mostly open sources. For the same reason, he had not written his report on the Operating Base but by hand, on paper. Officers were known to take offense at crew who poked into their affairs.

Born into the wealthy and powerful Ramamurthy family, which held the half-commandery of Eugenics-Input, the subject had scored well enough on his exams that when that posting became available through the unexpected demise of its incumbent, his appointment could be ascribed as much to his expertise as to his birth. He had cousins scattered in several departmental baronies in the Demography Division, and his sister had paired with Nelson Chandrashekar, who commanded the other half of Eugenics.

When both his parents died in a traffic mishap, Dumont Ramamurthy inherited the chieftaincy of his family, as well.

Bùxiè considered the intelligence. It was no great matter to experience two or three deaths among family, friends, and colleagues. His own parents had died years ago, and now also his Woman. But each death Qínfèn had reported had advanced the career of Dumont Ramamurthy.

A shadow fell across his papers, and Bùxiè looked up to see Dhik Spandhana looming over his booth. Not the man's fault. He could not help looming, no matter how he stood, nor casting shadows. What surprised Bùxiè was the attachment of Petronella Patterson to his left arm.

"Well met, brother," said the Enforcer. His huge paw engulfed Bùxiè's hand like a pile of rubble collapsing onto a helpless victim. "Peta is treating me to dinner because she thinks I saved her life in the Burnout."

"You did," Bùxiè allowed, but Dhik went on as if he had not spoken. "Would you care to join us?"

Usually, a casual request from the Big Dhik could come across as a threat because his voice sounded like rocks grinding together. "No, thank you," Bùxiè said. "I'm doing a spot of work."

Dhik's glance slid over the papers. "Checking up on a Ramamurthy? That can't be the healthiest of avocations. Is he a suspect in one of your investigations?"

Bùxiè hid his surprise. In his line of work, Dhik must have developed the skill of reading documents upside down. "No, there was something in his demeanor at the funeral service that piqued my interest. I don't even know what it was. An intuition—but a copper learns to trust his hunches."

Dhik grunted. "Trust but verify." He slid into the seat opposite Bùxiè, which took care of that half of the booth. Peta, perforce, sat herself beside Bùxiè.

Jambly, ever attentive, appeared by them to take an order. "A-hoigh. Peta. Your usual tipple?" She turned an expectant gaze to Dhik, who worked his lips and said, "Tall glass of the local."

When Jambly had hurried off, Dhik sighed, a sound much like a leak in a pneumatic main line. "You were right, Pet. No one at this end of Little Lotus recognizes me. Just as well I didn't wear my glad rags or tote my 'boo. My size makes people uncomfortable enough. Tell me, chief inspector, how are you getting on these days?"

Well enough, Bùxiè thought, *until someone asks me that.* "I'm going to the nick most days. My heart doesn't ache until I poke it."

The others nodded sympathetically as if they understood how he felt. Jambly returned with their drinks, and they ordered some food. Bùxiè asked for a shrimp-and-orange salad, Dhik, a large patty of beefstuff with the vegetable of the day. "Surprise me with the veggie," he said.

"Do I even need to ask?" Jambly said to Peta.

"Bangers and mash."

The landlady nodded. "I shouldn't even bother asking. Onion gravy and peas?"

"Of course."

"Why have I never seen you in here before?" Bùxiè asked her. "You're obviously a Known Person."

The medical examiner shrugged. "I usually drop in on Third-day. Today is a special occasion." She reached across the table to pat Dhik's hand. If Bùxiè had ever wondered if a rockface in Minetown could look sheepish, his curiosity was now sated.

Dhik spoke. "One thing I can tell you about Lord Ramamurthy, brother. He is known to Enforcers to organize orgies for unpaired colleagues."

Bùxiè wondered if Winnie knew about those. "How many blows of the 'boo is that worth?"

"Don't be silly. No one wants to get demoted. Capewalkers do what they wish. Regs for you and me, my brother, not for them. So, we just look the other way."

But Bùxiè recalled the bruising he had noted on both Rama-murthy and Winnie. If the Enforcers had not broken up the party, then who? There was no record of the incident in the Ship-wide Incidence Report.

When he mentioned it to Dhik, the man just shrugged. "You don't know about that, do you? Eugenics matched me up with the Princess of the Air."

"What? But she was supposed to pair with ..."

"Aye. Well, I didn't want it, and sure as tensors, she didn't want it, but you can see how either Masterson or Barnstable might want to teach Ramamurthy a lesson."

Jambly brought their meals, and Bùxiè cleared his papers from the table. For a time, they chatted amiably about their experiences in the Burnout, which led Dhik to comment that their "brother," Too Tall, was coordinating an incursion by First Platoon to confiscate the teasers some of the Dwellers seemed to have gotten hold of. "Though Too Tall doesn't think they were Dwellers. A lotta special-ized training needed to handle them without electrocuting yourself."

"Who, then?" asked Bùxiè.

Dhik shrugged massive shoulders, and plates and dinnerware rattled several tables away. "Renegades, maybe? He asked our broth-er Little Face to act as guide, but he turned the gig down."

"I just remembered," said Peta. "Back when I was pathologist third up in Jade Terrace, your friend Ramamurthy was briefly a per-son of interest in a murder inquiry."

Bùxiè gestured toward his neatly stacked papers. "Qínfèn did not mention that."

"Nothing came of it. His Special Woman, Ah Kum Kenworth, had been brutally beaten, and the Man is always interrogated in such cases."

Bùxiè nodded. "Standard practice. Did they catch whoever did it?"

"It was a while ago, and my involvement was marginal, but I think they recycled a vagabond who had been breaking into billets for quick money. But Ramamurthy and his Woman did have a right barney that very evening."

"Over what? Did you hear?"

"Nothing important. The quality of a mulligatawny she had prepared for him."

The go-captain and the in-captain walk into a wayhouse …

"Wait a minute," said Ling-ling. "Is this a joke?"

Venables scowled and gestured at the screen. "Don't waste time."

Ling-ling returned her attention to the question. It was only a practice exam. What difference did it make how long she took?

The go-captain and the in-captain walk into a wayhouse and order a glass of the local. Who will be served first, and why? Explain your reasoning in a six-legged essay set in iambic pentameter.

There were only two possible answers. The in-captain would get served first (because she oversaw wayhouses). Or the go-captain would be served first (because he guided the ship and the in-captain was simply a passenger). Or …. She thought of a third answer. They would be served simultaneously because, while separate in jurisdiction, they were equal in dignity. Or …. Maybe there were other reasons. Whichever captain placed an order first would be served first. That made sense, too. And unless they entered side-by-side (which, having met the in-captain, she thought logistically improbable), whoever entered the premises first. First come, first served. Right? What kind of stupid question was this?

Ling-ling tossed her stylus to the desk. This was not like the earlier questions on pneumatics or air filtration. Flow, torque, and pressure; millibars and pascals …. Those made sense. If she was to be one day Commander of Air, she ought to know such things. She could see that, but … "This question is stupid. I mean, who cares who gets the first drink? There doesn't seem to be any right answer!"

Venables spoke gently, "Perhaps that is the right answer."

Sunlight dawned in Ling-ling's mind, and for a moment, she sat dazzled by its brightness. A great many odds and ends lying about in her mind were revealed by that light, and she began putting them together. The Commander of Air ought to know not only *air* but also *command*. She must make a decision and justify it. There would be underlings to handle the air filters, the circulation fans, the lithium scrubbers, and the like. The Commander didn't do any of that personally, but the Commander ought to know to whom to serve the first beer.

"It's a null question," she said. "Neither captain would ever walk into a wayhouse, let alone to walk in together. If anything, they would send someone to fetch the beer for them. Or summon the landlord to bring one to the Palace—or to the Golden Horn."

Venables nodded and made a notation in his notepad. "Iambic pentameter," he reminded her. "This is only the Practice Examination. You will sit the regulars when you are sixteen, but it is never too early to practice. The Board will examine not only your answer but your reasoning in arriving at your answer. You can sit three times with the Board of Examiners, and if you don't cover the nut, even your father's *yin* privilege won't help you."

Ling-ling swallowed. For the first time since reaching womanhood, she understood what it meant to be a grown up.

"DCI deSōuxún," said Winsome Alabaster when she answered the hoigh plate. "To what do I owe the honor of this visit?" The detective appeared tired and worn. There were bags beneath his eyes. Remembering her own struggles following Jaunty's disappearance, she could empathize with the man. She wondered why he'd dragged his sorry body up to Flowing Silk.

"Why don't you come in, Chief Inspector?" She spoke a little loudly because she could see Vishwakarma's door cracked so the old busy body could see and hear what was happening. At least Bùxiè was no capewalker, but any finite set of facts could support a multitude of rumors.

The inspector flashed a smile as fleeting as her own and he ducked through her hatchway. Winnie made a point of *not* scanning the pass'way for witnesses before she shut the door. "Have a seat. Would you like a cuppa? I've got a kettle on."

DeSōuxún lowered himself into the chair that had once been Jaunty's. She had now six years to grow accustomed to the chair's vacancy, but oddly, since the foray into the Burnout, she had become more keenly aware of it than before. She welcomed any distraction from the emptiness of her quarters, indeed sought it through exercise at the gym, jogging in the pass'ways, or stepping out with Dumont. Bùxiè had been fortunate to find her at home. But then he had probably checked her locator chip beforehand.

She busied herself with the makings, choosing a black tea and steeping the ball the requisite ten minutes. "How are you adjusting?" she asked over the clatter.

"Life goes on," he said. "And you either go on with it or not."

Winnie remembered similar thoughts years ago. "I wish I could have met her."

"She would have liked you, I think."

Winnie brought two cups to the front room and handed one to the inspector. "So, to what do I owe this honor?"

Bùxiè reached into his pouch and pulled out a teaser. Winnie tensed for a moment. *Had he come to kill her? But why?*

However, he offered the teaser butt first. "This is yours," he said. "I wound up with it when Goliad gave you Vermain's weapon."

Winnie had returned the Marine's weapon. Now, she imagined returning the dog-kicker to Dumont. She would have to reach into her pouch and pull it out as the inspector had just done, but she would have to do it in the presence of One or Two, who were ever attuned to the sudden appearance of a weapon. She pushed it away.

"No, inspector. You keep it. You may need to jangle a feral dog for me again one day."

The inspector looked at the weapon, and returned it to his pouch. "I doubt I'll be going back out there any time soon."

"Always the story: 'Have dog-kicker, no feral dogs; feral dog, but no dog-kicker handy.' Maybe someday they'll wander out of the Burnout looking for prey. Little Lotus abuts the Burnout; Flowing Silk does not."

"Speaking of the Burnout, I'm curious. You told us that Eugenics has three goals: prevent overpopulation and prevent in-breeding, but you never mentioned the third."

"I was chattering." Bùxiè simply waited, providing a receptive silence into which she could drop her words. Winnie thought he would make an interrogator most formidable. "The Departure Generation," she continued, "was comprised of scores of ethnoi. Polonis and Roos, Chinos and Malayas, Yurpans and Roomies .... Diversity was our weakness. Sooner or later, the bonds of the common enterprise would weaken, and a descendant of one ethnos would rediscover an ancient grudge against another. Si, si. I know it makes no sense. Descendants are not guilty of an ancestor's crimes, and you cannot change the past in any case. That's what makes those grudges so intractable. They are always there. So Eugenics set about ..."

"Crossbreeding ethnoi to wipe out group identities."

Winnie nodded. Bùxiè was quick on the uptake. "That's one criterion that MOBI uses when matching pairs. Given genetic compatibility, a potential pair from different ethnoi gets weighted more than one from the same."

"Like Dhik from Billy's Gate and the Princess from Zephyrholm."

"Oh, you know about that?"

"It seems to me that as you smudge the stem ethnoi out of existence, new ethnoi are springing up among the *Whale*rs. There lies something in the human heart that abhors homogeneity, and deprived of one kind of distinction, we will conjure up another."

"So long as pass'gangs from Highsteeple don't fight battles with those of Billy's Gate, or Minetown invade Pigwhistle."

The inspector grew wistful. "Still, I can't help but feel something has been lost."

"Yes, the potential for inter-ethnic fighting. Tell me, have you ever had a meal of hoddawgs and judni? Shnizzel with bog joy? Something has been gained, as well."

The inspector laughed and they fell into more quotidian discussions. DeSōuxún described a couple of cases he was working on. Winnie had mastered a tumbling routine. As Bùxiè was taking his leave he asked about Dumont, and Winnie told him Lord Helix had asked her to prepare a meal for him: his mother's mulligatawny recipe.

15 SEARCHINGS

Wilderness Road—Down among the pipes—It's hard
to follow someone who knows you by sight—Recruities

The Burnout bustled with more activity than it had seen in
eighty years. HVAC fans began turning once more, overhead sun
panels flickered into renewed life. Maintenance and Power techs
labored long hours to create this oasis and, when they were done,
regarded their accomplishment with justifiable pride. A small
portion of the darkness had been reclaimed for the Ship. The
pride was tempered only by the knowledge of how much vaster
was the remaining darkness.

"We can't clear any more of the pass'way, sah," a Maintenance chief
reported to First Sergeant Goliad, who stood with his squad sergeants
around a map table. "When the pull-dozer removes any more rubble,
more just slides down through the rent from Twenty-One Deck."

"What do you recommend?"

"Raise new bulkheads and wall it off. We ain't clearing the whole
Shiva-dammed Burnout, after all. Just clearing a road."

"Very well, Chief. 'Do it to it.' What is it, Lucky?"

Staff Sergeant Lutz had been standing off to the side, waiting for Maintenance to finish its report. She scratched her cheek and looked down the length of the now brightly lit pass'way. In the distance, the illumination faded, and the rubble receded into shadow.

"Looks just like back in quarters, doesn't it?"

"Except for the wreckage."

"Except for the wreckage. But even then, it could be a normal pass'way undergoing renovations."

"Very extensive renovations," said First Sergeant Goliad. "Do you have a report?"

Lucky proffered her MOBI, and the First sucked up the report. "You ain't never gonna find those teasers," she ventured. "Not while you announce yourself with sound and light. All the Dwellers hafta do is sidle off a little farther into the gloom if we even get close at all."

Goliad looked off to a brightly colored tent. "Tell the lieutenant. This is his carnival. What would you do?"

Lucky gave that some thought. "You don't believe the Dwellers have the teasers."

Goliad shook his head. "No, I surely do not. Using a teaser is not like using a crossbow and maintaining one in good working order wants a qualified weapons tech or gunnery sergeant. So, I think they were stolen by crewmen who knew their nuts, maybe this Brotherhood of the *Whale* we've been hearing of."

"If they're crewmen, not Dwellers, they have MOBIs."

"So. We call them and ask them to bring in the stolen weapons?"

"No, First Sergeant. When the Power techs throw up our comm bubble that projects a sphere, and if the renegades are anywhere within that sphere, we'll spot them."

Goliad glanced at the squad sergeants, who were listening with keen interest. "If they are out here hiding," he suggested, "they'd have their MOBIs turned off."

"Too Tall, you know there's always one cholo in the group who forgets. Besides, they're used to being in a comm shadow, so they may not see the need."

Goliad bent over the map table and toggled the 3D view. The original design grid sprouted, and Goliad superimposed a modification, showing where passageways were known to have collapsed, twisted, or become blocked with rubble. "This is the route we took on the body recovery," he told them.

Lucky leaned in with the others and studied the track. Up, down, starboard, port. It looked like their guide had been leading them on a merry dance. She pointed. "Why didn't you go this way?"

"Fanghsi told us it was impassible."

"What's *this* volume?" asked Fishaven. The original schematics showed a large open space. "An old mess hall?"

"Now just a mess," joked Kent.

"Maybe," allowed Goliad. He turned and beckoned the Power tech and pointed out the region that Fanghsi had led them around. "Can you arrange the network to project a bubble covering this volume? But don't activate it until I give the order."

The Power tech nodded and started to tell them how he would do it, but Goliad cut him short. "Anyone who works for Lord Thantos knows his nuts, but it's all beanstalk to us. Just 'do it to it.'"

Lucky nodded with satisfaction. That should net any active MOBIs in the zone. The Dwellers were another matter entirely. She ran a finger around the collar of thix armor she had devised for their necks. It chafed, and she noted that half the Marines had removed them. Lucky didn't know whether the bolt that had killed Vermain had been skill or dumb luck, but if she were to err, it would be on the side of caution.

Ling-ling wore a nondescript pair of dark blue coveralls, the sort worn by any technician or petty officer in the Water Department. She hated its ugliness, much preferring her usual colorful and airy garb.

"Where are we going, Megs?" she asked her Man, who was similarly clad. He had already led her through the reclamation duct from Undine Palace, so no one back there knew where they had gone or, indeed, that they had gone anywhere at all.

In answer, Megwan held a finger to his lips and lifted a manplate in the narrow back-passageway in which they presently found themselves. That meant they were about to go back down into the dank network of water tunnels that underlay primary decks. She braced herself for the smell and hoped it would not be a wastewater tunnel. Nevertheless, she clambered down after Megs, then waited while he replaced the manplate above them.

That plunged the tunnel into temporary darkness. Then the section lights reacted to their presence, and Megwan said, "This way." The pipes gurgled and occasionally banged. The first time she had heard it, she had jumped in sudden fright. Megs told her that was a "water hammer" caused by variation in water usage by the crew.

To Ling-ling, one direction looked very much like another, but she trusted the Water Prince to know his way around his realm. She was due to be tutored on the air ducts starting next month. Ba-ba's bo's'un was to take charge of that aspect of her instruction. She hoped the ducts were more pleasant than the pipes.

The pipes in this particular tunnel carried fresh water to quarters as well as wastewater away. The former pulsed with the pumps; the latter flowed primarily from precisely positioned gravity patches.

Shortly, they came to a supply cache, and the tunnel widened into a broader space crammed with people, both male and female. The volume of their hubbub was diminished by the fact that they spoke in whispers so that, on the whole, they sounded like a nest of hissing snakes. One of them broke off and faced the newcomers.

"What d'ye desire most of all?"

Ling-ling was inclined to say her pleasant, dry, airy apartments at Zephyholm, but Megwan had cautioned her before they had set out, and she answered in unison with her Man, "The *Whale* as she was."

Twenty-Third and Tenth was sparsely populated, so Bùxiè took a manlift down to Twenty-Fourth, where the bustle was greater, and a man could pass unnoticed if his uniform blended in. These were the servants' entrances for the elaborate estates on Twenty-Third, and his quarry was more likely to exit here. Jones had secured for him a copy of the watch rotations of "Peng's Poodles." How he had done so, Bùxiè had not asked.

He waited patiently, watching the reflection of the servant's entrance to Helix House in the window of a noodle shop, noshing the while on a cup of noodles. According to the watch rotation, Two was due for R&R beginning at end-of-watch.

When he saw Two's reflection exiting the quarters, he almost failed to recognize the man, dressed in mufti rather than his Ship Security uniform. He waited to see which way he turned—starboard—before he chucked his noodle cup and sticks into the recycle and set off to follow.

Two walked along the fore side of the traverse pass'way, so Bùxiè shadowed him on the aft side. He also allowed several other crewmen to get between him and his quarry. When Two stopped abruptly to study the display at a confectionery, Bùxiè did not break stride but continued past until he came to the longitudinal. There, he hurried around the corner, whipped off his jacket, and turned it inside out. It was a reversible jacket, and the reverse was a different color and design than the obverse. He yanked a decorative beret from the pocket and clapped it on. To casual observation, he would now appear to be a different man.

Emerging from the longitudinal, Bùxiè glanced about as if to get his bearings, but Two was nowhere to be seen. He no longer admired the confections in the shop window, but neither had he continued down the pass'way. Had he gone into the confectionery? If he lost his quarry now, it would be many weeks before his next opportunity.

But when he turned the corner with the intention of scoping the various shops into which Two might have stepped, Bùxiè found himself face-to-face with the man himself.

"It be passing hard, Chief Inspector," Two said, "to shadow a man who knows you by sight."

"Not at all, my brother. In fact, I was counting upon it."

Fanghsi led the recruities to Fort Freedom, where he turned them over to Group Leader Chang. Aside from nervous chatter on the recruities part, he had guided them in silence, cautioning them only when they came near Desola territory. The Brotherhood had worked out a truce with the Desolate, but Fanghsi was none too sure how seriously Dwellers took such agreements.

He also had not engaged with them because he had no wish to know men who might soon be dead. Whether from training accidents working with teasers or more directly from fights with Marines or Ship Security, also working with teasers, the stink of death was already on them.

Chang looked over the roster Fanghsi handed him. "A raggedy bunch," he said in Běifāngwóng wá, "but we'll whup 'em into shape 'fore long."

Fanghsi, having seen both blackbirds and Marines in action, thought an awful lot of whupping was in store if the Brotherhood planned to take them on. "Who Dwellers?" he asked, pointing at three men whose ragged clothing and pallid skin marked them as unacquainted with sunlamps or tailors.

"The one in the middle with the geegaws in his ears and nose is Chully, son of Venslaw of Desola. He and his two oath-brothers have agreed to join the Brotherhood militia to seal the truce."

"Hostages, then."

"Little Face, you are a cynic."

"So, how many hostages you give them?"

Chang sighed. "Three, for their diversity."

"Ah, *those* sound like volunteers. Doesn't that leave you short-handed on corporals for training?"

"We'll make do," Chang said. He turned to address the recruits, and Little Face tuned him out. He knew why they had joined up from their chatter while on the way here. Tired of stepping aside for arrogant officers, tired of being treated as servants rather than crew, tired of petty extortions and evictions. Tired of paying bribes to get a simple license. Tired, most especially of being told when and with whom to copulate.

He idled over to the table where the artifacts sat. There were more than usual, he noted, and supposed Desola had helped collect them. He noticed a silver condiment dish with inlaid cups labeled in raised lettering—salt, turmeric, anise, licorice, fenugreek, cumin, and hing. It demonstrated how the stem ethnoi had already been co-alescing, even back then. A card tied to its handle listed the quarters in which it was found, namely, those of Lieutenant (jg) Vance Belaji. Fanghsi sucked in his breath. The hero who had personally rescued forty-six crewmen trapped at Fifteenth and Fifty-Fourth during the Burnout and last seen going back for a forty-seventh.

Fanghsi's pulse hammered. Likely, neither Chang nor the Dwellers realized the pricelessness of the find, whose value alone might finance the entire Mutiny. It lacked only the tiny sprinkle spoons to make the setting complete, and Little Face searched for them in vain among the remaining pieces on the table. He tucked the dish into his specimen bag and tried to look nonchalant.

"Hoigh!" he heard one of the recruities say. "My MOBI just connected!"

Fanghsi and Chang exchanged startled looks before Chang shouted. "Shut it off! Now!" Then he called his corporals together. "A comm bubble?"

Jek Buddhathal said, "The Marines are building a road two decks down and four traverses sternward. We been keeping an eye on them. They must have thrown up a comm bubble for themselves."

"They'll detect the ping and come looking. Cuòle!" When he got blank looks from half the recruities, he added, "Bug out! Vilo, Hitch, go pull in the sentries." He went to fry the memory bubbles with an EM pulse,

Hasten slowly, Little Face thought. Too slow and curious meant Marines might get here before they were gone, but too much haste would risk leaving crucial intelligence behind.

Jek snapped at the recruits. "Each of you grab one of these back-packs. We ain't leaving our teasers behind to be confiscated. We went to too much trouble nabbing them to give them up. Where to, Group Leader?"

Chang did not hesitate. "Across Hanging Bridge. Chully, find your people and have them meet us there."

Jek looked at Little Face. "You're coming, too, courier. You've the recruits to shepherd."

Fanghsi thought that Jek had serious weenie against him, and a possible firefight was an ideal occasion for revenge. The best place to hide a corpse was on a battlefield. He also thought that Big Blue ought to be informed, but he saw no way to duck the assignment, so he fell to considering how he might put distance between himself, the pending fight—and Jek.

16 CONFRONTATIONS

The tripartite oath—In Pass' Christine—Battle at Hanging Bridge

Bùxiè found a wayhouse farther down the pass'way and offered to buy a beer for Two. But the blackbird led him aft through a longitudinal, then a manlift two decks down. "Less likely," he said, "we run into anyone who knows us." In response to Bùxiè's quizzical look, he added, "I taken it from the trouble you gone to that you want to talk 'down in the orlop.' If so, just remember that I took the tripartite oath."

Bùxiè nodded. "To the Ship, to Ship's Security—"

"—and to our Client."

"In that order, I've been told." Two made no reply to this but tilted his head in interest.

"So, what be on your mind, Chief Inspector? Naught ordinary would warrant the pains you taken."

Bùxiè paused while the beermaidle set two thick steins of lager before them. The wayhouse called itself The Dorfschenk and evidently intended to imitate an ancient stem ethnos, although Bùxiè was unsure which it was supposed to be. He took a sip of the lager and found it passable. "Were you working for Lord Helix when his wife was murdered?"

Two considered his answer. "Straight to the point—but what point? That's old news and out of your jurisdiction. They recycled the man who did it. Like they say, 'Lid closed, monkey dead.' But no, that was before my time. What be your interest?"

"I'm not entirely sure. There was something in Lord Helix's demeanor at my Woman's funeral: a disconnect between his words and his expression. It was as if he did not really mean what he said."

Two shrugged. "No mystery. Lord Helix has trouble expressing emotion."

In other words, thought Bùxiè, he's *faking it*. "Tell me," he said, "does he often speak in past tense or passive voice?" When Two scowled, Bùxiè prompted him. "Come, brother, surely public behavior does not fall under client confidentiality."

Two finished his lager and set the stein down. "Tain't that, but the oddity of the question. Can't say I ever noticed."

"Have you ever seen him *lose it*?"

"You mean *flip his lid*? Get angry? Maybe that does fall under client confidentiality."

Bùxiè finished his own lager and dabbed his lips with the napkin. He took a shot in the dark. "I've heard that he gets angry when his meals are not prepared to his taste."

"Oh, that. I hadn't thought that incident generally known."

Bùxiè cocked his head. "Which one?" Pretending a wider knowledge often elicited a narrower response.

"A couple of dekadays past, he fired his cook, but I can't say he 'flipped his lid.' It was more like he was coldly furious."

"Dekaday?"

"Sorry. Metric time. One dekaday is just over a week, standard time."

"Do you know the cook's name?"

"You are a curious fellow, Chief Inspector."

"It goes with the job. But none of this is Chief Inspector business. I'm just your old brother-in-arms, Bùxiè."

Two visibly relaxed at that and said, "Cook was Yufreni Dox. I don't know her contact particulars."

"Thank you." Bùxiè rose and extended his hand. Two looked at it a moment, then shook it, although he remained seated. As Bùxiè turned away, Two said, "Friend? Don't try to interrogate One. He be not so affable as I."

Ling-ling emerged from the water distribution tunnels on Pass' Christine, named for a once powerful Commander of Water but not one well-liked. Posterity had taken its revenge by placing her name on this narrow and little-used passageway. Most of the quarters that lined it showed their backs, presenting their fronts to the busier traverses one block over.

The light panels had been turned down to "evening," so everything was limned in silvery "moonlight." Ling-ling tried to remember what a "moon" was. Tutor Venables had covered it, she was sure. It might be on the Exam.

Megs had gone up first. Little-used pass'ways tended to attract the sort of crewmen who preferred little-used pass'ways for their avocations. The surveillance cameras here were painted over or smashed outright.

She and Megs would return underground at the next longitudinal pass', Babbling Brook, which led to the back of Undine Palace and, more importantly, gave access to a pipeway that would enable them to reenter the palace without passing through the main gates. But for the moment, they paused to catch their breath.

"It's not quite what I expected," Megs confessed. "There was less talk of restoring the *Whale* than of tearing down the officer corps."

"Are they true, the stories they told?"

"With probably some exaggeration. I know Mother told me Maintenance has been extorting shop owners."

"She should talk. She was ready to throw a dozen petty officers out of their quarters to make room for us."

"We would not have moved into those quarters." Megs spoke with conviction. "But I hadn't known that crewmen and petty officers had to step out of the pedestrian way into the cartway if an Officer required passage. That seems a little degrading."

"They have to salute, too," said Ling-ling

"But the Officer has to return the salute, so I'd count that as even." Meg gestured at the smashed cameras. "I think the constant surveillance is a greater irritant, along with being told who they can pair with. After all, weren't you told to pair with some oaf from aft frames?"

"But I didn't."

"That's just the point. Officers—at least Commanders—can defy Eugenics. I doubt crewmen or petty officers could get away with that. Come on, let's get out of here. Pass' Christine gives me the jeebs."

But when they turned the corner onto Babbling Brook, a swarthy man with a scar across his right cheek was leaning patiently against the bulkhead. He wore the aquamarine coveralls of Hydro. Ling-ling sucked in breath, and she reached instinctively for Megwan.

Megwan, for his part, stepped between her and the stranger and pulled a quillon dagger from his belt. But the stranger had the reach and the weight, and he towered over her Man. Ling-ling learned in the emptiness of her stomach how much she wished for Megwan's well-being.

"If it isn't little Lord Hydro," the stranger said. "What were you doing at a meeting of the Brotherhood? Spying for your mama?"

Megwan drew himself up as if he were trying to make up the inches he lacked. "Mam—Mother does not even know we've left the palace. I was told the meeting was open to the public. Informational."

The man grunted. "Recruiting, more like it. Well, none else seemed to recognize you, a bit o' luck there. Some at that session would have handled you less kindly than me."

Megwan stared more closely at the scarred face. "Jimcas?"

"Wouldn't expect the mighty Lord Hydro to recognize a mere bo'sun's mate, second class. Though I would have thought my calling card"—he ran a finger along his scar—"woulda introduced me."

Megwan's dagger had disappeared, not that it had seemed to faze Jimcas. He turned to Ling-ling. "This is Jimcas Nearwell. He's assistant strawboss of the palace staff. We call him the 'underbutler.'" Turning to Jimcas, he said, "I'm sorry I didn't recognize you sooner, but the pass'way is dark, and you startled me."

Jimcas said, "Follow me. We'll sashay through the main gate. I'll sign us in. There's been a change of watch, so the sentry on duty now won't be the one who saw me sign out alone. No one figures the likes of you for log-signing, so your thumbprints won't be missed. If anyone asks, I took you out for training, and the little Woman insisted she come along."

"That's well enough, Master Nearwell," said Ling-ling. "But why were *you* at the meeting?"

The bo'sun's mate turned and smiled at her, though the scar prevented his entire face from participating. "Why, that's for me to know and you *not* to find out."

Lucky Lutz directed the squad gleaning the abandoned mess hall for intelligence. The hall had been deserted in haste, which meant *something* had been forgotten and left behind. A computer remained, but the bubble memories had been slagged by an electromagnetic pulse. She had the bubbles collected anyway. An electromagnetic wipe sometimes missed things, and you wouldn't know if you didn't check.

The hall was well-lit. All but one of the camp lamps had been left in their fixtures.

"I think you were right, First." She handed him the bag. "This looks way too sophisticated for your Dwellers. That lighting is ad hoc, but I don't see where a gaggle of barbarians coulda hooked it up."

They studied the graffiti on the walls. Much of it was personal, mocking unfortunate bodily traits or wishing good fortune in coupling. But one of her corporals found a scrawl that announced, *Fort Freedom* and another proclaiming, *The Whale as she was!*

Lt. Dingbang did not think much of it all. "Are you certain, Goliad, that you pinged a MOBI from this location? It looks like it was once used, but how long ago?"

Lucky answered for her boss. "Not so very long ago, sah. These scratches on the hatchway are fresh-made." She pointed to a mark at about waist level. "You can tell because they're still shiny. But what can scratch bulkhead material?"

Goliad and the lieutenant had come over. The First Sergeant grunted when he saw the chevron mark. "An adamantine stone set in a ring, worn on a hand, held loosely at the side."

Lucky frowned. "You read all that from a scratch?" She thought the First possessed some arcane tracking ability.

Goliad bent down. "Ola, Little Face," he whispered to the mark. "Scouts. Memorize this. It tells us to go that way." He pointed to portside. "Watch the bulkheads, especially at corners, for further fresh marks. Alright, jùggies down! We're marching into the night."

Lucky remembered wanting to go into the Burnout in the worst way. Crowley had gone into the Burnout, and in the worst way, too. She remembered feeling envy at Vermain's good fortune. Maybe if she had gone with her, she could have prevented her death. Jeez, how she missed the little pest!

Lt. Dingbang brought the platoon to order and arranged each squad in blocks as if they were on parade. First Squad—Jen-jiao's Janglers—proceeded behind the scouts, followed by Second Squad—Kanada's Crackerjacks. Weapons Squad had been left behind in the Redoubt to watch over the bolt cannon and provide a safe space to fall back upon. The lieutenant did not think deploying the squads into their fire teams was necessary when going against savages or a rabble. A show of force was all that was needed. He was a by-the-Book officer, but Lucky was pleased that he hadn't found it necessary actually to open the Book for study.

Headquarters Squad—The lieutenant, first sergeant, staff sergeant, and life guards—walked between the Janglers and the Crackerjacks. It had no official *nom de guerre* but Lucky had privately dubbed it "Dingbang's Dingalings."

"You never do see them," Goliad whispered to Lucky.

"What?"

"Something Pathfinder said about the Dwellers. They've lived out here for four generations. Time enough to learn every nook and cranny in these pass'ways."

"The scouts will check out all the nooks we pass."

"But maybe not all the crannies. I wish the Janglers weren't strutting like they were on review."

Only Singh, Lucky noted, was stepping warily, his teaser held ready in his hand, his gaze swiveling from side to side. Goliad, too, walked careful steps. But then the two were the only ones in the platoon ever to encounter Dwellers in combat.

Lucky liked to trade insults with the First, but she respected his savvy and his ability to learn from his experiences, so Lucky too walked in a semi-crouch, scanned her surroundings, and held her teaser ready in her hand. She snugged her thix collar against her neck and waited for the unheralded crossbow bolt from the surrounding night.

The scouts followed the chevron marks down the traverse, then aft down a longitudinal, then following some confusion, up a stairwell. Goliad thought this Little Face person was a captive and was surreptitiously leaving signs for the Marines to follow. Lucky was less certain. He might be a *member* of the Brotherhood luring them into a trap.

The Crackerjacks sang the bouncy *Vikramaditya*, an ancient song that had become the Marine's marching song. "Proud to be a Fleet Marine ..." Marching strides broke into dancing steps.

"Silence in the ranks!" hissed Goliad, but the lieutenant overruled him.

"Let them sing. It's good for morale."

"It's also good," Goliad pointed out, "for announcing our approach."

"To a bunch of riffraff? If they hear us coming, all the better. Their dread will build."

Lucky thought there were several holes in the lieutenant's reasoning. But from all she had heard from Goliad and Singh, the Dwellers would know they were coming whether the platoon mimed or chanted in four-part harmony. The operative question was: Would their quarry prepare to flee or prepare an ambush?

Lucky sent some of the corporals in the Life Guards to warn the scouts to keep an eye open for possible ambushes. In the dim light of their jùggies, bogeys could leap out of the darkness just beyond their range. She kept thinking of Crowley and hoped everyone was wearing their thix armor. She adjusted her helmet, anciently known as "Corinthian," from its "cap" position to full facial protection. That left openings for her jùggies as well as her nose and mouth so she could breathe. The openings were narrow, but she felt exposed, nonetheless. Dweller crossbowmen couldn't be *that* good. Could they?

And what about the Brotherhood? The ones they were tracking from the grandly named Fort Freedom. They had the stolen teasers. She wore dispersal mail under the thix for that reason, but she didn't think many of the others did. Dispersal mail *plus* thix was heavy, hot, and chafed in unfortunate places. And a teaser bolt that struck exposed muscles, like the hands, would still paralyze those extremities.

They came at last to an old park. The trees and grass had long ago shriveled in the darkness, but stone benches and playground equipment staunchly testified that this was once an area for play. Now, it was just one more gray and derelict ruin within the Burnout.

Seated on the teeterboard was a man in parti-patched clothing possessed of a wide, fleshy face in which his eyes, nose, and mouth huddled closely together in the middle. He was guarded by three scouts, and the Janglers had bunched up around this remarkable sight.

"Little Face!" said Goliad.

"Do you know this tramp?" the lieutenant asked.

Goliad confronted him. "You always knew the Brotherhood was out here, didn't you, when the body recovery team came out?" It wasn't quite a question. "Are you mixed up with the Brotherhood?"

"Don't act friend, you. Eyes watching." Little Face spoke low with his head bowed.

Lucky looked past the park and saw that part of it had shifted, opening a chasm spanned now by a primitive bridge. A few gravity plates hung by cable suspenders from the overhead. She supposed the Dwellers had raised it sometime in the past. On the far side of the bridge, she could discern shapes.

"Stumble on Brothers, me, while artifact-hunting. 'Join or die' not time-consuming question. Waiting across Hanging Bridge, them. Twenty-four recruities, not trained, and six cadre, good-trained. Dweller allies come soon." He held his wrists out. "Bind me like your prisoner, me."

"You *are* our prisoner," the lieutenant told him. He made a sign to the lifeguards, then turned away and strode toward the bridge.

"Sah!" said Lucky. "Take care."

"You heard the prisoner. Only six trained fighters. They wouldn't dare take on an entire platoon of Fleet Marines. Kent alone has twelve."

Who were, Lucky remembered, just as untested as their opponents.

Lucky upped the magnification on her jùggies and saw human beings flanking the far side of the bridge, hunched behind stone benches and other barricades. She glanced at the bridge and saw that the Marines could cross no more than two abreast. So much for greater numbers. She wondered if Ding-ding realized that.

"Gunnery Sergeant Chang!" said Dingbang. "I am sorry to see you there,"

Goliad, standing beside Lucky, muttered, "More than sorry. Reggie Chang was my gunny before Vòng. If *he's* been training those people …"

"It's been alleged," the lieutenant said, "that you are in possession of stolen teasers."

"I reckon so," said a voice from the darkness. "I stole them."

Lucky remembered that Chang had run last year's live fire exercise. Who better position to organize the shell game with the two pallets?

"We don't want a fight," said Chang, though one of his companions grumbled, "The hell we don't."

Sgt. Kent said, "Janglers. Present arms," and First Squad pulled teasers from their bandoliers. "Set voltage at half." Lucky turned and saw some of the Crackerjacks had followed suit without orders. "Belay that," she whispered to Sgt. Fishaven.

The lieutenant had turned his head at Kent's action. Now he again faced Chang.

"We don't want a fight, either. We only came to collect our stolen property."

Someone in the Brotherhood ranks called, "Come and get 'em." Chang made a hushing gesture and said, "We believe that an armed crew might be treated more politely by the Officers.'"

Perhaps Lt. Dingbang had gauged the futility of attacking across the narrow bridge. At any rate, he seemed determined to subdue the militia with words. Lucky wished afterward that he would have chosen those words with greater care.

The lieutenant drew himself up. "As an Officer of the Fleet Marines, I *command* you to turn over your weapons. NOW!"

Someone in the opposing ranks shouted, "Death to Officers!" and a teaser bolt took Dingbang in the chest. He was wearing a thix vest, but apparently, no dispersal mail, for he dropped like a grain sack from a lorry and splayed across the bridge approach.

Lucky heard Chang cry, "Who fired?" Then, a fusillade of bolts was unleashed by First Squad, and a lesser volley responded from the Brotherhood.

The Brotherhood had not set their teasers to half power, and those Janglers who were struck learned that while dispersal armor might chafe, teaser bolts did far more. Lucky heard cries of "Corpsman!" Some Marines tipped over the stone benches to use for protection. Some, indeed, were cowering behind them. Well, this was a new experience for them as well as for the Brothers. Sighing, Lucky produced her own weapon but did not fire.

Abruptly, a camp lamp lit up in the Brotherhood ranks, and its focusing panel produced a spotlight, which played across the front ranks of Marines.

The problem with light-gathering goggles comes when there is too much light to gather. Half the Marines on the front line were dazzled. They shrieked and clawed at their jùggies, dropping their weapons as they did so. Unfortunately, the half that were not blinded were precisely those cowering behind barricades.

Lucky, who was in the rear and not in the path of the light, immediately flipped her jùggie up and ran toward the front.

"Where are you going, Lutz?" Goliad shouted. "Get your ass back here!"

But when Lucky judged herself within range, she dropped to one knee, braced her left arm on the other knee, and steadied her gun arm with her left hand. She took a bead on the camp lamp and prayed that her hours of practice on the range would pay off.

She didn't have a clear idea what sort of pulse a teaser put out, whether particle or wave. That nearby personnel—or the shooter himself—would sometimes feel a penumbra of the shock argued for a wave, but Lucky liked to imagine microscopic ball lightning.

In any case, her aim was true—or her luck held good. The lantern sparked as it shorted out, and its wielder howled at the shock.

As everything went dark again, Lucky flipped her jùggie back down. She scurried back to Goliad's position, hoping no one across the bridge would pot her as she ran. *Motion is the enemy. Motion betrays your position.*

When she reached Goliad's side, she said, "Sorry, first sergeant. What was it you said?"

But Goliad was busy directing the fire teams from the Cracker-jacks forward. One of them, as he passed by, clapped Lucky on the shoulder, saying, "Good work."

"Hey, Too Tall," Lucky said. "You see any Dwellers over there?"

Goliad pressed his lips together and narrowed his eyes. "Lutz, I'm in command now. Why are you bothering me?" A crap load of weight, Lucky decided, had just fallen on his shoulders. Maybe it was true what Officers sometimes said. Command was a burden.

"Little Face said that Dweller allies were going to meet the Brotherhood here."

"And ...?"

"From which direction will they come? If they are as Burnout-savvy as you said they are, my money is on *behind us*. Our way forward is ef-fectively bottlenecked at Hanging Bridge. A half dozen sharpshooters can pot us off as we cross—and I wouldn't be surprised if the bridge were booby-trapped. I don't trust those suspenders. I say it's time to advance to the rear before the Dwellers catch us in a pincer."

"We can prevail," said Goliad, "if we press it."

Crap, thought Lucky, *he's channeling the Dingbat.* "Sure, and our victory will be almost as impressive as our casualty list."

Too Tall pondered the situation, then nodded sharply. "Sgt. Fishaven," he said. "Face about and send out scouts. You are point. We are returning to the Redoubt. Sgt. Kent, disengage from the Brotherhood and pull back on us. Take rear guard." He turned to their prisoner, who had been standing by in silence. "Lifeguards, take charge of our prisoner."

The withdrawal to the Redoubt proceeded without incident, and Lucky was beginning to wonder if she had spooked the First Ser-geant unnecessarily. She glanced at the autogurneys the corpsmen were guiding. Three dead, including the lieutenant. Gunny Chang had tried not to fight, but he would be made to pay the butcher's bill regardless. She knew that back on Earth, there had been bat-tles involving hundreds, thousands, tens of thousands. She could not imagine fights that large.

When they came to the Redoubt, however, they found every-one in it dead.

17 RESTORATIONS

A cry in the night—Caraway—In the fo'c'sle—"Put the two propositions together."

Tongkawa Jones entered the quarterdeck at start of watch to find the deck crew in great agitation. His usual seat, astrogator, was occupied by his senior, Second Officer Berylplume, who in turn had been bumped from the centerline seat by the First Officer himself. Skybones waited with an implacable patience for the change-of-watch bell to relieve Fourth Officer Brahmadharma. A flick of his eyes told Jones that the steersman's seat, the "Saddle," bore the chief steersman rather than the senior quartermaster.

The World's turned upside down, he thought and looked to Berylplume for enlightenment.

But the Second made a wait-and-see sign. The engineer's mate at Higgs wet her lips and looked about the room as if seeking help.

Snowy Mountain's death had filled Jones with a peculiar emptiness. That was a koan, surely, for how could an emptiness fill? And yet it did: so vast an emptiness that his spirit could not contain it, and some of it spilled over to touch those nearest to him. He wondered if even her Special Man felt half so great a loss.

Jones settled by default at the empty astrogator's-mate console, where he ran his hands across the relays and toggles, thinking how *her* fingers had but so lately touched them.

"I relieve you," Skybones said to Fourth Officer Brahmadharma when the chimes finally sounded.

"That's a relief," said the grizzled old man, whose penchant for irreverence was one reason he remained at Fourth despite his seniority. He rose slowly, saluted, and the First Officer sat down rather less slowly. But Jones noted that Brahmadharma did not leave the quarterdeck but strode off to the side, where Jones was surprised to see also Third Officer Tang, atypically awake at this end of the clock. *What is he doing on deck?*

Skybones, after casting his stony glance about the quarterdeck, said, "Steersman!"

"X/O, aye!"

"Find me a course solution toward the Visser Hoop. Put us dead in the center."

Number One should have asked that of the astrogator on duty, who was Second Officer Berylplume, but he was unpracticed in the protocols. Chief Steersman Honeytong was equally uncertain and had no idea what to do until Berylplume coughed gently, and the steersman passed the order on to him.

"Chief Chartsman!" said Berylplume.

"Astrogator, aye!"

"Take a bearing on the anomaly. Here." He boxed the location of the Visser Hoop on the Sky Ahead. Then he spun his console to face the X/O. "I must register my objection to the proposed course. It is an unacceptable risk to the Ship."

Jones said nothing, but his nothing backed up the Second Officer. And he could see by the set of their lips that Tang and Brahmadharma also disapproved.

Whale had been bearing away from the ringularity for several days. Sharp turns were no more possible in a vacuum than banks or swoops, no matter how fancy one worked the Higgs projector. Steersman knew this, so did the Higgs engineer.

"It is our last chance," said Skybones. "It may be a shortcut to Tai Ceti."

"May be," said Berylplume. "But it may lead somewhere else, like Andromeda Galaxy, and though we may travel like a leaf floating on a swift current, the transit may be longer than the warranty on the ship. We don't even know if it *is* a tunnel. It may be a cone, and we will be spaghettied to a single point. No, diving into the Hoop would be taking too great a risk. 'Dead in the center' may be exactly that."

Skybones laughed. "Where is your sense of adventure, Number Two? I believe it is a risk we should take."

"You have no right to take such a risk for forty thousand passengers. They may not have your sense of adventure."

"Reynaud, we are hurtling through an endless vacuum beyond the grip of any star, in a hollowed-out pebble precariously supplied with air, water, power, and food by a gaggle of squabbling bluecapes who have no visceral grasp of the situation. The whole generation-ship project was fraught with failure from the egg. *And you speak of great risks?* Your fears would be mirthful were they not so tragic." Skybones turned and said, "Signals!"

"X/O, aye!" Signals answered.

"Read the communication we received."

After an initial murmuring at the novelty of a communication, the quarterdeck gradually fell into silence as each grasped its import. It was not from Earth.

"*All ships and stations!*" Signals recited the transcript.

"This *is* Ship Imperial Red Dwarf. *Our string engines have failed. Go-captain Huang, hoping to reach Proxima sooner, ordered an increase in acceleration but, in so doing, exceeded engine design limits. We can now no longer project the requisite Higgs field, and without its constant deceleration, we cannot slow our velocity into Proxima capture orbit. Our ship will skid past into the Big Empty. We have laser-beamed this message to the computed trajectories of* Whale, Indiaman, *and* Big River *so that someone—anyone—may learn our fate.*"

There was no question of going to help the Dwarf or even of answering her call. *Red Dwarf*'s fate had been consummated before her message had been received. Chances were that *Indiaman* had not received it even yet.

"Ach," said one of the chartsmen, "she must have been nearly there."

By dead reckoning, *Whale* had covered two and a half light-years of her transit to the Tau. *Red Dwarf* had cast off from Beanstalk twenty years before *Whale* and must by now have completed ninty percent of her much shorter transit. To fail when so close to their goal compounded the tragedy.

Skybones broke the silence. "So you see from the message, the entire generation-ship project is doomed to failure. *Red Dwarf* was traversing a mere four-plus lights. Our transit is three times farther. We've already had the Big Burnout. How long before our Higgs engines fail, or the air plant fails, or some other catastrophe envelopes us? Nothing has a warranty period of a millennium. Better to seize a wild chance now than to drag matters out for another eight centuries."

The X/O's eyes were as wild as the chance he was proposing. *He's gone mad,* Jones thought.

Skybones appealed to the quarterdeck. "You all see that, don't you? You caught the import of the message? Even should diving into the ringularity destroy the ship, that would bring our doom upon us only a little sooner."

Berylplume rose from his seat and to Jones appeared to swell. "If the Audorithadesh Ympriales was feckless in sending out the generation ships—if we *are* doomed—let that doom come upon us when it will. It is written: We will know neither the day nor the hour. But by the Bood! Let us not seek it out. All men die, but that is not a call to suicide. The Way is narrow, long, and hard, but what I heard in *Red Dwarf's* message was the danger of straying from the Flight Plan in the hopes of shortening that Way."

"Your objections are noted."

"It is understandable that after a few centuries, some may panic and give in to despair."

"Panic? You forget yourself, Number *Two*." Skybones, too, had reared up from the center seat and swelled even more than Berylplume. Jones thought there was serious danger that both men might pop like overinflated balloons. "Remember, I am your superior officer!"

And a voice from the rear of the quarterdeck, from under the very Sol projected on the Sky Behind, said, "As you have forgotten that I am yours!"

Jones twisted his seat and saw, wearing his first-class uniform, Pedro san Grigor, ninth go-captain of Ship Imperial *Whale.* By his side stood the execrable Yves san Pedro, Prince of *Whale.*

Skybones sneered. "The Executive Officer has for generations charge of the day-to-day operation of the quarterdeck."

"Serving," said the old man, "at the pleasure of the captain. It no longer gives me pleasure that you should do so. Sergeant-at-arms!"

"Captain, aye!" responded the security guard.

"Please take Skybones Eframof san Waykesh under arrest and confine him to his quarters."

The sergeant-at-arms stepped toward the X/O and clapped his hand on his shoulder. "Sahb! If thou wouldst come with me. There's a good fellow."

Skybones shrugged off the hand and glared defiantly around the quarterdeck. But if he sought support, he found none, only relief in the faces of the deck crew—quartermasters, chartsmen, even the engineers. "Mutineers!" he told them. "All of you."

The go-captain reproved him mildly. "A fine point. Can a *captain* mutiny? We are simply restoring a constitutional order which has been awry far too long."

Of a sudden, the sand went out of the X/O. He sagged and followed the sergeant-at-arms from the deck. No one spoke.

Only when he was gone did Jones turn to Berylplume. "I wasn't told."

Number Two mopped his face with a kerchief. "If it had all 'gone to the orlop,' san Jimmy, you could have denied any knowledge afterward and kept your post. Only Tang and Brahmadharma knew. And the captain, of course. Even the Prince was kept in the dark until the last possible minute. Had the engineers rallied to support the X/O, the Restoration might well have collapsed, but we would have had you and Yves still in place."

But Jones wondered how Pedro would reorganize the deck in the wake of the X/O's demotion. Tradition, the Democracy of the Dead, wanted another engineer in his stead, and he noticed some hooded glances from the engineering consoles.

Winsome Alabaster hummed as she shopped, although she did not know she was humming until old lady Vishwakarma stopped her in the spice aisle of the commissary.

"I did not know I was humming," she told the busybody.

"It's not allowed to sing *that* song. Peng sent out a notice yesterday. *It Doesn't Matter* is classified as subversive."

Winnie shrugged. "It's a catchy tune. I don't know the words. Besides, I thought you didn't care for capewalkers."

The old lady humphed. "Don't mean I want to be hassled by their poodles."

"Why would they hassle *you* if *I* hummed the tune?" She turned her attention to the spice rack. "I cannot find the coriander."

Vishwakarma's vocation as a busybody fit well her avocation as a know-it-all. "Seed, powder, or leaf?" But when Winnie fumbled for the recipe, she added. "Don't matter no how. Flowing Silk hasn't stocked coriander in donkey's years. Maybe some people still grow it in their window boxes. Maybe other neighborhoods have it. Ask your rich boyfriend."

"Seeds," said Winnie in triumph. She had found the recipe in her scrip at last.

Vishwakarma reached past her and snatched up a small jar in her claw. She dropped it into Winnie's basket. "Here. You can use caraway seeds in place of coriander. Trust me, you'll never notice the difference."

Yufreni Dox, Bùxiè learned, lived in Humpback, one of the original villages set up by the Planners. Clustered around Eight Deck starboard afore Five Frame in the fo'c'sle, it had served originally as quarters for electronics mates, Higgs technicians, and others working in the bow, but the Brownian motion of crewmen since and the irresistible human tendency to fiddle with their quarters, had dispersed the departments, and poor, tatty Humpback now provided run-down single-room servants quarters for the Excellent upper decks. Maintenance appeared to have forgotten them. Though the commissary was well-stocked when Bùxiè paused there, much of its stock proved past its use-by date. The water from the drinking fountain, his reason for stopping in, had a metallic tang.

Residents had attempted their own repairs and refurbishments, though with indifferent success. People he saw about wore clothing long out of fashion, even in Little Lotus, and Bùxiè gathered a few curious stares as he walked down the traverse. Even the surveillance cameras were of an antique style.

There was no police nick nor even an Enforcer's station, and Bùxiè reckoned that Humpback was serviced from some larger village nearby. Poorly served if the bars on the windows of many private quarters were any clue.

He found Yufreni Dox's quarters in a sort of half pass'way that deadheaded against a bulkhead. It was surprisingly well-lit and swabbed, so he had no trouble identifying the hatchway number. The surveillance camera there looked new, also.

The woman who answered the hoigh was not so new. She was about sixty and looked like a bread loaf that had not risen properly. "Yufreni Dox?" he asked.

"Nay," The woman answered. "Me sister be dayd." Her accent was very nearly beyond comprehension.

The village that time forgot, Bùxiè thought. "I'm sorry to hear that. I had wanted to ask her about Dumont Lord Ramamurthy. I understand she was recently his cook."

"Thou art a stranger by the fo'c'sle, aina." It was not really a question. She studied him through squinted eyes, taking in his clothes and bearing. She had not invited him in and had not offered the inevitable tea ritual. Bùxiè grew increasingly aware of the surveillance camera in the pass'way.

"Art thou workin' an *him*?"

"Who?"

"Lor' Dumont."

"No."

Several additional moments went by while the old woman made up her mind. Finally, she shrugged bony shoulders and stepped aside, allowing him to enter. "Narakattil. What mought thou be a-wantin' here?"

The inside of the quarters was tidy but cramped. There was a cot in the corner and a second one, folded, propped against the wall. No separate kitchen but a heating cabinet atop the dresser, presumably to warm up rations fetched from the commissary. A mass-produced print of guru Krishna graced one wall; a crucifix, the other. A half-empty bottle of yellow wine held pride of place by the cot.

"I don't know if you can help me," Bùxiè admitted. "I wanted to ask your sister about the circumstances of her termination."

The woman laughed bitterly. "That be the right word, a'right. Termination. They paid me good money, they did, and told me not to flap me gums on it. But, aye, she was 'terminated' right enough."

"You promised not to speak about it." Bùxiè felt the deep frustration he always felt when a line of inquiry sidled up a dead end.

"Narakattil. Promises be *given*, not *purchased*. A promise ain't bindin' if'n it be bought. What kin he do a me? Kill me? Me life ended when me baby sister died. The body-stop be just a formality. What art thou wishful a knowin?"

Well, what did he want to know? All his questions had been lined up; but they had scurried into hiding at this woman's dusty grief. He wanted to tell her what he had told himself: Life goes on. But he saw that in Mistress Analika Dox's case, it had not.

"What were the circumstances that led to Yufreni being fired?"

"Thou plavver fancy. Where be thou from?"

"Little Lotus."

"A cut above this shit-hole, but nay much. No need for fancy, then. Yuffie screwed up a soup she cooked fer 'im, an' *he* done beat her within an inch of her life. Put 'er in an autocart and sent 'er home, but it was more'n an inch to home. She staggered in th' door, lay doon on her cot face tae th' wall, an' she died."

Mistress Dox was dried out, a husk, but a tear nevertheless squeezed itself from her eye and dribbled down her cheek. Either she was unaware of it or did not care, for she did not bother to brush it away.

Bùxiè asked a few more questions, but he did not think the old woman could tell him much more. He was already confirmed in his working hypothesis.

Dumont Ramamurthy was a psychopath.

Other people were not quite real to him. If they furthered his wants, he could be as charming and loving as any other man and use them. Or, more precisely, he could simulate the words and behaviors he had observed in other men. But if they got in his way, he would remove them as dispassionately as other men might remove a stone from their slipper.

Ramamurthy had not beaten Yufreni in a rage but had coldly and methodically chastised her for her poor preparation of a soup, although it remained unclear why the soup meant so much to him.

As Bùxiè left the fo'c'sle for the tram station, he instructed MOBI to transfer two hundred credits to the account of mistress Analika Dox. He was not sure why he did that.

He left the tram at Jeezburr Pass' and walked to his quarters, still mulling the information he had gathered. Spinning open his hatch, he found a man seated in his own favorite chair.

Ling-ling did not know why her lessons continued. Somehow, she had gotten the idea that once she had been Paired, all that childhood foo-foo would cease. Yet, Tutor Weepwillow continued to visit Undine Palace to instruct Megwan, and so Tutor Venables came to instruct her. She thought that greater efficiency might be achieved if the same tutor instructed both of them together, but Venables quickly disabused her.

"You stand at different levels in different topics and are destined for different Offices."

"Fine, fine," she said, but the truculence in her voice announced that all was not fine. Especially when he asked her to produce her homework from the prior session.

Her classes were now held in Undine Palace, although her baba continued to pay Venable's stipend. The arrangement was more formal as well, with tutor and pupil occupying plush facing chairs, each with an arm-desk, and Ling-ling now was expected to maintain notes. She did not know if these changes reflected her status or the venue.

One thing that had not changed was her aversion to hard work.

"The mind is like a muscle," Venables scolded her. "If it is not exercised, it atrophies. Your exercise was a simple essay in logic, and the habit of logic will carry over into many areas of life. So, explain to me why Shang-Di must be triune."

Ling-ling was not sure about the "must" and wondered if she could open her search screen without Venable noticing.

"No," he said. "Don't touch your Notes. You should be able to answer from basic principles. Can you give to another something you do not have yourself?"

"Uh, no, *pandit*?"

"Was that an answer or a question? Never mind. Shang-Di has given men, both males and females, the powers of intellect and voli-tion. Put the two propositions together."

Ling-ling floundered a bit. "Erm ..."

Venables leaned back in his chair and steepled his fingers under his chin. "I'm waiting ..."

Then she had it, a simple conjunction of the two. "If Shang-Di has given us intellect and volition, then Shang-Di must have intel-lect and volition to give."

"Close enough. We like to say that 'there is something in Shang-Di that is *like* intellect and volition in men.' Now, what is the *product* of the intellect?"

Why did Tutor always ask her the questions? That seemed back-ward. She should ask him the questions. Then, she could memorize his answers for the Exams. She was very good at remembering. "The intellect produces ideas?"

"Close enough," he said again. "I would have said 'conceptions.' Since you are an old married woman now, you should know all about conception."

Ling-ling flushed and almost missed his next question. "How are concepts expressed?" When she was slow in answering, he lost patience. "In *words*, you little bobble-head. In *words*. So, if the Sub-ject of intellection is Shang-Di himself, the Object must be ...?" He waited, but her tongue knotted itself, and he supplied the impatient answer. "Shang Di's *Word*. But the Word is Shang-Di, and Shang-Di is his Word because He is Celestial Li, so there is nothing in Him that is not actually Him. Before our next session, I want you to work a similar analysis of the second procession, Shang-Di's volition. What does volition produce, and what are its subject and object? Do you understand?" He sighed and rose, preparing to leave the palace. "Perhaps I was wrong," he muttered to himself. "Perhaps she is still too much the little girl to handle this topic."

Nothing else he could have said, no thunderous command or pleading wheedle could have moved Ling-ling. But that half-heard remark sparked a fierce determination in her heart which, had she suspected, Venables knew quite well.

18 AFFLICTIONS

Goliad's Retreat—A parking ticket—Beneath trees

The Redoubt was more than a shambles; it was an abattoir. Weapons Squad was obliterated, wiped out, made not to be. Lucky could not think of a verb monstrous enough to encompass the slaughter. Bodies littered the pass'way—some evidently fleeing, some with weapons in hand, some clustered around the chow floater. The same fate found each of them. She had thought the three deaths at Hanging Bridge a terrible loss. She had no words for this.

Some were pinned by crossbow bolts, others chopped by hatchets. Most had not even had time to draw their teasers. Vòng had died by his bolt cannon, as had three electrocuted Dwellers who had tried to seize it. The unarmed power techs and maintenance workers had been slaughtered as well, which was strictly against the usages of war.

"So," said Platoon First Sergeant Too Tall Goliad. "It seems we have some work to do." And he directed First and Second Squads to gather the bodies.

"Vòng!" cried a young Marine named Spencer Ku, who ran toward the gunny with arms outstretched and tear-blurred eyes. "Vòng!"

Lucky grabbed him before he could touch the body, wrapping her arms around his struggles. "Stop," she hissed. "He shorted the cannon, and the capacitor is still discharging. Touch him and you die, too."

"I don't care," wept Ku.

"Ah, but I do, and the rest of your mates, too. We need every Marine we can muster." She looked over his shoulder and saw the scorch marks down the pass'way that marked the impact of the ball lightning. Vòng and his crew had gotten off a few shots at least.

But while they had fired on Dwellers before them, they had been taken in the rear and overwhelmed by Dwellers from behind. Lucky read the battlefield with cold insight, noting where the fallen lay and who lay atop whom. A classic feint-and-ambush, like Herman the German had pulled off in the Teutoberger Wald over the proud Roman legions.

The Romans had never gone back but then the Romans had not been Fleet Marines. Lucky had always thought of anger as hot, but she realized now that it could be cold as ice. She would find the barbarians who had done this, and she would make them howl. She had played Crazy Eights with Vòng, who tended toward high bets on low chances. She would miss him, too.

The Dwellers had been led by a warrior with an innate savvy for combat. She could salute his skill while yet wishing his guts for garters.

The Redoubt was to have been a Safe Space, and Lucky could see that Weapons Squad had embraced that belief. None of them were wearing their thix armor, and the commissary float was surrounded by a heap of corpses. Had Vòng even placed outposts at the crosspasses?

Complacency fills the funeral urn, she thought.

Goliad was still working the scene when Lucky saw Fanghsi's ears twitch, and the burnsider suddenly looked up at the overhead.

Even before Fanghsi could cry out, Lucky hollered, "First guns, both squads. Fire on the overhead!"

Goliad turned to her. "Why? The material is impervious to the ray."

"The metal framing will carry the charge."

The First Sergeant didn't question her right to issue tactical orders. As staff sergeant, she ought to have advised the First to issue it, but there was no time for a line-versus-staff debate. Little Face had heard something in the overhead, and she didn't think it was friendlies.

Four guns from First Squad unloosed and four from Second, including Spaceborn Te, who having taken a teaser shot in the left thigh at Hanging Bridge, lay in the wounded cart. The charges ran like fire around the framework, and two light panels shorted out. Howls from the overhead and rapid thumps announced Dwellers hidden in ambush now either dropping from electric shock or crawling rapidly away.

"Second guns," she called over the whine of the first guns recharging, "watch the intersections. First Squad to port, Second to starboard." If she had been the Dweller war leader, she would have used the overhead ambush to fix the defender's attention and then unleash a flank attack, a maneuver used by the Carthaginians at Cannae and by the Zulus against the Shona and the British.

Sure as taxes, Dweller warriors burst screaming from the longitudinals fore and aft.

A hissing of crossbow bolts followed by throwing hatchets gave cover to the rush. The Dwellers followed, brandishing chopping hatchets. Thix armor stiffened on impact of bolt and blade, but the kinetic energy still punished. That was how the English had used their longbows against the French chivalry at Agincourt. The arrows could not pierce the plate armor but pummeled the knights repeatedly with their impacts and, by sheer volume, found chinks and gaps.

Thix did not protect everywhere. Arms and legs were oft exposed, and several Marines dropped with dart or blade sunk into thigh or bicep. Harjo MacDonald from Second Squad had not donned his thix—"Too damned uncomfortable"—and discovered how much less comfortable a hatchet in his chest could be. A fortuitous crossbow bolt found the T-slit in First Sergeant Goliad's helmet and impaled him in the eye. No degree of self-control could stay the shriek from leaping off his tongue.

And just like that, Lucky Lutz was in command of First Platoon, Imperial Fleet Marines.

Some Luck.

Better luck than poor Too Tall had had. Then the attackers were among them. Scanning the battle space, Lucky saw that numbers were about even. Theoretically, this was an advantage to the defender, though that presumed defensive preparations. She sent the lifeguards off to buttress the fire teams of the First and Second and ordered Second Squad to fall back on First.

She saw Spencher Ku, shouting "For Vòng!" draw his Sykes knife and leap upon a knot of Dwellers. He yanked a hatchet from a surprised warrior and began chopping with his right hand and slicing with his left. The serrated blade of the Sykes knife left terrible wounds; the hatchet left worse. The fury of his assault drove back the Dwellers, and his squaddies joined in the counterattack.

Close combat called upon skills learned in countless wayhouse brawls, and the Marines punched, and stabbed and gouged the enemy. Nor were Dwellers unfamiliar with hand-to-hand, though they did learn that in close quarters, the knife was superior to the hatchet.

Throats spewed battle cries, screams, blood, gurgles.

Abruptly, the Dwellers disengaged and ran for the longitudinals. One paused and turned, waving a teaser on a severed lanyard. Several teaser bolts were loosed at him, and one must have struck his foot, for he limped badly as he completed his getaway.

Then Kent and Fishaven were with her. "Are you alright, Staff? My God, Goliad!" Kent dropped to his knees and cradled the First Sergeant's head in his lap.

"No time for that," Lucky said. "The Dwellers might be back. Set pickets to watch the longitudinals. Aim the searchlights down them so the bastards can't approach unseen. Put Goliad in the dead cart. Where's Ku? Still alive? Shang Di watches over children, fools, and the Fleet Marines. Dump the supply floater and load it with any wounded who can't walk. The sooner we're out of here, the better I'll like it. Thank Jeez and the Bood that Wilderness Road is clear and lit."

"You sure you're okay, Staff?" Fishaven looked worried.

"Why? What's wrong?"

Fishaven waved an arm up and down. "Well ..."

Only then did Lucky become aware of the crossbow bolts and the hatchet embedded in her thix. They had not penetrated, but she would be sore and bruised come morning. At her feet lay three Dwellers, one with her own Sykes knife, "Sweet Betsey," in his chest.

She shook her head vigorously. She could not remember any of it happening. It was as if it had befallen someone else.

She worked the hatchet out of her corselet and turned it over in her hands before shoving it in her bandolier. She recovered her knife. "Scouts fore and aft as we march. Ricochet flash-bangs down every intersecting pass'way before we cross it. Find the gunny's wooden pole and pry Vòng off the cannon. *No one stays behind.*" She looked each sergeant in the eye and said, "Do it to it."

They responded with dispatch, and Lucky marveled. She had walked into the Burnout with inexperienced niyōs, but she was leaving with hardened veterans.

Dhik strode down Lotus High Gang, the main gangway through Little Lotus. Most of the action in the village took place along here, and therefore, the most correctable behavior. Also, being wide enough for two gangs of crewmen to pass each other at a full run, gangways gave Dhik more room for action. Signage at intervals proclaimed EMERGENCY ROUTE NO PARKING OR OBSTACLES. It did not occur to him that he might himself constitute an obstacle.

He noticed Blossom Elderborn outside the Horn O'Plenty Commissary weeping. He stepped up to her, causing great alarm to cross her tear-riven face. But Dhik only placed a meaty arm around her shoulders in what he meant as a gesture of comfort and said, "What's troubling you, Bloss?"

Blossom inhaled a sob and accepted the intended comfort. "My wean, Jhara, has the Red Rot, and there be no cure for it, and this morning the medics come from Recycle to take him awa' but he had *days* left tae him tell me that ain't right."

Her grief came out in a great rush, without the usual punctuations. Dhik listened more slowly than she spoke, but he grasped the nettle of it.

"Ah, Blossom, it's sorry I am to hear such a thing, but you know how the final days of the Rot run. Your Jhara will be spared the pain, and you will be spared the agony of caring for him."

"Ah, ye great hulking clod, caring an't no agony, but he being taken from me like that was, those are days I'll ne'er hae wi' me bairn."

Dhik tightened his grip, but not too much—he knew his own strength and crushing Blossom Elderborn would hardly be a comfort to her. Instead, he continued to mutter platitudes, knowing from his brother Bùxiè's experience how uselessly the words would slough off her. In the end, he could not assuage her grief, though he could let her know others shared it.

He touched her MOBI with his, transferring his contact data, and told her that if she needed anything, she should let him know. But the only thing she needed was her Jhara hale and whole, and that was a thing that he could not provide.

A man burst from the commissary behind them, clutching a tote of groceries from which a bread loaf projected like a student raising his hand. The dukāndar ran out behind him and shouted at Dhik. "He did not pay me! Oh, I shall be bankrupt from his theft, and my children will starve. Stop him!"

The long arm of the law is proverbial, but in Dhik's case, it really was long. He stretched and seized the miscreant by the neck. The man howled and grabbed his shoulder, dropping the groceries in the action.

"See here, Chaoxiang. What's all this in aid of?" Dhik prided himself on knowing most of the Lotusans on his beat,

"Thief!" cried the dukāndar, but Dhik knew Chaoxiang was a hard-working mechanics mate, third class.

The man stared at Dhik with resignation. "Go ahead, Dhik. Wale me with your 'boo." He continued to nurse his shoulder.

"What happened to you?"

The dukāndar cried, "Beat him! Thief!"

Dhik eyed the thieved goods. A long loaf of bread, a bag of milled 'ponic, a dozen eggs—those last were a loss, smashed as they were by the dropping—a bag of snow peas .... Hardly the high-end goods a thief would try to carry off.

Before his excursion into the Burnout, Dhik had never concerned himself with questions beyond What? and Who? *What*, in this case, was theft, and *Who* was Chaoxiang. What else need an Enforcer know? But since the Burnout, since discovering fellowship—and Peta—he had begun to ask ...

"Why?"

Chaoxiang looked puzzled. Indeed, the small crowd that had gathered in hope of witnessing a chastisement murmured to one another. One of them said, "Tell him, Chao."

"Prices going up," Chao said, "but *leftent* still demand same kick-back from pay. That leave less for me feed family. I refuse kickback last pay period and he swat me with his baton. Now I cannot raise arm so well to do work, and *leftent* relieve me of posting. Now, no pay but still hunger."

"Thievery is no solution, Chaoxiang. You can go to your church or your relief bank."

But the man was already shaking his head. "Too ashamed."

Dhik turned to the dukāndar. "How much is it worth, the groceries?"

The shopkeeper ran a practiced eye upon the groceries Chaoxiang had dropped. "Fifty credits," he said.

Dhik spoke in a voice like the imminent seizure of a fan bearing. "Are you certain?"

The dukāndar swallowed and discovered his uncertainty. "Allow me to be examining more closely the contents." After rummaging through the tote bags, he said, "A thousand pardons, honorable sahb. The eggs were of a smaller size than I had initially supposed and the bread loaf shorter. The value is thirty-eight."

Dhik proffered his MOBI. "Replace the smashed eggs and double his order. I will pay it. No crewman in the *Whale* should ever go hungry. Perhaps someone here can find employment for a machinist mate?" He sent a look around the small crowd and saw that several of them were smiling. This was a new experience. As an Enforcer, he had more often encountered frowns and fright.

As he took his leave, he noticed a cart parked on the other side of the pass'way and a little bit farther down to portside. He sighed. No rest today, it seemed, and he strolled over to it. "Vehicle parked on Lotus High Gang contrary to Regulations," he told his MOBI and scanned the time, location, and cart registration. He did not send the report quite yet, wondering if there were grounds for leniency.

"Hey, you. Boy!" cried a lieutenant exiting a fabric dukān across the 'way. "What do you think you are doing?" The crowd that had gathered to watch Chaoxiang and the dukāndar had not dispersed but were watching this new development with great intensity. Some of them hooted. One called out, "That Chaoxiang boss!"

Dhik glanced at his MOBI. "I think I am logging a parking violation, sahb. Why? Am I mistaken?"

"Damn right, you're mistaken, boy! Don't you see my cuff rings?"

"Sah! All are equal under the Regulations."

"Insolence!" The Officer struck him across the cheek with his baton.

So Dhik brained him with his 'boo.

And the crowd cheered.

"The time is ripe," Venables told Organson. "There comes a pulse in the heartbeat of the *Whale* when everything is poised on the cusp, and it seems as if the next beat will never come."

The two were once more in their old discussion grounds in Greenfields, this time in the grove called Beneath Trees. The trees were as old as the ship and had been selected from species thought, as near as telescopic study and glimpses from swiftie fly-bys could ascertain, to be suitable for the projected colonization of Vishnu. Organson thought the trees were looking more haggard over his lifetime and doubted they would endure for the centuries awaiting. Trees were long-lived, but not *that* long-lived. Sometimes, he wondered whether *Whale* herself would endure.

But that was futile speculation, a problem for their grandchildren's grandchildren. The future did not yet exist, and the past was irretrievably vanished. All that remained of all infinite time was now.

It was a chore, listening to Venables' chatter. He seemed to grow more nervous—and hence chattier—as the Day approached. His erudition, especially in matters historical, had proven useful in the planning stages. He knew what had worked and what had failed in the past on Old Earth, but Organson suspected the man had no bottom to him. He could not find the ruthlessness in him that circumstances might require and would check his blows at the very moment when they ought to be carried through. He would not stand upright in the gale that was coming.

Organson returned to himself and tuned in again to his companion. *What am I to do with you, old friend?*

"Because, you see," Venables was saying, "the best parents can hope for is to pass on about ninty-five percent of their vision to their children. Their epigones will be that much less in thrall to their beliefs."

"What's an ay-pig-onay?" Organson asked in some irritation. Venables could not just be smart; he had to let you know he was smart.

"What? Oh, it means 'successor' in one of the stem languages, usually with a connotation of 'less worthy.'"

Then why not just say "successors?" Organson wondered. "And how does that means the time is ripe?"

Venables had the irritating habit of holding his forefinger upright when he was making a point. The first time he had done that, Organson had looked at the overhead, thinking Venables had been pointing to something above them.

"Because if the Departure Generation held their ideals with one-hundred percent zeal—"

"How do you measure something like that? With a zealometer?"

Venables pursed his lips briefly and said, "It's a notional quantity. Work with me. Their children would have only ninty-five percent zeal, and the grandchildren only ninty-five percent of that. You follow?"

"Grandchildren, ninty-five percent. Right. Go on."

"Well, then the dedication to the original ideals will decay by a similar amount with each generation, so that—"

"Generations are not discrete," Organson pointed out. "They overlap and blend."

"Yes." Venables was growing testy. "It is only a simple model."

And all models are wrong, Organson recalled, but he did not voice this thought. He had toggled the old man's switches enough for one day. So, he said merely, "Go on."

"So that ninty-five percent of ninty-five percent and so on reduces in the twelfth generation to fifty-seven percent of the original ideals."

"And this is significant because ..."

"Because it is about in this generation that their own ideals begin to outweigh the founding ideals. It is a 'tipping point,' and there is an opportunity to supplant the old *Whale* order with a new *Whale* order."

Children liked to play a MOBI game in which they called a voice message from one to another, and what the last child in the chain heard was often quite different from the original. But that assumed too many things. That the signal loss between generations was ninty-five percent and not ninty-nine percent or some other amount. That generations were discrete entities, like the children. That the signal transmission was from generation to generation and not acquired from a central source, like the schools or the MOBI archives. A central source resulted in a different decay curve than unit-to-unit.

Organson shook his head in irritation. He knew the moment was ripe because he could hear it in the wayhouses and pass'ways and see it in the arrogant behavior of his colleagues. He didn't need a mathematical model to tell him the iron was hot and eager for the hammer.

He saw that Venables had stood and plucked a fruit from the tree they sat beneath.

"You're not going to eat that, are you?" There was something unclean about eating a thing growing out of the dirt.

19 AFTERMATHS (I)

Perhaps he seduced an Excellent's Woman—A surprise visit—No words would ever do

After their workout at the dojo, Jones and Berylplume relaxed in the sauna. The Golden Horn had a great many amenities, and Jones availed himself of all he could. Of course, there were those who might not regard being knocked about and pummeled and then gasping in live steam as luxuries, but it did help soak off the tensions of the watch. And he had defeated Berylplume at long last. The Second Officer would sport some puissant bruises tomorrow!

Jones wondered if Reynaud would remain Second now that there was no First. It made sense to bump each officer up a rank, which would leave a vacancy on the dog watch for a new Fourth Officer. Jones did not think it egotistical to regard himself as the best qualified of the junior astrogators to fill it. No brag, just fact.

But if, by long tradition, the go-captain was elected from among the astrogators, the X/O was chosen from among the E]engineers. That being the case, with an engineer at First, there would be no advance among the astrogation staff.

Though it might quiet engineer grumblings.

He wondered who Pedro might pick. The post did not require great expertise in engineering. It did require skill in personnel and management. So, he might pick even a junior and raise him up.

"The solution that comes to me," he told Berylplume, for they had been discussing this very issue, "would be to split the X/O office from the First Officer. The First ought to stand watches, but the X/O needs only to deal with personnel problems, scheduling, execution of the captain's orders, and the like."

"I don't know if that's an 'only,' " Berylplume answered. "Tensions in the staff may be just as difficult to resolve as tensors in the space-time manifold." But Berylplume spoiled the mood by adding, "Of course, he could name the Prince of *Whale* as X/O. As heir-presumptive, he ought to be given experience in managing the stewpot."

Jones felt positively ill at the thought, so he was glad to hear the Second Officer muse, "But I very much doubt he would do that."

> *"The eyes see afar*
> *But the feet scamper and skip.*
> *Let harmony reign."*

Si, thought Jones. *Exactly so.*

"Meanwhile," Berylplume continued, "this one is much puzzled when an astrogator spends so much time reviewing surveillance footage."

> *"A man in chase of two prey*
> *Splits himself thereby in twain,*
> *Catching neither."*

Jones did not ask how his boss knew of his investigations. "Sensei, I have identified the man responsible for Snowy Mountain's untimely passing."

"We know who that was. He was tried and convicted—though many of us had hoped for a more severe sentence." He dipped the ladle into a clay pot of scented water and dribbled it over the heated stones, replenishing the steam with the odor of almonds.

"No," Jones told him. "There was another man who cravenly held her as a human shield. He must also answer."

"And you have learned this other's particulars."

"It was not easy to find his image. His locator chip had been spoofed and returns a false identity on Facemaker."

"You are working with a policeman, then. Someone with access to the Dataface. I will guess it is Bùxiè deSōuxún, whose Woman our Snowy Mountain was. Ship Security is a delicate bed partner. One must always check afterward to find if one's been buggered. Ah, I see in your eyes I have guessed correctly. Perhaps I should apply for a detective inspector's billet. But tell me how it is, given that this man's chip returns a false identity."

"O Best One, I took his face from surveillance a block distant from the riot as he scurried off with the others. Then another, one learned in the anthropological arts, 'regressed' the face to a younger appearance."

"A police sketch artist."

"Once we had an image of the malefactor as a younger man, MOBI, that best of all trackers, seined the archives, for somewhere in the past was his true identity."

> *"Though a man goes now a-tip toe*
> *Yet he leaves a footprint on his backtrail."*

His name is Jek Buddhathal who once worked in Transshipment but has now disappeared. We believe he has taken refuge in the Burnout, where even his spoofed chip does not register."

"He knows you are tracking him?"

"I do not see how he can. He must have gone dark for other reasons. Perhaps he seduced an Excellent's Woman or injured a man in a wayhouse brawl, and he is hiding from their vengeance." Jones shrugged. "But we know him now and should he ever surface, we will bring him to accounts."

"Pray tell me, which Regulation of the *Whale* did he violate?"

"None. But he violated the Regulations of Shang Di by his craven and callous act."

Berylplume considered that. "Should you and the inspector not leave that punishment for the Dalai Papa to impose, or at least to his village bonze or parish priest?"

Bùxiè closed the hatch door behind him but did not spin the locking wheel. "I won't ask you how you got in here," he told the stranger.

"Good. A certain mystique ought to overlie my persona. I should not be perceived as too quotidian."

Bùxiè grunted. Only a short leap from there to the man's identity. Lord Peng. He turned to his kitchenette. "Shall I prepare the customary cuppa?"

But Peng waved a hand. "I shouldn't bother. I thirst for knowledge, not leaf-flavored water."

Meaning he had come to interrogate Bùxiè. "But you will not begrudge me my own, I trust. The day has been long, and interviewing witnesses dries the throat." But instead of pulling the tea ball from its drawer, he pulled the bottle of his favorite brandy from the cupboard. There was thirst, and then there was *thirst*. He did not know what Peng wanted to hear, though he expected to learn shortly, but the presence of the Head of Security induced a need to brace one's spirits with spirits. Peng was a universal presence. He lurked always in the background. His image was not public, and his particulars could not be found on MOBI. It portended trouble when he stepped into the foreground.

"Ah," Peng said. "I had not known your offer of a cuppa was for a cup of brandy. Perhaps I will have one after all. A small one, if you please."

Bùxiè placed his brandy by Adrienne's chair and shortly returned from the kitchenette with a shot. It was a fine brandy boiled by Jambly, and he begrudged serving it to his unwelcome visitor. He was conscious that Lord Peng had just made him "jump through hoops" but did not see how he could have politely refused.

Peng sipped the brandy and remarked, "A short measure wants small sips to prolong its savor." He placed it on the side table by his chair. "Now, about 'interviewing witnesses.' To what crime was Mistress Dox witness?"

233

That told Bùxiè not only that the camera by the Dox quarters was working but that Security was working it. To what end? Bùxiè considered several answers to Peng's question while he sipped his brandy, but which he chose would depend on what Security already knew.

Before he could open his mouth, however, Lord Peng said, "Please don't tell me you are investigating the death of her younger sister. That is so far off your manor that it may as well not be aboard *Whale* at all."

"I don't want to see my brother hurt."

Peng raised only one eyebrow, a curiously inquiring gesture. "I was unaware you had any brothers."

"Anyone who defies danger at my side is my brother, no matter what his rank or station."

Bùxiè could almost hear the wheels tumbling in Peng's thoughts, like the wheels of a slot machine. Should they stop in alignment, words would issue from his mouth.

"Ah," said Peng after a moment. "The members of the team you took into the Burnout are now your 'brothers.' For whose safety do you worry? Not One and Two Ramamurthy, the two surviving Marines, nor even that hulking brute of an Enforcer. Surely, they can handle themselves."

Peng had the most wonderful kind of mouth, for what came out of it never meant one thing. In addition to asking for clarification, the Commander had told him that he knew the composition of the body recovery team.

Well, Two had likely reported his encounter with Bùxiè. No wonder they had been watching when he called on Dox. That was a lot of telling to pack into such a simple statement.

He saw no way around it. Telling the truth made remembering easier. "Winsome Alabaster."

Again, Peng raised a single eyebrow. "I've met her. She braced me at the Captain's Table once. Why do you suppose she might be hurt? You cannot suppose that I would have her hurt based on what you have not yet told me."

A gentle reminder, that. Bùxiè took a deep breath and said, "What do you know of Dumont Ramamurthy?"

The second eyebrow joined the first. "Oh, my dear. Are *you* interrogating *me*? Isn't that rather wrong end 'round?"

"I fear it is our common profession. Lord Ramamurthy has asked my brother, Alabaster, to prepare his mother's mulligatawny."

"Goodness! That is serious."

Was Peng mocking him? Bùxiè spoke severely. "So far as I've been able to determine, no one has ever prepared it properly, and Lord Dumont ..."

"Expresses his dissatisfaction by murdering the perpetrator. That is probably because he had not expected his mother to die when he assassinated his father. Not that he feels guilty. We don't think he feels at all. But that does not mitigate the psychic harm of the error."

This matter-of-fact comment unsettled Bùxiè. "*You know?*"

Peng blinked at his outburst. "Why, yes, old boy. We are Ship Security. We know everything."

"Then, why haven't you recycled him? Beating a mere domestic cook to death may count for little among the Excellents, but murdering his own Excellent parents must weigh something."

Peng laughed and slapped his knee. Bùxiè had never seen anyone actually do that before. "Oh, what you must think of us! How it must dramatize your lives! Tell me ..." And he leaned forward with his arms across his knees, "how do you suppose I secured my post?"

Bùxiè was unsure how to answer the non sequitur. Birth or Examination were the two usual paths, assassination a third, but MOBI was silent on anything touching Lord Peng. He swallowed the remainder of his brandy in one gulp, depriving it thereby of its being savored. That stink he detected was his own sweat. "I would suppose by Examination." He spoke with care. To cite Birth might be deemed insulting.

Peng chuckled. "Half-right, chief inspector. The one thing the Commanders fear above all else is that Security becomes hereditary. The Examinations provide them with a pool of qualified candidates and, when the post becomes available, the Electoral College selects one."

"What is the Electoral College? I've never heard of them."

Peng waved a hand as if shooing a fly. "My private name for them. The selection is their only duty. The Collegium consists of the paramount Commanders: Power, Agro, Air, Water, and Maintenance. And the Captain, of course. She holds two votes, and so breaks all ties. Would it surprise you to learn that I was crewborn and raised in Greater Harwich?" He pointed to the overhead.

"My lord, to learn anything about you would surprise me."

"Hmm. I was chief petty officer at the time. The College probably believed I would be so grateful at being raised to Commander that I would be pliant to their desires. But like they say, 'the Office makes the Man.'"

"I'm sure they chose the best candidate."

Peng snorted. "What is that smacking sound? Are you trying to kiss my arse? That ill becomes you, deSōuxún. No, they selected the least candidate with the qualifications."

"Then, sah, they must have been terribly disappointed. 'The Office makes the Man,' as you said."

"Don't get too clever. Since your nose is already halfway into the tent, I am going to tell you certain things that are not for general knowledge."

"That sounds—dangerous. sah."

"Oh, it is. But less dangerous than for you to blunder about blindly as you have been doing. Sooner or later, Lord Helix will twig to your inquiries—and to your sorrow. You have no protector against his—him. I almost said, 'his wrath,' but as I said, he feels nothing. It would be for him only the removal of an inconvenient obstacle."

"Are not all obstacles inconvenient by their very nature?"

"Take care, deSōuxún. Take care. Ramamurthy was useful to us. He could derail the plans of Air and Water to form a powerful Commandery. They are powerful enough in their own right. For them to join their powers would be supererogatory."

Bùxiè said, "I don't want to know this. 'A little knowledge is a dangerous thing.'"

"Then you should 'drink deep.'"

" 'Or taste not.'"

"Oh, too late for that. But I continue. Ramamurthy overplayed the hand. He chose a pairing that was so outré that Water simply ignored the draft notice. After that, his usefulness ended."

"So now you can charge him?"

"Oh, Bùxiè. There is the little matter of evidence. We cannot charge on a mere superfluity of probabilities. And no, before you say it, we do not make people 'disappear,' though the reputation for doing so is as useful as the deed. Tell me, if Security made an offer of a posting, would you accept?"

Electricity shot through him. Peng, it seemed, was a master of the non sequitur. His sentences were as stealthy as his agents and could come upon you from unexpected directions. "I am hardly of a disposition," he said, "for selfless bodyguarding."

"We have investigators, too. They work on high crimes, not mere criminal malefactions. Come, old boy, I think you'd enjoy it."

In the silence that followed, Bùxiè heard a lorry roll past his door. Peng's offer was the last thing he had expected; nor was Peng himself what he expected. "Could I have time to think about it? There's my rank and seniority to consider." Another lorry sped by. Surely exceeding the speed limit in Little Lotus. Where were the Enforcers?

Peng again waved a hand. "Take what time you need, but your rank will be raised, and your seniority will carry. What ..." he turned his head as yet another lorry passed. "What is all that in aid of?" He strode to the door, pulled it open, and peered out.

After a moment's study, he said, "By their shoulder patches, that is the Second Platoon of the Fleet Marine Company."

"Where are they going in such a tearing hurry?"

Peng shrugged, palms upturned. "I don't know."

"But you're Security. You know everything." Bùxiè paused, then took a chance. Perhaps Peng was not so drastic as his reputation, "What about Ramamurthy?"

"That's taken care of."

"What about the Widow Alabaster?"

"That's taken care of, too."

Blood possessed a peculiar metallic odor, and bodies began to stink after a few hours. But Lucky spared no time on the carnage at the Redoubt. Drawing a deep breath to numb her nose, she gathered the sergeants and corporals. "The difficulties of entering the Burnout,"

237

she told them, "will be nothing compared to the difficulties of exiting. Or do you think the Dwellers have given up?"

Kent and Fishaven looked at the deck and shook their heads.

"Kent, you're senior. You want command?" *Please, please, take it,* Lucky telepathed. She treasured, above all things, the avoidance of responsibility.

But Kent demurred. "No, thanks, Staff. The middle of an intersection is no time to switch carts."

Lucky glanced at Fishaven but found no joy there, either. "Alright," she said. "This is how we'll do it. First, everybody wears thix."

"I don't think you'll get any pushback on that now," remarked Corporal Te.

She looked at Goliad's body and the misfortunate bolt that had found the eye slit in his helmet. That was what did it for King Harold at Hastings. There was no point to wishing the First Sergeant good luck. Wherever he had gone, he was not coming back. Fortune played an antic role in any fight. Was that why the sergeants had deferred to her? Because she was "lucky?" Enough of that! "Scavenge thix off the dead and use their armor to improvise shields."

"Wish we'd brought our riot shields," Fishaven said.

"If wishes were carts, swabbies would drive. Dead and wounded floaters in the middle. Kent, you take the left flank, Fishaven, the right. Deploy your fire teams in echelon. Maintain fire discipline. What is it, Kent?"

"Not all my fire teams have three shooters."

Lucky glanced at Fishaven, who nodded. "Second Squad, too."

"Combine and reform your teams, then. I want three-man fire teams in both squads. One firing, one ready, one recharging. If that means three teams instead of four, so be it. If you still fall short, slot a Marine from the pioneers or the headquarters squad. Everyone's trained on teasers. But tell me before you do. Singh, take headquarters squad and act as rear guard."

"That's your lifeguard," Singh pointed out.

"Sometimes, a staff sergeant's life is not the most important thing to guard." *Oh. Lucky, what are you saying?* "If I fall—If I fall, Kent's in charge."

"If you fall," said the sergeant, "Kent's in deep kimchee." Then, noticing Lucky's gaze, he fell silent and nodded with a jerk.

"Pioneers ahead. Have your hockey pucks handy."

What was left of the platoon set forth at the double-quick. Lucky noted that the walking wounded had rejoined their squads, and she swallowed a lump. Baptized in blood, they had been reborn, and, like iron, they had become harder for having been hammered.

She stopped them short of the first intersection and asked Little Face if he could hear anything down the longitudinal pass'way—a cough, a shuffle, heavy breathing, anything. She told Singh to have the rear guard make noise so that any potential ambushers would think the Marines were farther back.

Little Face cocked a fist and pointed right, aft. He gave the left a thumb up. A pioneer crept to the corner and skidded a hockey puck into the indicated pass'way. It exploded with a bang and a blinding flash of light—amplified by the light-gathering goggles the Dwellers used. Howls of distress echoed from the longitudinal, and Second Squad picked off the dazed and disoriented Dwellers.

Fishaven exulted. "And *that* for Goliad."

But the Dwellers were not especially stupid. Two pass'ways later, they waited inside closed compartments until after the flash grenade, then burst forth to unleash a crossbow volley at the column as it passed the intersection. The impacts staggered the men even when they failed to penetrate, and inevitably, some bolts found gaps in the armor. Spaceborn Te was wounded in the elbow, and "Chilly" Papa was killed when a bolt sliced his carotid artery. But everyone knew the likely price of dropping out of the column. The Dwellers were not taking prisoners at this point. Plucking low-hanging fruit for their genetic diversity was one thing, but some fruit was more plucking trouble than it was worth.

After each ambush, the Dwellers screamed in triumph and fled down a parallel pass'way to set up another. But Wilderness Road had been cleared, and the other pass'ways had not, so the Platoon steadily pulled ahead.

Finally, Kent cried, "Network comm bubble."

Lucky activated her MOBI. "First Platoon to Headquarters."

"Headquarters. Go."

Lucky detailed the situation, but headquarters did not grasp how deep was the kimchee and asked to speak to Lieutenant Ding-bang, then, after an awkward explanation, to First Sergeant Goliad.

On finally apprehending the magnitude of the disaster, Head-quarters said, "Rendezvous with Second Platoon, Little Lotus entry."

"They must not enter the Burnout, sah. Nothing in our training will have prepared them for fighting Dwellers."

When the First Platoon—Lucky had taken to calling them "Go-liad's Goons" and the name was catching on—staggered from the Burnout and saw their comrades waiting with ambulances, some of the survivors could not withhold their tears but wept unashamed. If the Second had been inclined to mockery, they withheld their comments. Perhaps they sensed the toll exacted by the grueling running battle.

Second Platoon formed two lines for Lucky and her people to walk between to the waiting lorries and, as they proceeded, began to clap and cover them with cheers of welcome.

Lieutenant Gupta of the Second stepped forth and saluted Lucky. "Welcome, Marines of the First. You have fought bravely against a foe both wily and depraved and emerged victorious ..."

So, this is 'victory?' Lucky wondered.

Gupta droned on, stroking her and the First with soothing words. He even threw in several heroic couplets and a haiku. But it was all boilerplate. Gupta had no idea what they had come through. She glanced behind at her men. They, too, stood at ease with the same patient looks that had borne them down Wilderness Road. They were waiting for the ambush.

Lucky suddenly realized that Lt. Gupta had finished his pan-egyric and was waiting for her to respond. She looked at Fishaven and Kent, at Ku and Singh and Spaceborn Te. She looked at the dead cart and Too Tall Goliad. She did not know what to say, but words came to her.

"Thank you."

She knew then that for the rest of her life, there would be those who had been there and those who had not. For the former, no words would ever be needed; for the latter, no words would ever suffice.

20 PROMOTIONS

A labor of love—With enough predictions, some are bound to come true—Organson receives a briefing—Lucky's luck runs out

Winsome Alabaster sweated over a hot stove. More accurately, she watched as the chef box cooked the ingredients she had inserted. As in chemistry, so in cooking, order of addition was a key factor. It mattered what ingredient you added at which time. To prepare herself, she had visited numerous eateries and asked about their preparation of mulligatawny and discovered, to her distress, that, among those willing to share their recipes, no two of them had the same. And thus, no two of them tasted quite alike.

So, without a standard, repeated practice at home may or may not have hit the gustatory target. She had no way of knowing.

Placing the mustard, cumin, and caraway seeds in their hoppers, she pressed the "execute program" button. The chef box presented a skillet and toasted the seeds over a high heat. She watched the timer closely. After three minutes, the toasted seeds should be dispensed to a grinder, where they would be milled to a fine powder.

But Mama Ramamurthy's recipe had read, "until they smell toasted." Experiment had proven this to be three minutes, but she couldn't really be sure.

Meanwhile, the vegetable oil in the pot had come to a simmer, and the chef box dropped the salted chicken thighs into it, skin-side down. Mama Ramamurthy had written, "Simmer until the skin is golden-brown," but how could she know that if the chicken pieces were lying skin side down? She thought Dumont's mother had not used a chef box, but there were so many things to track that Winnie could not imagine preparing the soup entirely by hand.

She glanced at the remainder of the recipe. She had already put the carrot and celery sticks through the autodicer. That could be done off-line ahead of time. But did Dumont prefer potatoes or turnips? The recipe allowed for either.

She wanted to impress Dumont. She wanted this to be a good soup, the best he had ever tasted. And so, she had practiced again and again until she was heartily weary of the taste of mulligatawny.

But how wretched would it have to be for Dumont to lay down his spoon? He would recognize it as a labor of love and applaud her efforts.

The wonderful thing about predictions was that if you made enough of them, some were bound to happen. Less wonderful but still to be wondered at was which ones those would be. Jones had heard through the whisper circuit that the Deck Officers had each been bumped one grade and that the Chief Fusion Engineer had been named X/O. So Berylplume was now first officer, and Hathaway Boronfuse was X/O. Reynaud had predicted the two offices would be separated. And when Jones reported for duty on second watch, he found Pete Tang already dozing in the centerline seat. Tang explained that he was now Second Officer and that Brahmadharma had taken his slot at Third.

Jones congratulated Tang, and Tang snapped his fingers in recollection. "Oh! The captain sends his compliments and desires you call upon him at 1400 hours, at your convenience."

Jones felt light-headed. He was to be raised to Fourth Officer and placed in charge of the dog watch! He knew it. With

Brahmadharma raised to Third, there was a vacancy at Fourth. For the remainder of the watch, while he ran the quartermasters and chartsmen through the normal refinements of ship's motion, he could barely contain his joy.

Yet, his ambitions had been surprised once before when Snowy Mountain, not he, had received the promotion for spotting the ringularity. So perhaps he ought not enumerate poultry prematurely.

Still, when the chimes sounded five bells, he leapt up from his console and asked the Officer of the Watch permission for an early dismissal. Tang granted it with a smile and a whisper of "Good luck."

The captain's cabin was directly below the quarterdeck. Jones made his way to the aft hatchway, where he slid down the ladder, too impatient to climb down. He knocked on the captain's door and, on hearing the brusque "Enter," stepped inside.

Pedro sat behind a broad mahogany desk, a relic brought from Earth itself. It held a built-in link to the OB, a stack of neatly squared hard copies to one side, and a few manuals. The accouterments of a busy man with matters well in hand. Flanking him were X/O Boronfuse and the Prince of *Whale*, the execrable Yves san Pedro. Off to the side, First Officer Berylplume wore a worried frown. With that frown, Jones' anticipation withered like a flower in vacuum.

He stood to and saluted. "Astrogator (jg) Tongkawa Jones, reporting as ordered."

"Wrong," said Pedro. He opened a drawer in his desk and withdrew two arm patches. "Astrogator First Class Tongkawa Jones."

Numbly, Jones took the patches in his left hand, and when the go-captain extended his right hand in congratulations, took that as well. The captain said, "So say I," and the three officers with him responded, "So say we all."

Jones compared the simplicity of the ceremony with the grand induction of Snowy Mountain into the Guild and ascribed that difference to the smile that curled the wretched lips of the abominable Prince of *Whale*.

"You will report on fourth watch to the officer of the deck, Fourth Officer Yves san Pedro."

You could not blame a man for putting his own protégé forward, but once again, when a hatch had swung open for him, Jones found that Yves had darted through it first. He placed a smile in front of his teeth and said, "Congratulation, sah." But he saluted in lieu of shaking his rival's hand.

"I had been instructing Yves in the contemplation of the sacred Flight Plan," said the captain, "but in light of the Restoration, I thought it fitting that he be instructed in the practices of the quarterdeck as well. I am an old space dog, myself, and it is too late to teach me new tricks, but when my last watch comes 'round—"

"Not for many years," the other officers assured him.

Pedro accepted the well-wishes with a fatalistic shrug. "When the time does come, I want my protégé properly prepared to step into the new, more active captain's role. Your duties, Astrogator Jones, will be to teach him all that is needful for leading the quarterdeck."

In other words, Jones thought, *teach this* niyō *my job so he can play the role I have trained for years to play.*

Upon dismissal, Jones left the grand cabin along with Berylplume and Boronfuse. The engineer, oblivious to the power play that had just taken place, pumped his hand vigorously and congratulated him on the grave responsibilities he had been assigned. "Tain't gi'en tae everyone tae mentor his ain future captain."

"You better get some rack time," Berylplume told him. "Fourth watch starts in six hours."

"Did you know about this, Number One?"

The new First Officer tossed his head. "Not in enough time to forewarn you. But you must admit, the postings make sense, and it was our own fault for restoring the captain. Just remember, when Yves becomes captain, he will need to relinquish his post as Fourth Officer."

"Not for many years to come," Jones reminded him.

Hamdu Organson reviewed his notes on Gold Crew for the briefing he would give the in-captain. Some sort of turmoil had run through their ranks. A great many postings had been shuffled about. Skybones had dropped out of sight. Whatever had gone down, the goldcapes had not filled him in. The senile old man who commanded Signals had said something about a catastrophe, but Hathaway

Boronfuse, the new X/O, had assured him the catastrophe did not affect *Whale*.

In which case, why call it a "catastrophe?"

Captain Ming-ti would want to know more, and Organson found himself in the unusual position of not actually knowing more.

His hoigh plate chimed, and the camera feed showed Baozhai Henderson, nominally his secretary but who kept greater secrets than most. She had a stocky man with her, dressed in a motley assortment of clothing. Curious. Organson said, "Enter," and released the catch.

The man who entered had a head too large for his face. Prominent ears flared out to either side, but his eyes, nose, and mouth were positioned close together, guarded by wide expanses of cheeks, forehead, and chin. Had Baozhai brought him only to exhibit this curiosity?

His office was Peng-proofed, but his secretary nonetheless consulted her squealer to assure herself that she could speak freely. Organson became more alert. That probably meant Brotherhood business.

"Yes, your business, man?"

"Alessandro Fanghsi, me, courier from Fort Freedom." He sketched a mockery of a salute, which Organson overlooked. "Big Blue, You, not so?"

Organson shot Baozhai a sharp look.

"No one told him so, sah. It's his own conclusion."

"Your information must be important, indeed, if you could not leave it with your usual contact."

"Told contact me. He pass me on. Passer-on pass me on. No one wants tell Big Blue, so Little Face takes nettle in hand."

"Wait. Who is Little Face? Oh, I understand. So, what is this hot potato that no one wanted to take?"

"Fort Freedom is fallen."

The news struck him like a body blow. "When? How?"

"Guiding new recruities, me. All brave and dedicated but also stupid. One leave MOBI active. Marines on expedition to find little lost teasers throw out comm bubble for selves, notice stupid MOBI signal and come looking."

"Did they grab the teasers?"

"Group Leader Chang, smart fortune cookie. All teasers kept in backpacks, so quick-quick he gets recruities carry them off while cadre run guard. Oh, and he fry bubbles before we go. Guide 'em, me, to Hanging Bridge, where they build barricade. Good thing, too, since Marines follow somehow. Battle ensues. Captured me, but later help Marines in battle with Dwellers, so they release me. Random burnsider co-opted by rebels."

Organson realized his mouth was hanging open, and he snapped it shut. He had heard nothing about this from Chang yet unless this burnsider was, in fact, Chang's message. If he had allowed his cadre into a firefight with the Marines, no wonder he had not reported!

"How did this firefight come about?" he asked the courier. "Chang was under strict orders to avoid conflict."

"Not entirely up to Group Leader Chang. Marines have some say. They follow and catch up at Hanging Bridge. Their Officer demands we turn over stolen teasers. Then someone hollers, 'Officers die!' and burns down Marine lieutenant. Marines open fire, and cadre returns fire."

One of the Brothers had fired first? Organson could guess who, too. Damn. He would have to get Venables busy on countering that news. "Casualties?"

"Don't know for Brotherhood. Captured by then, me. Two other Marines dead, several burned. But Hanging Bridge nothing compared to running fight with Dweller allies. Marines led by mere staff sergeant before manage escape."

The Dwellers were allies of the Brotherhood? Chang had certainly exceeded his remit. But Venables could recast the Dweller attack as something independent of Brotherhood action and divert crew anger from the Brothers to the Dwellers. Maybe that first shot had been fired by a Dweller wishing to foment trouble between the Marines and the peaceful Brotherhood. Yes, that line could work.

But Organson could not evade the feeling that circumstances had run away from him.

Lucky, when she had been summoned to the Commandant's office, expected the most royal ass-chewing of all time. First Platoon was wrecked, and she was the only one left to blame, Dingbang and Goliad having had the forethought to die before facing the music.

But instead of an ass-chewing, she found herself faced with an affable, doddering chatterbox who digressed constantly into arcana and irrelevancies in a dialect rarely heard outside Pigwhistle, full of drawls and with an appalling lack of rhotic consonants. Lucky could barely understand him but paid him full attention for, gaffer or no, he was the Commandant. Yet the man she had spoken to over her MOBI while escaping down Wilderness Road had been firm and decisive. Unless Commandant Yueh became so when crises struck—an eventuality on which she harbored grave doubts. Irresistibly, her gaze was drawn to Company Master Sergeant Laalamani Popof, known in the Company as "Lollypop."

"It ain't fitting," Yueh went on, "fo' a sergeant to head up a platoon. The Table of Organization calls fo' a leftenent in that there billet. Yessir, it does that."

Lucky breathed a sigh of relief. They had found a suitably Excellent candidate to put in place of Dingbang. Lucky desired, above all things, the avoidance of responsibility. She had discovered during the Retreat how much the lives of others could weigh upon one's shoulders,

M/Sgt. Lollipop said sharply, "Stand, Staff Sergeant Lutz." When she did, he stepped forward and tore her stripes from her sleeves.

So, that's it, she thought. Her fabled luck had run out at last. *They need a scapegoat, and I'm elected.* It wasn't really fair. Hanging Bridge and the massacre at the Redoubt had happened before command had pounced upon her, but as Too Tall had been fond of saying, where is "fair" in the manual?

The Commandant tossed a package at her, and she caught it reflexively. "The Commandant and his staff," said Lollipop, "listened quite closely to the debriefings you, Kent, Fishaven, and the other survivors gave us, and the conclusion is that you—and Goliad and Dingbang before you—played the hand you were dealt about as well as anyone could hope under the circumstances. Go on, open the damned package."

Lucky had been turning it over in her hands. Now, she peeled off the wrappings and saw two gold bars.

"Sit, *Lieutenant* Lutz," Lollipop said.

It was a good thing she had been commanded to sit because her knees gave way. Her luck really had run out.

21 COMMOTIONS

A new Number Three—Battle honors—Peng agreed
to do me a favor—Do you know how deep the *fen-fen*
is that you've stepped in?—A humiliation—Holy shit

Winsome Alabaster found the kitchen of Helix House well-stocked
with nearly all the ingredients and utensils she would need. Lord
Dumont himself conducted her there. There was henstuff fresh from
the Pigwhistle vats, carrots and celery from the hydroponic farms, a
spice rack endowed by the window boxes of Greater Wooser and
Highsteeple. Only the coriander was missing, but there were plenty
of caraway seeds to substitute for it. The chef box was of unfamiliar
design, but she believed she could master it.

"Do you have everything you need?" Dumont asked her, and
she replied yes, though she would like to practice a bit program-
ming the chef box.

"Take your time. Mama's recipe is unique and it is important that
it be gotten right." He left her to practice. The scullery maid seemed
about to speak but pressed her lips tight instead.

She told the maid to fetch some bowls for her to mix the ingredients and began measuring them out. She hummed, realized she was humming "It Doesn't Matter"—what an earworm!—and stifled herself.

She ran through the manual for the chef box, identifying the hoppers for the ingredients.

The hatch to the pass'way opened and closed. You needed a household pass key to do that, and she looked up and saw that it was Two.

"A-hoigh," she said. "Your leave over already?" He was still dressed in mufti, so she figured he was not yet on duty and could dispense with the Great Stone Face.

"Aye," he said. "Are you prepared to make the soup tomorrow?"

"I am," Winnie replied. "I practiced at home. I just have to get used to this model chef box."

"It be an antique, right enough. Should be in the Museum. It belonged to his mother."

"I've got all the ingredients except the coriander, but my neighbor said I could substitute caraway, and no one would taste the difference."

Two scowled. "No coriander? When did you say the big day was? Tomorrow?" He snatched a biscuit from the pastry table before the pastry chef could stop him. "My favorite. Sugar cookies. We call 'em 'cookies' back home, not 'biscuits.'" He took a bite. "Oh, by the way. Three has been reassigned. We're getting a new Number Three tomorrow. You won't know him."

Winnie laughed. "I don't know any of you, not really."

"No, mistress. That sentence was imperative, not declarative."

And then he left the kitchen for the Security room, where he could change into his uniform and put on his friendless mask, leaving Winnie to puzzle over his remark.

Lucky accompanied Lollipop into the wardroom for First Platoon. Kent and Fishaven were there, but they were not sitting at the card table. Lucky had not sat herself there, either, since returning from the Burnout. The reminder was yet too painful that Goliad and Vòng had customarily occupied two of the seats.

The squad sergeants showed surprise when the company master sergeant entered, a surprise evidently heightened when they caught sight of the shiny gold bars on Lucky's shoulders and the single ring on her cuffs.

Surprised but not impressed.

"Smell *your* feet," said Fishaven.

"What, were they scraping barrel bottoms, looking for a new loo?" said Kent.

Lucky accepted their razzing because she knew that the Commandant's action had been based in part on their own testimonies regarding the Retreat. The sergeants of First Platoon had been a cozy bunch. Lucky knew that their relationships would shift, given her new rank, but she hoped they would not shift too far nor too soon. She was going to need all the help she could get.

"At ease," said Master Sergeant Popof, surely the most needless command ever issued in First Platoon's wardroom. "Ye mighta noticed that Lutz here been promoted. Lucky, I seen yer file, and you was a screw-up and slacker the whole time in the Company."

"Gosh, thanks, Master Sergeant."

"Always knew that," Fishaven added. "Nice to get independent confirmation, though."

"But something came over you at the site of Vòng's Last Stand. Maybe it was the spirit of Too Tall Goliad. But whatever that something was, we can only hope you keep it with you."

"Amen," said Kent. "None of us would be here today if it wasn't for you, and that there is a fact."

"We didn't know you had it in you, Lucky. Oh, can we still call you Lucky? I mean, now that you've gone all grand on us."

"Escaping down Wilderness Road with minimal losses must count as lucky. So, sure."

Lollipop coughed, and Lucky added, "Here in the wardroom, we can talk unbuttoned. But in front of the troops, it might be best to maintain military decorum."

"Yes, sah, lieutenant, sah!" said Fishaven, saluting smartly. Though seated, he stamped his heel.

"The Loo made recommendations for platoon First Sergeant and staff sergeant, which I am grieved to say were you two. The Commandant seconded me to Acting Platoon First Sergeant to make an independent assessment of both of you. Meanwhile, in the unlikely event that you are promoted, give some thought to who you gonna recommend to take over your squads."

"I knew it," said Fishaven. "You're trying to take away my Crackerjacks. Well, you can't have 'em. They're Kanada's Crackerjacks, and that's that."

"It would mean a hefty increase in pay grade," Lucky pointed out.

"I'm in," said Fishaven.

"Lucky," Lollipop handed over the ribbons, "you wanna do the honors?"

Lucky took the ribbons and attached them to the pole for the Platoon's colors. Each bore an inscription: Hanging Bridge, The Redoubt. Goliad's Retreat. Lucky stood facing the banner for a long time, swallowing her sorrow, holding back tears by main force. Then, she saluted their flag and the Great Yellow Banner with its black three-headed eagle, turned smartly about-face, and hoped the others had not seen her struggles.

But Kent and Fishaven were both quietly sobbing, and even Popof, who hadn't been there and who wasn't even a Goon, had allowed a single tear to run down his cheek.

When she thought she could speak without choking, Lucky said, "That will give us bragging rights over Second Platoon."

"For a while, at least," said Master Sergeant Popof in a gloomy voice. "Until the crap impacts on the air-conditioner. The problem with battle honors is that winning them requires a battle."

Bùxiè finished clearing out his desk, marveling at how little his years of service had accumulated. That was the problem with a devotion to de-cluttering. There was little left to take with you. He studied his coffee mug for a while, remembering the numberless cups of really bad coffee that had occupied it. He wondered if Peng's people made better coffee. It was hard to imagine worse. He sighed and placed the mug in his tote.

Qínfèn had been watching him the while. "I still can't believe you're packing it in after putting in all that time."

"Don't worry, sergeant. I was assured that I would keep my seniority and my pension would transfer. After all, like they say, 'it's all one *Whale*.'"

"But how far can you trust Ship Security? They give me the jeebs. I can't help it. I wouldn't like it if *you* started giving me jeebs."

Bùxiè paused in his packing and looked at his sergeant. "I'll try to remember not to do that. Besides ..." he resumed packing, "you really don't want to disappoint a man who can show up in your quarters unannounced. Don't worry, you'll get along famously with DCI Harjo."

Qínfèn shook his head. "It won't be the same."

Bùxiè lidded his tote and thought. *No, it never would be.* "Who's our boss?" he asked of a sudden.

"What? You don't know?"

"Humor me."

"Kogee, the precinct lieutenant."

"And his boss?"

"Chief Constable Idom."

"And *his* boss?"

Qínfèn paused. He had seen where Bùxiè was going. "Commander Peng," he said, drawing it out.

"*Shi de.* That's right. So, I'm not going very far, am I?"

"I don't know, sah. The Constabulary deals with local crime. Little Lotus, or wherever the nick is. Ship Security deals with—I don't know what you want to call it—inter-neighborhood cases?"

"A different set of malefactors is all. Bigger and stupider than ours. Besides, Peng agreed to do me a favor."

"What favor?"

But Bùxiè did not say.

"Do you know how deep the *fen-fen* is that you've stepped in?" CPO Ippolito Okoye asked. Lightning flashed in his eyes, and thunderclouds lowered on his brow. He balled his hands on his desk.

Probably, thought Dhik, *to stop them from leaping forth to strangle me.*

"Do you know how deeply connected his family is? An uncle is a senior lieutenant in the medical corps, and his father is a lieutenant commander in Communications."

Dhik tried to look away, then thought, *To hell with it.* "Sah, he parked his cart illegally, in violation of the Regs. The penalty is one blow."

"Normally applied to the buttocks, not the skull. You're lucky you didn't kill him."

"I would say *he* is lucky."

"Don't try for cute, Spandhana. You're far too big and far too ugly to pull it off."

"He struck me with his baton, sah. It is against the Regs to strike an Enforcer or any peace agent. He deserves five more strokes."

CPO Okoye sighed and picked up a paperweight from his desk, perhaps to throw at Dhik. He certainly looked as if he were contemplating that. "Did it escape your notice, Enforcer, that the man was wearing a cape?"

Dhik heaved a huge breath, and small items fluttered in the gale. "It reads in the Constitution of the *Whale* that 'Officers as well as crew are subject to the same conduct regulations.'"

"Spandhana! Have you become a constitutional scholar since I last chewed you out. Blast force and lightning bolts! I shouldn't have to tell you this. Capewalkers follow their own rules, and yes, before you tell me, I know it is contrary to the Regs, but wealth plus power equals they get away with it. That you don't like it— Thunder-weather! *I* don't like it, either—doesn't enter into it."

"No wonder we long for the *Whale* as she was."

"Be careful with your choice of words, there, and who hears you say them. The Officers were always an aristocracy, even in the Departure Generation."

"Aye. But now they've become an oligarchy."

Okoye shrugged. "It is what it is. Turn your head to the gale. It's never a good idea to anger the rich and powerful, no matter who they are."

Dhik gave Okoye one of his Looks, though his supervisor did not quail. "The solution might be to make them less rich and less powerful."

"And who will do that, Spandhana? You? Me? Flying snakes! A parable regarding cats and bells comes to mind. Why do I see you in front of my desk more than any other Enforcer in my squad? Riddle me that."

Dhik shifted his stance, though only a little. "What are we going to do about it, sah?"

"*We*, Spandhana? Did I hear you use the plural form? *I* didn't brain anyone—though it is growing more tempting by the minute." He made a throwing gesture. Dhik looked around for a bus under which he might be thrown. "It's out of our hands, anyway, Spandhana. Lord Kennett has filed a grievance, and the whole matter has gone up the sweet chain of sorrow to Lord Peng himself. Lots of luck dealing with *him*. Commanders scratch one another's backs."

Ling-ling had to stand idly by and watch her Man be humiliated, not once, but twice. His mother, the Egregious Sophie, had asked—no, told—her to be here. Ling-ling had a sudden vision of what it must have been like for Megs to grow up under the woman's regimen. She longed all the more for her gentle, lost realm of Zephyrholm.

"I don't want you *ever* to go to one of those meetings *again*," she said in that high-pitched harpy's voice that was an ice pick in Ling-ling's ears. They were gathered in Sophie's sewing room, a volume she used for a great many purposes, none of them involving seamstressing.

"Why not?" Megwan muttered. Ling-ling wished he wouldn't sound so truculent. She also wished Megwan's father were present. He was kindly like her own father. But Sophie had dispensed with him once he had done his duty and helped her produce an heir. He now haunted remote passages within Undine Palace, searching for his lost relevancy. That was too bad; a lad needed a father in his life, and Sophie was not very good at providing one.

"Why not! Meggy, those men were talking mutiny. They're dangerous, 'lean and hungry.' If they had recognized who you were, who knows what they might have done?"

Perhaps, one would have slip-tongued to Lady Water, as Jimcas Nearwell had evidently done. He had accused Megs of spying on the Brotherhood for his mother, and people often accused others of their own sins.

"Maybe," said Megwan, "they wouldn't be so 'lean and hungry' if they were paid more." His defiance of his mother thrilled Ling-ling, and quite suddenly, with no warning, she wanted to Do It with him.

"And now mutinous talk in my own house! I won't have it." Sophie pulled back and slapped her son with the back of her hand, a sharp crack in the still air. Megs said nothing. He did not even reach his hand toward the bruise.

Just as suddenly, Sophie embraced Megwan, holding him tight against her and rubbing his hair. "Oh, Meggy, my darling baby, my beautiful child. Look what you made me do."

And that was the second humiliation, thought Ling-ling. The slap was bad enough; the embrace was worse. Megs was fourteen, a grown man, and hardly a child or a baby to be disciplined *or* coddled by his mama.

As they left the sewing room afterward, Jimcas was standing by the hatchway. When Ling-ling stung him with a venomous look, he said in a low voice. "It weren't me, young mistress. Jimcas never said aye, yea, or maybe."

Ling-ling wondered if he spoke truth. But if not him, then who? And if Lady Water had informers within the Brotherhood, so did other Excellents, including Lord Peng. She had a sudden vision of a conspiracy comprised entirely of informers, eagerly turning one another in to Security. The image was so ludicrous that she burst into laughter, greatly puzzling both Megs and Nearwell.

Lucky entered the Armory with the sensation of returning to familiar ground. The smells of packing grease assaulted her. Even the sounds of the Armory—dead silence—pleased her in some indefinable way. Only the recruiting poster, prominently displayed to the left of the service counter, rankled her.

First of all, what good did a *recruiting* poster do in the freaking Armory? Everyone who saw it was already a Fleet Marine.

And second of all (unless it was really first of all), it portrayed *her* dressed in her class B uniform up to and including the thix collar around her neck, all superimposed over an imaginative rendering of the battles in the Burnout. Prominent lettering announced that "Lucky wants YOU if you want to fight."

How in the *Whale* had such a humiliating defeat become a great victory? The defense of the Redoubt and the fighting retreat down

Wilderness Road had somehow captured the imagination of the ordinary crewmen and borne Lucky herself on its wave as a hero.

She fingered the medal that hung on a crimson ribbon around her neck. The Military Star. *What did I do to deserve this?*

Vòng had received *The Wounded Lion* posthumously, for his act of staying by his bolt cannon and spiking it in the face of overwhelming attack. *That* had been heroic. Private Ku had received *The Defiant Lion* for his wild attack upon superior numbers, which had, maybe, turned the tide at the Redoubt. That, too, had been heroic. She had done nothing like that. She had only shouted desperate directions.

Well, and killed three Dwellers who had broken through to her command post while receiving crossbow bolts and a hatchet in her thix. But that had been incidental. She had only done what she had to do, and that was that. Had she her druthers, she would have been in the wardroom playing Crazy Eights with Goliad and Vòng.

"Nice bit o' bling there, Sarge."

She turned away from the poster to greet the Armorer. "Hoigh, Tony. And it's 'Lieutenant' now." She touched her gold bars.

Tony touched his forehead, lips, and chest, "Nice bit o' bling there, Lieutenant Sarge."

Tony was a small man, almost elfin in stature, and was widely reputed to shave twice per day. His "five-o'clock shadow" made its appearance shortly after lunchtime and bid fair to being a permanent feature of his visage. He was said to use his chin for sandpaper and his cheeks for emery cloth.

"Okay, Tony. I'll bite. What is 'bling'?"

"An ancient word for schmutz, jewelry. Do you know what 'lieutenant' meant originally?"

"No, and I don't care. Today it means 'the shit stops here.'"

"It meant 'substitute, deputy, placeholder.' Lieu-tenant—in place of the holder. And sergeant originally meant 'servant.'" He tittered. "Isn't that *awful*? Servant? Say, you don't care much for the new recruiting poster, do yah? You think the gory background will scare folks away?"

"I insisted on it. I don't want troopers in my Platoon who are not ready, willing, and able to fight. It's one thing to march in fancy parades on Departure Day and other holidays or even to put down riots, like back in '53. But to go toe-to-toe with the Dwellers, you need sand. I gotta build up a brand-new Weapons squad and fill the holes in the Table of Organization. I'm not gonna fill 'em with pusillanimous chicken livers."

"Pusillanimous?"

"You heard me. Which brings me to why I'm here. When we were fighting our way down Wilderness Road, I learned that Dweller crossbows have a greater range than our teasers. Problem was, the Dwellers learned that, too, and staged their ambushes from deeper in the cross-pass'ways. So, every intersection, we got a rain of bolts from outta the darkness. And all we could do was take 'em on our thix and shields we improvised from dead men's armor."

"Bad cess to 'em, sez I. The Dwellers, I mean."

"They would tremble in their boots to hear you say that, Tony. Beware the Angry Elf! I can't blame them for doing their best and learning from their experiences. But I want the right to do the same. Seems to me I remember from Weapons class, years ago, we have longer range personal arms. They weren't in the stockroom, 'cause I inventoried that ..."

"More or less, the way I hear."

"... so that means they're buried deep in the Armory, and I can't ask the inventory-taker for that volume if he saw 'em."

"Why not?"

"His name was Vòng. As a former gunny, you might know what I'm talking about."

Tony twisted his face to the side. After a moment's thought, he said, "The coil guns, mebbe. They use magfields to fling kinetics at the target. Like a carpenter's nail gun. But they never been used. Mightn't still work. Even packed in protective grease, two hundred years is a long time to sit idle."

"Then let's find 'em, clean 'em off, and test 'em."

Tony shrugged again, "You're the Lieutenant, Sarge."

And so it was that Lucky found herself on the firing range later that day with a three-stage coil gun. Hacker and Moore Model 312A. *Auto and Semi-auto Modes. Launches a Size F5 Flechette. QuikQuench™. No sliding Contacts! No Suckback. Warning: High Voltage FastDump Capacitors. Danger: Do Not Remove Ceramic Shell.*

After all that, Lucky was wary of opening even the carrying case.

The coil gun consisted of a stock, support bipod, a replaceable flechette drum, and a grooved rail onto which the flechettes were loaded. These were small solid metal darts with fins. *(LoXSection™ to reduce drag on the projectile!)*

"A lot like miniature crossbow bolts," Lucky commented. "Don't look very ferocious." Tony, standing behind her at the spotter's binoculars, said nothing.

The rail was encircled—barreled, the instruction manual said—by three coils. When the launch button was pressed, the A capacitor would dump current into the first coil, creating a magnetic field that would draw the flechette forward into the coil. When the flechette reached the midpoint of the coil, the current was quenched—otherwise, the projectile would be held stationary—and at the same instant, the B coil would be activated, pulling the flechette forward. Lucky tried to guess what happened then with the C coil and was pleased to find she had guessed right. The net result, if the timing was set properly, was a smoothly increasing acceleration so that the projectile departed the gun with considerable velocity. Primitive early flechettes, the manual read, dropped from biplanes struck with enough kinesis to pierce the helmets of soldiers in the trenches, and Hacker and Moore promised comparable terminal velocities with the Model 312.

Lucky hefted the gun. Kinda heavy. Definitely a specialty arm. She powered it up. Pretty lights announced readiness. She laid the barrel across the sandbags, supported on its bipod. Then, she exhaled slowly and pressed the launch button.

Nothing happened.

Lucky resisted the temptation to look down the barrel to see if the flechette had gotten trapped in one of the coils. Maybe it needed to be retimed.

"Would the lieutenant care to attach the magazine now?" said Tony.

Lucky muttered something face-saving about dry-fire for practice, and the Armorer pretended to accept this.

She selected semi-automatic and launched a single round. The gun went *whrrr* and *chuff* like an air gun, and the projectile sped downrange. A miniature thunderclap accompanied it. *A sonic boom, by the Bood!*

Tony slowly straightened from the binoculars. He swallowed. "It penetrated the thix. One inch, high-density thix armor."

Lucky nodded and flipped the selector to automatic. A press of the button launched a furious flight of flechettes. Their sonic booms were a roll of thunder on the range. When she looked at the target, she didn't need Tony's binoculars. It was shredded like a piece of paper. Pieces of it fell even as she watched. The darts had penetrated faster than the thix could stiffen.

She waited a moment to regain her composure. Kinetic energy increased with the square of the velocity. Double the terminal velocity, you quadruple the impact energy. "Holy shit," she whispered.

"Divine doo-doo," Tony agreed.

22 RESOLUTIONS

At Comm Central Plaza—A great wave of thirst—"By the Bood, there's another one!"—The true coriander

Bùxiè left the tram tube at Quarterdeck Station and took the manlift to Twenty-Three Deck, where he emerged on the corner across from Comm Central. He quickly stepped off the pad, for other commuters were rising after him, and one didn't want to cause a jam at the manlift. Scores of crewmen hustled about. He dodged a cart. Little Lotus was a much quieter neighborhood, and the pre-watch rush there was primarily pedestrian. He did not know if he could accustom himself to the bustling gang'ways of Centrum.

He looked about for the entrance to the local tube, where he could catch the tram forward to Ten Frame. Well, to Nine Frame and walk the rest of the way to his assignment. The commute from Little Lotus was wearying in itself. He ought to look for quarters in Centrum. He could afford it now. But the milling crowds were—if not unfriendly, more indifferent than he cared for.

And it would mean giving up the quarters he had shared with Adrienne for so many years.

The unexpected sight of Jek Buddhathal stopped him in mid-stride. The crewman who had used his Woman as a human shield.

Anger swept through him as surprising as it was sudden. He had thought he had made peace with Adrienne's death, but the red rage caught him up, and he almost—almost—ran to throttle Buddhathal on the spot.

But to cross Comm Plaza would be to expose himself, and the man would be ever after vigilant to Bùxiè's presence.

In fact, standing still amidst the busy commute itself drew attention. Buddhathal might have noticed something from the corner of his eye, for he turned toward Bùxiè, who quickly snapped his MOBI to his face and peered at the intricately decorated façade of Comm Central, where intaglio carvings of twisting vines represented the interconnection of the *Whale* net. Bùxiè became in an instant just another *turista* from the aft frames visiting Centrum.

Besides, he did not want to be late at his Post-of-Duty, certainly not on his first day. He made a show of consulting his time and hurried off to the local tram line. He did not look back at his sometime quarry.

But why in all *narakas* had Buddhathal been taking images of Comm Center? Surely, he was not also aping a tourist.

The Big Dhik was feeling large when he walked into Arfwendsen's Wayhouse. In part, this was because he *was* large and standing in the hatchway had much the same effect as an eclipse, but in part also because he felt expansive. He almost said, "The drinks are on me," but no man, however generous he was feeling, would make that misstep in so thirsty a venue as Arfwendsen's Wayhouse.

Some patrons had applauded his entrance. A few even called out his name. In the past, few had ever tried to draw his attention to themselves, but now they reacted with something akin to affection. Courtesy, not trepidation, now caused them to make a Dhik-sized hole at the bar. Not that he had ceased to enforce filial piety. There were several in this very room who had recently felt his 'boo on their backsides, but since he had begun to inquire about reasons and had begun to *talk* to those he chastised, they had begun to take their swats, if not with joy, at least with resignation. Since that day on Lotus High Gang' when, in short order, he had comforted Blossom Elderborn, paid for Chaoxiang's groceries, and whapped the lieutenant sharply on the pate, attitudes toward him had shifted. He wasn't sure which of those acts had earned him the affection of the neighborhood, but that day had surely marked a sea-change in his life.

He said as much to Little Face, who was looking very much like a feral feline sated on *Serini canariae*. "No mystery, friend. You do some of the Seven Good Things."

"The Seven Good Things?"

"Yas. There fourteen of them."

Dhik thought the burnsider numerically challenged but used a Look rather than a question.

"Seven for soma, seven for atman. I not list all. Yes, you welcome. You comfort sorrowful, feed hungry, and admonish offender. All in one day, too. Is also give drink to thirsty, but I do that for you." So saying, he bought Dhik a glass of the Strangler.

"You suddenly become wealthy?" Dhik asked at this unlooked-for generosity.

"Beyond dreams of avarice, brother. Beyond dreams of avarice. Big find in Big Burnout; sell to Museum of *Whale*." He rubbed his fingers together to signify many credits deposited to his account. But then his visage changed.

"Trouble come, friend," he murmured.

Three large men wearing the livery of Maintenance had walked through the hatchway. They each brandished a *pilli* club.

"Which one o' youse guys is Dhik?" the leader hollered, which brought a halt not only to the chatter that had filled the place but even to the gaming at the tables. Hidaki paused with a rook in mid-air. Kunigund reached for something under her bar, though she did not pull it out.

Dhik turned and faced them straight on, holding his 'boo at ready. Little Face said, "Uh-oh," but did not leave Dhik's side.

"I gave you a beating last time we met," Dhik said, pointing his 'boo at one of the three.

"Yeah?" the singled out guy answered. "Now I come t'give it back."

"There are three of us this time," the leader announced in case Dhik could not count. Being large, Dhik was often thought slow, both physically and mentally. It wasn't true, but Dhik found it useful to allow people to think so.

"Three?" he said. "Then it will take me fifty percent longer. No wait. Incitement to brawling carries a *two*-stroke penalty."

But when the three stepped forward, separating to attack from all sides and thus incidentally separating themselves from easy coordination, an astonishing thing happened. Almost every man in the wayhouse stood from the tables or away from the bar and faced the intruders.

"You three," Fanghsi announced. "We twenty-three."

The patrons of Arfwendsen's were no strangers to brawling and, sometimes, on encountering a fight upon their entrance, would join in without inquiring into the causes or the sides. Their readiness showed in their faces and stances.

One of the Maintenance thugs wagged a finger at Dhik. "You beat an Officer, and you'll pay for it."

"Lord Peng is handling that," Dhik told him.

"Peng!" The Leader sounded less sure of himself, but he could not lose face. He reared up. "Watch your back, you. You'll not always have a mob around you to save your pigstuff."

"I'll mention that to your widow."

When the Maintenance goons had gone, Dhik finally did say the words he had been dreading. "Drinks are on me."

And a great wave of thirst swept the wayhouse.

It irritated Jones beyond measure to instruct a man in the very job to which he himself had aspired. It was bad enough that Yves had wormed his way into Pedro's affections to be named Prince of *Whale* and the designated successor to the captaincy, but he had also convinced Pedro to reward Snowy Mountain for a feat of detection that had also belonged properly to Jones.

And now he was to be instructed as Officer of the Watch for no better reason than that Berylplume had convinced Pedro that the captain should take more active command. Hitherto, Pedro had been schooling Yves in the contemplation of the Flight Plan, which had at least kept the Prince decently out of sight. Now he had to learn about taking bearings and calculating the speed and position of the Tau, as well as the minutiae of launching swifties, coordinating with Higgs, computing the minor corrections to their trajectory, and the telemetry from the go-aheads received by Signals.

At least, Yves knew his tensors. Jones had satisfied himself on that score early on by running the Prince through some exercises. In fact, the Prince was well-versed in the math and could cast a poem as easily as his mentor.

"Is that the anomaly that spooked Skybones?" Yves asked.

The Visser Hoop on the Sky Ahead had been highlighted by a bright red ring-and-slash. Do not enter. Strictly speaking, Skybones had been spooked by *not* entering the ringularity, but Jones did not correct his future liege.

"Yes, now pay attention. When we take a fix, we select three slow-moving stars in the Deep Sky. It's bad enough that the Tau is screaming across the sky like a banshee, but we want greater stability in our benchmarks, and we choose different benchmarks now and again so we can cross-check our results."

"You know, Tongky. I'm not entirely stupid. I know the Tau's proper motion. I even know the Tau's apparent position is where it was ten years ago because light speed is finite. I even know the stars we use as benchmarks are where they were hundreds or even thousands of years ago, and that's why we pick sluggards. They won't perceptibly move in our lifetimes."

"I'm sorry, Yvesy. Have I given the impression I thought you were stupid? I don't think you are." *Sneaky and mendacious*, he thought, *but not stupid*. He did not give voice to the thought, however, as it was seldom a good career move to insult your future captain.

Yves turned to look at the Sky Behind. "Which one is Earth?"

You mean Sol, Jones thought. "Quartermaster!"

"Astrogator, aye!"

"Please highlight Sol on the Sky Behind at the request of Number Four."

"Highlighting Sol, aye."

Jones pointed. "There, in the constellation Boötes, southeast of that bright star, Arcturus."

Yves pondered the sight for a moment. "So that was our ancestors' home. I wonder why they flung us out here."

Jones glanced at him, then back at the sky map. "Why did the Imperials do anything? Because they could. There, south-by-west of Sol, that's Rigil Kentaurus. *Red Dwarf* was proceeding to its companion, Proxima. A better question might be: 'Why send a ship *there?*' Proxima is a flare star, dim, with a narrow goldilocks. I doubt they would've found a suitable world there. We got the prize. Of all the nearby stars, the Tau is most like Sol. Our destination, Vishnu, is likely to be a very suitable place for our descendants to settle."

"*Indiaman* and *Big River* are headed toward binaries?"

"Epsilon Indi has two brown dwarf binary companions at a considerable distance, but Epsilon Eridani is a solitary, though one less Sol-like."

"Well," said Yves with a shrug. "Not our problem. We only have to maintain constancy of purpose for the next eight hundred years. You think that likely? Already, officers and crew seem to regard who gets to be captain or how power will be divided among the Commanders or how much they get paid as more important than they do reaching the Tau and colonizing Vishnu."

Jones wondered if that was a sly insinuation against him. "That's not an astrogational question, I'm afraid."

Yves pointed to the sky. "Why are there no stars southwest of Sol?"

Jones started to say that they must be too dim to register on the sensors, but then he said, "Chartsman!"

"Astrogator, aye!"

"Can you give me a long-distance scan of that area?" He used his light wand to outline it.

"Long-distance scan, aye."

Yves shoved his hands into the pockets of his uniform jacket. "By the Bood!" he said. "That's another one, innit? Another Visser Hoop, I mean. The sky is full of holes."

Jimcas Nearwell leaned close to Megwan Masterson and whispered, "You understand why we can't fully trust you yet, for all that you call yourself 'Crewman Masterson.' It be the name, y'see. 'Masterson.'"

265

The underbutler was walking Megwan through the motions of inspecting the great water pump at Third and Forty-Second. He did not understand why the man whispered since the pump made enough noise to mask any nearby microphones.

Jimcas pointed to a valve, which Megwan knew to be the primary diverter valve, and Megwan nodded as if he was receiving instruction. Peng's eyes and ears were everywhere. "They want to see you *do* something," Jimcas said. "Nothing is cheaper than talk except a human life in Pigwhistle."

"Yes, but what do I need to *do*?"

Jimcas clapped him on the shoulder. "You'll think of something, my man."

Later, when Megwan cuddled with Ling-ling, his Woman had another slant on matters. "How do you know Nearwell is not an agent of Peng trying to coax you into mutiny and bring down House Masterson?" And he thereafter found sleep elusive.

At the goldcape facemeet, Organson contemplated the great shifting of personnel around the table. The go-captain himself chaired the meet. The engineer, Boronfuse, was the new X/O but did not seem to wield a mite of the might that Skybones had deployed. The Prince of *Whale* was introduced as Acting Fourth Officer but, despite the lower office, sounded now more confident.

Lord Signals ran through the routine telemetry from the go-aheads—eighty percent had achieved orbit around Vishnu, and half had already deposited their terraforming payloads, but when he made his expected report of "no other messages received," an air of gloom settled over the assembled goldcapes.

Why now and not before?

He listened to the chatter with more than his wonted interest. But all they talked about was some technobabble about a "second anomaly."

How many anomalies did there have to be, he wondered, before they ceased to be anomalous?

The captain entertained them with a poem concerning a meal of rice noodles.

"Hor fun absorbs the flavor
Through porous bands.
How eats one chǎo fěn *with a knife?"*

The riddle would seem trivial, but the goldcapes, especially the astrogators, received it as if it were a great insight.

"Can one slice a noodle without creating two noodles?" asked Jones, who had been raised in the meantime to full astrogator.

A wise observation indeed, thought Organson with more than a grain of sarcasm. But again, the others nodded and bobbed at its import. What in the *Whale* were they talking about? Surely not *chow fun!* A wave of *ektóvróchouphobia* swept over Organson. He hated to be out of the loop on anything.

Winsome Alabaster arrived early at Helix House so she would have time to prepare the soup for the evening meal. She was already arranging the ingredients in order when Two appeared at the hatchway from the residence.

"I done brought yuh a present," he said. "Searched fore and aft to find it, Were some old lady in Shenville grows it."

The package contained seeds. She looked her question at the blackbird.

"That be the true coriander. I knew you needed it for the sacred recipe, and I knew the Boss done let his supply run out, so I thought you could use that. Boss, he don't like it if'n the soup's off."

Winnie gestured at the grinder. "I'm using caraway seeds."

"Last person who tried got terminated."

Winnie laughed. "I'm his friend, not his employee. He can't terminate me."

"Don't be too sure what Lord Helix can or cannot do." Two snatched a sugar biscuit from the bakery table, dodging a ladle that the pastry chef swung, not too seriously, at his knuckles.

"What does that mean?"

"I've said too much," he said around a bite from the biscuit. "I took an oath to protect client confidentiality." He had to repeat himself because he had taken a big bite. "But you oughta know that you have more friends than you might think."

Later, she and the scullery maid brought the tureen to the dining hall in a cloud of savory aromas. Turmeric, chili, cinnamon tickled her nose. Dumont sat at the head of the table in his ornately carved wooden chair, scribbling on some papers.

She had the maid set the tureen on the table and ladled the red soup into two bowls, one for herself and one for Dumont. He had glanced up briefly at Winnie's entrance, but Two, standing beside him, placed another paper before him for his signature. Then, he picked up Dumont's spoon and tasted the soup. Lord Ramamurthy waited to see if he would drop dead.

When he did not, Dumont said, "Enough," and brushed the papers aside for Two to gather up off the floor. "The mulligatawny awaits its destiny." He beamed at Winnie.

It was only then that Winnie noticed Three standing at her side, ready to help her into her seat. With a start, she recognized him: DCI deSōuxún. She parted her lips in greeting. What was he doing in a blackbird uniform, anyway? But she caught the almost imperceptible toss of his head and remembered that Two had cautioned her that "you won't recognize him" was a command, not a prediction. So, all she said was. "Thank you, Three," and took her seat at the foot of the table, greatly puzzled.

This theater was lost on Dumont, who, if he recognized Bùxiè at all from their one brief meeting, gave no sign of it. Instead, he dipped his soupspoon into the mulligatawny and brought it to his lips. He slurped loudly, sucking in air along with the soup to enhance its flavor.

Then his brow furrowed, and he tossed the spoon down, splashing the tablecloth. "Caraway!" he said. "You used caraway in place of my mother's coriander!"

She had not. She had used the coriander that Two had given her. What was Dumont talking about? He stood and stalked to the foot of the table, where he loomed over her. She noticed then that while his words and tone bespoke anger, that anger did not reach his eyes, which were icy. Behind him, Two had rolled the papers into a tube.

Dumont wrapped his hands around her throat and bore down, cutting off her air. She could not draw a breath, and her vision blackened around the edges. This couldn't be happening! Dumont would not do this, not to her! But his hands were huge, and she could not breathe. She tried to say something. *Stop!* But the words could not struggle from her throat.

Suddenly, she was outside herself, floating in midair, watching her body writhe and pound its fists against Dumont's impervious bulk. It seemed to go on for a long time, but it was only instants before Bùxiè shouted "No!" and pulled him off of her.

Winnie snapped back into her body and pulled in a sharp and grateful breath. She coughed repeatedly and saw in her supervisor's eyes neither sorrow nor regret, nor even anger, but rather frustration.

Dumont turned to Bùxiè, "How dare you lay hands on me!" Two tapped him on the shoulder, saying, "Sah!" and Dumont turned to look at him.

Two placed his thumb over one end of the tube he had rolled from the papers and jammed the open end into Dumont's eye. Stiffened by the air column trapped within it, the paper tube might as well have been a rod. It pierced the cornea and vitreous humor.

Dumont shrieked, and his hands flew to his face. "My eye! My eye!"

And Winnie cried out, "No! You're hurting him!"

Bùxiè clapped his hand on Dumont's shoulder. "Lord Dumont Ramamurthy, I arrest you in the name of Ship Security for the attempted murder of Eugenist Second Class Winsome Alabaster and for the suspected murder of Senior Cook, Yufreni Dox. Additional charges may be filed pending further investigation."

Blackbird One burst into the dining hall with his teaser drawn and pulled up short as he took in the scene. Bùxiè had manacled Lord Ramamurthy, who continued to shriek about his eye. Winnie's wheezing, gasping breaths had collapsed into sobs. Two was trying desperately not to vomit. One holstered his teaser.

"Peng called," he said. "He wanted to know if it was done." He glanced at Dumont. "You let him live."

"It was Three's price for helping us,"

"Bu- bu- but I used the coriander. I did," Winnie insisted.

"Aye, ej'mā̱ni brother," Two responded. "But sometimes a man sees—or tastes—what he expects and not what is actually presented to his senses."

Winnie wrapped her arms around Bùxiè. "I was coming to love him," she said.

"Aye, ej'māṉi," said Two. "We all loved him, even One." One snorted derision. "Lord Dumont was good at that. He knew how to seduce."

"Was he born that way," wondered One, "or did he acquire the trait after killing his mother by accident?" He turned to Dumont.

"My eye!"

One shrugged. "We'll get nothing coherent from this one, not for a while. Well, let's find out what Lord Peng wants to do with him." And he and Two led Ramamurthy from the room.

"Would you like to sit down?" Bùxiè asked her.

She still could not wrap her mind around matters. She was half-way to seated—in the chair where Dumont had tried to strangle her!—and shot upright. "No. No, take me home. Are you allowed to do that? I mean, now that you've become a blackbird?"

"Actually, I'm in Peng's Criminal Investigations Division, not the Life Guards. This posting was my price for agreeing to the transfer. I wanted to be close enough to protect you."

"In case another dog jumped out at me from the dark."

"As one did."

23 DISRUPTIONS

A trigger warning—"What be da meaning o' dis bustle?"—In the dark—That can't be good—What the hell is going on?—A pair of eyes

Hidaki Thomason had lifted too many mugs of the Strangler, otherwise the midwit from the clinic would not have irritated him so, and the whole matter would have passed with no more than a friendly exchange of insults.

"All I'm saying," the medic repeated, "is that not all Officers are bad eggs."

The observation was true, but Hidaki had seen the images of Dhik getting a baton across the face and was in no mood to make concessions. "Most of them just lolling in they palaces," he retorted, "while the rest of us do all the work. Crewmen in a department should be picking their own Commanders."

"I would rather be ruled by an Officer lazing away up in his palace than by a score of work rivals living in my pockets."

So, Hidaki punched him.

271

That was all that was needed to start things going in Arfwendsen's Wayhouse. Shortly, the mayhem burst out into the pass'way like pus from a squeezed pimple.

Huyo Ghontzal left his quarters in Lower Black Jade to make his usual stroll to his duty station in the firehouse. Fire was rare in the *Whale*, but in a closed ecology, it was better to have firefighters and not need them than to need them and not have them. Meanwhile, he could polish and clean the equipment against the possibility, play *go* with his *compadres*, and extend his rack time until someone let their cooker run dry, and the buzzer rang to call them out.

But the pass'way outside his home was crowded with crewmen in an almighty rush.

"What be da meaning o' dis bustle?" he asked of the passing throng.

"We gone a th' brig!" one of them answered.

Ghontzal thought that was the usual destination for an unruly crowd. "Why you gone a dat brig?"

Someone else answered, his original respondent being now out of earshot. "They's a man," she said, "wot tried to strangle a crewman. We gone bust him out—*an' hang 'im!*"

Ghontzal scratched his beard. It sounded like good, clean fun, but if he punted his watch at the fire station, a mighty conflagration would surely engulf Lower Black Jade.

His duty station was to starboard, the direction in which the crowd was running, so he had no option but to run with them. He had read once of an ancient custom of his ancestors called "the running of bulls." The custom sounded especially invigorating and thereby especially stupid. But this crowd reminded him of the ancient video clips, and he found he had to jog to keep from being trampled. They began a-singing in a ragged unison.

> *"So, you Whalers; so, you brothers*
> *Bound as one to one another,*
> *No matter what your rank as crew.*
> *Everyone who sings this song*

The old ones and the very young
We'll make, yes, make a difference when we do."

And so it was that he was rounded up by the coppers at the next longitudinal intersection. When he tried to explain that he was just going to work, the constable hit him upside the head with his baton, after which all conversation ceased.

When the lights went out in Fu-lin's wayhouse, a great groan went up, and someone cried out, "Who didn't pay their electric bill?"

Another voice hollered, "Better lock the till, Fu!" Then there was a rustle as people fumbled for their jùggies. Those who had neglected to bring theirs added colorful oaths to the hubbub.

Organson grumbled, too, though for other reasons. Venables would never find him in the dark. He felt his way to the entrance and threw the hatch open, hoping to gather light from the pass'way, only to find that the outside lights were off, too.

Then someone said the B-word. "Hope this ain't another Burnout."

Bùxiè deSōuxún was enjoying an end-of-watch pastry and tea at a small café on Comm Central Plaza when a score of men in brown coveralls and wearing brightly colored scarves rushed the doors of the comm center. *That can't be good*, he thought. He contacted Peng over his MOBI, told him what he had seen, and sent him the video he had captured. "I don't think they were delivering advertising copy."

"Wait there," Peng replied. "Continue to observe and report."

Lord Thantos knew that the power grid was imperfect and that at some point, a transformer would blow, or a circuit would short, or some idiot would park something electronically opaque smack in the path of a power beam. And, of course, it took time to trace the malfunction, and more time to identify the component that had failed, and still more time to repair or replace it. Crewmen and even Officers oft failed to appreciate this.

"So, what does the Highsteeple Substation report?" he asked his MOBI. "Have them send out a line crew as soon as they identify the locus. How would I know what they need? They haven't diagnosed it yet. Acknowledge!" He pressed the connect button several times. "Nǐ hǎo? Hello? MOBI, my connection was lost."

But MOBI answered him not.

"What the devil is going on?" asked in-captain Rajalakshmi Ming-ti.

None of the Commanders she could reach and summon to Palace Mainouvertes could answer her, though some suggested the Brotherhood of the *Whale*.

"What the devil is going on?" asked Hamdu Organson, who had finally made his way to his office, where he found his advisors waiting for him.

"Sometimes," Venables said, "if one would lead a mass movement, one must hustle to get out in front of the masses."

"We not ready yet," said Baozhai

"What about the commando that seized Comm Central? They're hanging out to dry."

Baozhai shrugged her perfect shoulders. "Sometime sacrifice for premature action. With MOBI down, we cannot reach them to order them back."

Venables said, "I think it is Peng's doing."

"What the devil is going on?" asked Peng.

Blackbird Master Chief flipped his hands palms up. "No one seems to know. No one has been able to get through."

"What about the gang that deSōuxún saw rush into the Comm Center just before MOBI went down? Saboteurs, maybe?" Peng pondered the matter some more. "Get me my cloak," he decided. "No, the black one."

"What the devil is going on?" Bùxiè muttered, but since he sat alone at his observation post thinking how many hours in the dojo he would need to work off the pastries he had consumed, he could ask no one but himself and the waitress who kept him supplied with the pastries. He didn't expect the waitress to know, and she didn't.

"What the devil is going on?" asked Brig Master Chief Petty Officer Kemynder.

"Sah," replied the bo'sun's mate who had charge of gate security, "a large and unruly crowd has gathered at the main gate demanding entrance."

"Well, then, open the gate and show them to their cells. If only all our clients were so proactive! Next time, don't wear yourself out. Just call me over MOBI."

"Ah, sah," said the bo'sun's mate, "seems there's a problem with that."

"What the devil is going on?" Little Face asked, but he got no joy from MOBI. So, he hollered to the wayhouse at large.

Kunigund Arfwendsen answered. "MOBI down fer you, too? My daughter's a steward's mate *first* class, and her post is waitressing at a café on Comm Central Plaza. She said a bunch of strange men rushed into Comm Center."

"What happened then?"

"MOBI's down, ya ijjit. So how would I know? My daughter called just afore the crash. I bet you Peng got something to do with it."

Little Face thanked her. It would take more than a system crash to take down Kunigund Arfwendsen. Was today the Mutiny? He had not been notified.

"What the devil is going on?" Lt. Lutz complained. "I can't get through to anyone."

M/Sgt. Lollipop made a face. "Why complain to me? I don't got no special beamcast."

"How am I to know my duty? Where should I go?"

"I would say our first duty is to sit tight. It's probably a technical malfunction, and Fleet Marines would be no more help than a swabbie in a China shop."

For some little while, Bùxiè had become aware of a pair of eyes watching him. At first, he thought it was the waitress waiting for him to order another tea, but when he looked around, she was nowhere in sight, so he set himself to study his surroundings.

He checked the windows in the quarters across the Plaza from him, but the only people at them did not appear to be studying him especially. The men who had occupied Comm Central had come back out and thrown up barricades of furniture, which struck Bùxiè as ungood. But those manning the barricades did not seem to pay him any more attention than they did the other gawkers.

Less, because many in the crowd seemed to hold them, not unreasonably, responsible for MOBI being out of service. Some shouted abuse at the barricaders, and a few threw objects at them. That could go orlop mighty fast.

He finally located the eyes he had felt upon him and discovered that that was exactly what they were, a pair of eyes floating in the air. Green eyes. They were hard to make out against the background. He gathered his composure from wherever it had scurried.

"I can see your eyes, y'know," he told the disembodied oculars in what he hoped was an insouciant tone.

"The drawback of the cloak," said a voice, "is that by diverting light around itself so its wearer becomes effectively invisible, neither can the wearer see out. Hence, the eyeholes in the hood become necessary."

That Peng's voice answered was at once disturbing and a relief. A relief because it meant the floating eyes had a rational explanation; disturbing because it meant that Peng had capabilities previously unsuspected. Bùxiè wasn't sure how he felt about that and settled on "uneasy."

The eyes floated to a shadowed alcove, from which Peng emerged clad in a plain black cloak. He had thrown its hood back and settled into a seat opposite Bùxiè. His gesture to the barricade stood for the question.

"About fifteen minutes ago," Bùxiè reported, "two goods lorries arrived, one from starboard, one from port, and unloaded all those sandbags."

"They expect a teaser attack, then. Sand is non-conductive. Those are the lorries?"

"Yes. They were incorporated into the barricades."

Peng grunted. "They are aware the building has a rear entrance?"

Bùxiè made a helpless gesture. "I could not go back there to check without drawing attention to myself. But I assume they did not suddenly become stupid when they passed through the building."

"Don't be too sure, DCI deSōuxún. Many a crewman, upon entering Comm Central, has become stupid. Or don't you follow the news vendors?"

"What can I bring you, sah?" The waitress had found the table again.

Peng pointed to Bùxiè's plate. "I'll have what he's having."

When the waitress had vanished once more, Bùxiè asked, "Sah. What should we do?"

Peng smiled without humor. "The hardest task in the *Whale*. Absolutely nothing."

At that moment, his MOBI and Bùxiè's screeched and, from the echoing around the Plaza, so did everyone else's.

24 EXHORTATIONS

WHALERS ONE AND *WHALERS* ALL.

IN SHANG DI'S NAME AND OF OUR GENERATIONS DEAD AND GONE, *IMPERIAL SHIP WHALE* SUMMONS HER CHILDREN TO STRIKE FOR FREEDOM. HAVING ORGANIZED AND TRAINED THROUGH THE BROTHERHOOD OF THE *WHALE*, HAVING PATIENTLY PERFECTED HER DISCIPLINE, HAVING RESOLUTELY WAITED FOR THE RIGHT MOMENT TO REVEAL HERSELF, SHE NOW SEIZES THAT MOMENT. RELYING ON HER OWN STRENGTH, THE *WHALE* STRIKES IN FULL CONFIDENCE OF VICTORY.

THE TIME HAS COME TO THROW OFF THE SHACKLES OF DEGENERATE OFFICERS AND STAND UP FOR OUR RIGHTS AS CREWMEN OF THIS OUR NOBLE SHIP. FOR TOO LONG HAVE WE TRUCKLED, STEPPED ASIDE, DUCKED OUR HEADS, ENDURED THEIR PRODS AND SWATS.

WE HAVE CO-OPTED COMM CENTRAL SO THAT OUR MESSAGE WOULD NOT BE SUPPRESSED BY THEIR LYING

MINIONS, THE NEWS VENDORS. EVEN NOW, OUR COMPA-
DRES ARE OCCUPYING OTHER KEY CENTERS. SOON, THE
TYRANNICAL REIGN OF THE OFFICERS WILL BE ENDED!
THE *WHALE* AS SHE WAS!

Peng tossed his head. "Very derivative."

Captain Ming-ti laughed. " 'The time has come to throw off the
shackles of degenerate Officers' and submit to the shackles of a degenerate rabble!'"

Organson looked to Baozhai. "Have any other units occupied their
assigned targets?"

"None have reported. Should I tell them to move?"

Organson shook his head. "If they've mobilized, tell them to
stand down and if they have not tell them to stay put. What possessed
Li Son to occupy Comm Central and broadcast the Manifesto?"

"That crowd out front," said Brig Master Kemynder, "must be another of this Brotherhood's commandos. They're here to seize the Brig
like their compadres seized Comm Central."

"But why, sah?" said his staff sergeant, who chewed nervously on
a flavored turpene stick. "What possible benefit would they gain?"

"They must have a reason. The only thing we got are prisoners,
so that must be what they're here for. Why would they possibly
want them?"

"Maybe they only want them released?" The sergeant popped his
chewed up turp, a sound which irritated Kemynder to the edge.

"Who do we have?"

With MOBI up and running once more, the list came only an
eyeblink after the sergeant's thumbprint on the screen. "Twelve
drunks and disorderly, mostly from Little Lotus. A score of street
marchers rounded up in Lower Black Jade. An Excellent murder
suspect awaiting trial. Five assaults with intent ..."

"Why are they in my bin and not their local? Never mind. How many security guards are on watch?"

"Five, no six. But there must be a hundred madmen out there yammering." His sergeant hooked a thumb at the security screens.

"Why couldn't Peng have assigned more guards? Never mind. If wishes were carts, swabbies would ride. Release 'em all. If we got no one in here, the mob got no reason to break in."

"What about this Excellent? Attempted murder, suspicion of murder."

"Release him on his own recognizance. We've got his tracker ID, and he can't exactly leave town."

Lucky Lutz listened to the Manifesto to the end. She turned to Lollipop. "Any word of other mutinies?"

The Master Sergeant tossed his head. "A riot was reported at the Central Brig, but that's all."

"Tell the Commandant to send the Third Platoon over there and calm things down. It'll be good training for them. We'll take First and Second over to Comm Central and stop this nonsense."

"You giving orders to the Commandant, now?"

"No, Master Sergeant. You are."

25 MUTINIES

Hamdu is a big boy—Lifted out of the press—What is the difference between a surgeon's scalpel and a sledgehammer?—"Hit the deck!"

Baozhai thought Florian Venables very much an old fuddy-duddy, or at least as something that might translate as "fuddy-duddy." Perhaps something stronger. Privately, she had named him Lǎo dàjīngxiǎoguài, which meant something like "elder who fusses over nothing" in the Běifāngwóng wá. But the Excellent Hamdu Organson set much store by the man's advice, and so she put up with his nattering.

Venables, for his part, thought Baozhai was a talking doll with little effect in her voice and manners. Though perhaps he ought to have studied the portrayals of talking dolls in the historical literature. It is not a comforting trope.

"The burden of the Remembered Past," he opined, "grows more burdensome the more past has passed, until finally, one must lay down the load or be broken by his remembrances." He then imagined pulling a string on the doll and waiting for her prepackaged response.

But Baozhai's response—*how jejune*—was not what she voiced, saying instead, "Do you think he will be safe?"

Venables' face crinkled irritation at the derailing of his discourse. "I don't see why not. No one knows he is Big Blue, save our inner circle. Certainly, neither Li Son nor his platoon know."

"But he's an Officer, and the Brotherhood has been agitating against Officers. Going to the Comm Center ..."

"He has to find out what's going on. Hamdu is a big boy. He can take care of himself."

Ling-ling found herself jostled and shoved in the crowd facing the barricade. She clung to Megsy's hand so they would not be separated. Why had he thought it a good idea to come aft to Comm Plaza? They could have stayed safely at Undine Palace or, better still, at Zephyrholm.

"Why are they so angry?" she asked her Man. She could see, between the pushing, shoving, shouting crewmen, that a similar crowd had gathered at the starboard end of the Plaza, where the Brotherhood had thrown up another barricade. Such nice furniture, too, now carelessly tossed in a heap. Oh, the scratches and chips that must be marring such lovely pieces!

"When the Brotherhood shut down the links," Megwan explained, "crewmen missed some of their favorite morning streams, especially the newsertainment shows. That's why they need the Brotherhood. Most crewmen can't see past their own immediate nose, so the Brotherhood must be their vanguard and lead them. Oof!"

Somebody had shoved Megwan from behind, and Ling-ling almost lost her grip on his hand. She wondered if the crowd on the other side was less unruly or at least less smelly. She regretted leaving her scented facemask behind, but Megsy was probably right. She did not want to appear Excellent in this mob!

Another push, and she and her Man were separated. "Megsy!" she cried as the swirl of humanity pulled them apart. "Megsy!"

She stumbled and nearly fell, adding to her fears that of being trampled. She cried out a third time, though she could not form Megsy's name, and only a high-pitched "Eeee!" came forth.

Then, rough arms gripped her, and, though she twisted and kicked against them, they lifted her and then set her down again, and she was suddenly free of the jostling press. A line of grim men in colored scarves stood to either side of her. She spun wildly. She was out of the crowd but inside the barricade.

"Megwan!"

"I'm here, Ling!"

She nearly collapsed, so great was her relief, and they fell into each other's arms.

A grizzled man with white sideburns and a saffron-white-and-green scarf said, "What were you kids doing out there? You coulda got stomped."

Megwan drew himself up. "I'm fourteen, a grown man, and my Woman is twelve, a grown woman. We heard that the Mutiny had broken out here, and we came to offer our services."

The man—he seemed to be a leader of some kind—had large, milk chocolate eyes, and he looked them over for a moment in silence. "Can you handle a teaser, young man?"

"I was a junior cadet!"

The man opened his mouth and seemed about to say something but shut it again. "Enforcers will be showing up soon, and I don't think even junior cadets can handle a two-hundred-pound Enforcer."

"We can collect snacks and drinks inside the building and bring them out to the Brothers."

Finally, the man surrendered and held out his hand. "I'm Lieutenant Li Son, commanding. You haven't heard of other Risings, have you?"

Megwan shook his head and said, "There was a power outage in Highsteeple and some sort of protest at the Brig. That's all."

"We thought the power outage meant ... well, never mind. Try and stay indoors as much as possible. This is not a game. When the Enforcers come, tell them you were trapped inside the building when we occupied it. Understand?"

Megwan and Ling-ling nodded and set off on their errand of mercy. The woman at the concession stand wanted fifty percent over the posted price. "Supply and demand, sweeties. Once these treats are gone, when—if ever—will I get more? I stayed at my post when others left because I couldn't leave my treats unguarded."

Instead of paying the exorbitant prices, Megwan led Ling-ling on a search for self-vending machines. They found the machines close to the front to be intact, while those nearer to the rear were smashed and looted. Ling-ling suspected the third group of men, barricaded at the back door, of robbing the machines.

But Megwan had a pay-card and filled a tray box with kolu-kattai, Chettinad paniyaram, pretzels, cream wafers, murqan-style jogjip "cookies," and deep-fried thin potato slices. They made several trips like this, and Brothers requested favorite snacks or candies until Ling-ling appreciated what the concessionaire had meant by supply and demand.

The day was waxing hot, and Li Son and his men were shouting to one another. Apparently, some were having second thoughts. "If'n no other platoons have acted," said one man. "we'll be facing mighty long odds."

"Hold fast and wait for orders," said Li Son. "Big Blue won't forsake us."

Ling-ling and Megs filled three tubs with drinking water and hung ladles on their sides. They trundled to spots midway along each barricade so the men could take quick water breaks. The third tub, they placed in the center of the Plaza, atop the manplate there.

Lt. Li Son dipped his scarf into the tub and wiped his face down. "Why here?"

Megwan answered him. "In case any attackers are hydro techs. They can scuttle through the water tunnels and pop up right in our middle."

Li Son eyed the hatch. "One man at a time," he said. "Appreciate the thought, kid, but we could handle it."

"He's no 'kid,'" Ling-ling told him.

"One man with a flash-bang," Megwan said. "A strike from the water tunnel needn't be overwhelming; it just needs to disrupt our defenses."

Li Son turned thoughtful. "Good thinking, ki—I mean, Brother." He continued to mop his face. "Pretty sure Lord Thantos upped the heat in this sector."

"We could search the Center for portable fans, blow the hot air off us."

Li Son turned back toward the barricade. "Nah. What sort of wussy mutineers would we be if we couldn't take a little heat."

On their fifth visit bringing snacks to the men, Megwan nearly dropped the tray-pack. "Lieutenant?" he called. "A-hoigh to starboard. They're coming."

But it wasn't Enforcers.

Peng saw the lorries pull up in a screech of rollers. "Uh-oh," he said to Bùxiè. "Trouble." He opened his MOBI and said in small, intense syllables. "Ship Security. Teams One and Two stand down and disperse. Team Three continue infiltration."

A half dozen men, scattered among the crowd at the barricades, slipped away and departed the Plaza.

The Imperial Fleet Marines had arrived.

"Tell me, DCI deSōuxún, what is the difference between a surgeon's scalpel and a sledgehammer?" Bùxiè had just returned with two mugs of lager from the stoobie next to the café. He glanced at the departing blackbirds in mufti, then at the Marines disembarking from the lorries, who formed a line facing the barricade.

The deployment attracted the attention of the crowd, which began themselves to disperse. Between the Marines and the barricade was not a very enticing place in which to loiter.

"One is blunt," Bùxiè guessed, "and the other is sharp."

"You can't do brain surgery with a sledgehammer."

Bùxiè mulled that over. "Actually, I think you can. It just wouldn't be very precise brain surgery. Should we leave now, sah?"

Peng took a mug from the agent's hand. "Certainly not. I have not yet begun to drink. And this is the best seat at the venue. Or could be." Several of the dispersing crowd must have had the same idea, for they eddied and settled in front of the table at which Peng and deSōuxún sat. They chattered and nudged one another with their elbows and exchanged mutual exclamations of their ignorance. Peng cleared his throat. "Excuse me, gentlemen. You are blocking our view."

One husky female turned and said, "Tough nuts, honey-buns."

Peng had never allowed his picture to circulate, so she did not recognize him, but there was something implacable in his eyes that gave her pause. She swatted her friends backhanded and said, "Step aside, Gormy, Stachy. Show a li'l courtesy, wouldja?"

As a space opened up, Peng turned to Bùxiè once more and said, "This should be entertaining."

"Or, at least, instructive." He had noticed several Marines in the second line carrying unfamiliar weapons.

Lucky Lutz was gratified to see that even the recruities had learned how to deploy from lorries into line. They cocked their arms on their hips to get their spacing and kept their hands away from their teasers. First Squad deployed on the right, Second, on the left. She placed the first guns in the first line with the second guns and third guns backing them up. One Marine had deployed with the wrong squad, and shamefacedly trotted to the other part of the line while Lollipop growled comments on his ancestry, his upbringing, and his personal hygiene.

Some fool among the mutineers let loose with his teaser, but Lucky had carefully lined them up several paces beyond teaser range. In the weeks since Goliad's Retreat, she had replenished the ranks of First Platoon and trained them. She had expected to be sent on a punitive expedition into the Burnout, not a reprise of Hanging Bridge, but if the niyōs were to get a baptism of fire, better to get sprinkled by the Brotherhood than dunked by the savages.

"Sah," said Kent. "The line is ready." At a barked command, they presented their riot shields. Thix armor draped with dispersal mail … just in case. The grunts were, in part, a tribute to shield weight, but they could rest them on the deck, and the grunts also served to intimidate. Now they could inch forward into teaser range. Damn, but she wished she had had the shields at Hanging Bridge.

Lucky hoped she looked more confident than she felt. Act the part well enough, she told herself, and you became the part. "Gunny Ku."

"Aye, lieutenant?"

"No itchy fingers in Special Weapons."

"No itchy fingers, sah."

Lutz looked at the other sergeants. Everyone thinks they're ready until you ask them. That's when they get second thoughts and make bonehead mistakes, like Rosecrans at Chickamauga. Poor old Rosie had been one of the best generals his side had had, but he had taken his finger off the dime for an instant, and everything went to the orlop on him.

Readiness was also why she had a First Sergeant and why that First Sergeant was still Lollipop. No point in *both* the lieutenant and the First being niyōs. She summoned her Squad commanders—Kent, Te, and Ku—as well as her Staff Sergeant Fishaven.

"The Commandant," she reminded them, "told us to give them the chance to surrender. So, have your people prepared to cover me."

"Remember Lieutenant Dingbang," said Kent.

Lucky nodded. "I'll stay out of range. But this is why they pay me the big credits. Just remember. These aren't Dwellers, and that means someday we've all got to live together again. It helps if we haven't piled atrocities on their asses." She stepped forward, and many in the watching crowd must have recognized her, for she heard her name amidst the murmuring.

That was the problem with having a reputation. At some time, you stopped bearing it, and it began bearing you. Yet, all she had done was pull Dingbang's nuts out of the fire, and the poor fellow was not even around anymore to resent it. She wished she were wearing a top hat so she could pull a rabbit out of it.

"Who's in charge there?" she called in her best parade-ground voice.

"I am," replied a high and reedy voice.

"My name is—."

"I know who you are."

"Which puts you at an advantage over me."

A voice in her ear whispered, "He has no locator chip, and his mask foils Facemaker."

"Thank you, Fishaven," she replied. At least she was not facing Reginald Chan. "We've come to collect our stolen equipment, sah."

"Do you really think we went to all this trouble just to hand in our teasers?"

Lucky sighed. "You've had your chance."

"We mean to have a Mutiny, so let it start here."

She flashed a sad smile. The rebel commander must be a schoolteacher. She replied, "We mean to *stop* a Mutiny, so let it end here." She turned smartly about-face and shouted, "Kent! Advance the line!"

"Advance the line, aye!" The Marines began to chant their haka with Fishaven's booming bass calling the measure. Each time they came to a HAH, they pushed their riot shields a step forward.

Li Son stared in dismay at the implacably advancing lines. "What do we do now?"

He had intended the question rhetorically, so he was surprised when a cracking voice squeaked at his elbow, "Dump the drinking water over the barricade."

Li Son looked at Crewman Masterson. "You think they'll quit because their feet get wet?"

"No. I think they'll step in the puddle."

Comprehension dawned, and Li Son and Private Gundermanu lifted the tub by its two handles and tipped it over the lip of the barricade. The water splashed to the deck and spread.

"What the hell," said Bùxiè, watching from the sidelines.

At first, Lucky thought the mutineers were dumping boiling oil on their attackers, but if so, they ought to have waited until the battle line was closer. She watched the rivulets meander and spread. She watched her Marines step into the puddle. She understood.

"Marines! Retreat to dry deck! Do not stand in the water!"

Most of the line stepped back, but some watched in bemusement as the water ran around the souls of their boots. Those who twigged dropped their shields and turned to run.

Just as the mutineers fired their teasers at the water puddle— which *was* well within their range—and the water carried the charges to the Marines—who were not. Several Marines jerked. They all wore dispersal mail—Lucky had seen to that—but no one wore mail on the soles of their boots.

Three. Four. Five Marines were down, spasming in the electric current as the mutineers continued to fire their charges. Their squaddies tried to pull them out only to learn the nature of connectivity. Seven down, No, eight.

But the mutineers had no fire discipline. They had not held some teasers in reserve while others recharged but had "poured it on," and now all that came from their barricades was the hum of recharging.

Unless they were waiting for other Marines to splash forward.

What the hell. Lucky ran forward, grabbed a fallen Marine, and dragged him back to safety. She heard a few snaps as mutineers fired prematurely. Other Marines, seeing this, also came forward to pull their compadres from the puddle.

Lucky fell to considering. It seemed the enemy commander was a smarter cookie than she had thought. If you don't have the range, alter the range.

Two can play at that.

"Ku! That barricade is in my way. Remove it, please."

"Aye, sah! Special Weapons, step for'ard. Set semi-auto, and aim at the base of the barricade. Try not to hit any of the mutineers."

Thunder rolled across the Plaza as the coil guns opened up. A cloud of flechettes smacked the furniture forming the barricade, striking off splinters from chairs, tables, desks, even the lorry. Shredded sandbags spilled their contents onto the deck.

And by shredding the lower courses of the barricade, her coil guns had undermined the whole façade. It teetered, and holes opened up.

"Merde!" said Peng. "What are those things!" But Bùxiè shrugged helplessly; he had thought being a spectator might be educational and had not been disappointed. The crowds that had lined the Plaza margins evaporated, their fleeing screams echoed off Comm Center.

"Damme," said Li Son. "Hit the deck!" He turned, saw Megwan behind him, and, placing a hand on the young man's head, pushed him prone. He glimpsed his Woman—the men had called her the Angel of the Barricades—running into the Center. Half a dozen freedom fighters had toppled from the firing step, holding their feet or ankles where missiles had broken through the barricade and smashed them. Li Son beckoned to the men at the portside barricade, which was not under attack. "Second squad. Odd numbers. To starboard."

A projectile ricocheted off the deck and buried itself in Corporal Chowdary's abdomen. Li Son gritted his teeth. He wanted to stop his ears against the thunder of these weapons, and other freedom fighters were cowering behind the barricade, but one of the penalties of being thrust into a leadership role was that the leader was not allowed to show his own terror.

Private Jensen peered out through the loophole in the barricade. Then he fell back with a dart in his face. The problem with loopholes was that a hole worked both ways.

He would be lucky if half his men dared expose themselves to fire back. Their teasers were recharged now, but the Marines with the strange weapons stayed resolutely beyond the puddle. His men had envisioned standing safely behind their barricade and firing through the loopholes. But "he that would lose his life the same would save it." Cowering was no guarantee of safety. Quite the contrary. Only by hazarding it all could one hope to pass through safely to the other side.

A quick duck of the head showed him one of the gunners and his terror weapon had stepped into the puddle. Another quick bob, and he fired his teaser.

The charge passed through the water and jolted the gunner, whose hand spasmed, on the firing button. As he fell, his weapon continued firing, and some of the projectiles took down his own compadres. Li Son smiled.

A wave of shouts arose from the barricade behind him, and Li Son turned in time to see a wave of Marines overwhelm the half-squad remaining on the portside. Lucky Lutz was a clever putz. She'd had a second platoon in reserve and, when the Brotherhood's attention was firmly fixed on the fight to starboard, had unleashed her reserves into his rear.

The other commandos had been supposed to tie down any extra troops, but it had now become quite clear that no other risings had taken place. He called the third squad, manning the staircase at the rear of the building, but was not surprised when he received no answer.

Ling-ling, who had sheltered in the confectionaries' booth and cowered now with the older woman, watched the play unfold.

A voice filtered through from outside. "Surrender, you mutineers, in the captain's high name."

"We don't surrender to Peng's Poodles. Ya wanna try charging up a flight of stairs?"

The booth attendant nudged Ling-ling with a package of cream wafers. "Not like inventory gonna matter much now," she said.

Ling-ling tore the wrapper off, realizing suddenly how hungry she was. All morning, she had toted snacks for the Brothers and never once snagged one for herself. Thus, her mouth was stuffed when the overhead panels quietly shifted aside, and half a dozen ropes snaked out of them. Blackbirds slid down the ropes in eerie silence. No one at the barricade saw or heard. They were too busy insulting the blackbirds in front of them.

Ling-ling swallowed and sucked in her breath to warn them, but the woman with her clapped a hand over her mouth. "What do we owe the likes of them?" she said.

And by then it was too late. "Why would we charge up a flight of stairs," said one blackbird, "when we can wriggle through the air ducts?"

The unexpected voice behind them threw the Brothers into consternation. The teasers that the blackbirds held on them threw them into silence. They glanced one to another. "*You gonna fight or what?*" But no one wanted to be the only idjit to fire, so the answer was "or what," and one by one, they dropped their weapons and linked their hands behind their necks

Ling-ling was near weeping at the ignominious end to their brave stand, but the woman she had sheltered with growled, "Serves 'em right."

When he saw the Brothers who had been manning the staircase on the other side of Comm Center herded out by blackbirds, Lo Sin knew it was time to surrender. He had been well and truly boxed. He pulled out his white scarf and flapped it, crying, "Cease fire! Cease fire!"

The thunder rolled away as if into the distance, leaving the moans of the wounded in its ebb. He could hear Lutz shouting for medics.

It was only then that he noticed the dart in his shoulder. For a moment, he wondered why he had not been shredded, then realized that sometime during the battle the Marines had changed projectiles. It was an anesthetic dart. The Plaza began spinning as the drug fought the adrenaline in his body.

"C'mon, kid," he said to the still prone Masterson. "Time to play your role as hostage."

But when he rolled the lad over, he saw that one of the earlier projectiles had skittered across the deck through a hole in the barricade and shattered the boy's skull. Brains and blood had spattered all about him.

He had been very sensitive about his age, but he was an old man now, for he would never grow any older. *I should not have made him lie prone,* Li Son chastised himself.

Foul liquids rose in his throat, and the Plaza dimmed. The last thing he heard before he passed out was a high-pitched wordless scream wrenched from the throat of Ling-ling Barnstable.

26   AFTERMATHS (II)

Her tactics had succeeded—"What is *he* doing here?"—No words would come—The scalpel and the sledge—"He's very good at that."

Lucky Lutz found that her luck had held. The pincer movement had very nearly worked as planned, although she thought the rebels would have surrendered even without Second Platoon swooping in as they had. Still, it was good for the Second to have been blooded. She could console herself with the thought that casualties had been light, especially when compared to the storied battles of Old Earth—Verdun, Boise, The Pass of Jelep La. But then, they had fielded massive armies on an entire planet. The mutineers seem to have modeled their tactics on the Easter Rising in Ireland— which was foolish, for the Rising had failed—or on Philip Habib's Seizure of Paris, which had at least succeeded. Both had employed multiple commandos occupying multiple strongpoints in their respective cities.

"I don't think this was coordinated," she told Lollipop. "I think this crew here jumped the gun."

"I try not to think on that kind of crap," her Acting First commented. "Too much to do with the crap right in front of us. Our job was to take down the barricade, not worry whether other barricades were being built somewhere else."

All well and good, thought Lucky. Unless the first barricade had proven a diversion meant to draw her attention, as she had drawn the mutineers' attention to one barricade and away from the other.

But the boy bothered her. How depraved were the mutineers that they pressed young boys into their ranks? Later, when the medics had identified the corpse, she grew even more uneasy. *What in the name of the Whale had Lord Hydro been doing here?*

"What is he doing here?" Peng asked.

"Maybe the mutineers took him and his Woman as hostages," Bùxiè answered. "They thought they could bargain themselves out of the hole they'd dug themselves into."

"No," said Peng. "I meant *him*." He pointed across the Plaza to a tall man in a blue cape. Bùxiè had seen him before, but his name did not come immediately. The capewalker strode among the witnesses, prisoners, and Marines, pausing now and then to pass a few words with one or another. On some, he laid a comforting hand.

"He really does like to keep up on all the gossip," Peng continued. "Probably because he has no real duties of his own."

"Idle hands are the devas' tools."

"Eh? What's that?"

"Nothing, an ancient folk saying. Oh, wait! He was at my Woman's memorial," Bùxiè suddenly remembered. "The Excellent Hamdu Organson, right? He delivered one of the eulogies."

"Did he?" Peng seemed intrigued. "That seems unlike him. What did he have to say about a woman he did not know?"

Bùxiè gathered up the empty beer glasses. They did not belong at the tea shop, and he saw no reason to burden the waitress with the duty of returning them. "I don't remember," he admitted. "I was still encased in my own misery, and nothing outside that bubble could touch me. Oh. He lauded her fellow-feeling in joining the protest at Undine Place."

Peng studied Organson with renewed interest. "Did he? Strange."

Bùxiè remembered too that Lord Hydro also had come to the memorial and offered his own clumsy condolences. He had blown the young man off, and now that the time for apologies was irretrievably gone, regretted having done so.

Ling-ling Barnstable could find no words for the pain in her heart, and therefore, no words made their way to her lips. She cried like a baby when she saw her Man's shattered skull; she cried like a baby when they placed his body in a bag. She cried like a baby when the lorry took him off to Recycling. Yet, what baby had ever experienced such a loss as hers?

The namelessness was a void that could never be filled. The Plaza was blurred; the figures moving about on it were strange, impressionistic streaks. A rinse poured down upon her as if the very overhead had joined her tears. Swabbies had come and were dutifully washing up the remnants of the fight, including the last gory remnants of her Man, reduced now to a mere stain on the deck. There would never be anything more of him, not even within her womb. He was gone and had left not a trace of himself behind.

Someone draped an arm across her shoulders. But it wasn't *his* arm, and she shrugged it off. Her tears blended with the tears of the overhead sprinklers until she felt as if she were drowning in the Great Pond in Greenfields. She looked here, there, down, up, searching for the light so that she could swim toward it. A waterproof cape was thrown over her head, and the cleansing rinse was replaced by an endless spattering of drops as if she were a drumhead. Her hair, wet and sticky, clung to her neck, chilling her. Her hand was taken, and she was raised to her feet and led from the Plaza onto a waiting cart.

A time then passed in rocking and bouncing until she found herself once more in Zephyrholm, in the rooms of her childhood. It seemed obscene. These rooms had been once a place of a child's happiness, but she would nevermore be a child and nevermore be happy.

Sophie Water Masterson did find words when she received the news, though they were few and inarticulate. "No!" she cried as she dashed pointlessly from room to room within Undine Palace. "It can't be! Oh, my boy. Oh, my beautiful baby boy!" Her Man, the Excellent Jobe Consort Deng, could scarce keep up, let alone catch and console her. Instead, he rushed uselessly in her wake, his own heart cracking the while. Megwan had been *his* son, too.

"Behold the scalpel," said Peng as his blackbirds flocked to him. Bùxiè searched their faces, but none were known to him. "They took the third position at the staircase in the rear of the building. The great Lieutenant Lutz was not such an idiot as to mount an attack up a flight of stairs, but the mutineers could not leave it unguarded."

Bùxiè said, "I heard no sound of fighting from back there."

Peng smiled. "That is what you must expect to hear when my men fight." He thanked his blackbirds, who departed then by various means, no longer flocking. Only three of them lingered. "What sound does a scalpel make when it performs its appointed task? Surely not the same sound a sledge makes." He waved a hand toward the Marines, who, having shackled their prisoners, were stowing their equipment aboard the lorries. Peng explained the tactic the blackbirds had employed and looked pleased with himself.

But Bùxiè could not see how the same tactic would have worked on the Plaza itself. There was a time and place for scalpels and a time and place for sledges.

"I have an assignment for you, DCI deSōuxún. Ship Security is taking custody of the prisoners, and you will conduct them to the Brig."

Bùxiè swallowed. "Sah, there are a score of prisoners and only one of me. What if they decide along the way to unsurrender?"

Peng introduced the three blackbirds who had remained behind. "Meet Blackbird One deSōuxún, Blackbird Two deSōuxún, and Blackbird Three deSōuxún. All of them are temporarily seconded to you for the task. You will all be armed, and the prisoners will be shackled. Do you have any more concerns?"

Bùxiè sensed that he was being tested in some manner. Should he ask for more blackbirds to show careful analysis of risks? Should he perhaps request fewer to show he had matters well in hand?

He turned to his One and said, "Go and get a receipt from Lutz for the prisoners, then cover the rear of the group. Two and Three, you will take the flanks. Keep the injured and the stragglers in line. Or do we get a lorry, sah? Sah?" But when he turned back to Peng, the Commander had vanished. That meant they would walk to the Brig.

"No worries, Chief Inspector," said One. "There will be more of us than you think. MOBI has featured Ship Security in enough dramatic presentations that the prisoners will multiply our numbers in their imaginations. They will see blackbirds in every shadow, at every intersection." A moment later, he added, "All hyperbole, of course."

The Brig was guarded by a squad of Marines from the newly raised Third Platoon. Bùxiè turned his prisoners over to Brigmaster Kemynder and exchanged receipts with him. Bùxiè hooked a thumb at the Marines and let that serve as a question.

"Ach," said Kemynder. "They was a bit o' ruckus here earlier. Mob come up from the aft frames and demanded one of my prisoners what they come here to lynch. We thought a first they was mutineers like this bunch." His staff sergeants and their corporals were processing Bùxiè's prisoners through the gate.

"Must be getting crowded in there," Bùxiè remarked.

"Nah. Cells held a bunch of drunk and disorderly from Little Lotus, a couple B&Es, a forger, ... oh, and even an Excellent suspected of attempted murder. He's the one the mob come for."

"More than suspected," Bùxiè told him. "I nabbed him in the act."

Kemynder pursed his lips and looked down to his left. "That's not the way he told it,"

"Why, what did he say?"

"That you were mistaken in what you saw. Peng ..." He glanced at the blackbirds, wet his lips, and continued, "Peng has some sort of grudge against him. He were very persuasive, sah."

Bùxiè scowled. "Well, that is for the courts to decide, not his jailor or arresting officer."

Kemynder relaxed visibly. "That 'twill be, sah. That 'twill be." As Bùxiè turned away, he added, "He surely convinced the mob that were here."

Bùxiè turned back. "What's that you say?"

" 'Twere him the mob come to lynch. Did I not say that? But he talked 'em smooth, he did. Told 'em what I just done toldja. Mobs be fickle, and it flipped from wantin' to rip 'im to shreds to weepin' over the injustice Peng had done 'im. Understand, Deadly Ones," he added to the blackbirds, "Only reportin' what he said, not agreein' necessarily."

Bùxiè spoke through gritted teeth, "Where is he now? Tell me he's back in his cell."

"An' my staff an' me saw that honkin' mob banging on our gates, we released all the prisoners with bench warrants. The Excellent demanded to address them, which we thought real ballsy, seein' as they come to kill 'im. He's a silver tongue in his head, no denyin'. At the end, he walked right through 'em, an' they slapping him on the shoulders and wishin' 'im good luck at his trial."

Bùxiè seized the Brigmaster by the blouse. "*Tell me you're tracking him.*"

Kemynder freed himself. "Course we are. Staff Harriman, where be the Excellent?"

The petty officer spoke into his microphone, listened to MOBI for a moment, and said, "Taking the tubes aft, sah."

Three interrupted, "Sah, I've just received an on-call request from my client. Permission to re-deploy?" Bùxiè fluttered his fingers at him, mimicking a bird in flight. He turned to One. "Peng will want to know."

"Already informed, sah." He stowed his MOBI. "Tube drop is this way, sah. Not too far from here."

"He's a very dangerous man," Bùxiè told his blackbirds. "Take care when we approach him."

"Charmin' an' well-spoken, he was," said Kemynder.

Bùxiè gave him the squint-eye. "Yes, he's very good at that."

When Dhik escorted Peta into the *Glowering Tiger*, heads turned. Dhik thought their eyes drawn by the remarkable woman attached to his arm. "Are you certain you can afford this?" he asked her once more.

"Yes," she answered once more.

"Because you know I've been suspended without pay for two weeks."

Peta let out a soft laugh. "Don't worry about it. This is my treat. Here's our table."

When they had been seated and were consulting the menu screens, she added, "Two weeks seem a remarkably light sentence for striking an Officer."

"It is. If *I* had caught me at it, I wouldn't be sitting for a month, no matter how soft the cushions. But Peng is a notional creature. Maybe he wanted to show Lord Kennett his place in the grand scheme of the *Whale*. Maybe he didn't like one of his Enforcers being batoned. Bood! I can't even read this menu! What language is it in? 'Le tigre de zibeline.' And why are there no prices?"

"Forget it, dear. If you have to ask, you cannot afford it. It's an Old Earth lingo, only used in high-end restaurants, where they prefer their customers not to realize it's just meatstuff from Pigwhistle."

Dhik shuffled a little on his chair, wondering what to do with his hands and feet.

Peta solved one problem for him by ordering for him. *Poitrine de poulet au four a la Russe.* He was no wiser after she ordered than before.

It proved on arrival to be a slab of henstuff baked in sour cream, mushrooms, paprika, and sundry spices.

"It's all in the sauce, you know," she told him.

He did not know, but she had ordered the same meal for herself, and he set himself to study how she conducted the orchestra of knives, forks, and spoons that escorted the plates. Why were there so many forks? Surely, one was sufficient for the task.

It was too fussy and elaborate, but Dhik went along with the gag. The *poitrine* was, in fact, tasty, and he began to enjoy the meal, chatting pleasantly with Peta about everything in the *Whale*, save the Mutiny.

They must have been the only people in the Tiger who were not nattering about the Manifesto and the combat that followed at Comm Center. Dhik had thought the former needlessly bombastic and self-important and the latter needless, full stop. What Peta thought of it, he knew not, for he never broached the subject with her. Instead, he learned that while she had no talent herself in flower arrangement, she enjoyed viewing the arrangements of others. She did have some talent in pencil sketches, which she used sometimes in her autopsies.

"They can be more revealing than MOBI images," she explained, "because they can highlight features otherwise difficult to make out."

Of course, her art would never grace the screens at the Cetean Museum. Her sketches were much too repulsive to be popular. Or at least Dhik hoped so. But the abnormalities of dead bodies were her fondest avocation, and she could speak endlessly about swollen livers or extra coronary arteries. This bothered Dhik not in the least since he allowed the words to wash through him while he enjoyed the music of her voice.

Diners at neighboring tables, if they had been listening, might have been "put off their feed" by her conversation, but the only snatch he caught was an irrelevant reference to an ancient fable, "Beauty and the Beast."

Evenings, however enchanting they may be, must come at last to an end. So, after the last post-prandial wine had been drunk, he bundled Peta up and escorted her from the restaurant. Outside, he scanned the pass'way for signs of a public cart-for-hire, but none were in sight.

"Don't worry," Peta said. "One will come along soon."

"I'd like to thank you for the dinner."

"You'd *like* to thank me, or you *do* thank me? Never mind. Wipe that puzzled look off you face. You look like a mine shaving about to peel off. The price of a dinner at the *Glowering Tiger* was the least repayment I could make for saving my life in the Burnout."

"I toldja, I didn't—"

"Of course, you did. You didn't see things from my side. I know when my life has been saved and by whom."

Dhik gave it up. He would never convince Peta that he was not her hero, however unheroic he felt. But she was the first person, other than perhaps Little Face, who had ever treated him as a friend. And he did not feel about Little Face as he felt about Petronella Patterson.

The sun panels had dimmed from eventide to night. Only the "night lights," which were supposed to simulate "streetlamps," cast their jagged shadows. Three figures stepped from alcoves to the left and right as well as directly across Tiger Pass.' Dhik heaved a weary sigh.

"You guys never give up, do you?"

The man across the street snickered. "What sort of Erinys would we be if we did?"

The remark sailed right past Dhik's left ear but did elicit a surprised laugh from Peta. "What manner of vengeful Furies do you attract, dear?"

"The matter's settled," he told the trio. "I'm on two weeks unpaid leave because of it. Lord Kennett chopped his agreement with Lord Peng. Peng agreed to punish me, and Kennett agreed to Lady Purser's ruling that his 'tax' was contrary to Regulations."

The spokesman across the passageway scoffed. "We didn't sign no Concordat."

"Your Commander did."

"To the orlop with Lord Kennett. And with Peng, too. We know what Lord Maintenance *really* wants, and that's your gonads on a tray."

"I'm off duty, so I don't have my 'boo with me."

"Then that will make this easier."

Dhik shook his head. "No," he said. "It won't."

"Hey, woman, what're you doing?"

Dhik turned to his companion in time to see her whisper into her MOBI. She looked at the leader. "I am recording this. I think both Kennett and Peng will find your consignment of them to the orlop deck, in the light of the recent mutiny at Comm Central, to sound a trifle mutinous itself."

"To the narakas with that! We was sticking up for Lord Kennett, not trying to overthrow him."

"No, you were only trying to force him to forswear himself *with Ship Security*. I did not say what it was. I only said what it would *sound like* to the Officers."

The thug on the left said, in low, trepid tones, "Zach …? Maybe we should …"

"Nuts. Just grab her MOBI before she can send."

"That would not be a good idea, friend," said a fourth shadow.

"What? Who are you sticking your nose in the compartment?"

"I am Blackbird One Patterson." The man leaned out from the shadows so that the streetlamp highlighted his black coveralls. "Time to run, boys. We have you surrounded."

The three Maintenance toughs 'rankled their ankles' and fled in various directions. One of them tripped, but he bounced up and scrambled. Quiet descended on Tiger Pass'way. Then the blackbird said. "Are you quite alright, milady."

Dhik unclenched his fists. He looked first at the blackbird, then at Peta. "Milady? You never said."

Peta bowed her head slightly. "I'm sort of the 'black sheep' of the family. I have a job, and I'm good at it. Don't tell Bùxiè or Qín-fèn or any of the others. I swear you to secrecy." She traced a wheel around her heart.

Dhik knew that the number of blackbirds in a flock depended on the rank of the person guarded. He had sudden difficulty finding his voice. "How, erm, how many bodyguards do you have?"

"Just the one, and he's 'on call,' not full time."

"Ah." He faced the blackbird. " 'We have you surrounded'?"

One grinned and looked sheepish. "It worked."

Dhik nodded. He liked the fellow's attitude. Turning to Peta, he said, "Would milady care to be escorted back to her quarters, or would her bodyguard be sufficient?"

"If you promise never again to call me milady, you can escort me *into* my compartment for some tea."

"And what about your blackbird?"

"What blackbird?"

Dhik looked around and saw no sign of the bodyguard. He had vanished as silently as he had appeared.

27 ESCAPADES

A burnsider learns patience—A true captain—On the tram platform—Justice or mercy?—Why are you smiling?

Alessandro Fanghsi walked lonesome steps deep within the Burnout, alert for the slightest sound or light. Since learning of the Dwellers, he had begun to sense them everywhere. That couldn't be true, he knew, because if they were that plentiful, he would have come upon them long before, or they, upon him.

No, the Dwellers must be like him. A few seeds rattling in the maraca of the Burnout.

He set up camp in his favorite spot, the grand, multi-deck plaza at Sixteenth and Seventy-Fourth, where a gangway led up from the public square across a façade of moss-encrusted balconies and overlooks. Decks from Twelve down to Sixteen had been dismantled in the Long Ago between the Seventy-Fourth and Seventy-Fifth Frames to provide for the townhouses for rear-quarter officers.

Unlike much of the Burnout, the Great Plaza had lighting, although it was dim and uncertain. Nonetheless, Fanghsi set up a camp lantern, and its brightness chased the shadows from all but the upper reaches. He sat with his back to the light so his eyes would not be dazzled and hung a bag of jerky from the gangway railing. Then, he settled himself to listen.

The background rustling of the memory metal formed a constant insect-like chittering against which he tried to make out stealthier sounds. After a time, he noticed without surprise that the jerky bag was gone and announced in a loud voice, "I would be willing to trade diversity for picking relics." What the hell. It had worked for Pathfinder.

He waited, for if a burnsider learns nothing else, he learns patience.

"Something is going on in Blue Crew," the Prince of *Whale* said when Jones came on deck and took his seat at the astrogator's console. Jones glanced at him. Something was always "going on" with Blue Crew. He wondered if Yves could possibly be so disconnected that he had not heard of the abortive mutiny.

"Any reports from Brahmadharma?"

"About the Blues?"

"No, about ship status." Who, after all, cared about the Blues? As Dominic Dhruvs had written: *Blue Crew are cargo.* (Aphorism 83).

The Fourth Officer scanned the end-of-watch report. "Nothing he told me in the briefing. Except a malf reported in Engineering."

"That's not nothing. The Officer of the Watch must pay attention to all aspects of ship running, not just astrogation." Jones missed Berylplume, who now held first watch, and who was altogether a more agreeable conversational partner than Yves.

"The timing was off on one of the fusion engines during the test firing."

"Well, that's why we test-fire them. Equipment out of use can fail—the dust-and-rust effect, the engineers call it—and we wouldn't know until we called upon it at a critical juncture."

The Prince attempted to appear thoughtful, an attempt which, in Jones' estimation, fell short. His brow furrowed, his lips grew pinched as a thought attempted to squeeze its way out of his cortex. Jones thought he appeared constipated and was heroically trying to de-constipate himself.

"If we continue to test-fire the fusion cages for the next seven-hundred years," Yves said at last, "we will deplete our boron stores and have insufficient supplies left to decelerate the ship when we enter the Tau."

"The Tau *system*," Jones corrected him. "Why tell me? Shouldn't you tell Pedro?"

"The captain will not hear of any deviation from his precious Flight Plan."

"Certainly not after that message from *Red Dwarf.* What did X/O Boronfuse say about it?"

"If a problem is not immediate, he does not consider it a problem. The depletion of the boron stock is so gradual that it will remain unnoticed for generations."

"But you are certain of it?"

"I've run the material balance. Boron is something we cannot mine from the *Whale's* shell. At least, not in sufficient quantity. Some exists in the chondrites, but it's thin soup and difficult to isolate and concentrate."

Jones saw genuine concern in the prince's face. He really was worried over a crisis that would not materialize for centuries. As much as he hated to admit it about a man who had undermined his every ambition, that marked him as a true captain.

Blackbird One deSōuxún consulted his MOBI link while they hastened to the tube station. "Facemaker caught Ramamurthy exiting the tram at Flowing Silk Junction," he reported. "We'll never find him in that maze."

Bùxiè knew despair. Winsome Alabaster lived in Flowing Silk, and her testimony could put Dumont Ramamurthy in the Brig for many years. And Lord Helix did not hesitate to remove obstacles to his happiness. "I know exactly where he's going. One, Two, your secondments only covered our delivery of the mutineers to the Brig, so I cannot order you to accompany me."

Two waved his own MOBI. "But Peng can. I filled him in, and he extended our term to Lord Helix's apprehension. Dead or alive," he added. They jumped on the manlift and rode it down to the starboard tram tubes.

An agonizing time went by while they waited on the platform. The tram tube moaned like a vast organ pipe with the slight breezes that wafted through it. Now and then, Bùxiè thought he heard the creak of tram cars from the darkness. When the tram finally arrived, many of those waiting suddenly decided they were in no hurry to board a tram with blackbirds on it. Passengers who exited at Centrum Station took one glance at Bùxiè and his escorts and hurried toward the manlifts.

Some of the glances were hostile.

What did I ever do to them? Bùxiè wondered. But he put it down to a generalized dislike for the regime. The Bood be praised that Lt. Lutz had promised lenience and dignity to her prisoners, even after that nasty trick with the water.

The audience chamber of the Palace Mainouvertes was packed tight. Organson did not believe a single Commander had ignored the summons, save only Eugenics-Input, of course, and that was special circumstances. In Organson's estimation, there was genuine sorrow over the boy's death, even among those like Lord Maintenance, who might otherwise have derived satisfaction over Water's misfortunes. There were limits even to shame-joy.

Some among the Commanders did not yet realize that they were all in the crosshairs, and their internecine squabbles were as the clucking of the captain's live chickens while the axe was being sharpened.

"I don't care what some numb-nuts lieutenant of Marines promised the mutineers," Lady Sophie cried to the captain. She stood stiff as a frame rod and streamed out her rage as from a fire hose. "I want them all executed, every one of them. If it were possible, I'd resuscitate their dead bodies and execute them twice for what they did to my boy."

Organson was reasonably sure that Lord Hydro had joined the mutineers willingly, but how do you tell a grieving mother that her son had quite likely been a traitor?

Lord Agro spoke up. "The evidence seems to show that it was an unlucky ricochet from the Marines' coil guns that …"

He had not finished his observation before Lady Water rounded on him, screeching, "I don't care! I don't care! *I don't care!* The mutineers created the situation that put my boy in danger. They must pay the price. What say you, Most Excellent Captain? What do the Regulations state as the penalty for mutiny?"

The captain said nothing, though fear chased worry across her face.

Organson did not think that any Officer in attendance had failed to read the relevant Regulations before coming to this face-meet. He was just as certain that the sub-paragraphs had been skimmed over. Provocateurs and leaders faced recycling. Followers faced Brig time and fines. Organson shivered as he realized that he was in the former group, should anyone learn his role. He knew that his anonymity had been based partly on the need to preserve secrecy as plans were laid, but in large measure, too, it had been based on his own cowardice.

He saw the fear also on the faces of others: Lord Logistics, Lady Purser, up to and including the Captain herself.

"Recycling," Captain Ming-ti eventually said.

"All of them?" demanded Lady Water.

Captain Ming-ti did not answer but dipped her head in assent.

"And the second group, the one that stormed the Brig?"

Again, silent assent.

Alone in that assembly, Organson knew that the second group had been spontaneous and unconnected with the Brotherhood. It had been directed against another goal entirely: the lynching of Lord Ramamurthy. That the smooth-talking bastard had walked right through them was a tribute both to his eloquence and to the gullibility of the crewmen.

But Lord Agro spoke up. "The crew are not our friends," he said, "but we may yet keep them from becoming our enemies. It may be there is room for mercy, at least for some participants." Gregor Vishwakarma mopped his soft, round face with a kerchief, which Organson suddenly noticed was tricolored in black-red-gold. Did anyone else recognize its significance?

"Never!" cried Lady Water. "Most Excellent, there may be other Brotherhood teams lurking among the crew, waiting their moment. Showing weakness now is tantamount to an invitation to strike."

Lord Agro said, "Mercy is not weakness, but strength."

Peng spoke up. "I'm curious what Lord Liaison thinks."

Organson felt the query like a punch in his gut. "What? Me? Why?" What did Peng know? Worse, what did he suspect?

Peng replied in smooth tones. "Because of all of us, you are the most detached. None of your duties touch the crew; few of them touch even us. What are the thoughts of the disinterested observer?"

Organson saw by the way everyone leaned into him that he could not avoid answering. He searched within himself and found, much to his own surprise, a small, deeply buried nugget of courage.

"I went aft to Comm Central," he confessed. "I wanted to know what drives a man to such a desperate state that he would risk death for its sake. I spoke to witnesses and to Marines, and yes, I spoke to mutineers."

"Why bother with them?" Maintenance asked. "All we need know is did they mutiny or not."

"I am sorry, Lord Kennett, but that is not all we need to know. We also need to know *why* they did so. Otherwise, as a practical matter, how can we be sure the incident will not be repeated? And what I learned is this. They revere the Departure Generation as much as we do. 'The *Whale* as she was' is their motto. But they believe that Officers have ceased to inspire and lead and turned inward to their own wealth and power. No, hear me, hear me. I am only telling you what they believe. They see Maintenance extorting tenants and staff, building up a secret fund for who-knows-what. They see Water callously dispossessing tenants of their freeholds. They see …"

"How do they see me, Lord Liaison?" The captain spoke with adamantine eyes, darkened under the furrows of her brow so that they seemed not so much to look at him as to take aim.

"Your pardon, Most Excellent. They see you as a plaything fought over by squabbling factions who whiles away her time in idle parties and amusements." He spoke up over the growing mutters of outrage. "I say only that this is how they perceive you, that this is one of many perceptions that have nudged and elbowed them until they believe they have no recourse save to mutiny." He did not tell them these had been his own conclusions after years of thinking and discussions with Venables.

The mutterings had swollen into a flood of objections and denials from all but Lord Agro, Lady Purser, Lord Air, and a few others. Curiously, Peng too was among this silent minority, and his glance darted lively from Commander to Commander, noting the reaction of each.

What is his game? Organson wondered. And it said a lot about the Officer Corps that he thought that there must be a game, and Peng, a player. Even those otherwise devoted to an old-fashioned honor and duty, as Power was, found themselves forced into the dog pit of the struggle for the sake of self-preservation.

"It sounds like you are stirring up a mutiny in the very palace." Peng had quietly come to his side and spoke for his ear only. Organson started.

"You asked for the disinterested observer," he said. "You can hardly complain that you have heard him."

"Oh, I'm not complaining," Peng replied. "I'm just wondering. Before you spoke, the Commanders were split between justice and mercy. Now, all but a handful will want justice—as they see it. I wonder if you did that on purpose since you always struck me as rather more sympathetic to the crew as not." Peng's face settled into a neutral, expectant mien, and Organson had to remind himself that he need not respond.

In the end, the captain was carried like a leaf on a rushing stream of Officer outrage, and Sophie Water Masterson received the joy of her desiring. *Forgive me, Li Son,* Organson prayed. *And all you Brothers of his commando.* But he had seen a way to expand the Mutiny beyond the Brotherhood and had taken it.

Winsome Alabaster was returning from the gymnasium, still dressed in her workout clothes, still with the stink of sweat on her. She had spent the morning pummeling the sandbag, imagining alternately that it was Dumont Ramamurthy or that it was Blackbird Two, the latter for destroying Dumont's beauty and the former for revealing himself a psychopath. There were other ways of working off the rage and sorrow she felt than furious exercise, but none so swift and direct.

People she passed in the 'ways were chattering about a mutiny put down that morning by the Imperial Fleet Marines. A remarkable eruption, but it did not affect her.

Vishwakarma intercepted her as she stepped out of the drop tubes.

"Vish! What are you doing here?" They were paused in Littlepark Plaza, an entrée to Flowing Silk, but well off the old nosey parker's usual orbit. Other crewmen, chattering like magpies, swirled around them. Vishwakarma smelled of lilac water, a marked contrast to Winnie, who smelled of acrobatic workout. She wanted, of all things, to shower in the safety of her own quarters. She had developed a marked reluctance since Dumont went off his gyros to make herself vulnerable in public spaces.

"What's this I hear about a mutiny?" she asked her neighbor.

"Don't go home," the old woman replied. A sequitur so familiar that, at first, it struck Winnie as a fragment from another conversation that had fallen by chance into this one.

"What do you mean?"

"Were my words too long? That capewalker what tried to strangle you been hanging about your door."

"You must be mistaken. He's in the Brig."

"So, I should not believe my own lying eyes? A posse of your neighbors went up by the Brig intending to beat him, either because they loved you or because they despised capewalkers, or both. Straws and camels! It don't matter. Each one in the mob had his own reason, an' they needn't have been the same."

"What happened? They didn't hurt Dumont, did they?"

"Don't fret yourself over the likes of him. 'Slick' talked his way out of it. A mob be the only critter with a hundred bellies and no brains. The Brigmaster let him go. He released *all* his prisoners, the pusillanimous little skite."

"There you are, my dear!" The words flowed from the honeyed throat of Dumont Ramamurthy, whose swift strides carried him into the park. "I have been waiting by your door for ages."

Dumont could make an eyepatch look good and, even without his cape, project an air of confidence. Winnie's heart thudded in her chest. "What were you waiting for, a second attempt?"

Dumont placed a hand over his heart. "You wrong me, dear." Then, as if just noticing Vishwakarma, he added, "This is a personal matter, milady."

"I just bet it is." The old lady stood her ground, and Dumont snapped at her.

"Begone, hag!" Startled, Vishwakarma backed away, hesitated, and then scurried up the pass'way. Dumont dipped his head to Winnie. "I'm sorry to have been rude to your friend, but there are certain matters you need to get clear."

"I think you made matters clear enough when you tried to strangle me."

Dumont reached out to grasp her hands, but Winnie danced back and avoided his grip.

"You were choking on a piece of chicken, and I was trying to dislodge it when Peng's minions attacked me."

"And why would they do that?"

"I had done a favor for Peng, but my usefulness had become a liability. So, he instructed his minions to recycle me."

Winnie wondered. Could she really have misunderstood the events? She remembered floating above herself and watching Dumont choke her, but had that been a genuine experience or a hallucination brought on by choking from some other cause? She wanted to believe Dumont, but while she might believe any wickedness of Peng, she could not believe so of Bùxiè.

He had explained to her that Dumont was a psychopath, and while psychopaths need not be violent and may lead ordinary, organized lives, their relationships were artifices intended to manipulate others to the psychopath's own benefit. Dumont had paid her no attention until she had discovered his tampering with the Air-Water pairing. She wondered if his attentions afterward had been motivated less by attraction and more by distraction. Had she been no more than a pawn in some contest between Dumont and Peng?

"You must believe me," Dumont pleaded. He spread his arms, and Winnie very nearly stepped into his embrace.

But she paused to think, and thought is fatal to impulse. Why *must* she believe him? She was the chief witness in his upcoming trial for attempted murder. He did not have to kill her to remove her as an obstacle. In fact, it was safer for him to take a more velvet approach. If he undermined her confidence in her own testimony, he stood a good chance of acquittal. So, was he only trying once more to manipulate her?

The eyes are the windows of the soul. Jaunty's eyes had been like two candles in the windows flanking the entry of their quarters. Bùxiè's eyes were like searchlights; Dhik's were the large, liquid eyes of a devoted hound. But when she looked into Dumont's eyes now, she saw …

Nothing.

She did not know why she had never noticed that before. Perhaps her mind had not been prepared to see it, or perhaps because *nothing* is hard to see. But the vacancy repulsed her now and as he continued to advance on her, she continued to back away.

"Don't retreat," he pleaded.

In answer, Winnie executed a double backflip, placing herself suddenly two body-lengths from his grasp. She vaulted atop the rail that separated Littlepark from the lorries and carts rolling down Silk Way and danced along it as on a balance beam.

To catch her, Dumont would need to run down into the swale, past the culvert under the Silk Way, and up the embankment on the other side. She did not dare break her concentration to mark his progress. Dismounting the rail onto Littlepark Plaza, she possessed a clear dash to the drop tubes.

And Dumont was in front of her,

Blood ran from his mouth, where she had kicked him during her backflip. He howled, "My tongue!" Or as close to that as he could, her kick having snapped his jaw on that organ.

She did not pause to wonder how he had crossed the swale so swiftly but dealt with the fact that he had. She launched a furious series of jabs, left-right-left-right, raining small fists on his body like a nail gun.

Dumont gasped at the concentrated pummeling on his heart. He was a big man, but years of indulgent lifestyle had sapped his constitution, and he was much softer than a sandbag.

That did not stop his hands from seizing her wrists. "You've become more trouble than you're worth," he slurred through clenched teeth.

"Much more," she said and delivered a head-butt to his nose.

In a contest of brute strength, the brute always wins. The key to close-in fighting was to concentrate your strengths on your opponent's weaknesses. There was a great deal of pain to be found in the body's humbler organs.

He released her and stepped away, holding his bloody nose and weeping. He hauled back a fist and punched her in the face. "Why ah you smiwing?"

Winnie had not been aware of her smile, but it broadened as Bùxiè deSōuxún, swinging a quarterstaff like a stickball bat, scored an over on the back of Dumont Ramamurthy's skull.

28 EXECUTIONS

Are you one of us?—The curse of Winsome Alabaster—
Pale men and crossbows—The execution of Li Son—
The Orphans—The sergeants—Regulation 18.3

Lucky Lutz polished her brass with a special intensity. Not that she took particular pride in the upcoming parade, for the crushing of the Mutiny had held little of which to be proud, but to honor the First Marines and those who had died in its suppression. Lapel tabs bearing the crossed antique rifles of the infantry, the gold collar bars of a second lieutenant, the buttons that ran down her red uniform jacket bearing the three-headed imperial eagle. Lucky wondered for how many more generations the Marines would maintain their allegiance to an Imperium now so distant in time and space. Was it nostalgia? Inertia? Was nostalgia, in fact, only emotional inertia?

There were so many geegaws to brighten that the polishing became a deeply-meditative task that might occupy her until next Departure Day.

So she would not have to think about her orders.

"I gave my word," she told First Sergeant Kent. "I told Li Son that he and his men would be used with honor."

Kent, Fishaven, Ku, and their corporals were occupied in their own brightwork, and the wardroom was redolent with the odors of polish. Kent glanced up. "Picked the firing squad yet?"

Lucky shook her head, "I have a good mind to decline the assignment."

"Not too long ago, Loo," said Fishaven, "you was doin' damn-all to kill him."

Lucky frowned and studied her buttons. It was different, somehow, in battle. Execution seemed too much like murder. She thought it mattered if the other fellow had a weapon. Executions would be rather less popular were the condemned man armed.

"I'll be in my office," Lucky announced, and she gathered her things. Fishaven looked up, then returned to his busywork.

In her office, a hardbound copy of the Ship's Articles laid on her desk. She could not remember having left it open but saw without surprise that the text was CHAPTER 18: MUTINY. TAB 1:

Whosoever shall incite or lead a mutiny against the Whale or her Regulations shall be, having been duly convicted in court martial or court civil, recycled.

She read it once more and sighed. The words had not changed.

"Those are hard words to read," said a voice.

Lucky spun round and saw a thin man seated in the corner wearing a tattered black cloak. "Who are you?" she demanded. "And how did you get in here?"

"I have no face in public" was not much of an answer to either of her questions, but Lucky was not slow of wit.

"You're Peng," she said, pointing a finger at him.

He neither affirmed nor denied. Instead, he bobbed his head toward the Regs. "They don't leave much wiggle room."

"I don't like it."

"No one asked that you should, least of all Li Son. He took an oath. He pledged his life to 'the *Whale* as she was.' He has no complaint if that pledge has been called due. What matters if it is the battlefield or the firing squad that cashes it in?"

"Probably little," Lucky said, "but I can't help but feel that there *is* a difference."

"Maybe for you, not for Li Son." Peng fell silent while he studied Lucky with piercing green eyes, "One often hears the *Whale* compared to a flying apartment, but there is another comparison that is apt."

"What's that?"

"A flying prison." When Lucky made no response to this, Peng continued, "We are here without our consent, nor is there any possibility of escape. And like all 'lifers,' we have all gone a little 'stir crazy.'"

"Is that a defense of the mutineers? Innocent by reason of insanity?"

Peng tossed his head. "Understanding is not forgiving. There are three ways to rule men, lieutenant: by one, by some, or by many. Everyone creates in his own image, and the Planners of the Imperium were no exception. So, they gave us an aristocracy like themselves. But every regime decays into some form of anarchy. Monarchs become lawless tyrants; aristocracies, squabbling, self-interested oligarchies; and republics decay into democracies."

Lucky shifted in her seat. "Why are you telling me this? Will there be a quiz later?"

Peng smiled without humor. "In a way. You know, it is easy for the Brotherhood to comfort themselves with the idea that the oppressive regime will be swept away and replaced with one of their own devising. But whoever builds the new *Whale* order will have known only the old order and cannot help replicating it, as the Planners replicated their own aristocracy. Overthrow the Bourbons and get the Terror and, shortly, an Emperor with secret police. Topple the tsars, and you get the commissars."

"What about the Murqans? That worked out well, if I rightly remember."

"That mutiny started over heavy taxation, didn't it? How long was it before the new regime was levying taxes that would have made the old kings blanch? They did their best to limit the powers of their government, after which their government did its best to ignore those limits. Eventually, they wound up with the president-emperors of the Granpublic Americano. They delayed their decay, but they could not prevent it. We think there must be a cleansing when the old is swept away, but is it not more horrifying to think that matters after the Mutiny will proceed pretty much as before? They will wear different costumes and bear different titles, but, otherwise they will be the 'same old, same old.'"

Lucky was taken aback by this speech, and it was a moment before she found her voice. "What's the answer, then?"

"What makes you think there is an answer? What is the end state of a juggling act? Tell me where each ball will end up. You cannot because if they do not remain in continual motion, they will all drop to the ground. The *Whale* may be thought of as many kinds of artifacts—political, social, economic—but we must never forget that she *is* an artifact, pure and simple, and therefore, behind all the scrimmaging for power—the anarchy of the crew or the anarchy of the Officers—there stands always this constant: *care of the artifact herself.* The air must be filtered regardless of who wields power. The water must be refreshed, equipment repaired …. There stands, in short, our duty and honor. A few of us remain dedicated to those ideals—we who honor the three-headed eagle—for whom honor is not a smirking joke, and everything is not a game of power and status. So, my question to you, Lieutenant Ynigo Lutz, is whether you are one of us."

Winnie Alabaster knelt by Dumont Ramamurthy and checked his neck for a pulse. Perhaps it was her imagination, but it seemed to her that his body was already growing cold. "He's dead," she announced. To Bùxiè, she said, "You killed him."

It was mid-watch, and the rush of crewmen to their posts of duty had slowed to a trickle, but a small crowd was accumulating, nonetheless. Two young boys were staring at the body and nudging each other. Wait until they told their classmates!

"Did you have to kill him?"

Bùxiè studied the quarterstaff in his hands. Blood ran in rivulets down its shaft. Scalp wounds bled freely, she knew, and often seemed worse than they were. "I didn't intend to," he said. "I must have struck harder than I thought, but the sight of him beating you was too much to bear."

317

Crewmen coming off the drop tube from the tramway eddied about the scene, murmuring and pointing. Winnie could hear them exchanging their mutual ignorances. "Don't apologize for that. It's only that I wanted to kill him myself. But, though he was less strong than I feared, he was stronger than I hoped, so I thank you for your help."

Bùxiè turned to one of the blackbirds with him. "You had better inform Peng."

"Done and done, sir. A Recycling crew is on its way." He glanced down at the body. "He talked his way out of the brig and through a lynch mob. Let's see him talk his way out of this."

And he had come within an eyelash of talking her into thinking that her testimony might be mistaken. Winnie realized that she had *wanted* to be mistaken, that she had enjoyed the attentions of an important man. "I know he was only mimicking," she said, "but am I fated to see every man who shows me affection die horribly?"

Bùxiè said in a strange, tight voice, "I certainly hope not, milady." But shortly after, Vish returned with a mob of Flowing Silkers, and they hoisted Bùxiè deSōuxún to their shoulders and cheered him through the village.

Hidaki Thomason, standing watch over the forest of porcine vats, worked in his undershirt because of the hissing steam. He had labored so long on the pigstuff that he no longer noticed the odor. This was both fortunate and unfortunate; the former because it spared his olfactories the oppression of the odor, the latter because he failed to notice how that odor impregnated his clothing, indeed, his very skin and hair, so that he carried it with him wherever he went.

He was a conscientious crewman and kept a weather eye on the meters, monitoring the feed rate and the accumulation of pigstuff on the rotating skewers. Temperature and moisture content were critical, as also pH, steam pressure, and a host of other variables. Much of it was automated, but it never hurt to check. Once, a valve had failed to open; another time, a water runoff line had clogged.

He did not bother with the monitor screens. Condensate from the steam had long ago crusted over the camera lenses. But this precluded his noticing the pale men with crossbows and hatchets drifting out from the Burnout and slowly surrounding his control room.

The execution of Li Son was staged on a platform erected outside the Brig. The backdrop was a metallic sheet designed to carry and focus the charge of the firing squad. When Li Son was brought out, the gathered crowd jeered and laughed. Dhikpārușya Spandhana, watching the proceedings on the screen at Arfwendsen's Wayhouse, did not join in the hooting. The mutineer had led an uprising and so had earned his fate. It had to be done, but Dhik saw no call for the mockery.

Lt. Lutz, in command of the firing squad, tied the condemned man's hands to the post and said something that Dhik could not hear. *That might have been me up there*, he thought, had Peng ruled differently on his braining of the Maintenance lieutenant. That could have been construed as an act of mutiny. The operative difference was that he had been doing his duty while Li Son had not.

The mutineer faced the crowd. "I'm sorry our brothers were killed in the battle, especially the volunteer, Crewman Masterson."

"Liar!"

Dhik saw that the voice belonged to Lady Water, dressed in the white of mourning. Beside her stood the Princess of the Air, likewise garbed in widow's white. She said nothing but glanced at her mother-in-law with poorly concealed hostility. *My unintended bride*, Dhik thought. How might matters have transpired differently had he followed through on Eugenics' meddling?

"I have only one life," Li Son continued, "and though I'd gladly keep it, I lay it down willingly for 'the *Whale* as she was.'"

"One life?" cried a voice in the crowd. "Fortunate you'll be to be reborn as a cockroach."

The captain might mandate that the execution be shown live on every stream, but the captain could not mandate that Dhik's eyes be glued to the screen, so he focused instead on his mug of the Strangler, which was in grave danger of depletion. Elsewhere in the wayhouse, customers were concentrating on their go stones or chess pieces or were engaged in whispered conversations, but they could not help casting occasional glances toward the screen. Why did Kunigund not simply turn it off? Or did Comm Central have a way of determining whether screens were tuned in as mandated? The entire crew was supposed to witness punishments.

Dhik cast a morbid glance at the screen, and he saw Lutz cut a formal salute. Was she saluting the mutineer? No. The strains of the Imperial Anthem welled up from the speakers, and a translucent, computerized image of the Great Yellow Banner was superimposed over the scene. Graphic effects made it appear to be billowing in a breeze, and this, in turn, made the three-headed eagle appear to be striking with one head after another. Dhik had learned in training that each head represented a different group of ethnoi: the crowns of the kings of Yurp, of the rajahs of Inch, of the huangdi of the Middle Kingdom. No one in the wayhouse braced to attention.

> *"Great Yellow Banner, furl*
> *Your folds across the world.*
> *(God save us all.)*
> *Bind us with brother-bands*
> *People of all the lands*
> *From icy north to southern sands*
> *God save us all!"*

Dhik felt no longing for an Imperium that might or might not be yet standing far behind on Earth and might or might not have lived up to the lofty ideals of its anthem. And so, it surprised him when a close-up revealed a tear on the cheek of Lucky Lutz.

> *"Three-headed eagle, fly*
> *Piercing the highest sky!*
> *(God save us all.)*
> *Safely beneath your wing*
> *Hark, while your people sing*
> *'Til mountains and valleys ring:*
> *God save us all!"*

Though after the execution, as they carted Li Son's body to Recycling, he did mutter: "God save us all."

Hidaki held his arms carefully in the air, not wishing to give the Dwellers—for such he judged the bandits to be—any reason to lose their bows. He wasn't sure which stank more, the pig vats or the Dwellers. "What is it you want?" he asked the man by whose accouterments he took to be their leader.

"We'uns want ham," the man said. "You give us ham."

Hidaki did not hesitate more than a fraction. Lieutenant Offelberg would be unhappy if the material balance were off, but Offelberg was not here, preferring to oversee pig production from his more comfortable and less noisome quarters. And Porktender First Class Hidaki Thomason would be even more unhappy if he were used as a pincushion by these savages.

"Let me select a prime ham for you. Ain't healthy to eat unfinished pig. Do you want it shaved off the roll, or do you prefer larger pieces?"

"Big chunks. We'uns got packs. Carry 'em, *jildy*."

"Can I lower my arms? I gotta lower my arms to carve the pseudo-carcass."

The leader gestured with his crossbow, but neither he nor his men uncocked their weapons. Hidaki led them to Vat #14. He thought he could concoct a meat failure on that one to explain the shortfall in mass.

As he led them there, he said, "It's no use hanging back, Little Face. I see you. How you mixed up in this?"

The burnsider stepped forward, and Hidaki saw that he wore a rope in a bight around his neck, the bitter end of which was held by one of the Dwellers.

"Stylish necktie," Hidaki commented.

Fanghsi shrugged. "No noose is good noose. My compadres— they call themselves the Orphans—do not trust me. I promise you give them meat and not make fight. Otherwise, they skewer you and your co-workers and grab what they can."

Hidaki thought that over. "I appreciate your eloquence."

"But they do require a price. You must contribute your diversity."

"What does that mean?"

"You must lie with their women."

Hidaki thought that over, too. "I appreciate your eloquence."

Only then did the Orphans uncock their crossbows, and with grins and handshakes, welcome Hidaki into their gene pool, and only after *that* did Lord Agro's blackbirds drift out from the forest of meat vats with their teasers held in a cautionary mode.

The next day, the captain's guards marched Li Son's three sergeants from the Brig. Each had been in charge of a barricade at Comm Central and so could be construed among the leaders of the Mutiny. One of the sergeants, L.L. Lakhani John, had been badly injured in the fight and was, for that reason, strapped into a wheelchair. Lucky and her squad balked at shooting an injured man, though she could not say why it would have been more humane to await his healing and then kill him. Nonetheless, despite her distaste, she did her duty.

The next day after, they brought out the common Brothers, and Lucky quoted the Regs on mutiny, 18.3, *"Whosoever assists, or engages in any mutiny against the authority of the Whale or the Regulations thereof, or gives aid or comfort thereto, shall be fined or imprisoned not more than ten years, or both, and demoted in rank two grades."*

Clearly, the Planners had distinguished between the leaders and the led. Consequently, Lucky refused to execute the common mutineers, and Peng backed her up. Nor would he permit blackbirds to act in their stead.

But Captain Ming-ti, incited by Lady Water and other Commanders, was not mollified, and their personal guards replaced the Marines as the executioners. But since under the Peace of the *Whale*, only Marines and blackbirds were allowed to carry full-power teasers, the guards used their quarterstaffs to beat the prisoners to death, an altogether more savage mode of execution. Some of the militia checked their swings or backed out at the last moment— and found themselves thereby accused themselves of mutiny. Some vomited afterward, but others seemed to enjoy the duty.

On the fourth day, the spectators, who had previously jeered the mutineers, began to applaud them. But the tipping point came when they executed Huyo Ghonzal, a man so clearly innocent and bewildered that the punishments for mutiny had clearly shifted to an unreasoning fear of the crew itself.

"You can always depend on the ruling classes," Venables told Organson, "to push things over the edge." He cited historical examples from Old Earth, ranging from eighteenth-century Ireland to the Paris Jihad, but Organson stopped listening. He tapped the MOBI link he had reserved against this day.

"Go," he said and deleted the link.

"Go," said Group Leader Chang.

"About bleeding time," said Jek.

29 INCIDENTS

Highsteeple and Hexenplaza—The Storming of the Brig—Incident at Power House—The Siege of Undine Place—Maintenance first of all—You may need to evacuate—Only madmen.

Like the spattering of droplets that precedes a pass'way cleanse, incidents here and there throughout the *Whale* accumulated.

Orson Lieutenant Patel supervised power distribution throughout Highsteeple, which he did from his comfortable townhouse just afore that once pleasant community. Not that he did any electrical work himself. He had petty officers, bo'suns, and electrician's mates in plenty for the scut work. As long as he reported the proper voltages and currents, outages and malfs—there really was a lot to keep track of—Lord Thantos remained satisfied. The blackout just before the Mutiny had been a real black eye for him.

Consequently, he must now make site inspections of each of his substations and discuss equipment wear with the district electricians. He could not wait to win his second ring, to be raised to lieutenant commander, when he could be shut off from such annoyances.

As he guided his cart down Steeple Chase, the main gangway through the village, a knot of crewmen milling about blocked his way. They shouted and gesticulated to one another. Patel was a patient man, so he waited a few moments before he leaned on his cart's warning buzzer.

That drew everyone's attention. They stopped their argument, whatever it had been, and stared at him. No one moved, and he buzzed them again, more insistently. But instead of saluting and stepping aside, they swarmed his cart and dragged him from it. Nor were they gentle about it.

"But the Mutiny is over," he protested, and someone in the crowd answered him.

"No, the Mutiny is just beginning."

When Tongkawa Jones eased his cart through Hexenplaza, he saw a large and unruly crowd brawling there. Quarterstaffs clacked. Punches smacked flesh. Two males and a female lay on the deck. Behind them, he saw that the Mural had been defaced once more, this time much more crudely.

"What in the seven hells is going on?" he exclaimed, which proved to be a tactical error on his part.

Scowling faces turned in his direction, blood dripping from their noses and from cuts on their bruised cheeks. Mentally, Jones' question repeated itself, but this time he did not give voice to it. The answer no longer seemed urgent. *Get off the Hexenplaza!*

But before he could shift the cart into reverse, the brawlers had surrounded him and begun rocking his cart. Some grabbed at his clothing. "It's a capewalker," one said, and another cried, "Get the lousy Officer!" Fear ran through Jones like an electric shock, and he clung desperately to the tiller. Why did these strangers want to hurt him?

He absorbed several blows on the body, twisting so as to receive less damage. His training at the dojo had included several martial arts, but, seated and against so many, he was reluctant to employ them. It would be futile. Besides, the Art was intended for balance and inner peace, not brawling. Nonetheless, he was also reluctant to be beaten to a pulp without a blow in his own defense.

Other brawlers rallied to him. "Protect the Orficer, boyos!" they called. Jones no more understood his defenders than his attackers, although he was more grateful for them.

But his twisting had revealed the color of his cape.

"Hold up!" someone shouted. "He be goldcape!"

"So whut? He still be Orficer."

"We gots no quarrel wit' them goldcapes. They don't touch us."

"They's arrogant and look down they noses at the rest of us."

"Nose-looking, I can live with. They look down on Blue Orficers, too."

A beefy, battered face shoved itself into his. "What say ye, matey? Where ye stand on the Mutiny?"

Jones could hardly avoid such a direct question; he took refuge in naivete. "What mutiny?"

Both sides of the scuffle laughed. "See? What'd I tell yuh? Totally disconnected."

Another man said, "Only the most important thing to happen to the *Whale* since the Big Burnout."

"Oh, then you haven't heard."

That earned him frowns of incomprehension. "Wot yuh mean, capewalker?"

"We passed perilously close to a ringularity recently, and our sister ship, *Red Dwarf,* is lost."

They backed away from him with scoffing and derision. They did not know or care what a ringularity was, nor likely what *Red Dwarf* was. Jones restarted his cart. "I should be very careful, were I you. We are living in a tiny bubble of air, water, and power, hurtling through an infinite ocean of vacuum and hard radiation. You may want to ensure that the ship remains intact while you sort your differences. Meanwhile, I'll do my best to pilot you to your descendants' intended destination."

When he finally reached the quarterdeck, he advised his colleagues to stay close by the Coisters and the Golden Horn until matters had settled down among the cargo.

The second time a crowd swarmed around the main hatchway for the Brig, Brigmaster Kemynder did not go out to meet them. For

326

one thing, they seemed better organized this time. They wore brassards with rank insignia, and some were armed with teasers. For another thing, he had been chewed over royally by no lesser teeth than those of Peng himself regarding the previous incident. He thought this was because freeing his Excellent prisoner had led in short order to the man's death.

But in any case, he was not inclined to indulge a mob again. This time, however, they had not come to lynch anyone but to set free the remaining rioters and mutineers from the Comm Center debacle.

Staff Sergeant Jui popped his turpene chewing stick and studied the visuals from the pass'way outside the Brig. "Ya think they'll be mad if they see how few remain in custody?"

"You mean madder than they are because they be in custody in the first place?" Kemynder thought that Ship Security should have authorized a staff increase for him if this sort of thing were to be a regular occurrence, but judging by the size of the mob outside, he would have needed a small army to defend the Brig, so he must put his faith in his small staff of jailors and stewards—and the reinforced bulkheads that walled his domain. He tried to remember how much food and other supplies they had in the cafeteria and asked Jui what the inventory showed.

"Don't think it matters, boss. They got themselves a cutting torch."

"That can't be good," said Kemynder. The Brig was built to prevent breakouts, not break-ins. "Open the arms cabinet and distribute the air rifles and a couple of magazines of anesthetic darts. Put a few of that crowd to sleep and let 'em wake up in cells. The rest will disperse."

Staff Sergeant Jui expressed uncertainty but went to do as he was told. Shortly, he returned with the air rifles and most of the jailors.

"Where are the others?" asked Kemynder,

"Disinclined, sah."

Kemynder pumped his air reservoir and chambered a dart. The rifle clicked with satisfying authority. "I'll deal with them later. They won't like sharing cells with their own prisoners." He led the jailors to the Brig's anteroom, where the hatch boomed with the impacts of a battering ram, and the edges glowed from the flame of the cutting torch.

"We don't want to wait until the door is knocked in," the Brig master said. "Jui, spin the wheel. The rest of you aim for the hatchway. Soon as a rioter steps through, dart 'im."

Air rifles came to the ready. Jui waited for the high sign. Kemynder took a deep breath, let it out, and nodded to Jui.

The staff sergeant spun the locking wheel, and the door swung out. Rioters backed away. But before Kemynder's people could loose their darts, rioters began firing their teasers into the anteroom.

Goldfish in a bowl. The Brig staff went down like corn stalks in the hydroponic farms, the bolts paralyzing their muscles. Legs gave way. Arms dropped weapons. Lungs and hearts ceased to pump. The last thing Kemynder saw was rioters swarming into the Brig and the last thing he heard was their triumphant cries.

Thantos Chan gazed out from the second-floor windows of Power House at the chanting mob below. Like all the commanderies, Power House was a congeries of residence modules connected to one another. Unlike most of the others, the modules were connected in a maze-like complexity. The palace had grown haphazardly over the generations.

The Excellent Thantos sipped from a tall glass of yellow 'ponic wine. "I shouldn't worry over that crowd," he told his sons.

Burly men in their late thirties, Lord Volt and Lord Amps stood to either side of their father and matched his sip with their own. Fine, strong sons, Thantos had often thought. "They can't get in," said Volt, the younger of the two. It was not quite a question.

Volt's birth had complicated family dinners at Power House, since with mother and father, they comprised an unlucky Four, forcing Thantos either to invite a guest—usually a cousin or uncle—or hold dinner without the Lady Onora at the table. Her death three years ago had simplified matters considerably, although Thantos and his sons knew a lingering sadness because of it.

"And what if they did?" his brother laughed. "They'd get lost in the maze."

The crowd was throwing rotten vegetables and fruit, eggs, and miscellaneous bric-a-brac. Nothing, at any rate, that would break down the gates. Just more work for the swabbies when they came to clean up. A line of blackbirds faced the crowd from the fenced courtyard, and their teasers dissuaded the rabble from any more ambitious acts.

Thantos raised his right arm, the one not holding his drink, above his head, and his sons hid their smiles over their father's idiosyncrasy. "Other mobs have assaulted junior officers here and there," said Amps, "but that's what happens when you mix with crew."

"Lieutenants' duties require them to be out and about," Volt answered him, "someone has to keep an eye on the crew. Can't trust crewmen a fly's testicle. We're safe enough in here."

Amps waved his wine glass at the window. "They'll tire of this futile exercise soon enough and retreat to their quarters."

"Don't be too sure," said Thantos. "I've heard reports over MOBI that other Houses have been attacked, some with disciplined platoons of armed crewmen. I think this is the Mutiny, the real one. And the rabble out there is simply marking time until Brotherhood troops arrive." He brought his MOBI to his face. "I'm pulling my blackbirds inside the palace. They're too exposed in the courtyard, and Peng would not like it if we lost too many of them." He signed with his right hand, and one of the deaf-mute servants came and took his empty wine glass.

"Why not cut the power in the pass'way? Volt suggested. "Let them mill about in the dark."

But Lord Thantos shook his head. "When the worker bees are agitated, don't poke the hive."

Amps tossed off the remainder of his drink and placed it on a salver held by his deaf-mute. "And what if armed Brothers do break in?"

His father shrugged. "Then we fight. We arm the servants—with steak knives if need be—and fight to the last man."

Thantos then learned three things new to him. The first was that the servants had already armed themselves with the cutlery. The second was that at least one of those servants was not, in fact, deaf. And the third was that they were disinclined to be the last man fought to.

The knives were very sharp, and Thantos barely felt the blade as it sliced his right carotid artery from behind. It tickled, almost like a feather. His last sight was of his two sons—his babies!—dropping in their own blood. But it pleased him in some indefinable manner that they would be once more reunited with Onora.

Fighting broke out at Undine Place between Brotherhood troops and the Water Department militia. The crackle of teasers and the electrical whiff of their discharges filled the air. Lieutenant Astradian, who led the Brotherhood platoon, had deployed his men behind various obstacles in the forecourt—the carts they had arrived in, now toppled to present their rubber rollers for protection, and sheets of bulkhead material, impervious to teaser rays, torn up farther to portside.

To his rear stood a solid line of residential quarters. No longitudinal pass'way opened directly onto Undine Plaza. Ordinarily, this would be a poor tactical situation, without lines of retreat save to the sides of the Plaza, but each residence had an entrance on the main traverse aft of the Plaza and had been cleared of internal obstacles. His men could pass straight through these quarters should the need arise. Some of the occupants had willingly granted the Brotherhood access, others, perforce unwillingly. All had to sacrifice for the Mutiny. Most, whatever their allegiances, had fled.

"Pour it on them poodles, boys," Astradian cried. "But remember your training. Odd numbers firing while even numbers recharging. Then switch." He didn't know why he was shouting these things, only that Reggie Chang had told him how people under stress could forget even the most elementary matters.

Like other great Commanderies, Undine Palace stood in solitary splendor, quarters to all sides of it having been demolished generations ago. The quarters on Four Deck had been joined to those on Three Deck, and Three Deck itself dismantled in the vicinity, so the Palace towered two decks up.

The defending household militia had deployed behind the balustrade that separated the Plaza from the Courtyard. This low wall was topped by a fence of tall iron spikes. That made gaining entry to the palace a tricky tactical problem. Astradian's platoon had brought climbing ropes and bolsters to pad the spikes, but none of it did any good if they could not even get close to the fence.

Furthermore, a teaser bolt hitting that fence would electrocute anyone touching it. He hoped the blackbird defenders might forget this in the heat of battle and grab hold of a bar, but he didn't think they would do so.

The fight had been a stalemate so far. The attack was supposed to have been a surprise, and their first rush would secure the gates before the sentry could close them, but the problem with simultaneous strikes was achieving simultaneity. Jump-off had been delayed, and fighting elsewhere had alerted Undine to a possible attack, so the defenders were already positioned in the courtyard when Astradian's platoon had arrived. Four bodies now decorated the Plaza in an eerie reprise of the Massacre.

Astradian's only previous battle had been a fracas with a Dweller band at Conniption Pass', and he had not been in command there. "Think of it as on-the-job training," Reggie had suggested when he passed out assignments. Astradian thought he should have laughed, but he hadn't.

Of his original commando of forty, three lay dead—one of the bodies on the Plaza was that of the gate guard. He had sent six down to Five Deck to watch the servants' entrance, and another six to Two Deck in case there were a roof exit.

A residence in the row behind his position disgorged a crouching man in aquamarine coveralls. Water Department uniform! Astradian turned his teaser to cover the intruder. But the man wore also a red-white-blue armband, which marked him a Brother. He glanced left, right, noted Astradian, and scurried to his side behind one of the carts.

"Do you want to get into the palace?" he asked.

"No," Astradian replied. "We're just idling away our time at target practice." Why did people always ask stupid prelim questions?

"I can show you a way in."

"Unobserved?"

"Did you see me walk out the main gate?"

Evidently, it was Astradian's turn to ask stupid questions. "How then?"

The man hooked a thumb at the quarters behind them. "Leave a squad for covering fire. Withdraw the rest to Babbling Brook, down into the water tunnel in the interdeck."

"We'd get lost down there," Astradian objected.

"You might. I won't, and I'll guide you. The tunnel gives access to a pipeway that lets us enter the palace. We come up in a washroom—It'll be empty—the washing women have all skedaddled—and take Sophie by surprise. There will be a few blackbirds, three or four, guarding her person. If you can keep quiet, we should be able to take them. I call the passage 'Megwan's Gift.'"

Astradian made up his mind and offered his hand. "Lieutenant Adrian Astradian."

The offer was accepted. "Jimcas Nearwell."

Lord Kennett had been preparing his coup for years, biding his time until the proper moment. He had been skimming kickbacks from his tenants, from his crewmen, from independents who needed maintenance work. All to fund a private militia. He had convinced himself that other Officers must be likewise engaged, so it was only self-preservation.

Yet events had knocked the *Whale* on an unexpected course. The Mutiny had taken him by surprise. So, instead of seizing the captain hostage and deposing Air and Water, he found himself improvising. He told Lieutenant Commander Shon Militia Banerjee to gather Maintenance departmental troops in the Shops with their weapons, and Lord Kennett addressed them from atop a planning table where they could all see him. He looked over a sea of red coveralls sprinkled with the white of Manufacturing, the yellow of Inspection, and the black of Mining and Construction.

"People," he said. "Anarchy has raised his pointy head among our crew, and no one knows better than you and me how dangerous that is to the life of the *Whale*. Vital work will be neglected while crewmen riot instead. Infrastructure will be damaged. I know that may sound like good news to the repairmen since it would mean more employment for them." That raised a few chuckles among the red-suits. "But the *Whale* cannot afford to wreck itself, to create, as it were, a new man-made Burnout. We are all that stands between our homes and that bleak desolation. So, be prepared to fortify the Shops and defend them against the mob."

And to defend me, he added silently before grasping the nettle. "I know crewmen, including many of you, have good reason for disaffection. The arrogance of Water and her sock puppet Air have taken advantage of their control over our two most vital systems to strongarm our hapless captain. Ship Security spies on our every move and listens to our every whisper. Eugenics tells us who we can or cannot couple with. Enforcers swat us for breaking the least archaic rules. Oh yes, Officers, too, are subject to these banes. Does that surprise you? We breathe the same air and drink the same water as crewmen. We, too, are spied upon and chafe under the arrogance of Eugenics. Once this Mutiny is put down, once order is restored, there will be a reckoning. But … first things first. You have been assigned your posts?" A chorus of *ayes!* answered him. "Now we must make the Machine Shop an impregnable fortress! Yes, even where we abut the Burnout. Afterwards, we will consider how matters lie in the belly of the *Whale* and take appropriate action."

He unfastened his blue cape and flipped it around so that the scarlet lining faced out, making it a red cape. Taking their cue, his lieutenant commanders did the same. He thrust his fist in the air. "Maintenance, first of all!"

Cheers and the fist-in-the-air salute erupted from the ranks as his militia dispersed to their posts. Lord Kennett jumped from the table and confronted Banerjee. "Well, Shon, it seems 'the die is cast.'"

"Indeed, sah. Though we may hope the dice are loaded."

Kennett chuckled. "How goes production on the teasers?"

"We're out of start-up and into full production. I've put as many machinists and machinist mates on the project as I dared without increasing the backlog of repair jobs."

Kennett looked around the shop floor at the humming lathes and whirring drills and squeaking 3D printers. Somewhere out of sight, a stamping press was a marching giant. "We can afford some backlog, Shon. The mutineers are armed with teasers. I won't have my people fight them with quarterstaffs."

"Aye, sah. I'll be checking the punch list to see what can be delayed." He turned away, but Kennett grabbed his arm.

"And how goes it with the coil guns?"

"We can convert our nail guns to launch more aerodynamic flechettes. That'll give 'em greater range. But we can't match the Earth-built guns the Marines have."

Rajalakshmi Ming-ti sat in her captain's day cabin and spoke on her MOBI with a simulacrum of Peng. She did not know whence he had contacted her. Being difficult to find was part of his mystique. She selected a chocolate-covered apricot from her bowl and bit into its juicy sweetness. She asked Peng why he was wearing a crewman's plain coverall.

The head of Ship Security generally cast a serious mien, but today, his simulacrum seemed especially solemn. "This is not a time to swan about the pass'ways gussied up," he said. "If you must flee the palace, I recommend similarly anonymous garb."

"Flee the palace?" Captain Ming-ti was incredulous. "Why should I want to flee the palace?"

"It is not a question of 'want to.' MOBI reports mobs demonstrating outside Power House, Undine Place, Zephyrholm, and other commanderies. An armed platoon of the Brotherhood has stormed the Brig, and another is assaulting the Machine Shops where MOBI tells us Lord Maintenance is forted up. We have recordings of assaults on a score of junior Officers while going about their business, including a goldcape who stumbled into a brawl between mutineers and loyalists."

She would have to set Lord Liaison to contact the go-captain and sort matters. Tedious. "Don't forget Lord Helix was murdered," she said.

"That was a separate issue, milady. A criminal matter unconnected with the Mutiny."

"Then why are the mutineers celebrating the man who did it?"

"Because, like others, they have misconstrued the incident. Or their leaders have taken advantage of it. Mutineers did kill a senior lieutenant in Admin when they tried to grab him and he fought back with his baton." He hesitated a moment, then continued. "You may take some little comfort, milady, in that a third of the crew, by our estimate, is still loyal."

Captain Ming-ti leaned forward toward the hologram. "Do you mean to say that two-thirds are against us?" She did not want to believe that. Surely, Peng was mistaken!

"No, milady. The mutineers and their fellow travelers comprise less than a third. But there is a third faction." Peng reached outside his camera's view and returned with a cup in hand, presumably of tea. How could the man remain so calm in the teeth of such turmoil? There was *for* and *against*; what possible third option was there? After a sip of tea—she wondered what the blend was—he sated her curiosity.

"There are those who fear the disruption of Ship systems caused by mutiny, but who also believe that the Officers triggered outrage amongst a crew initially indifferent or even hostile to the Mutiny by the indiscriminate executions after Comm Center. If you recall, I advised against that."

Rage burned her, and she struck the arm of her chair with a fist. "Do you say this is my fault? Outrageous! I won't have it be my fault!"

Peng turned his head. He must be getting another report. When he faced the captain once more, he said, "It matters not whose fault the situation is; it only matters *that* the situation is. MOBI reports that the mob has taken Undine Palace. Lady Sophie, her consort, and several lieutenants are their prisoners. Apparently, the under-butler opened a basement door to them."

The shock was like a pail of ice water thrown in her face. For a moment, fear held her immobile, though secretly, she was pleased that Sophie Masterson had been removed from the chessboard. "What of her bodyguards?"

"Two of my blackbirds and four of her house militia were killed defending her."

"Could they not have done more?" As troublesome as Sophie was, she *was* a Senior Commander.

"My blackbirds are bodyguards, not an army."

"Speaking of which, where are the Marines?"

Lucky spoke to Kent as she hurried from her office. "Put the Goons on alert," she said. "We may be moving out any moment. Send Fishaven down to the Armory and tell Tony to be ready to issue weapons."

Kent saluted. "Lieutenant, aye. Go on alert. Inform Armory. Where you rushin' off to?"

"Commandant's called a meeting. All the lieutenants. Comm Center is gonna look like a picnic compared to this."

But when she reached the Commandant's quarters, her instructions were not what she had expected. Commandant Yueh sat at the head of the conference table with Lollipop at his side, both of them looking angry and frustrated. Lt. Patel of the Second was already seated, and Lt. Morsel of the Third entered just after Lucky. No place in the Barracks was very far from any other place.

"Thank y'all for coming," the Commandant drawled as if the invitation had been optional. *The Commandant requests your attendance at your earliest convenience,* meant in militarese *Right here, right now.*

" 'Sup, boss?" she said. "What are our targets?" Patel nodded, but Morsel, whose platoon had seen only riot control thus far, seemed more uncertain.

"We received ouah orders from Peng himself," he said. "Stand down. Defend the Barracks if need be, whethah from mutineers or loyalists seeking weapons, but take no offensive action until instructed."

A chorus of objection erupted from the lieutenants, but Lollipop's voice overrode them all. "Sometimes," he said in a voice that asserted without shouting. "Sometimes yuh have to let a fire just burn itself out. We're better armed than the mutineers and militias— we got bolt cannons and coil guns—but there just ain't enough of us. We got three platoons, and I wouldn't feel real confident in raising a fourth. An ancient fable of Trojans and horses comes to mind. And tempting as it may be to march between mutineers and militias and 'shoot both ways,' that would be like rushing into the Burnout and hoping for a copacetic outcome."

The lieutenants added grumbling to their repertoire. Lollipop passed on the Commandant's assignments for posting sentries and monitoring the surveillance cameras covering the approaches to the Barracks. Lucky suspected Lollipop had made the assignments, and the Commandant had rubber-stamped them.

"And by the by," the Master Sergeant added. "Yuh may wanna suss out the loyalties of the troops yuh do have. Marines ain't immune to the sweet talk of the mutineers."

As Lucky hurried back to the wing that housed First Platoon, she knew a sense of relief as if a heavy load had slid off her shoulders. The troops might be disappointed at their more passive role, but only a madman runs to a battle.

30 CAPTIVES

"We must be removing ourselves from this place"—
An altogether tougher nut—"He thinks we're in the
Imperial Fleet Marines."—Lǎo dàjīngxiǎoguài—"We
can handle ourselves."

The bang reverberated through Zephyrholm, and Ling-ling
wondered what it meant. She did not ask Tildy, her duenna, for she
had not spoken a word since her Man had been killed. She thought
that she never would speak again. She would wear widow's whites
until she herself died, though she knew some distaste at the way it
showed dirt and grime.

The room she sat in was no longer called a "playroom." She
would never play again. It was now her "salon," but she had not
held any receptions nor received any visitors. Having nothing better
to do, she had begun reading some of the material with which her
tutor had burdened her and found, much to her annoyance, that she
became interested in it. She wondered why the Riots of '53 had not
been called a mutiny while those going on now were. Was it only

338

because the current riots were planned and purposeful while those following the Burnout had been spontaneous?

Another bang disrupted her thoughts. Tildy frowned, folded her own screen, and bustled from the salon.

Ling-ling thought she really ought to hold a reception, perhaps a tea party—once a decent interval had passed, of course. There were other young males and females she could invite: Ginger Transport, Agni Medic, and others that she and Megwan had played with when they had been children.

But the thought of Megwan expunged the idea before it was ever more than a notion. She would never come out of her seclusion. She would never betray Megwan.

Tildy came rushing back with Mama and a blackbird in her wake. "Quickly, little *ej'māni*," the blackbird said. "We must be removing ourselves from this place. Make haste; oh, make haste."

Tildy looked at the front hatchway. "Where is Lord Luis?" Ling-ling noticed how Mama and the blackbird looked at one another.

"He'll be along in a moment," Mama said, but Ling-ling wondered how he would do that when the blackbird—Number Seven, she suddenly remembered—closed the hatch cover and spun the locking wheel. Perhaps Baba was coming by a different route, and they would meet when they had reached the back entrance.

The rear hatch of her salon led through several storage rooms and servants' pass'ways to the kitchens and thence to the delivery hatch for food and other goods. But when the four of them reached the prep area, they found strangers waiting there, and Baba stood among them with his hands bound and his face bloodied. One of the strangers said, "Grab them!"

Several things happened then at once. Baba cried, "No!" and one of the strangers struck him with a baton. Tildy began to cry. And Seven stepped between her and the strangers with his teaser up. But before he could fire, a stranger had drilled him with a teaser of his own.

Seven dropped to the floor, unable to breathe, and was able to gasp only, "Sorry, ej'māni," before he died. And the first thing

Ling-ling did since Comm Central was also the last thing she had did at Comm Central.

She screamed.

Reginald Chang had deployed two commandos around the Palace Mainouvertes, both fresh from victories elsewhere. Lieutenant Astradian's fighters had taken Undine Palace with minimal casualties and captured Lady Water with several of her lieutenants. Assault leader Jek Buddhathal had seized Zephyrholm in an equally bloodless *coup de main*.

Chang expected the captain's palace to be an altogether tougher nut. Indeed, her household troops had already repulsed several attempts to gain entry. But the palace was such a sprawling complex that somewhere, there must be an unsecured door. He had sent squads to various points around and below the towering jumble of quarters.

The problem with these towering "skyscrapers" was that, by removing all the quarters around them so they could soar in isolated splendor, they were left with entrances only on the main deck and, for servants, on the subdeck. And while this meant the defenders could be "bottled up" more easily, it also meant the attackers had fewer potential access points.

Maybe we can throw hooked ladders to catch on the second deck balconies.

The blackbirds that had been guarding the Plaza outside, shooting from the cover of the big planters, had been killed or driven back into the palace. Some had surrendered when they had found their position hopeless. Chang hadn't known they were allowed to do that. He had always thought of blackbirds as fight-to-the-death automatons and was oddly surprised to discover they were men like anyone else. Most were males, but a few—perhaps dictated by the necessities of bodyguarding the captain—were female. The teaser was a great equalizer in combat.

He and Lt. Astradian crouched behind an *ad hoc* barricade of wood and rubber just beyond teaser range. Oh, for a bolt cannon! Some days, he missed his time in the Fleet Marines. He would never have been surprised and massacred as Vòng had been at the Redoubt.

But one never knew. Who would have thought that a screw-up like Ynigo Lutz would walk out of the Burnout a freaking hero?

He looked over his shoulder, expecting at any moment to see Lutz and her terror weapons approaching in his rear. *Where were the Marines anyway?* He hoped his pickets would give warning in ample time for his fighters to scatter. And where was Jek Buddhathal? He had not returned yet from his mission.

"Why does that courtyard look a mile wide?" Astradian asked.

"Because we need to cross it under fire?" Chang guessed. "The greater the defending fire, the greater the distance."

Astradian snorted. "My biggest problem may be to get my boys to charge the palace at all."

Chang pointed through the loopholes in the barricade. "I been watching the fire patterns. I think there's a blind spot between the third and fourth windows. If we rush that point, their teasers can't touch us."

Astradian looked at him. "You find that argument persuasive?"

"No."

"You going to test it?"

"No."

"I wish we had those coil guns the Marines have. They would make short work of the façade."

"If wishes were coil guns, Mainouvertes would be a smoking ruin." He turned and looked again for any sign of the Marines. He was not anxious to be caught between an anvil and a hammer. Instead, he saw several forklifts lumbering toward him. They had been plated with bulkhead material so that they resembled turtles with tusks. Assault Leader Buddhathal, who had fetched them from Milkhoney, reported. He did not bother to salute, and Chang did not ask him to do so.

"Took you long enough, Assault Leader. I was beginning to worry you'd been ambushed."

"Barnstable had MOBI close the airtight doors on all the main longitudinals before we bagged him. And Rich Minyan—what calls hisself Lord Transport—shut down the tram lines. We had to wend our way forward through longitudinals big enough to accommodate the forklifts and open doors manually wherever we could."

"Well, you're here now," Chang said. "That's all that matters."

"The Stern is virtually cut off abaft the Burnout," Buddhathal persisted. "The only way to get back there is on foot, maybe in carts. Or through the Burnout. The Machine Shop and Agro are out of reach."

"Not our assignment, sergeant. Did you disable the auto-braking on the lifts?"

"Do I look stupid? These are the heaviest ones I could liberate that didn't depend on gravity plates. They lift stuff mechanically with the slats in front."

"Good. Now, Adrian." He gathered the platoon leader. "D'yah see those big wooden doors to the captain's palace? We are going to hit them as fast and hard as we can with these lifts. The slats will act like rams, and the bulkhead material will shield the drivers from teaser fire. We should breech the doors after a few hits."

Astradian nodded. "Those are genuine Earth wood? Seems a shame to smash them."

"Whose side you on?" asked Buddhathal.

"Oh, ours, of course. But it's still a shame."

Buddhathal grunted and addressed Chang. "I'd like to drive the first ram. I used to work Milkhoney Hard, and I brought me a couple guys from the union."

Chang decided to grant Jek his suicidal wish. After all, an assault should be led by an assault leader. But the hard work would come after the breech was made when the foot soldiers would rush into the narrow opening made by the rams.

That courtyard was looking wider by the minute.

A freedom fighter scurried to the command post. "Sah," he said. "A whatchamacallit, a lady's maid, done showed herself at a hatch on the port façade waving a white flag."

"Surrendering," Chang wondered, but the private shook his head. "Truce. They want us to evacuate the servants."

"Alright, bring her here, and we'll talk."

As the private hurried off, Jek turned to him and said, "You can't be serious!"

Chang raised his eyebrows. "Why not? Servants are crew like us: able spacers, petty officers, and the like. At most, the head butler and the housekeeper—and, maybe, the cook—hold warrants, but our quarrel is with the Officers, not the middle ranks."

"So what," Jek responded? "Some of them poodles actually love their officers."

Chang said through clenched teeth, "That's no crime. Some of the Officers are okay, like Agro and Liaison. Lady Purser always disbursed our pay in full and on time. Besides, I've got a notion about this truce that may save a lot of bloodshed."

Jek repaid the glower with interest. "Sometimes I question your loyalty to the Mutiny."

"Sah," Chang suggested, and after a moment, Jek added, "Sah."

Chang led a detachment to the manlift. Lord Transport had shut them down in an effort to hobble the Brothers' movements, but some of the Brothers were manlift techs and could restart them manually. Chang and the others floated down to the next deck and hurried to the servants' entrance to Mainouvertes.

"They be gathered in the staff break room," Jezka, the lady's maid, said. "Remember, we're under a truce. I ain't wishful of seeing no one hurt."

Chang worked his way through the grammar and decided she meant the opposite of its formal meaning. "No one is going to start shooting when they open the hatch."

"Don't see why not," Jek grumbled, not quite under his breath.

"We agreed to a truce, Assault Leader," Chang reprimanded him. "We won't break our word."

"If this is some trick of Rajalakshmi ..."

"Then, the dishonor is hers. The Officers gained us a lot of goodwill among the crew by their indiscriminate executions. I won't see that squandered through intemperance on our part. Remember, these are the crewmen the Mutiny wants to liberate." He turned to the sergeant whose squad had been guarding the servants' entrance. "Posie! Stand down. The servants are evacuating. So, hold your fire, but stay alert in case it's a trick."

"I still say this is a golden opportunity to force entry," said Jek. "Sah."

"Assault Leader, you'll report to Sergeant Posie here."

Buddhathal threw him a salute that was so precise as to border on the insubordinate and from the wrong side of the border. Jek's problem was that, for him, the Mutiny had become the end rather than the means to a greater end. He bore a hatred of Officers, not of their oppressions.

343

Jezka went to the hoigh plate, looking excruciatingly aware of the nervous, teaser-armed men behind her. She spoke briefly into the grill, and shortly the locks unlatched. Chang knew the sound was minimal, but it rang in his ears with a great mechanical clang. He fingered his teaser but kept his eye not on the lady's maid but on his assault leader. He was morally certain that Jek had gunned down Dingbang at Hanging Bridge, and so brought on a premature fight. Would he try the same now? That might all depend on what came through the hatch: footmen and maids—or blackbirds and militia.

The hatch cover swung out, and a short, a very frightened girl stepped out waving a white towel fastened to a rod. She wore the uniform of a scullery maid. Chang wondered how they had chosen who would exit first: the bravest among them or the most evidently harmless?

Whichever, it had worked, and Chang could actually *feel* the tension ease out of his men. Even Jek visibly relaxed. He might have demons aplenty wrestling in his brain, but among them, kitchen girls were not to be numbered.

After her, a dozen or so others scurried out, most with their hands linked behind their heads in the traditional fashion. Noting those whose hands were not so encumbered, Chang suddenly realized why even the innocent were ordered to do so.

A chubby, white-haired woman in a cook's uniform brought a smile to Chang's face. That cooks sampled their own work was proverbial, but they were not alone in doing so. For a moment, he admired the sheer—and uncharacteristic—gutsiness of the ploy. *Xuzba*, they called it. Then, with a sweep of his head, he gathered his staff and approached the cook.

Close up, Chang could see the white hair was flour and the wrinkles expertly drawn. He decided the limp was enforced by a shard in her slipper and the bent posture by some sort of harness under her uniform. That was too many traits, by far. The best disguises are the simplest. He saluted the cook.

"Most Excellent captain," he said. "*Atari*, and checkmate."

The Brotherhood commando outside the Palace Mainouvertes debated what to do. Their aversion to Commanders had cast its shadow as an aversion to commands, and so every act was debated, questioned, and second-guessed. This was fine for laying plans, not so fine for executing them once laid. Curiously, both Chang and Jek longed for orders given and received, though they disagreed on the giver and receiver.

"I just don't see the need to sack the palace," said Chang. "Residences are not our foes; those who occupy them are."

"So me and my people, what brung you the forklifts, wasted our time," the Assault Leader replied.

"It's just that with the captain in our hands, there's no need now to ram the doors."

"I was looking forward to that."

Astradian looked from one to the other with a cautious look on his face. "Those charging in the rams could get hurt," he ventured. "Whiplash."

"Scared?" Jek sneered.

"No. Only if'n we can get the captain here to order her household guards to lay down their weapons, we can take the palace without bloodshed."

"What's wrong with a little bloodshed?" said Jek.

"Who cares about taking the palace?" said Chang.

Captain Ming-ti smiled. "Not so easy, being in charge, is it?"

"Shuddup," said Jek and slapped her across the face. That, more than anything else that had happened, seemed to break the captain's hauteur. She blinked, and surprise, anger, and worry chased one another across her features.

"What about the blackbirds?" asked Astradian. "Can she order them to lay down their arms?"

The captain spoke up. "They are sworn to guard my person, but they belong to Ship Security. Only Lord Peng can release them from their oath."

"They are sworn to guard *the captain*," Chang told her. "Which you are not any longer."

"Who is," asked the captain. "You?"

"Shuddup," said Jek again. His hand flew up, and Rajalakshmi flinched. Jek laughed.

"Blackbirds are sworn to guard the *Whale* and her security first of all," said Astradian.

And what would that mean? wondered Reggie Chang, former gunnery sergeant of the Imperial Fleet Marines. Whose side would the blackbirds take? And what of the Marines? Why were they still sitting on their butts in the Barracks? What was Peng up to?

He had a momentary impression of a pair of green eyes regarding him from behind Jek, but when he looked again, he saw nothing.

When they brought the captain to the Brig, the bodies of Kemynder and his staff lay on the deck of the anteroom like so much cordwood. A single staff sergeant remained on duty from the original complement. He had cowered instead in the cellblock and so had avoided the slaughter. Since he knew how to work the system, log prisoners, and open and secure the cells, he had been co-opted into the Brotherhood.

Chang studied the bodies with distaste. "Won't they begin to stink in a few hours?"

The Brothers in the anteroom looked at one another and shrugged. They had no prior experience with dead bodies. One of them said, "Recycle ain't come by yet."

"I suspect most of the crew has stood down," Ming-ti said,

Jek said, "What part of 'shuddup' is proving difficult to grasp?"

Ming-ti smiled silently but then risked a slap, "Everyone's waiting to see how things settle out, and no one is giving orders or assignments. You desired the rule of the *Whale* but were I you, I'd not accept neglect of watch duties very easily."

Jek cocked his arm, but Chang seized his wrist and checked his swing. Jek glared at him.

I can almost see the steam hissing out of his ears, thought Chang. "She's not wrong, Assault Leader," he said. "We do need to keep the *Whale* shipshape. Our lives depend on it. I'll consult with Big Blue. It may be time for Phase III."

They chivvied Ming-ti to the big holding cell, where one of the other holdover sergeants hesitated before opening the door.

"Problem, sergeant?" said Jek.

The man's eyes flicked briefly to Jek's tricolor brassard but said merely, "Quite a change from the drunks and disorderlies we usually get."

"And from your political prisoners."

Another hesitation. "Yeah, them, too."

When the hatch opened and Chang escorted the former captain inside, he saw a fair number of Commanders crowded in together. Cdr. Barnstable bore substantial bruises on his face, and Lt. Cdr. Sewage's uniform was torn, but the others seemed unmolested. In addition to the Officers, Chang noticed their consorts, a few retainers, and ...

"What are the children doing here?" he asked Jek. The Princess of the Air clung to her father, weeping. He saw the son of Transport, the daughter of HVAC, as well as others.

"They would not leave their parents," Jek replied. "Are we a mutiny or a daycare provider? Besides, nits make lice."

Chang turned away from the prisoners and frowned at Jek. "They are children, Assault Leader."

"They are the children of privilege," Jek snapped back. "They grow up pampered and indulged and sneering at the rest of us. Then they feel they have the right to molest us."

The last remark puzzled Chang, and he said, "Sneering is no violation of the Regs. For that matter, the consorts had no role in our oppression."

"No direct role."

"Sah."

"Sah."

"And the servants? What was their crime?"

"Those are the ones who stood by their masters when we captured them. Sah."

"Yet I don't see Peng here. He was a prime target and dangerous. He controls the Marines and blackbirds. If he's running around loose ..."

"My teams haven't found him—yet."

"No, you were too busy rounding up consorts and children."

He spared another glance at the prisoners, harvesting from their faces hate, fear, despair on the bounceback. As well as a few smirks of pity.

"There is no job more simple," said Ming-ti, "than that of the other man."

Jek stepped forward and planted a solid punch on her jaw. The ex-captain staggered back a few steps and was caught by Nelson Chandrashekar. The Vice-Commander of Eugenics-Output glared at them. "You could at least have used a baton," he said.

Chang turned away from them and said, "That's quite enough, Assault Leader. Consider yourself on arrest."

Jek smiled. "Hear that, boyos? Group Leader Chang thinks we're in the Imperial Fleet Marines."

"We'll take these matters up with Big Blue."

"You'll find that hard to do from in here." Jek nodded to his assault team, and two seized Chang's arms while a third unclipped his teaser from his belt.

Taken by surprise, Chang struggled too late. His MOBI was taken from him. "What are you doing?" he demanded. "Unhand me! Now!"

"I think you are insufficiently devoted to the Mutiny, Chang. You think these people are innocent? Fine. Stay here with them." He laughed, turned his back, and left the cell. The door clanged shut behind him. A few minutes later, it opened again, and Astradian was pushed, stumbling, inside.

He and Chang looked at each other. "I guess we gotta be careful what we say from here on." Chang could not tell him he was wrong.

Ming-ti laughed. "Aren't you so glad you overthrew the Excellents?"

Hamdu Organson studied the transparent three-dimensional image of the *Whale* that floated above the map table. Red showed regions of the ship controlled by the Mutiny; blue, the opposite end of the color spectrum, those still controlled by Officer militias.

Baozhai took another report off her MOBI, and a region of the map changed from blue to yellow. Organson glanced at her.

"What was that?"

"Whoever holds Agro," she said, "just drove off a loyalist militia."

"Then Ku secured his objective? We hold it?"

"No, Excellent. Lieutenant Ku's commando was driven off earlier. The best we could determine from Ku's reports is that the meat vats and 'ponic fields are defended by Dwellers."

"Dwellers!" Organson was puzzled. Why were Dwellers meddling in the Mutiny? "What happened to Lord Agro?"

"No one seems to know, or at least no one in touch with us seems to know."

"Have MOBI keep searching. Gregor Vishwakarma may come over to us. And tell Ku that securing the food production sector remains a key objective."

"He may already know that," Baozhai said.

Organson paused and bobbed his head. "You are correct as always. Ask Ku his casualties and whether he needs reinforcements. Who is available?"

"Wait, one." She listened intently to MOBI then activated two red dots within the holomap. "Undine Palace and Power House have fallen." She could barely keep the glee from her voice but then quickly sobered and announced, "Lieutenant Astradian's commando is free. And we took the palace and the captain!" She shoved a fist into the air. "The *Whale* as she was!"

"Who took Power House? That wasn't on the first-wave list."

"A spontaneous mob attacked it, and apparently, a revolt by the palace servants assassinated Chan."

Organson frowned. That was too bad. Thantos was a man he thought he could have worked with, but an ancient proverb about omelets and eggs came to mind.

The hoigh plate sounded, and Organson saw Florian Venables in the peep screen. He wagged his stylus at Baozhai. "Let him in."

Baozhai tripped the lock from her desk, and the hatch swung out. Venables staggered in and almost fell against her desk as he was pushed from behind. Organson stared at this strange eruption. Baozhai shot up, alarm twisting her face.

Five mutineers pushed their way into his office. They wore their tricolors in black, gold, and red. One of them checked his MOBI, then looked Organson in the face. "Hamdu Organson?" He did not salute.

Organson did. He raised his fist and said, "The *Whale* as she was!"

One of the other mutineers giggled and said, "Aren't they cute when they do that?"

The leader glanced at her, then back to Organson. "Hamdu Organson, you are arrested by order of the Crew Council."

"Crew Council? On what grounds?" Organson asked.

The man smacked him. "On the grounds that you're a freaking bluecape."

"But ... I'm Big Blue. I planned and organized the Mutiny!"

"Yah, right. Cuff him, boys."

"Ask Group Leader Chang! He knows me!"

"Not the best name to conjure with," smirked the third mutineer.

As the mutineers hustled Organson out the door, Baozhai spoke up. "He's telling the truth."

The leader smiled. "Then it will probably turn out alright. Take it up with First Councilor."

The second mutineer said, "What about those two?" She hooked a thumb at Venables and Baozhai.

"A schoolteacher and a secretary? They's crewmen, not Officers. We got no orders concerning them." He gave them the stink eye. "As long as ye keep your noses clean and your loyalties clear." Then they were out the hatch, their chatter fading with distance.

Venables looked to Baozhai and said, "The Revolution always eats its young."

Hate flared on her face as if she had been painted over in dull red. "Lǎo dàjīngxiǎoguài," she snapped. Then she, too, was out the door and calling, "Hamdu!"

The regulars were huddled in Arfwendsen's Wayhouse, waiting out the tumult that roiled the pass'ways. Now and then, a stray pressed into the wayhouse seeking respite—and a stiff drink. But the Little Lotus neighborhood was less interested in the Oligarchy than in warding its border with the Burnout. Ever since their existence had been revealed, the Dwellers had grown bolder in their raids. Dukāndars had taken to armoring their storefronts. It seemed to them that neither Officers nor mutineers were interested in combatting these incursions, so Little Lotus,

Greater Harwich, and other villages along the frontier had taken a keen interest in self-defense.

Dhik was enjoying a mug of the Strangler and teaching his fellow patrons the finer points of quarterstaff play when Petronella Patterson ducked in, breathing heavily.

"Dhik," she said. "Help me! They're after me!"

Dhik did not even ask who was after Peta nor why. He turned to Kunigund and asked a question with his frown.

The landlord triggered the hatch to the storage room below and said, "Down here, ducky." Peta hurried through the trapdoor and down the ladder. Kunigund closed the door after her, threw a bar mat over it, and stood casually upon it.

Less than a minute passed before three men in the now ubiquitous tri-color scarves burst into the wayhouse, drawing all eyes toward them. "Alright," said one, "where is she?"

Kunigund had begun to polish a mug. "Where is who?" she asked. "Your pronoun lacked an antecedent."

The mutineer said, "Hunh?" but the second spoke up.

"Don't play games, land*lord*," with just the slightest emphasis on *lord*. "The Officer what run in here ahead of us."

Kunigund pulled a long face and looked around the tap room, bestowing significant looks on the drinkers, looks which Dhik reinforced with his own. "Anyone see a ring-sleeve scuttle in here?" She was answered with a chorus of negatives.

The lead mutineer turned to his compadres. "You sure you saw her duck in here?"

"Well ... we thought so, leader, but we don't see her neither."

The three of them walked slowly through the crowd in the wayhouse, examining closely each woman, sometimes cupping her chin to lift her head. They received a number of glares, a few raised fist salutes, and one, "Oi! That's my Woman, innit?" Dhik had a bad moment when they looked behind the bar, but they did not ask Kunigund to step aside.

When the three mutineers had finished their walk-through and returned to the entry hatch, Dhik spoke up.

"Laying hands on another crewman's Woman carries a two-stroke penalty."

The three looked at him in surprise. One of them said, "Yer that Enforcer what waled on the Maintenance leftenant. I seen the video."

Their leader added, "So, you should be on our side."

"That lieutenant," Dhik said, "violated regulations when he stopped his cart in a designated gangway and again when he struck a crewman with his baton. Not to mention that he was collecting an improper tax from tenant dukāndars. What regulation did this woman you're chasing violate?"

The leader shook his clipscreen. "Her name's on the Officer roster. She's a lieutenant (jg) in the medical department."

"Oh, *that's* a threat to our liberties. It's not a violation of regs to be an Officer," Dhik pointed out.

"They throw their weight around," said the second man. "The Orficers do."

Dhik grunted. "How much does she weigh? A jg? What's next, ensigns, CPOs?"

"In the twenty year I been running this place," said Kunigund Arfwendsen, "I ain't never seen an Officer shoulder his way in with the arrogance of you three."

The mutineers' gazes danced from drinker to drinker, from bar to tables. They harvested naught but hard looks in return. The second mutineer swatted the leader on the elbow. "C'mon, she's getting away." He and the third man turned to the hatchway.

The leader held back for a moment or two. "You better be a-wearing a tricolor tomorrow, or you'll learn better."

"Throwing you weight around, are you?" said Dhik. "This is Little Lotus, the most cantankerous neighborhood in the *Whale*. We can handle ourselves."

When the intruders had gone and the chatter in the wayhouse returned to its usual incoherence, Dhik said to Kunigund, "Let Peta out of that dungeon of yours now, and we'll be out of your hair."

Kunigund cocked her head. "We can handle ourselves?"

"Maybe, with the right help."

31   EXECUTIONS (II)

The hauteur of Sophie Masterson—"We can defeat them in detail."—Tommi Two Stones needs a woman—Regulation 18.872—Two brothers—Tommi Two Stones throws a strike

They brought the prisoners out one by one to a temporary platform erected at Comm Center Plaza. The first was Sophie Masterson, possibly the single-most-hated Officer in the belly of the *Whale*. When she saw the firing squad, she said, "At least we held trials for the mutineers."

"Shuddup," said Jek as he slapped her. He tied her to the post, pulling the cords rough and tight. The big screen mounted on Comm Center showed her magnified to the size of an ancient culture hero. Her face twisted in a mixture of fear, resignation, and contempt. The crowd laughed and chanted in Spanglish, "How now, old cow?"

Haughty to the last, Lady Water contrived to look down her nose and said, "Nor did we mock the traitors."

Jek gave the rope an extra tug, and Masterson winced. He said, "We're only traitors if we lose."

"What difference does it make? You killed my boy. I have nothing left for which to live."

Jek laughed into her weary eyes. "Then the timing works out alright, dunnit?"

He took his place beside the firing squad, lined them up in loose order, and gave the order to fire.

The crowd cheered.

But the squad expected to hear "ready, aim" first, so they did not fire their teasers in unison. Instead, their beams drilled her one at a time. Sophie Masterson jerked and twisted against the rope, though Jek was unsure whether that was reflex or a vain effort to dodge the beams.

None of the shots proved immediately fatal. Jek considered letting her die of her wounds. Surely, enough of them had drilled vital organs. But the crowd's cheers had subsided to mutters. They had wanted Sophie Masterson dead, but they had wanted that death to be clean. So once his teaser had recharged, Jek walked over to her jerking body, placed the aperture crystal against the base of her skull, and pressed the button. He called it "giving the tickle."

Lightning shot through her head and fried her brains. After a single final spasm, Sophie Masterson hung still and lifeless from the post. Jek had learned at Hanging Bridge that when a man dies, his bowels and bladder relax, so Masterson left a noisome mess behind.

One of the firing squad scoffed and said, "I thought she was supposed to crap her panties *afore* we teased." Jek chuckled. He was disappointed because he had always imagined the bluecapes screaming and crying and begging. That Masterson had actually salvaged a little dignity while being put down irritated him.

Walking back to the firing line, Jek heard another of the squad, Brithny Riguez, say, "She kicked people outta their homes. Maybe we shoulda just kicked her outta hers."

Jek had dreamed of this day for years and wasn't about to let anyone diminish it. He turned on the Brother and said, low and intense, "Sounds like you may be slack on the Mutiny, boy."

Riguez quailed and looked away. She said, "This way, she didn't suffer as much, not as much as her tenants, anyway."

Lucky Lutz sat alone at a table in the canteen, sipping now and then from a steaming ceramic mug of kaff. It was still too hot to drink, but if she sipped enough, she thought she could increase the surface-to-volume ratio and hence hasten the cooling of the beverage.

The others in the canteen spoke in whispers and bestowed stolen glances in her direction. It was not difficult to deduce the bent of their whispers. They were waiting for the legendary Lucky Lutz to pull a rabbit from her hat and put down the violence. That would be a good trick. If she had a rabbit. Or a hat.

She flipped screens and read off the names of Officers known to have been captured by the mutineers and noted first, that it was a list of considerable mojo, and second, that Peng was not on it. Lucky pondered that singular omission and its probable connection with the continued idleness of the blackbirds, the Enforcers of Filial Piety, and the Company of Fleet Marines. Not to mention the poor, unarmed police constables. Peng was loose somewhere in the *Whale*. She did not know if that was good news or bad and supposed that it was both, though for different parties.

Her MOBI flickered into Command Override. "Lucky Lutz, report to the Commandant's office. Lucky Lutz, report to the Commandant's office."

She sighed. In the entire history of humanity, no one had ever had to add "immediately" to such a summons. She sighed and glanced at her kaff, still too hot to drink, and carried the mug to the Recycler, where she poured it into the oubliette. Not that it was any great loss. The Commandant, she knew from her staff sergeant days, served a much finer brew, small amounts of which had on occasion found their way to First Platoon's wardroom.

Lucky could think of three reasons why she might get called up, and all three of them were bad.

She found Lt. Patel of the Second and Lt. Morsel of the Third already seated at the table. But there was also in attendance M/Sgt

Lollipop and the thin, severe man she had on the previous occasion taken to be Peng Himself. She made no remark on his attendance but went to the sideboard and served herself a cup of the Commandant's Own. The others had cups already before them.

When she had settled herself, Commandant Yueh addressed her. "Leftenent Lutz, who would you nominate to assume command of First Platoon?"

That was coming straight to the point, wasn't it? She had been found deficient in some fashion—perhaps she had failed to dot a I or cross an T in her paperwork, or perhaps she was to answer at last for her long-ago diversion of the Commandant's Own—and would now be relieved of her beloved Goons. She looked in turn at Morsel, Patel, and Lollipop, searching for some hint and finding none. She did not bother looking at Peng, whose face had yet to display his thoughts. He was the new element at the table, though, and likely the prime mover in kicking Lucky out. "Lieutenant Patel has seniority," she suggested.

"Oh, no," said Patel. "You'll pry the Second only from my cold, dead fingers."

"Ah prefeh' to promote from within," Yueh added.

Lucky barely hesitated. "Kent is platoon First Sergeant, and he managed First Squad before that. I think he can step up quite nicely."

Peng spoke. "Does he have your nose for tactics?"

The question called for a pro forma, *yes*, but she hesitated until Peng raised a single eyebrow. "Well?"

"I've set him to studying the urban battles of the past, like Beirut—or Lodz, where they stopped the Paris Jihad. I thought those more pertinent than field battles like Gettysburg or the Marne. I'm satisfied his grasp will become a second nature."

"And how would you tighten the Table of Organization?" Patel put in.

"Move Fishaven to First, Ku to Staff, and promote Corporal Singh to sergeant Second Squad."

"You sure you wouldn't want to think it over?" Peng asked.

"Sah, I am always thinking about who is ready to move up should the need arise."

Silence hung like a heavy blanket as the others looked from one to another.

"Test?" suggested Morsel.

"Very well," Peng called up the 3D holomap of the *Whale*. "Red dots," he said, "are the locations of mutineer gangs—'commandos,' as they call them. They are slightly larger than our platoons, and they have six of them remaining. Blue dots are militias fielded by various Commanders. Yellow are apparent third-party bands trying to protect vital regions from takeover by either faction."

Loyal to neither Captain nor Mutiny. Lucky recalled Peng's earlier appearance and waited for the question she knew must come.

After a number of heartbeats as the lieutenants studied the map, Peng said, "How would you address the tactical problem?"

Morsel said, "They outnumber us two-to-one."

"Then we must shoot twice," Lucky suggested. When the joke failed to harvest any chuckles, she added, "But the mutineers are led by former Gunnery Sergeant Reginald Chang. He had the finest tactical mind in the Company of Fleet Marines and taught me everything I know. I don't suppose he's forgotten any of it since he resigned."

Peng steepled his hands under his lips. "Chang has been arrested by his own mutiny, according to a sergeant on the Brig staff who works for us."

Lucky's heart tripped, and her thoughts danced ahead. "Who's leading their forces now?"

"Apparently, an assault team leader named Jek Buddhathal."

Lucky searched her memory for the name and came up empty. "An amateur, then?"

"Good news for us," said Morsel.

"Not necessarily. An amateur can make moves a professional would never anticipate and so be successful—for a while. That's where we get the expression, 'beginner's luck.'"

"Like Philipp Habib?" suggested Peng. "Or Adolph the Wolf in the Great War for Yurp?"

Lucky nodded. "Exactly, sahb. As long as they were on the offensive, their improvisation was successful, but improv doesn't work so well on the defense, and their amateurishness became a glaring deficiency."

"So with Chang now off the board, how would you defeat them?" Peng asked.

For a moment, Lucky thought he meant how would she defeat Habib or the Wolf, then she shook her head clear and studied the map. "Display the tram tubes that are blocked and the airtight doors still shut on the longitudinals."

Lollipop toggled a few items on his screen, and black lines and bars appeared throughout the *Whale*. Lucky saw immediately that the stern of the ship was effectively cut off. Forces could transfer only in trickles or through the Burnout, where the Dwellers held sway. Lord Agro and Lord Maintenance—and the mutineers attacking them—were on their own for now. That took two commandos off the board. The other four were scattered in squads and fire teams, apparently chasing bluecapes or, in a few cases, loot. Lucky smiled and said, "Sahbs. We can defeat them in detail."

The trick, as an ancient general had once said, was to get there "first with the most." How fast could troops move on the various pass'ways? The idea was to concentrate overwhelming force on pockets of the enemy, positioning the attacking forces so as to prevent the enemy joining together. The logistics problem presented elements of both *go* and *chess*.

"Good," said Peng. "That was my conclusion, as well. Yueh? We've already discussed this."

The old man smacked his lips and said, "We'll be needing an overlieutenant to coordinate all three platoons. They must strike in unison so the Enemy cannot concentrate his assets."

"Like the beaks of the three-headed eagle of old," said Lucky. She turned to Patel and extended her hand. "Congratulations, Gunja."

But Gunja Patel shook his head. "Not me. We already agreed."

It could not possibly be Morsel, whose commission was junior to a shucked clam. Were they raising Lollipop to officer? Yueh could not be taking direct tactical command, could he?

It only proved how slow of wit she was when the Commandant handed her a package and drawled, "Well, put 'em on."

Peng said, "We have not had such a rank since the *Whale* cast loose, but special needs demand special actions."

Lucky looked at him, then unwrapped the package, where she found the double bars of an overlieutenant. She looked back to Yueh, her face full of questions. "Y'all are on my staff, overlieutenant Lutz. Yer staff sergeant will be my command master sergeant, Laalamani Popof."

For a moment, Lucky did not know who he meant. Then she nodded to Lollipop. Lollipop nodded back. "Are you certain you want me?" Lucky asked them. But she was already working the problem. Did they have enough carts and lorries to scatter the three platoons and bring them together at the critical points?

Peng harvested their faces. "Are we agreed?" and a forest of bobbing heads responded.

Lucky sighed. It seemed there was a fourth possibility for the meeting, and it was also bad.

Tommi Two Stones crept about in settled volume. He had not known there were so many people in all the world. Having lost contact with the remainder of the Forlorn raiders, he had no clear idea of where he was. He had already taken cargo from four storehouses and married himself to three females, but he did not know which direction the Jumble was. In this severely rectangular shipscape, with 'ways ever at right angles, one passageway looked very much like another.

His man-hair—full beard and long, greased locks—had garnered a few curious glances, though fewer than his camo pattern dead-suit. The irregular patches on his coverall did not make him invisible, regardless of what the hexdoctor claimed, but it did break up his silhouette and make it more difficult for a foeman to draw an accurate bead.

But he must never forget that *these people*, as soft and clean-shaven as they appeared, had savaged Clan Desola in what should have been a perfect ambush, and later, even as they fled in terror, they had sent a great many of the Desolate to join the Dao. They were led, according to Tiff deSola, by a woman warrior, though that point, Tommi did not believe, for who had ever heard of a woman warrior?

He hadn't seen any reason to kill the females he had taken. After all, he was not bringing any of them back to the clan, but long habits are hard to break. The third female was the exception. While the first two had fought and resisted being married, the third had actually seemed to enjoy it and had stayed by his side since then. He thought she might be guiding him back to the Jumble, but that was hard to be certain since she spoke a language opaque to him. On occasion, her womanly jabber tossed up a word that seemed familiar, but usually in a skewed fashion. When she said, "toṇtai," she apparently meant *throat* rather than *swallow*. And the name she had given for herself—Phugkyu Deddman—sounded like no name he had ever heard before.

Conflict surrounded them, a condition Tommi found familiar, and he supposed two clans of Outsiders were wrangling over cargo. Whenever they encountered these armed bands, his woman would tug him aside into a niche or a back passage. All of the passageways were strangely unobstructed.

Except that, at times, they found great hatchways sealed against their progress. Tommi, who had grown up among obstacles, believed this a sign they were getting closer to the Jumble.

A male and female stepped out of a crosswise passage behind them, and Tommi, by reflex, ducked into a shadow. He had discovered that Outsiders could not see in the dark so well as the People. The male possessed a hawklike visage. The female was rounder and well-fed, as Outsider females seemed to be. As she turned the corner, Tommi caught a glimpse of a sad, wan smile and felt an immediate desire to marry her.

He unsnapped the thong on his throwing hatchet, and Deddman looked from him to the couple now walking away. Perhaps she divined his intention because she *touched* him and put a finger to her lips.

The hawk-faced man said some jabber and pointed. Tommi understood only the single word *Burnout*, which he understood was the Outsider term for the Jumble. Sometimes, he thought he should have listened more closely to the stories the Fogies told around the camp light. They were told in a *lingo* nearly as incomprehensible as the Outsiders.

But if the Jumble was in the direction the hawk-man had pointed, the woman had been guiding him away from it. The woman must have noted his realization, for she stuck a shiv in his side, saying her name over and over: "Phugkyu Deddman! Phugkyu Deddman!"

Had her blade been a longer one, he might have joined his ancestors in the Belly of the *Whale*. But it was not, and he had received
more-serious wounds during his admission into the male room of
Clan 'Lorn and *far* worse in the tussle with Triple-X. It would not
be fair to say that he laughed at pain, but he did chuckle some as he
turned on her with his own knife and plunged it deep into her gut,
twisting it and slicing sideways so that her abdomen opened up like
an ancient food package and her sausages spilled out.

The stab itself had at first silenced her through shock, but lest
her cries attract unwanted attention from the couple he had just
seen or from roving bands of Outsider fighters, he clapped his other hand over her mouth and pushed her to the floor. Her muffled
screams hummed against his palm as he waited patiently for her
writhing body to still itself.

The Fogies sometimes told of the *Struggle for Existence* that
caused improvements among the People, so Tommi waited patiently until the woman no longer struggled to exist. Then he wiped his
knife clean and returned it to its scabbard. He refastened the thong
on his throwing axe and set off after Hawk Face and Sad Smile. He
felt in his bag for the two stones by which he was known within the
clan, the stunstone and the killstone. He hoped the man would lead
him back to the Jumble. If not, there was always his companion. He
needed a new woman.

Jek was an impresario of death. After the first big execution,
that of Lady Water, he brought out a few lesser "robber barons,"
Maintenance lieutenants, senior and junior grade, and an ensign,
who had been about their business of extorting kickbacks from
a shopping district owned by Lord Kennett when the Mutiny
caught them backfooted. The lieutenants faced their ends with
what dignity they could, but the ensign blubbered and cried in a
gratifying manner. He had been doing only what he had been told
to do by his parents.

"You should have known what they told you was wrong," Jek said
and gave the order to fire. "There's a difference between doing things
right and doing the right thing."

361

Riguez had not fired. She lowered her teaser and quoted the Regs.

" 'Any officer of the *Whale* who commits or attempts an act of extortion shall be fined or clapped in the Brig for up to three years, or both. Regulation 18.872.' Extortion ain't no capital offense, sah."

Catcalls erupted from the crowd. They did not want the executions to stop. But some muttered in agreement. Jek turned to the Brother and said, "The 'Excellents' write the Regs. So they made it a capital offense to *lead* a mutiny but not to *drive* the crew into one."

But the Brother stood staunch. "The Departure Generation wrote the Regs."

That increased the mutterings from the crowd, and Jek noticed uncertainty on the face of another executioner. He shoved his face into Riguez. "Sounds like you're not so sure which side you're on, boy."

The Brother stood only a moment longer before she gave way. "No, sah. I'm sure." It was one thing to stand for a principle, quite another to die for it, and the threat had been there in Jek's tone. Riguez had to know that a few commando leaders already languished in the Brig awaiting the tickle.

But Jek knew what the restless mob was awaiting, and, having teased their appetites, he called for the main course, the in-captain herself. Cheers erupted from a score of throats.

"Capital enough for you?" Jek whispered.

Riguez's nod was a jerky bob of her head. "Yeah, sure."

Lucky was in the map room when Sergeant Singh reported. He came to a sharp stop, snapped a salute, and clicked his heels. "Sah!"

Lucky lowered at him. "You're not going all formal on me, are you, Gavinder?"

The squad sergeant tossed his head. "Wouldn't dream of it, captain."

Lucky sighed. "Okay, one formality," She tapped her rank insignia. "There can be only one captain in the belly of the *Whale*. So, they made me an overloo. Marine ranks differ from the Navy. Their captain would be like our colonel if we had a regiment aboard. Our 'captain' is like their lieutenant."

Singh said, "Confusin'. What's *our* lieutenant?"

"Like their lieutenant (jg). Just be glad we're Fleet Marines and not Planetary Marines. Then you'd have Rissaldars and Subadars and Naiks."

"No, thank you, overloo."

"You came to see me," Lucky reminded him.

"Oh, right. I was coming to that. Sentry at Twelve Gate says we have visitors."

"Visitors?" Lucky glanced at the map, but MOBI showed no armed forces approaching the perimeter.

"Two of my brothers," Singh told her.

The "brothers" proved to be Singh's compadres at the "Siege of Conniption Pass'," the Enforcer, and the medical examiner. They had trudged all the way forward from Little Lotus to the Barracks, seeking sanctuary because the medical examiner was an Officer and was being hunted by agents of the Mutiny. Lucky interviewed them in the entry hall by Twelve Gate, where the banners of the Three Platoons, the Company of Fleet Marines, and the Imperial Authority itself were displayed for visitors. She seated them at a broad table in comfortable chairs, and Singh sent an orderly to fetch accommodating beverages.

"Why not seek sanctuary at St. Brendan's?" Lucky asked them when all was settled. "That would seem more traditional." The Cathedral, like the Barracks, the Hospital, and the Quarterdeck, was situated amidships. Most mutineer bands were forward, scouring Officer Country, but not a few roamed aft as well.

The Enforcer—his name was Dhik—shrugged his massive shoulders, and it seemed to Lucky that the banners in their display cases fluttered a little. "Two reasons," said Dhik. "First, a couple ensigns claimed sanctuary there when the mutineers combed through Accounting, but the Mutiny's posse barged right in and snatched 'em right from the arms of the Holy Ecumenical Mother Church of the *Whale*."

The very thought scandalized Lucky. "And the second reason?"

"The Dalai Papa ain't armed."

Lucky leaned back in her chair. "We don't operate a hotel, you know."

The medical examiner—her name was Peta—made a face. "How are you fixed for medics?"

363

"Most of the patients in our infirmary are still alive."

"Not an obstacle," she said.

"So far as that goes," Dhik added, "this whole mutiny business shows less than perfect filial piety."

"So …?"

"So, are you making use of the Enforcers?"

Lucky looked off to a corner of the room, where she saw, to her unsurprise, a pair of green eyes floating. She grimaced. Peng could be irritating. She turned to Singh.

"What say you, sergeant? You know these people? I don't."

Singh said, "I would stand anywhere if they were by my side."

Lucky nodded. "I'll take it up with the Commandant."

Dhik said, "The Enforcers and the medical examiners have different chains of command from the Marines. You'd have to go all the way up to Peng for a ruling."

Lucky glanced again to the corner of the room, where the eyes had now vanished. "Somehow, I don't think that will be a problem."

Quarters between Flowing Silk and Little Lotus were scattered and solitary. Most of the cubic was given over to workshops of sundry sorts, nearly all of them silent now but still smelling pungently of paints, wood shavings, soy sauce, and the like. Occasional 'ponic trays, part of the post-Burnout efforts at decentralization, laid ragged and untended. Winnie did not think that boded well. The *Whale* was a vast juggling act with tens of thousands of balls leaping through the air. Let motion cease even for a moment, and they would all drop, bouncing to the deck. Because *this* 3D printer sat idle today while its proprietor was off chasing bluecapes—or protecting them—*that* assembly plant would not receive the parts they needed tomorrow.

Because she and Bùxiè were making their way down a longitudinal, most of the hatchways were devoted to goods inward or goods outbound. One cubic laid open with stacks of cartons awaiting pickup by lorries that had not come.

Even those not caught up in the hoo-hah of the Mutiny had been forced into idleness. Winnie saw crewmen sitting on their stoops outside their residences. Wayhouses were hosting a lively and raucous business, and she heard snatches of song when they passed near one.

But most of their trek was conducted in dimly lit warehouse and fabrication districts. Only now and then did they hear the tinking and hissing that heralded an active workshop. What they were making and for whom, Winnie did not know. Perhaps they only wanted to keep themselves busy.

"If the trams were running," she said, "we would be there by now." It was a foolish complaint, as she knew even as she voiced it.

"You wanted," Bùxiè reminded her, "to escape your notoriety in Flowing Silk and find peace and quiet where nobody knows your name. Little Lotus is notoriously closemouthed. Even if they've heard about what happened with Dumont Ramamurthy, they won't bother you with it. Too much other waste has flowed through the pipes to obsess on a killing days ago and somewhere else." They walked a little farther, and, surrendering to a sudden impulse whose origin was unclear, Winnie stuck her hand into the crook of his arm.

He started but then relaxed. They still had to cross several more frames before they would reach his home village.

Bùxiè abruptly disengaged and chivvied her to walk in front of him. She grunted a surprised question. Had she offended him somehow?

"Dweller on our Six," he muttered.

"What? This far forward? What's he doing here?"

"What do any Dwellers do when they leave the Burnout?"

She turned and glanced behind but beheld naught save shadows and pools of light. "I don't see anyone."

"They don't exactly flaunt themselves. No, don't turn again. Look from the corner of your eye. He won't move if you're looking."

Winnie upped her pace slightly, trying not to break into a trot. Her heart flew back to Conniption Pass' and the howling pack that had besieged them. And to her, Jaunty's tortured and decaying carcass. "Only the one?"

"I saw no others," Bùxiè said. "But what does that mean?"

"Was he armed?"

"He's a Dweller." He pushed her gently in the small of her back. A little faster. "I saw a knife and two hatchets on his belt."

"No crossbow?"

"Not that I saw."

Winnie smiled to herself. "A good thing I'm packed."

"Delightfully so."

"Erm. 'Packed' is a term from those old street-thug dramas. *I'm packing heat.*" And in case this still did not clarify matters for him, she patted the holster on her belt. "I never gave the teaser back to One," she explained. "You expect him to throw his hatchet?"

"It's what they do. Why do you think I placed myself between you and him?"

Winnie twisted her head and looked into his eyes. She stumbled, and Bùxiè steadied her, "It's what *I* do. Besides, I'm wearing thix armor."

The Dweller chose that moment to step from the shadows, his arm hauled back like a stickball bowler. The rock struck Bùxiè in the back of his head, where he wore no armor, nor would it have mattered much if there had been. The stone hit with enough velocity to stun him, and he dropped, first to his knees, then face down to the deck.

The Dweller was already sprinting toward them, a bigger rock already in his hand for a killing blow. Winnie yanked her teaser from its holster and fried him in mid-stride.

The lightning took him in his torso, its voltage paralyzing his heart muscle and diaphragm. He tried to suck a breath and could not, though it mattered not at all, for his heart failed before he could asphyxiate, and he dropped, body jerking on the deck.

Winnie kicked the stone off to the side and unsnapped and discarded both his hatchets and his knife before she turned her back on the corpse.

She dashed to Bùxiè's side and felt the back of his head, bringing her fingers away red with blood. "Bùxiè!" she said.

He looked at her with pupils dilated to different sizes and said something incoherent.

"You have a concussion," she decided. "How many fingers am I holding up?"

"Five. No, two. Two Winnies. Twice as nice." His eyes fluttered closed.

"No," she said. "Don't go to sleep on me. Stay awake!" She rubbed him on the cheek. His eyes opened, closed again, and his breath sighed out of him.

Winnie clapped her hand over his mouth to contain the ghost. "No, you don't. Stay inside. Don't lose hold of your body." She was aware in a peripheral way that other crewmen were coming out of the latitudinals, attracted by the noise. Several were already on their MOBIs.

Bùxiè's eyes blinked and closed once more. Winnie cradled his head. Shang Di was everywhere, but Winnie always looked up to find him—to the overhead, to the deck above, past Greenfields and the asteroid shell, into the pitiless ocean of night. "Shang Di," she cried. "Krishna-Buddha-Christ! Must you take every male I care for? Keep his gust-ghost within him. Don't let him die!"

Winsome Alabaster owned a perennially sad visage, but she was not given to outright weeping. Only three times before had she wept without restraint. Now it was four.

32 COMPLICATIONS

The only thing left is style—Little Face scouts the rear—
She can keep a cool head in a firefight—The distress of
Hamdu Organson

Rajalakshmı Ming-ti, tenth in-captain of the Imperial Ship
Whale, was captain only because her great-grandmother had staged
a coup against the sixth in-captain after his inadequate response to
the Burnout. In this, she had shown an audacity, and courage that
Rajalakshmi had often imagined in herself. This only showed the
limits of her imagination. She had put on arrogance and imagined it
as courage. Only now, when led bound to the firing post and courage
was actually called for, did she find herself lacking.

Gazing into the pitiless dark eyes of her executioners, she knew
she would not leave the platform alive. And as an ancient author had
once written, when death is inevitable, the only thing left is style. She
was grieved now to discover she had no style. Tears blurred her vision.

"What did I ever do?" she blubbered to the men who led her
from the Brig, as if they cared or, if caring, could act. In truth, they
were as wary as anyone of getting on Jek's bad side.

368

"I always tried to play off the Entente against the Alliance! Those are the ones you should be teasing!" But perhaps (a traitorous part of her mind whispered) that was her offense. The in-captain was supposed to nurture the crew, not simply balance their oppressors. On the Day of Wrath, such judiciousness would be swept away along with the arrogance of Sophie Masterson or the extortions of Kennett Erlanger.

She saw now that her terrors had allowed the hard-liners to push her into overreacting in the executions of the premature mutineers. She should have listened more closely to Organson, Peng, Thantos Chan, and the others. Yet the Light Lord had been assassinated, and Organson sat in the Brig awaiting his own appointment with destiny, so there was no salvation along the pass'way of mercy, either.

Shang Di will bless the peacemakers, for no one else will. The Mutiny had already condemned some of its own more moderate members.

On the steps to the platform, her legs gave way, and she dipped in a parody of a curtsy. The mutineers on either side of her seized her arms under the pits and hauled her roughly to her feet. When they led her out onto the platform and bound her hands to the post, the waiting mob cheered. She twisted and squirmed and shrugged uselessly; but as she possessed a considerable mass, her struggles gave her captors a hard time. The waiting crowd roared its approval.

Finally, she gave up. The ending was foregone, inevitable. She prayed to Shang Di that she would be reincarnated as a bird, so she could crap all over the statues that the mutineers would one day raise to themselves.

Their leader, Buddhathal, approached her and said in a smarmy voice, "Any last words?"

She may have surprised him by saying "yes" in a calm, firm voice. She faced the mob howling for her death and waited a beat or two until they quieted. *Whatever was the fat old broad about to say?* She looked them over and her magnified image did the same on the screen. The microphones boomed her voice.

"Who is caring for the *Whale* while you take your petty vengeances? Who is doing your job?"

A sharp pain pierced the back of her head and a bright light blossomed in her vision.

Little Face led the scouting party seeking a path around to the rear of Ku's besieging commando. The meatpacking district was too broad to stop the Brotherhood from infiltrating, and Ku's commando, too few to sustain those footholds. And so, the struggle rocked back and forth with no resolution.

Lord Agro's people were posted in "pillboxes" with overlapping fields of teaser fire and among the meat spindles as well. No matter who ruled in the *Whale*, they would have to eat. A few pigs and beeves had already perished and would need to be re-cloned, but the one thing no one wanted back here was a "scorched earth" strategy.

Fanghsi led three Orphans through Pigwhistle, where Whistlers peeked cautiously through slits and slats. Those zealous for the Mutiny had long since run off to join it; those hard to preserve the old order had already joined a department militia.

You are lukewarm, he thought to the cowering remnant, *and so I vomit you from my mouth.*

That was not fair, he knew. Hidaki had told him that Lord Agro was sympathetic to the ends of the Mutiny but not to the means by which they proposed to accomplish those ends. The bulk of the crew had not chosen sides but were naturally reluctant to show themselves when angry men ran about with lightning in their fists.

Little Face supposed that he himself was now counted as a traitor to the Mutiny, although, like Lord Agro, he was sympathetic to their goals. But no one seemed disposed any longer to dispassionate debate.

He was not even overjoyed to find himself defending the meatpacking district. He would be much happier sitting the whole thing out in the Burnout sifting for relics. He could return to the *Whale* when the excitement was over, assuming there remained a viable habitat to which he could return.

He led his party past the shuttered eatery, the *Pig and Whistle*. Too bad, he thought. They had served a stand-out beefstuff there. He wondered if the owners and staff had gone off to fight in the Mutiny and, if so, on which side.

Finally, a longitudinal pass'way they were probing ended in a heap of collapsed bulkheads. Little Face thought he saw a sliver of reflected light running vertically down the heap, but his ears detected the whisper of a faint breeze. His nose, not to be upstaged, caught the whiff of stale air as he had oft encountered opening long-sealed quarters.

One of the Orphans had gone to his knees to study the thick dust in the pass'way.

"What is it?" Little Face asked him.

The Orphan did not look up. He pointed. "Many footprints go to Jumble, few return."

"That's the tale of Burnout, innit?"

But the Orphan shook his head. "Many footprints, same foot. Same fellow go in many times, seldom comes he out."

Meaning he somehow entered the Burnout here but exited elsewhere. Fanghsi deferred to the Dwellers' greater tracking ability. But that meant the pass'way was not as blocked as it seemed. He led his scouts closer to the rubble, and as he approached, Little Face realized that the sliver of light was not a reflection of the light behind him but a crack which showed a light beyond.

Before too long, the Orphans had found the way through the crack, and Fanghsi found himself in a pass'way that, saving only the skeletons lying about, might as well have been in the settled part of the *Whale*. The sunlamps in the overheads still shone, and Fanghsi could hear the faint whup of distant air-circulation fans. One of the Orphans, Scar Boy, fell to his knees.

"It's the very heaven of which our grandsires told!"

Little Face thought their grandsires had a low bar for their heaven. To him, the pass'way seemed desolate and, if one counted the skeletons, macabre. He opened one of the hatchways and looked inside the quarters thus revealed. The rooms were those of a petty officer third class, and one of the two skeletons commingled on the bed was undoubtedly his. Or hers. Fanghsi captured images of everything. The dust of eighty years overlay all. Treasures aplenty for a burnsider such as himself. A book on the dresser proved to be the diary of petty officer Ramona Harper. The paper had oxidized and turned brittle with time, but the experts at the Museum might be able to restore it.

Assuming the Museum and its experts survived the Mutiny.

Nonetheless, he had bagged the diary and some other small items to take with him when the thought struck him that whoever the footprinter was, he was not a burnsider. As often he had passed through this volume, he had not looked into any rooms for salvage.

The rear entrance to the petty officer's quarters revealed a mass of wreckage. Little Face opened two more portside quarters before he found one that led to a reasonably open pass'way. He was outside the region known to him and outside the "turf" of the Orphans, as well; so he and his scouting party felt their way carefully. After a few more blocks, the lights were out, and they resorted to jùggies to continue.

The mostly rectilinear arrangement of pass'ways and gangways enabled Little Face to maintain his spatial orientation relative to the meatpacking district and Ku's besieging commando. But just when he thought himself well behind the mutineers and two decks above them, a man with a shoulder-mounted teaser stepped out of the shadows and said, "That's far enough, I'm thinking."

Bùxiè deSōuxún awoke in a white room reeking with the odors of antiseptic. Looking about and fighting off the mild vertigo that entailed, he saw Winnie asleep in a chair. His double vision had faded, for he saw only one of her. He was surprised and a little discomfited at how the sight of her lightened his heart.

For a few moments, he lay in the bed, listening to the sound of her breathing. But he soon grew curious to learn how he had gotten here, not to mention where "here" was. He coughed, but Winnie did not move; so he coughed again, louder, and Winnie started.

"Bùxiè! You're awake!"

"Or else," he said, "I'm dreaming. What happened?"

"How much do you remember?"

"Not much. You and I were walking aft along a longitudinal. I recollect some sort of danger, but the details are not even hazy."

"A Dweller was stalking us. He threw a rock that hit you in the back of the head. It gave you an awful concussion."

Bùxiè winced, and his hand went to the back of his head, where it found a prodigious lump. "Did he? What happened to him? Why didn't he finish us off?"

Winnie shrugged. "He got teased."

When next Bùxiè awoke, he was alone except for a medic, whose badging named her Specialist Second Gruder. She checked his temperature, blood pressure, pulse rate, and a host of other signs that did not seem to him to have anything to do with concussion. But she also checked his pupil dilation, balance, and vision, which clearly did. So he concluded that she knew her business.

"Where am I? I forgot to ask Winnie."

"That the heroine what dragged yer sorry butt in here?" the medic asked.

Heroine? "Yes. Where did she go?"

"We packed her off to the resting room to get some zeds. She was a-setting here for two days until you regained consciousness. Oh. This here is the Urgent Care Unit in Little Lotus, somebody or other commanding if they can get all this nonsense sorted." The medic shook her head and said, "You wouldn't think so to look at her, but she must be a deadeye with a teaser, the way she took down that Dweller what beaned you."

"She did that?"

"Aye. Some crewmen who came a-running saw it all. I shudder to think of one of them nasties flitting about in Little Lotus."

Bùxiè bobbed his head and tried not to let the wince show. By "nasties." He assumed she meant Dwellers, not Winnie. "Yes," he said, recollecting the Siege at Conniption Pass'. "She can keep a cool head in a firefight."

Later that day, his former sergeant, Qínfèn, came to see him. "The word is gotten around the nick, sah. How you were beaned by a Dweller, and memsahb Alabaster saved your butt."

"Only fair, sergeant. I saved hers on a few occasions. From a feral dog, from a feral Commander ..."

"And that I would have liked to see. A constable from Flowing Silk told me you swung your staff with the grace of a master stickballer. Was Ramamurthy's head a ball, you would've scored an over."

Such talk made Bùxiè uncomfortable. He said, "I see you're packing heat, sergeant."

"Packing heat? Oh, I see what you mean. Very droll, sah. Almost every resident in Little Lotus—and up in Greater Harwich—'packs heat' these days. Dwellers have grown bolder. You remember Comfort Bhardwaj? Raiders pincushioned her and her whole family with their crossbows and packed up their larder. After that, the armory could not keep up with the demand for thix. I hope this mutiny business is sorted, one way or the other, because the borderframes need patrolling, bad. Oh, hello, sri Alabaster. You won't remember me, but ..."

"Sergeant Qínfèn. You were at the memorial for Snowy Mountain. Of course, I remember you."

"She means Adrienne," Bùxiè explained.

"Did you not arrange the memorial while Bùxiè was indisposed?"

"Indisposed? He was like a zombie, *mem*. But it was the quarter-deck made the arrangements."

"Jones?" Bùxiè exclaimed. "Why?"

"Yeah, that was his name. Jones. A nice chappie. Snow. Adrienne was his protégé, and I think he was nearly as devastated as you at her translation. You know goldcapes don't have children, so their protégés become their surrogate offspring."

Bùxiè knew all that but allowed Qínfèn to babble on. He had not thought of Adrienne for several days and immersed himself now in her memory. He recalled how she used to tilt her moon face at a slight angle. Adrienne. Her ghost stood beside his bed now and he thought, *I don't want to lose you.*

The oath was "until death parts us," pretty man. Past that dread barrier, all vows are ended.

He looked to Winnie. "Adrienne will always be with me."

"As Jaunty, with me. Maybe we could form a foursome and play pachisi together."

The thought was so ludicrous that Bùxiè could not contain his laugh, and it burst loose. He wondered if that was his first laugh since Adrienne had died.

Adrienne, he thought, trying to summon her ghost again, but she did not reappear.

Instead, two large crewmen in tricolor scarves entered the room. "And who are you, gentlemen?" he asked. "If this is to be a convention, I'll need a bigger room."

"You crewman Bùxiè deSōuxún?" The newcomers were badged for cargo-handling, and their name tags styled them able spacers, Chakraborty and Wing. "Assault Leader Buddhathal," Wing announced, "wants for to see yuh up on Comm Central."

Qínfèn whispered, "Comm Center is where he's been executing the bluecapes."

"A good thing, then, that I wear no cape. I've wanted to meet Jek Buddhathal for some time now, but I'm surprised that such a busy and important man has the time to see me,"

"He wants to give ye a medal fer executin' the bluecape, Ramamurthy," said Wing.

Bùxiè thought the fellow poorly informed. Braining Dumont Ramamurthy had had naught to do with the Mutiny. He had done it to protect Winsome Alabaster, the thought of whom drew eye to her momentarily. He told Buddhathal's men, "I can make arrangements once I've been released by the medics."

Chakraborty handed him a release form. "Councilor Buddhathal don't like to wait."

"We're supposed to escort yuh," Wing added.

Bùxiè dressed while Winnie and Qínfèn looked on. When he donned his black coveralls, Wing said, "Yuh work fer Peng, do yuh? Didn't know that. We was told you was a copper." Suspicion darkened their faces.

Bùxiè said. "I still am. I was promoted into CID, not into the blackbirds. When I was DCI, I investigated burglaries, assaults, murders, and the like. CID investigates crimes that cross police district boundaries, like serial killers or account hacking and identity theft. Like if someone in Pigwhistle siphons your personal account in Milkhoney and spends your hard-earned credits in Highsteeple, your local nick would be hard pressed to track him down. That's where CID steps in."

"Some poor fool steals *my* identity," Wing laughed, "he'll deserve all the bill collectors been nagging me."

"Might could be," Chakraborty added, "yuh can help us track down Peng."

Bùxiè thought that unlikely, given Peng's curious cloak, but said nothing. *Just put me next to the sunnuvabitch who used Adrienne as a human shield.* What might happen after that, he was unsure. It did not matter. Nothing had mattered to him very much since her translation.

Hamdu Organson was more distressed at the indifference of the mob than at his own impending demise. No one seemed sure of who he was, only that he was a "capewalker."

"Don't you know me?" he shouted to the jeering mob, "I'm Big Blue!" But all he received on the bounceback was laughter and disinterest. They had no idea who Big Blue was supposed to be and most of them were too drunk to care. And so, despite organizing the Mutiny, despite setting up the recruiting camp in the Burnout, despite orchestrating the liberation of two crates of teasers, despite all that he had done, he was to be denied even a hero's death.

This was not how he had imagined it. He had imagined a stalwart band of crewmen standing resolutely against a pampered and pompous commandery that had always laughed behind their hands at him and his liaison post.

"Yah got any last words?" asked the wretched Jek Buddhathal, and Organson thought they should have followed through and neutralized him when they had learned of his personal issues mixed into the Mutiny. Coulda, shoulda, woulda. It was too late now.

"Yes," he said, leaning close in confidence. "Did you review the post-Mutiny plans with Reggie before you threw him in the Brig? I don't think you've completed Phase II yet; nonetheless you ought to have started on Phase III."

Of the last words he may already have heard spoken, these perhaps surprised the self-appointed First Councilor. His mouth opened and closed like a koi, caught between spurning a reply and curiosity as to what Organson meant. Finally, he scowled and said, "What?"

"Have you even installed a provisional in-captain yet? If not, how do you propose to manage and coordinate the ship's systems? The balls don't juggle themselves, you know." The plan had been for Organson to carry that burden himself, but he did not mention that to Brother Jek. He knew it would serve no purpose. Besides, the scuttlebutt said that Lord Maintenance and Lord Agro still held out in the Stern. Neither, he suspected, would accept Lord Liaison as provisional captain.

As he looked out across the drunken crowd, a fable concerning Humpty-Dumpty and the king's horses and men came to mind. There stood Baozhai, his faithful assistant, with tear-drenched cheeks. And where …?

He finally located Florian Venables in the crowd, long-faced and solemn, looking on with something like sorrow and pity. *Farewell, old friend*, he thought. He had always wondered how his chief advisor would have reacted if Peng had caught him and that he wouldn't have the stomach for it when what had to be done had to be done. The old man would be amused to learn that it was not Peng they ought to have been wary of and that Organson himself was not constituted for the pitiless measures for which a successful mutiny called.

When Venables' face turned to one of horror, Organson braced himself for the lightning, though how exactly one was to do that was unclear. When the bolt to the back of his head did not come, at least just then, he turned and saw Luis Barnstable, his consort, and the Princess of the Air climbing the steps behind him.

Jek Buddhathal did not tolerate traffic jams, so he removed the speed bump forthwith.

33 PRESENTATIONS

"Two more, and I got the whole set."—"That won't last."—Unleashing hell—In the captain's cabin—"That's a suitably vague charge."—Heroes of the Mutiny

Just before Squad Sub-leader Jumdar could bang on yet another hoigh plate in the search for Ensign Chou-li, Fighter Kaur rushed up to him and grabbed his elbow.

"Crewman Jumdar! Marine squad to starboard!"

Jumdar was not impressed. "A whole platoon of them rusty-backs passed us in the night. Agarwal told me they was heading aft to patrol the Frontier. Dwellers been raiding the settled folk there."

"Nothing to do with us, then."

"Not that I can tell." He banged on the hoigh plate until the resident finally answered. She was an obese woman wearing only a nightgown. "G'day to ye, crewman," he said. "We's a-looking fer a bluecape ensign what's named Chou-li, Pharmacy Department."

The woman squinted pig-eyed at him. "Who wants to know?"

"Assault Leader Buddhathal, that's who. Yah seen him?"

"Buddhathal? No."

378

"Naw. The ensign."

"Oh sure, I collect ensigns. Got me four or five in my back room now. Two more, and I got the whole set."

"Sorry to trouble ye, crewman, but we's a-doing a door-to-door search for him. For Chou-li. Mind if we be coming in?"

The crewman squinched up her face. "Not much. My Man and me were just about to shag, and he's not very good at it. Mebbe you'd be better, honey-butt."

Jumdar swallowed. "Ah, no thankee, crewman. We's better keep a-going. G'day to yah, crewman." He thought there no compelling reason that a Whaler ought to look like a Whale and learned there were some mental images that could not be expunged.

When the hatch had closed, Kaur said, "According to the roster, she's a pharmacist's mate." He had his hand screen open.

"What of it?"

"Who better to be hiding a pharmacy ensign?"

"Kaur, if'n we a-pushed our way in there, only two things could've happened. No, three. And all of them bad. One," he posted a finger, "there be no ensign, just a fat lady in her nighty and her Man mebbe nekkid as a mole rat. Two," a second finger sprang to attention, "the ensign is in there, and we gotta cuff him, and fill out the paperwork, and a-shlep him up to the Brig—with no trams a-running, mind ye—instead of we just a-keep on knocking on doors an' sometimes getting ourselves a bit of tea and biscuits."

"And three? You said there were three possibilities."

"Yah, three. She really do have four or five ensigns in her back room, probably with knives, and there be only two of us."

"Marines to starboard," Kaur pointed. "Two fire teams between us and Argawal."

Jumdar sighed. "I already done told yah ..."

But he never got to tell Kaur what he had already told him because an anesthetic dart embedded in his back, his eyes rolled up, and he sagged to the deck. Kaur, calculating that three-to-one odds had just escalated into six-to-one, thrust both arms empty-handed into the air.

One of the Marines spoke on his MOBI, "Inform Patel that Lower Black Jade is cleared. Teams will now pivot up one deck to

379

interdict boogers in Shaolistown." He addressed one of his men. "Bring the Enforcer up and a medtech with an autogurney to escort our guests to the temporary brig, then report back, soonest."

Lollipop toggled the 3D map, and another mutineer pocket winked out. The red Marine dots moved up a deck, where another cluster of mutineers awaited. Lollipop touched his ear.

"Still no outcry, sah. Sending the Third to patrol the Frontier was a clever move. Enemy thought we were answering calls for protection."

"We are," Lucky reminded him. She wished her staff would stop reminding her how clever she was supposed to be. She might start believing them, and if that happened, her luck really would run out. "Is Kent in position yet?" That was the most difficult maneuver, and she wished she was with the Goons approaching Comm Center. She hated being back in Barracks directing the action rather than with the First Platoon in the thick of it.

"It's like a *go*-board in three dimensions," observed Peng with a gesture toward the map. "You're placing your stones to surround and isolate enemy stones."

Lucky said nothing and watched the map track Kent's progress. They were riding in closed lorries with florist or grocer or handyman logos, but sooner or later, they would need to deploy.

"And your opponent," Peng continued, "still does not realize the game is afoot."

Lucky exchanged glances with Lollipop. "That won't last," she said. It didn't.

All his life, Little Face had avoided taking sides, but of late, sides had been taking him. He had never had long-term goals. For a burnsider, the long term wasn't in the cards. What he had wanted was only an alliance with a Dweller clan, but one thing had led to another. The Orphans wanted meat, so Little Face had to lead them to meat. But Lord Agro had been looking for fighters and had co-opted the Orphans—and with them, Little Face—into his defense of the meat vats. When Agro sent him to find Wennel Ku's rear, Fanghsi had intended to slip off into the Burnout and avoid all the foo-foo. But the gods laugh at mortal intentions because Agro had sent three Orphans along with him, and the Orphans wanted the meat more than Little Face wanted the solitude.

Then, while searching for Ku's rear, he had found the Machine Shop's outpost. Now he stood on the "sharp edge" of an impending battle, the place he least desired to be, excepting only Jek's firing post up on Comm Center.

From his vantage point on Thirty-Seven Deck, a walkway overlooking the vast open Agricultural Sector on Forty Deck, he could see agro crewmen at work tending a complex and apparently chaotic array of meat spindles and 'ponic trays that stretched abaft to the frame boundary. Decks Thirty-Nine to Thirty-Seven had never extended their cover over the Agricultural Sector, so from here, he had a panorama of the whole field. It was the largest open volume in the *Whale*, Greenfields excepted.

H could see a motley of militia, Dwellers, and blackbirds quietly gathering behind the structures before Ku's siege camp, which was directly under him. One of them, a Dweller, extended a knife and shaved a slice of meat from a spindle, which he chewed with enthusiasm.

Ku was an idiot. He ought to have had an observer up here. But maybe he wasn't, and maybe he did—elsewhere, or perhaps on Thirty-Nine or Thirty-Eight because Fanghsi could see movement in Ku's camp, preparing to receive Agro's assault.

"The idea," Lord Kennett told him, "is that while Gregor hits 'em in front, we hit 'em behind and catch 'em between us like a walnut in a cracker."

Of course, that meant that Little Face would be between the two forces as well. He forbore pointing this out since Lord Kennett proposed to "lead from the front" himself. Whatever else you could say about Lord Maintenance, and Little Face had said plenty, you could not call him a coward. A weasel, maybe, but not a coward.

And what was the point of having a machine shop if you couldn't make yourself all sorts of useful shit? The redshirts had teasers of their own, fabricated in the Shops.

Little Face had sent Scar Boy back to Lord Agro to give that greasy hairball a heads-up on the lowdown. Agro would await Lord

Kennett's signal—*You'll know it when you see it*—and hit Ku's front at the same time the redshirts attacked his rear.

"No more complicated plan is needed," Kennett said. "The more complex a plan, the more things you can screw up."

"So, this way, we only screw up the simple stuff?"

Kennett glanced at him and laughed. "Just remember, scout. Once you yank the ignition cord to release the glycerine, throw the damn thing as far as you can. You've got maybe fifteen seconds before the reaction triggers. Trust me, you don't want to be holding it when it goes off."

Lord Kennett was a rat-faced bastard, and Fanghsi didn't trust him any more than he trusted Lord Agro. But then he didn't trust Wennel Ku, either, or at least not Ku's boss, Jek Buddhathal. Trust went at a premium these days.

The canister was packed with powdered aluminum and rust that was shaved off iron parts by the mills and lathes. It was called "thermite," and it burned like the fires of Hades. The redshirts used it to weld magrails in the tramways. You couldn't quench it with water since it possessed its own oxidizer and burned under water. In fact, it could break the water down and use its oxygen to sustain the reaction. Not to mention releasing the hydrogen gas. You just had to wait for the fuel—the aluminum—to exhaust itself.

Nothing is more terrifying in a ship than fire. Bulkhead material was non-flammable, but the steel framing could melt. Thermite burned *hot*. That was why Kennett had chosen this vast open area to unleash hell.

And—again—what was the point of having a machine shop if you couldn't make yourself all sorts of useful shit?

Fanghsi did not detest the mutineers, save perhaps for Jek, and that was personal. So, he did not share Lord Maintenance's zeal to incinerate them. He rather sympathized with their motives. Many Officers *were* corrupt bullies, Lord Kennett not least among them. Although once bribed, it was said, Kennett delivered. Could there be such a thing as "honest corruption?" Such considerations went above and beyond Fanghsi.

He could not deny that the Mutiny had betrayed its own ideals and had become the very thing they had rebelled against. He had heard that Reggie Chan and other leaders had been condemned for no better reason than that they had rubbed Jek the wrong way, and since Little Face knew he himself was abrasive, he was surely on Jek's to-do list, as well.

A bad business all around. What the Mutiny needed was Reggie and Lo Sin, maybe even that pompous ass, Big Blue. But what it had gotten was Jek.

"See you on Forty," Kennett said, clapping him on the arm before heading to the stairwell.

Fanghsi watched him go and wondered if he could drift back into the Burnout instead. The Orphans would not like that. Maintenance would like it less. Enough so that either would hunt him down? Who could say?

He sighed. He didn't know this region of the Burnout and the Orphans did, and it would be a crappy play to fade on them now. Stepping to the rail of the walkway, he looked down on Ku's camp, deployed now to anticipate Lord Agro's attack.

He was supposed to lob the thermite bomb directly into the camp, but he could not bring himself to do it. Wennell Ku was not a bad sort, all things considered. He could have ordered Fanghsi killed that day when he had stumbled into them standing over the body of Jaunty Alabaster, but he hadn't. So, Fanghsi owed him. And Ku had a brother in the Fleet Marines who had been a hero at the Redoubt fight.

So, in the end, he pulled the cord, waited a few beats, and threw the bomb as far as he could to starboard of the Brotherhood camp.

It caught fire in midair and burned with a furious fountain of sparks, flames, and molten metal as it fell.

Sorry, boss, he imagined himself telling Kennett. *I held on too long. Then all I could think of was getting the damned thing as far from me as possible before it went off.* But in his heart, Fanghsi knew the real reason. He was not prepared to commit atrocities for any Cause. He just could not think of the mutineers as *enemies.*

The persistent chiming of his MOBI brought Tongkawa Jones awake barely two bells into first watch. He peered weary-eyed at his chronometer. So, the reason he felt as if he had only just touched head to pillow was that he had, in fact, only just touched head to pillow. "Yes?" he snapped to his device.

Reynaud Berylplume answered. "Captain's cabin. Now."

The strangled urgency in the First Officer's voice was enough to splash Jones' face with cold water and throw on an off-duty uniform. He left the golden cape hanging. He had not worn it since the harrowing incident on Hexenplaza.

It was but a short scoot on a cart from the Cloisters to the Golden Horn, and when he arrived at the Great Cabin, he found a small mob inside. Four bodies lay on the floor, one in the uniform of a sergeant-at-arms. Two others were being treated by medics. All four deck officers were present—Berylplume, Tang, Brahmadharma, and san Pedro—as well as the Executive Officer. Yves san Pedro was weeping.

When a medic stepped aside shaking, his head, Jones saw why.

Pedro san Grigor, eighth go-captain of Imperial Ship *Whale*, slumped slack-jawed and vacant-eyed in his chair. *What is he looking at?* Jones wondered. *Something far, far away. Perhaps, the Tau. Maybe that's why he's smiling.* For a long moment, nothing made sense.

"What happened?" Jones asked.

In answer, Berylplume gestured to the bodies on the floor. "Those three came from the Mutiny to take the captain in 'for questioning.' Given the fate of the in-captain, the sergeants-at-arms were disinclined to submit. One of them said that wrangles among the cargo did not touch the Gold, and one of the mutineers said, then *we'll* touch the gold! They *manhandled* the captain, the mutineers did. They *laid hands* on his sacred person, and he meditating the while on the Flight Plan."

"They killed him?"

The medic looked up and said, "Heart attack."

"Brought on," said Berylplume, "by the manhandling. What now, captain?"

For a moment, Jones thought he was seeking oracles from the body, then he realized the First had addressed Yves, who was now, to the sorrow of Shang Di, the ninth go-captain of the *Whale*.

Jones studied the dead mutineers. They had evidently been unfamiliar with the Flying Mule and had not looked for a steel-toed kick to the side of the head. Armed as they were with teasers, they had automatically discounted the quarterstaffs of the sergeants. The martial arts were unknown to them.

"Fourth Officer, Jones," said Yves. "You had better get some rest before your watch begins."

And so, Jones received his promotion at last, though the circumstances were such that he almost wished he hadn't.

Returning to the Cloisters, his heart in turmoil, his MOBI chimed once more. "Yes! Bùxiè, this is not a good time. The go-captain has been murdered—by mutineers. What? Of course, I would, but we don't have that many sergeants. What? Yes, Gold can override Blue comm circuits. In case of emergency announcements. Why? What do you have in mind?"

When they brought Reggie Chang to the platform, the crowd did not cheer as lustily as before, or at least fewer of them did so. Jek wondered if they had become so jaded to the sight that one more execution no longer moved them.

"Reginald Chang," he said, "you stand convicted of betraying the Mutiny. How say you?"

"That's a suitably vague charge, Assault Leader. Difficult to prove, impossible to refute. I once longed to see the day when the Mutiny overthrew the Officers. I never thought to see the day when the Mutiny overthrew itself." Then he leaned close and whispered, though the microphones picked up his words, and the whisper became a roar from the great screen on the Comm Center façade.

"You should not have killed the girl, Jek. She was the Angel of the Barricades. She was here on the sharp end. Where were you?"

The crowd began to murmur, and Jek rebutted Group Leader Chang with a tease to the back of his skull.

He had given up on balky firing squads and administered "the tickle" himself these days.

Bùxiè watched them drag a body off the platform, and although he had no idea who it was, his stomach turned over. "I hope that's not in store for me," he joked.

Chakraborty laughed. "Naw, you're getting a medal, like the Enforcer who rapped that lieutenant in Little Lotus." He gestured to a second platform decorated in the various tricolors used by the Mutiny that stood before the entry to Comm Central. Bùxiè had deduced that the different color combinations represented different commandos.

"Oh, look," said Winnie, "it's our brother." She pointed at the stage, and Bùxiè saw the unmistakable bulk of Dhikpārusya Spandhana.

Wing said, "You guys members? You know he faced down Maintenance thugs three or four times."

Bùxiè was disinclined to share, yet again, the story of how the body recovery team had taken to calling one another "brother." No wonder Peng had been so curious since the Brotherhood also used that salutation.

Dhik sat in a row of seats occupied by others, though one hardly noticed because he was so large that the others faded from one's perception. Bùxiè supposed they were also to receive awards. Most seemed so swelled with pride that he wondered that their clothing fasteners did not burst apart.

Dhik, on the other hand, looked as if he would rather have been anywhere else. The fellow was uncomfortable with praise and adulation. His fingers twitched from time to time, and Bùxiè knew it was because the Enforcer was unconsciously grabbing for his 'boo.

Bùxiè and Winnie climbed the stairs to the stage, though he could not help but wonder if it was not all an elaborate ruse. He stole glances at the platform on the other side of the Plaza, where the bodies had been cleared away, and Jek Buddhathal was adjusting his uniform before replacing his smile with a friendlier one. He scurried across to the stage and *bounded* up the steps.

He is loving this, Bùxiè thought. Was it the power? Being the center of attention? There was a sort of crew council, and Buddhathal was styling himself "First Councilor." Bùxiè wondered if there were a Second or Third Councilor and how they felt about that.

Buddhathal was all sticks and strings and looked as if a good, hard shaking would scatter his bones. It was an interesting theory, and Bùxiè was more than willing to test it.

He and Winnie found seats beside a man named Nearwell. They exchanged perfunctory greetings and settled into the amiable silence of strangers while they waited for the ceremonies to begin. In the Plaza, a florist's lorry pulled up and parked.

Buddhathal danced to center stage and, with a whirl of his arm to the seated crewmen, announced, "Heroes of the Mutiny!"

That was a cue. Recorded music cascaded from the speakers: the lively old Departure Day Reel. Bùxiè did not know why he should have been surprised. Perhaps he had expected something more martial and bombastic.

> *"Oh, the Whale, she boosts in half an hour to cross the starry heavens.*
> *Our friends are watching from the Tower, their pride with*
> *   sorrow leavened.*
> *We're just about to slide away, and to the Tau, we're farin'.*
> *The Beanstalk is decoupling, and we're leaving dear old Terra."*

> *"And it's goodbye Krish and goodbye Chang and goodbye darling Mary.*
> *The Beanstalk is decoupling, and I'm leaving dear old Terra.*
> *Farewell to Tower, Taj, and Wall. I never more will see you.*
> *Farewell to Beijing and Chennai, and Paris, Rome, and Rio.*
> *And now the Higgs are folding space, I have no more to say.*
> *I'm bound for ol' Tau Ceti now, a dozen lights away."*

People in the crowd were clapping time. A few had linked arms and pinwheeled around each other. Bùxiè noticed that Winnie was tapping her toes. A plumber's lorry pulled in beside the florist. One for the memorial bouquets, Bùxiè supposed, and one to deal with the bilge that was shortly to flow.

The Whale as she was, he thought as he watched the dancers. The Departure Generation had known that they would never see the end of their grand adventure, but had they known it in their bones? Had they realized, deep down where even their dreams failed to sound, that they would grow old and die inside a box—and that they had condemned great-grandchildren yet unborn to a like fate? Had they danced this reel in celebration—or in desperation?

When it was over, Buddhathal patted down their cheers and whoops and called on "the Heroes," one by one, giving each a brief panegyric and draping a tricolor ribbon around his neck at the end of which dangled a ceramic star. One female had assassinated a lieutenant of Accounting; a male had sliced the throat of Thantos Chan. Nearwell, when they came to him, had guided a commando into the Water Palace. Most of the "heroic acts" seemed to Bùxiè acts of petty treachery, though a few really were feats carried out in firefights with household militias; two were received by numb-faced widows.

A handyman's lorry pulled into the car park across the Plaza.

When it came Bùxiè's turn, Buddhathal framed his act as a blow struck against the presumptuous arrogance of Eugenics. Bùxiè did not correct him but accepted his medal with a smile and a dip of his head.

A man on a two-wheeler spun into the Plaza, and after a few glances to get his bearings, ran up the stage and whispered in Buddhathal's ear. Whatever he said must have been startling, for the First Councilor jerked his head back, and Bùxiè heard him say, "And all his commando?" Buddhathal made a fist and struck his palm. "Tell the others to consolidate; consolidate now. Stop chasing capes and consolidate."

The messenger whispered again, and again shock ran across the face of the First Councilor. "The Marines? Are you certain?" he said. He noticed Bùxiè listening, pulled the messenger farther aside, and Bùxiè heard no more.

Buddhathal dismissed the messenger and came to Bùxiè. "What did you overhear?"

Bùxiè shrugged. "Naught I could make sense of."

"Good. Just routine field reports, but not for dissemination, you understand."

The other Heroes were leaving the stage, save Dhik, who lingered. *Now or never*, Bùxiè thought. He strode to center stage and announced, "Fellow crewmen!" and his voice boomed from the speakers. "There is one more Hero, but modesty forestalls him from announcing it. I am speaking of First Councilor, Jek Buddhathal."

That earned a few hoots and cheers from the crowd and a cry of "Go, Jek!" Buddhathal, who had turned at first with irritation, looked both flattered and curious.

"The Leader needs to be recognized for his heroism at Undine Place," Bùxiè declared, "which this surveillance shows." That was

Jones' cue to co-opt the internal network. This would be a hell of a time to discover he could not.

The screen rastered into fuzz, then clarified to the protests at the Water Palace. The crowd quieted to watch the infamous Massacre. Bùxiè heard a few voices pointing themselves out to friends.

"And here is Jek throwing the bottle that struck the sentry"—Someone hollered *Strike!*—"from safely in the rear."

Buddhathal's brow lowered as he caught the drift of the "praise," but Bùxiè did not stop.

"And *here* is where he heroically held Adrienne Mei-ti as a human shield." He turned and faced Buddhathal. "Adrienne Mei-ti was my Special Woman. She was the wind in my sails, and without her, I am becalmed. I plan to give you a sound thrashing because, by the seven hells, you deserve one!"

Jek laughed. He had not noticed that the crowd was no longer cheering him. "In the Mutiny," he said, "some are more valuable than others. That woman was a foot soldier in the struggle. She was expendable to ensure my escape."

Bùxiè punched him in the nose. Someone in the crowd yelled, "Coward!" and Jek looked wildly for the source. Perhaps he sensed that with the executions of the Princess of the Air and of the Mutiny's original leaders and now the revelation of his own pusillanimity, he had squandered his leadership. Only those utterly complicit would follow him now.

Though that might still number quite a few.

Fights had broken out within the crowd between Jek's supporters and anti-Jekers, hitherto too frightened to speak up.

Jek hated, above all things, humiliation. He pulled his teaser from its holster and pointed it stiff-armed at Bùxiè. "Traitor," he snarled.

And so Bùxiè would now join Adrienne. He hadn't supposed, deep down, when he had planned this that Buddhathal would take the humiliation quietly, but he hadn't expected the outbreak of anti-Jekist feeling, either.

Winnie cried, "Bùxiè! Drop!"

He did and saw Winsome Alabaster with her teaser pointed straight at Jek.

Jek saw it, too, and shifted his aim a fraction and fired. The blast took Winnie in the chest, and she spasmed and fell.

"Winnie!" Bùxiè turned his back on Jek and leapt to her side. "Winnie!" He took her in his arms. Behind him, he heard the whine of Jek's teaser as it recharged.

The sound had not been heard in the *Whale* for eighty years—the swirling howl of a humpback *Whale*'s distress song. MOBIs everywhere began to ping.

EMERGENCY WORK ORDER 218-16
ATTN: TRANSPORT
TRAIN 87 DERAILED AFT OF CHETTINAD STATION WHEN MAGRAILS QUENCHED. NO TRAMS CAN RUN ON PORTSIDE LONGITUDINAL UNTIL REMOUNTED.

EMERGENCY WORK ORDER 218-17
ATTN: AIR
IMMINENT SEIZURE OF FAN BEARING. MAIN CIRC. FAN, YANGBORO YARDS #3.

EMERGENCY WORK ORDER 218-18
ATTN: WATER
BILGE PUMP #763-27 HAS FAILED TO CLOSE. SEWAGE BACKING UP IN JADE TERRACE.

EMERGENCY WORK ORDER 218-19
ATTN: FACILITIES MAINTENANCE
MAJOR STRUCTURAL DAMAGE TO MEAT VATS AND 'PONIC TRAYS. 40 DECK ABAFT BURNOUT. ASSESS AND REPORT

EMERGENCY WORK ORDER 218-20
ATTN: POWER
BROWNOUTS IN HIGHSTEEPLE. POSSIBLE TRANSFORMER MALF. ASSESS AND REPORT.

Work orders cascaded into dozens of MOBIs. Work undone was piling up, and *Whale* herself was crying for help. The sounds of tumult died save for the groans of the injured or supine as crewmen paused their brawling to read them. Then, individually or in small groups, they hurried off to their duty stations, many shamefaced, some in open relief. A dozen gandy dancers at a dead run passed through the Plaza toward Chettinad Station.

Shortly, only a double handful remained on the Plaza, gazing about themselves bewildered. What had happened to the Mutiny?

When First Platoon burst from the backs of the parked lorries, even the holdouts knew no other course than surrender. A few teaser snaps and it was over.

Peng had been on a direct link to Lucky the while and said, "See? You can wield a scalpel, too."

Lucky grinned. She had heard the crowd sounds and Kent's shouted commands in the background. Peng was somewhere on the Plaza. His must be made of brass and weigh a pound each.

The drama on the Plaza played out beyond Bùxiè's attention, which was focused on Winnie's motionless body and the humming of Jek's charger.

Suddenly, the sound stopped, and Bùxiè, grabbing Winnie's "heat," rolled and aimed. He had never wished the death of another human being, not even poor, mad Ramamurthy, but he wished it now.

Blood had streamed from Jek's broken nose, but also a white foam graced lips spread wide in a fierce smile. His entire body was rigid, and his eyes bulged.

Jek dropped to his knees, then face down on the stage. Behind him on the Plaza a woman like a porcelain doll lowered a teaser. "He killed Hamdu!" she exclaimed. "He killed Hamdu!"

One of the Marines took the recharging teaser from her hands and deactivated it. Bùxiè looked from her to Jek's body and understood that he would live. Then he looked to Winnie and wondered why he should. "Oh, Winnie," he groaned.

"You know," Winnie whispered, "dispersal mail is not all that great."

Bùxiè's heart stopped, paused, started once more. "Inverse square law," he explained, striving to keep his voice controlled. "You were too close to the discharge." He took her in his arms and held her tight as if she might escape him.

"Mmph. Careful," she said. "My arms are still numb." Fortunately, much of the rest of her was not.

34 CONSTITUTIONS

A constituent Assembly—L'envoi

According to the Constitution of the *Whale*, on the infirmity or death of the in-captain, the captaincy would devolve upon the Purser. But Lady Purser did not want the post, and her first and only executive order was to call for a Constituent Assembly. Every department sent one or more delegates to meet in the auditorium at Comm Central.

Among others, the Constabulary returned the Big Dhik; Ship Security, Bùxiè; and Eugenics, Winsome Alabaster. She thought it was in recognition of their contributions to discovering the Dwellers or to ending Jek Buddhathal's reign of Terror, but Bùxiè did not think their contributions that important.

Oddly, while Food Production delegated Gregor Vishwakarma and Maintenance sent Kennett Erlanger, Power and Light delegated Adrian Astradian and Storage, Wennell Ku. Other departments also dispatched surviving mutineers, who made an uncomfortable mix with the surviving Commanders.

Non-voting representatives included legates of the Dalai Papa, the Gold Crew, and even the Desolate and Orphan Dweller clans. It was, on the whole, an eclectic gathering.

Florian Venables-*pandit*, sitting for the Tutors Guild, moved that the proceedings be private. "A great deal of sausage must be made," he said, "and people can get distressed watching it being made. No one really likes to read a work-in-progress, as it may progress to something quite different before its last coat of polish."

Venables possessed the saddest face that Bùxiè had ever seen. Someone told him that the renowned tutor never smiled again after watching one of his pupils executed by Buddhathal during the Terror, his grief exacerbated by the fact that he had helped set the Mutiny in motion. But it was Venables who produced the ancient texts that became the basis for the new Constitution.

Lucky Lutz was elected president of the Assembly, both for her prestige and the deft manner in which she had avoided a massacre at Comm Plaza (though Bùxiè suspected Peng's adroit hand behind that). Lutz had no ambitions and remained resolutely neutral during the debates, maintaining a mien of wisdom by the simple expedient of remaining silent, save on points of order.

No one ever found Peng. No image or presence of him ever surfaced, though the Constabulary and Ship Security continued to receive messages from him for many years after. Once, Bùxiè thought he glimpsed the man in the bustling crowd on Comm Plaza, but when he reviewed the surveillance footage, Facemaker returned a different name. A façade identity was not beyond Peng's abilities, however, and Bùxiè took to calling him the "Secret Name."

Since forbidding Commanders from using their offices to accumulate wealth had proven futile, the revised Constitution attempted the same goal by limiting the term of office and making Commander a temporary, elected rank. The crew would have a say in Regulations through a delegate Assembly, chosen by residential districts, and the synergy among departments would be maintained by a Commandery, chosen by occupational ratings. The captain would be selected by a Judge Advocates Court—lawmen delegated by Air, Water, Power, Food, and Maintenance—which would also rule on whether new Regulations were compatible with the Constitution. The whole thing was crafted with an eye to preventing that accumulation of power that had vexed the crew into mutiny.

That today's solutions become tomorrow's problems was not immediately evident to the Assembly.

The whole thing struck Bùxiè as overly complex, though Venables insisted that the complexity was needed to ward against tyranny. But Kennett Erlanger said during the debates that the more complex the plan, the more ways that it could go orlop.

Ship Security agreed to disable most of the surveillance network, saving only important public spaces like Comm Center Plaza, high crime areas, and critical infrastructure. Since private businesses could install their own surveillance, Bùxiè was unsure how much of a rollback this was, but everyone seemed satisfied.

Eugenics agreed to stop issuing draft notices, but in the interests of preventing overbreeding and inbreeding, would insist on licenses attesting to genetic compatibility and would provide lists of suggested mates to those who applied.

All in all, the Mutiny secured most of its goals, or nearly so, while the Officers preserved most of the best features of the Old Order. If no one got everything, all got something, and the level of satisfaction was sufficient that over time, wounds were healed and old friendships renewed.

Fanghsi, in his later years, lived among the Orphans and became a leader among them. The Assembly hired him to lead a cartographic expedition to chart the lower reaches of the Burnout, during which he discovered the body of Pathfinder. He contracted the Red Rot, but his Woman, Big Foot Bambi of the Orphans, treated it with poultices made from a mutated moss growing in an abandoned 'ponic flat. This folk remedy fortuitously cured him and, less fortuitously, made him and Big Foot rich. He used the wealth to develop Orphanstown.

Tongkawa Jones finished his career on the quarterdeck as Second Officer after first Brahmadharma, and then Tang retired. He became a key advisor to go-captain Yves and found him withal not such a bad sort to work with.

He spent the rest of his life studying the swiftie data from the Visser Hoop and determined that the one to their aft that Yves had discovered was, in fact, another segment of the same tube. Either something had sliced it, or the tube possessed entry points along its length. That it provided a shortcut to the Tau was demonstrated ten years later when they received telemetry from the swifties Snowy Mountain had sent through it. It opened exciting possibilities, but Jones still believed Reynaud had made the right decision in relieving Skybones. The quarterdeck simply had not known enough to hazard the entire voyage on the off chance.

He and Bùxiè remained ever-fast friends.

Big Dhik was placed in charge of training Enforcers in his New Model of enforcing minor transgressions. On-the-spot corporal punishment was de-emphasized, though it was not eliminated entirely. Many offenses now warranted a fine rather than a swat, and both were mediated by a village magisterial court in which the offender had the chance to submit extenuating circumstances.

He and Peta settled into Little Lotus, where Dhik became known as the Gentle Giant. Their son was not so large as Dhik—who was?—but trained with him in the dojo from an early age. Dhik hoped he would follow him into Enforcement, but he struck for medic instead after the Examination showed he had a bump for the Caring Arts.

About a year afterward, Bùxiè and Winnie were paired. (The fix was in. Winnie, by then was CPO in Eugenics-Input.) They moved into a "fixer-upper" billet in Highsteeple and settled in to learn about each other. Some of what they learned was surprising and pleasant, some was inevitably otherwise, but they never regretted their commitment.

Once a year, they would ride aft to Arfwendsen's Wayhouse for a meal in remembrance of the Siege of Conniption Pass' and renew old friendships with the Big Dhik and Peta and with Little Face, Sanech, Singh, and even One and Two (who by then had new assignments and hence new numbers. Eventually, when he became head of CID, Bùxiè learned their base names, but he continued to respect their need for anonymity). They would lift a glass to "Crawling Vermin" and to Goliad, and in later years to other absent friends.

Inevitably, their children would ask them, "What did you do in the Mutiny, Baba and Mama?" and they would answer, "Nothing much at all." The kids would answer, "Ho, ho! How droll! Nothing much? Why, you killed the monster, Jek!"

It hadn't happened that way, but the surveillance was ambiguous, and Bùxiè *had* aimed Winnie's teaser at the madman, so it looked as if he had. He was never able to convince the kids otherwise.

Venables became the *éminence grise* of the Mutiny, not only for his labors in revising the Constitution but for his more shadowy role advising Organson. After his death, they placed a statue on Comm Central Plaza showing him standing behind a seated Hamdu with an advisory hand laid on his shoulder.

He would not have approved. Florian Venables had disliked statues, especially noble and heroic ones. That's why they waited until he was dead before they did it. He did maintain a memorial, however. All his life, on his desk, he kept a still image of Ling-ling Barnstable, the Angel of the Barricades.

SCIENCE & TECH NOTES

1. **Meat vats.** Dr. Vladimir Mironov of the Medical University of South Carolina, as well as researchers in the Netherlands, are presently working on the growth of "in-vitro" or cultured meat.

2. **Swifties.** Hawking once suggested launching chip-sized "spaceships" pushed by laser on a solar sail. Our swifties are launched by coil gun to get an initial velocity with lasers to provide continual acceleration.

3. **Invisibility shields (cloaking).** "A recently published theory has suggested that a cloak of invisibility is in principle possible, at least over a narrow frequency band. In the first practical realization of such a cloak (2006); a copper cylinder was 'hidden' inside a cloak constructed with the use of artificially structured metamaterials. The cloak decreased scattering from the hidden object over a band of microwave frequencies while at the same time reducing its shadow, so that the cloak and object combined began to resemble empty space." "Metamaterial Electromagnetic Cloak at Microwave Frequencies," *Science*. Vol. 314, Issue 5801, pp 977–980.

4. **Teasers.** At Old Dominion University, nanosecond long, high-voltage pulses that punch holes in cell membranes could

be used for a Taser-like weapon that stuns targets because the pulse temporarily disables human muscles.

5. **Self-assembly and self-repair of equipment, and systems.** Researchers at the University of Michigan have developed a concrete material that self-heals cracks and recovers most of the original strength.

6. **Self healing** is being tested using polymer mixtures from Oak Ridge National Lab and the University of Tennessee, and nanoparticles assembled into complex arrays are being tested at Lawrence Berkeley National Laboratory. A University of Illinois polymer with self-sensing properties can react to mechanical stress, and Raytheon HEALICS Technology incorporates self-healing into a complex system-on-chip (SoC) design, providing the capability for the chip to sense undesired circuit behaviors and correct them automatically.

SONG NOTES

"It Doesn't Matter" is based on the old German Republican song from 1848, "Burgerlied."

"Departure Day Reel" is based on the Irish emigration song, "Goodbye Mick."